Brothers
IN ARMS
A STRIPLING WARRIOR NOVEL

Misty Moncur

Brothers
IN ARMS

A STRIPLING WARRIOR NOVEL

Misty Moncur

EDEN BOOKS — STANSBURY PARK, UTAH

Published by Eden Books, Stansbury Park, UT

ISBN-10: 0-9898959-4-7
ISBN-13: 978-0-9898959-4-1

Moncur, Misty Leigh, 1978-
Brothers In Arms / Misty Moncur
Summary: Sarai and Salome accompany a rescue party to the Land of Nephi.

ISBN: 978-0-9898959-4-1

Library of Congress Catalog Control Number

2015914987

WITH GRATITUDE TO

Maddy and Ashley

For your beautiful smiles

AND WITH LOVE TO

Anna, Christina,

Amber, and Shirley-Ann

For your encouraging words and sharp eyes
and for knowing my characters better than I do

Zeke grabbed my wrist. I tried to wriggle away, but he was too strong, and his grip was like a shackle. My feet scraped through the dirt as he dragged me back toward our parents, but they stood behind the gate and didn't make a move to help either of us.

"Let me go!" I slapped at my brother's hand, but it was no use.

"Captain!"

I froze, then slowly craned my head around to see a boy I barely knew sidestep the others as they shuffled back to let him through.

Zeke stopped pulling long enough to turn, too. I tried to yank my arm away, but he didn't let go of me, didn't even loosen his grip.

"Let her come. I'll watch out for her."

Lamech squared his shoulders in front of Zeke. He wasn't afraid of my brother's scowl. After a long moment, he reached out and actually pried Zeke's hard fingers from my wrist.

My heart was pounding when he took me by my hand and led me through the crowd toward the edge of the village.

I glanced back at Zeke. Hands on his hips, he was trying to reason with my parents, but Father only frowned, looking resigned. Mother stood away from them and waved me on. When I turned back to the road, Lamech caught the smile I couldn't quite hide.

"I can leave you as easily as take you, Princess," he said, sounding annoyed.

But he was still holding my hand. He wasn't leaving me in the village. I was in the band of warriors that would search for Gideon in the Land of Nephi, and that was all that really mattered to me.

I gave one last look behind me—thatched houses on two sides of the lane, bleating goats that cropped grasses in small courtyards, people, with their beloved, familiar faces, who were turning back to their morning chores—before I let Lamech pull me into the trees.

I nearly had to skip to keep up with him, as he seemed bent on putting distance between us and my brother, so I walked quickly along beside him, quiet and grateful, and wondering if he was perhaps more afraid of my brother's scowl than he had shown.

By midday, seven hours later, I was more tired than grateful, and I was hungry and ready to stop.

"When will we get to the farm?" I asked Lamech when the way no longer looked familiar.

His family's barley farm was to be our first stop, but I knew the way, and we didn't seem to be on it.

His dark eyes slid to me. "Shortcut to Orihah first."

"Orihah?"

"Didn't Keturah ever take you into town?"

"Sure, but why are we going there?"

He might have sighed. "Supplies."

Jashon jogged up from behind us. "Keep an eye on Keturah," he instructed his brother as he passed us.

It was soft, but I caught Lamech's snort. "She doesn't need looked after," he said under his breath.

Of course she didn't. But I apparently did.

I studied my hands, picked at a callous that had formed where I always held my needle. "So...how will we find Gideon? What is the plan?"

We had turned off the West Road over an hour ago, angling across the land to the southwest. Lamech said this narrow trail was meant to take us to Orihah, but I was beginning to think we would never get there.

Lamech didn't look at me when he spoke. "You came without knowing the plan?"

I didn't look at him either—I never did, when I could help it. Why should I? I already knew what he looked like.

Lamech had three brothers. Gideon and Jashon had gone to the war and returned home, but Shad, much to his annoyance, had not been old enough. For most of the past year, I had been living with Keturah and Gideon in their house on the family's farm. All of the boys had been trained up in righteousness, were strong from their work in the fields, were quiet and watchful when among strangers, and were considered handsome and unattainable by the girls in the nearby villages. But when Lamech came home from the battlefield, he was the only one my eyes had followed—as he chopped wood for the fires, as he threshed barley and threw the sheaves, as he carried water from the stream for his mother.

I definitely knew what he looked like.

"I trust you," I said. "I mean, I trust all of you. Jashon, Kenai—the men surely have a plan."

"And you thought you could be of some use in it?"

3

I didn't know. "Gideon's my friend," was all I said.

Our allies, the Nephites, were no longer actively at war with the Lamanites, but Lamech said men were still fighting in some places because the Lamanites were blood-thirsty. He would spend his life fighting them, until they left our lands for good or he was dead or taken prisoner like his brother. I doubted either of them would stop fighting even then.

"You don't have any idea what you're getting into," Lamech told me with a scoff.

"Do you?"

"More than you do."

"Lamech, you are four years older than me, and you've been in the army for all of them. Of course you have more experience than I do in traveling and life and making rescue plans. I'm not trying to compete with you. I just want to go and do what I can to help, even if it's just fetching the kindling for the fires. I would think you'd be grateful for the help."

"Why should I be? Now I have to watch you all the time and keep you out of trouble."

"Because Gideon's your brother, and you love him, and you want to free him from bondage."

Lamech didn't say anything to that, probably because he couldn't deny it, and disagreeing with me seemed to be all he wanted to do.

"Do you really think I'll be that much trouble?"

He sighed. "No."

"A burden then?"

"Sarai...yes, a little."

Then why had he shouldered it? Why had he defied Zeke in order to bring me along? He could have remained silent and left me in the village, and we both knew it.

4

"Have you ever had to look out for anyone before?"

"My brothers."

"That's why you're so miserable about Gideon."

He didn't reply.

"Gideon is a grown man, trained in warfare. What happened wasn't your fault."

"I know that."

Irritated. Defensive.

His jaw tightened and I could tell he did not want me to intrude on his feelings about what had happened, about how he had lost his brother in the course of the recent battle, so I changed the subject. "How many men do you think we'll get?"

"Maybe ten or fifteen more, but we don't want a lot."

"Why not?"

"Lots of reasons. We don't want to draw attention to ourselves for one."

"And what are the chances we won't?"

"Slim."

A lump formed in my throat, but I didn't say what I was thinking, that the thought of encountering enemies in Lamanite lands scared me.

After a while, Lamech said, "I'll take you home if you want."

"No. I'm going."

"I was afraid of that. If you don't want to go home, you can stay with my parents. Mother would like it."

"No." I paused. "But I do love Naomi."

"That's not going to get you anywhere with me."

"What do you mean?"

He grunted and held a branch out of my way.

"I don't understand you, Lamech," I said in confusion.

"You never will, so save yourself the trouble of trying."

I slowed, and when he sensed I was no longer next to him, he stopped and turned back to me, a look of long-suffering on his face.

I gestured for him to go on ahead. "I don't need you to look out for me," I told him. "I'm perfectly capable of walking along a path by myself."

He ignored the gesture and put his hands on his hips. "In the territory we're going to, there may not always be a clear path."

"And I'm sure I shall manage that just fine as well."

"Don't be naïve, Isabel," he said and turned to go, clearly ready to end the conversation—if the stupid things he had been saying could be called conversation.

My face burning, I let him take a few strides away from me before I said quietly, "I'm Sarai."

I watched his shoulders stiffen. He turned his head slightly so I could see his profile, but I doubted he intended for me to see his grimace.

"I don't accept your apology, so save yourself the trouble of making one," I said as I brushed past him. I would prove that I could walk a path on my own.

Eventually, I came to the crest of a hill and looked down on the town of Orihah. It wasn't as large as the city of Melek, but it was much larger than the village my family lived in. The town was busy at midday with homes and buildings everywhere and people out among them doing their various chores. Jashon was walking up the hill toward us.

I heard the others assemble behind me, Gideon's friends and kinsmen, as well as some of their wives. I felt

Lamech at my elbow. Breathing down my neck it seemed like. I took a step away from him, and I heard him snort derisively.

What was his problem?

"You sound like a horse when you do that," I said, my nose wrinkling.

I heard Isabel's giggle from somewhere behind me and took another slight step away.

Jashon spoke when he reached us. "I found Zach. He'll find some of the others and send them to the farm." He hesitated. "He...won't come. Beth forbids it."

"Go back and tell her she can come with him," said Eve.

"I did. She declined," Jashon said as he made his way to Keturah, but he spoke to Lamech. "Delilah is home. She sent Aniah with word to Enos and Jared at the mill."

Lamech turned to look toward the southwest, probably in the direction of the timber mill, and nodded. "Should we wait here for them?"

"Delilah said to bring you all for the midday meal. She's preparing it now." Jashon looked around to include everyone in the invitation. Then he ushered Keturah along in front of him and led the way toward his aunt and uncle's home in Orihah.

I had met Delilah and Joseph before. They were both very nice and had very nice children. Aniah, their only daughter, had become one of my best friends during my stay in Orihah. As Gid and Lamech's cousin, she had taken me under her wing and introduced me to the other girls our age and many of the boys, too. Their oldest son, Enos, had gone with the striplings to war. Now he harvested trees and prepared them for use in building houses and other structures. Almost eight years younger than Enos, Jared was the closest to my age. I liked them both, and during my stay with Gid and Keturah, they had all become like my own cousins.

Delilah was preparing a feast when we arrived, setting out large dishes of corn and beans and the sweet potato she was so fond of. She mashed the potato with goat cheese and served it wrapped in warmed chay leaves. Before the first time I had eaten at Delilah's, I had never heard of anyone serving food in warm chay. Just the thought of eating limp, wet leaves was disgusting, but Delilah's wraps were a favorite among her family and kinsmen and had come to be one of my favorite foods as well.

Aniah walked into the yard with her older brothers. The boys went straight to Jashon, but Aniah spotted me sitting alone on a bench at the edge of the yard and skipped over.

"Hi, Sarai," she chirped. Her cheeks flushed and her eyes bright, she was clearly happy to see so many handsome visitors at her home.

I slid over to make room for her to sit beside me.

"Enos and Jared wanted to come right away. Jared wants to go, too, to get Gid, but Enos said he had to stay and keep the timber mill going." As usual, she got right into the latest news.

"Can't your father run it alone?"

"Enos thinks he's too young to go."

"What does your father say?"

She shrugged.

"I think it's nice that he wants to go."

Jared had gotten food and grinned as he came toward us. It was not a grin for his sister.

I rolled my eyes when he squeezed himself between his sister and me and wriggled some space for himself until Aniah

8

fell off the end of the bench.

"Hey!" she protested, but after she stood and dusted off her hands, she gave me a wave and went to find her other friends.

Jared didn't even look at her. "Hi, Sarai."

I couldn't help laughing. "Hi."

"You're back early from the wedding."

I looked around at all the other people in the yard, the men who were preparing to leave for the Land of Nephi. What did he think I was doing here with them?

"I came with the others," I said.

He nodded and took a bite of the chay wrap. "I love when my mother makes these."

"Are you coming on the journey?" I asked him.

He swallowed and grinned again. "Of course."

"Enos said no," I reminded him.

Jared snorted and glanced after his sister. "Enos can't stop me."

"I didn't think he could," I replied.

"I'm not going to just let him have all the adventures."

"It's a dangerous journey," I said. If it was too dangerous for Jared, then it was definitely too dangerous for me, but I pushed that thought away because it made my heart beat fast. I couldn't let myself be afraid.

Besides, I would have Lamech looking out for me.

My eyes strayed to find Lamech in the yard. He was standing with some men, but he seemed alone. Lamech was leaning against the fence with his feet crossed at the ankle and his arms crossed over his chest. He wasn't talking to the others—barely seemed to be listening to them—and he was glaring at his cousin.

Some kids from the town had come into the yard—I guessed the large group of striplings was hard to ignore—and one of Jared's friends spotted us and made his way over.

"Hi, Sarai." He bent down a little and put his hand on my shoulder, and even though I could see red creeping up his neck, he kept his hand there longer than he should have.

"Hi, Daniel."

"I wanted to ask you, some of us are going down to the river tonight, and I thought if you wanted to, since you're back, maybe you might want to go. If you want to."

I smiled, and I was about to tell him thank you but I couldn't, when Jared got to his feet, and before I knew it, they were play fighting in front of me, having a good-natured scuffle and making me laugh.

Lamech was off the fence and coming toward us. Heavens, but I hoped he didn't think he had to watch out for me here in his uncle's courtyard. Couldn't he tell Jared and Daniel were just playing around? But he only made it halfway across the yard before Aniah and some other girls from church stopped him, and I gathered from the look Aniah sent my way that it wasn't unintentional. Her gaze flicked to her brother before turning back to Lamech, and I wondered why she had stopped him as I skirted past the boys who were wrestling now on the ground and went to find Delilah.

I found her near the house, and she smiled and put her arm around me. "Don't tell me you think you're going with them," she said in a stern, motherly way.

"I am going. I can help. Gid is my—"

I was going to say *friend*, but I choked up very suddenly and couldn't finish.

She hugged me tight again and just said, "I know." Her

eyes scanned the crowd in her yard, men who would try to rescue her nephew, and I followed her gaze to where it had landed, on Lamech, silent now while the girls chattered around him. He looked away when he saw we had noticed him staring at us. "But Gid is not your only friend, I think," Delilah teased me quietly.

"Oh," I said, feeling my face heat, realizing I had been staring at him too. "Zeke wouldn't let me come, but Lamech said he'd watch out for me so Zeke didn't have to. He's really annoyed about it." I nibbled on my lip. "He feels he owes it to Zeke."

She smiled at me. "He looks annoyed, but he is only afraid."

I looked doubtfully back toward Lamech who was trying to ignore us now that we were clearly talking about him, but it was almost comical how little he was succeeding in it.

I didn't think Lamech could ever, ever be afraid of anything, so I had to ask, "Afraid of what?"

"He is afraid to grasp what he wants, what he feels he does not deserve."

I stole another look at him. "What do you mean?"

"You will see," she said. "Have patience."

Giving one last glance to Lamech, I said, "Delilah, may I have your recipe for the chay wraps?" It was time to change the subject. "I could make them on the journey. I want to be helpful so the men don't regret taking me with them."

She squeezed me again and then led me toward her home. "Come inside. I will show you what to do."

The wraps were easy to make and as she showed me the steps, I told her how Jared and Daniel had ended up wrestling on the ground.

"You're going to have to start being careful which young men you encourage," she said. "Those two were trying to impress you."

"It wasn't very impressive," I laughed, and she laughed with me, but a sadness had crept into her eyes.

Lamech cleared his throat at the door. "It's time to go."

Embarrassed for having been caught giggling about boys, I wiped my hands on a cloth, bid Delilah farewell with a hug, and followed Lamech outside.

I looked around in the bright light. "Where is everyone else?" I asked.

"They already left."

"Why did no one call for me?"

"They didn't want you to come."

I snorted.

"Fine. They did call you. You didn't answer."

"I'm sorry. I didn't hear anyone call."

"You were giggling too loud."

"Just because you have no sense of humor doesn't mean I can't have one."

He grunted.

"And by the way, grunting is not a polite response."

He grunted again. "I've no need to be polite. We're not in the governor's hall, Princess."

Princess. The way he sneered it, it wasn't a compliment.

But I kind of liked it because I thought way down deep, he meant it as one.

"But I am a lady," I pointed out.

"Yeah, that's the problem with you."

"Only one problem? I'm flattered. I rank higher in your estimation than I thought."

We passed familiar buildings and people I recognized. I knew the way to the farm from here. I had walked it many times with Keturah or Naomi. If Lamech became any more insulting, I could leave him and walk alone.

"I can think of a hundred problems with you," Lamech said, and I thought I detected a small note of teasing in his voice.

I bit off a smile.

"And I can think of two hundred with you."

"Then I rank higher in your estimation than I thought."

I ducked around a branch as we entered the trees. "You can't believe that."

"Why not?" he shot over his shoulder. "I'm not exactly someone you should be looking at."

I thought we were teasing. Was he serious?

"What do you mean?" I asked slowly.

He stopped and all but rolled his eyes. "You're a princess. I'm nothing. Don't forget it."

"Lamech, are you trying to push me away from you?"

"I'm not trying." He turned away from me to stare sullenly down the path. "I'm doing it."

2

Lamech waited until I started down the trail before he fell in behind me.

I was feeling quite smug in my ability to follow the right path when there were several that veered off in other directions. Lamech would see that I could navigate on my own and that I was not helpless.

But in order for Lamech to see how capable I was, his eyes would have to be on me. When I realized that, I became self-conscious and wished I had let him lead the way.

Why did I feel as though I had to prove something to him? What did I care what he thought anyway?

I felt his eyes on me for a quarter of an hour, and it made my skin prickle. But I didn't glance back. I couldn't let him see he made me nervous. Of all the times we had been on the farm, eating meals or sitting at Naomi's fire, we had never been alone together, and today, under the dappled light of the forest, I was very aware that we were alone.

Finally, I came out of the dense forest and felt Lamech stop behind my shoulder as I paused to survey the green field and take a drink from my water skin.

I could see that the rest of our men were already standing in the little courtyard of the main house, which stood in the middle of the open fields.

"The fields are pretty when they're ready to harvest, but

I love them when they're green like this," I said.

I snuck a glance at Lamech as I reattached my water skin to my large traveling pack. I had trouble tying the leather thongs, and I felt clumsy and stupid for saying that about liking the fields.

"I prefer the fields to the forest."

Lamech's eyes were on the field, but they flicked to me before turning to the path ahead of us. He gestured me forward.

The lane through the field was narrow, like the one through the trees had been, but it was broad enough for two to walk abreast.

"Don't walk behind me," I said, feeling self-conscious again.

He didn't say anything, but in a moment, he was walking next to me.

The only person who seemed to notice when we walked together into the yard was Zeke. He gave me a hard look, but his eyes followed Lamech as if he had questions he would ask of him, but he didn't come over to ask them. He stayed with Eliza, his new wife, until Lamech's father led the men behind the house toward the old wash hut where they conferred, making their plans.

Liam was a quiet man. He seemed hard, maybe bitter, and I had sometimes heard him be brusque with his sons. But he was gentle to Naomi and demanded his sons treat her with the utmost respect, not that any of them would have ever done otherwise. And, surprisingly, he had always treated me the same way, speaking softly when he had reason to speak to me and seeing that his sons treated me with respect as well.

"Stay here," Lamech said, barely sparing me a dark

glance before he followed his father and the other men.

I stared after him for a long moment. Suddenly, I felt my travel pack being lifted from my shoulders.

"Oh!"

I turned to see Darius. He gave me a tentative smile, and a lump formed in my throat.

Darius was Keturah's handsome brother, the youngest son of my mother's best friend, and the whole reason I had spent a year away from home, on the barley farm with Keturah and the family she had married into.

His face fell. He set the pack at my feet and was gone before I could think to return the smile.

"Why are you so mean to him?" Isabel all but hissed at me.

I glanced at her over my shoulder, but turned back to watch Darius put distance between us with his lanky stride.

"He deserves it," I said when he had joined the other men.

"Dare?" Izz scoffed. "No he doesn't. What could he have possibly done to you?"

Done to you? To me. As if she thought I was beneath his notice.

I tried to glare at her, but I knew I wasn't very good at glaring. Most people just chuckled when I tried to look fierce.

"You look like a little princess stomping her foot because she didn't get her way," Zeke had said to me once, and it hadn't been that long ago. I was nearly sixteen, but everyone treated me like I was ten because I looked so young.

I tried another glare at Izz, because Darius hadn't been standing in the woods alone when he had hurt me.

Izz rolled her eyes and wandered away.

I loved my sister, I did. And maybe I was as naive as people thought I was, but sometimes Izz could be pretty clueless, too.

I spotted Naomi moving among the women. I had said goodbye to her only a sennight ago. I had grown to love her and her beloved, work-worn face, but today she looked stricken and scared. Perhaps no one else would notice, but her eyes were pinched at the corners even as she welcomed everyone with a cup of nectar she was pouring for them from a large jug.

"I can do that, Naomi," I said and tried to take the pitcher from her, my small hands covering her rough, hardened ones.

She gave me a tight smile and shook her head, but her eyes were warm.

"I'll cope better if I stay busy."

I offered her a smile too, though it seemed paltry. Her son had been taken captive by Lamanite soldiers and her other sons were preparing to go into hostile lands to get him back.

"Jashon and Lamech will see him free," I said. "You cannot doubt it."

She shook her head again. She didn't want to talk about it.

"I saw you come into the yard with Lamech."

I knew what she was doing. The whole family liked to hint at a possible match between Lamech and me. Shad was closer to my age, but he was already over the moon for one of the village girls, a pretty girl who had hair like sunshine. I told myself they only meant to tease Lamech, and because I was still heartsick over Darius, I had never paid it much mind.

But Lamech was handsome and had undeniably caught

my eye more than once. He worked hard, loved his country, his family, and his father's land. At first, when I had seen him on the farm, he had intrigued me with his long silences and the efficient way he went about his work, and how these things were so in contrast to the way he was with his family. He was affable and open with them, even teasing them back, but he seldom talked to me, and then, only when he had to. He said things like, "Don't touch that. It's hot," and "Fetch Mother some cloths from inside." I didn't really enjoy the thought of being stuck with his sullen attitude for the rest of my life, and comments like Naomi's always flustered me.

"He told Zeke he'd watch out for me so I could come."

Naomi turned to find her son in the circle of men. "I would think he'd want to keep you safe at home."

I wrinkled my nose. "He's probably dreaming of trading me to some Lamanite for a goat and two chickens."

Naomi actually laughed, put her arm around me, and gave me a squeeze. "You have to stay here forever," she declared. "I don't know how I will manage without your sweetness."

I could feel my face heat, and I looked down to hide the color I knew was rising in my cheeks.

"With only boys here, I forget what it's like. I need another woman on the farm."

"You've Keturah," I said, my eyes finding my friend in the yard, resting with her feet up at the outdoor table.

"We both need you."

Of course they didn't, but I said, "I will come back after our journey if Father allows it."

"I will see that he does," she said with another smile starting behind her eyes.

18

Something in that smile made me want to change the subject. "I don't see Shad." I made an exaggerated look toward the men.

Naomi sighed. "He's in Zarahemla buying seed. I expect he'll light out of here as soon as he hears of his brother."

"Liam told me you save your own seed."

She gazed toward the east. "We thought to try something new in the north field."

I nodded, but that was the first I had heard of it, and I had listened to much talk about farming during my stay here. It must have been a recent, perhaps sudden, decision to send Shad away. I agreed with Naomi—he would hate that he had been left behind, but we couldn't wait for him.

Even so, my feet were hurting and I hoped we might stay the night on the farm, but the men decided we should get a head start on the morrow, so we donned our gear again, bid Liam and Naomi a resolute goodbye, and headed south in the mid afternoon.

We didn't have tracks to follow, didn't know which tribe of Lamanites had taken Gid. We couldn't even be sure he had been taken prisoner, but Keturah insisted that if he was free, he would have come back to her. Thinking of the way they were together on the farm, how completely devoted he was to her, I did agree with her on that.

That first night, our camp was charged with a strange excitement that was mixed with sadness and worry. No one wanted to go deep into Lamanite lands, but everyone was dead set on it. Gideon was Jashon and Lamech's brother, but everyone thought of him as their own.

He was my brother, too. My friend. He had proved himself worthy to be called friend, and just his presence at the little house in the barley field had been enough to calm the questions and restlessness in my heart. Something about the way he listened to me and always offered his true, honest opinion after thinking the matter over—while he stirred the fire or strung up an animal for the skinning—made me feel comfortable with who I was inside. I didn't feel too young. I didn't feel too naïve.

That was the thing about Gideon, and I guessed it was the reason all these people were headed into enemy lands to rescue him. He made them feel comfortable with who they were inside, too, and if Gideon was gone, how would we ever feel that way again?

I had my own little tent attached to my travel pack, and when it was set up at the edge of camp, Lamech walked deliberately over and spread his bedroll in front of it with the quick flick of his wrists.

I watched him from where I knelt inside the tent. "What are you doing?"

"Making sure you don't sleep walk," he said succinctly as he sat cross-legged on his bedroll.

I thought it might be a joke, his way of making a joke, but he didn't laugh or smile like Darius and my brother, Jarom, would have done.

Without thinking, my eyes sought Darius across the camp, and Lamech followed my gaze.

"Don't even think about going out to meet him in the moonlight," he said dryly as he rummaged in his satchel. "I can't protect you out there."

I certainly wasn't planning on anything of the sort, but I said, "I should think Dare could keep me quite safe."

"Everything but your heart," he said, and then looked

like he wished he hadn't said it.

Long moments passed between us in silence. What he had said was cold, calculated to be so or not. I had never said I was on the farm because of Darius, but Keturah and Gid knew, and it embarrassed me to realize they had told the rest of the family. Probably even Liam knew. Surely they had told him why I was there on his farm, eating of his food and helping with the work in his home.

"And I suppose you think *you* can protect my heart?" I asked.

He stared into his satchel another moment before looking up into my eyes, but I let the flap of the tent drop between us and wished I hadn't asked such a stupid question.

The journey had been long and arduous, and I would have fallen directly to sleep, but I took a few moments to smooth some healing salve over my shins. It burned at first and the smell was strong, but after a few moments, the sensation began to soothe the sharp pain. I silently thanked my mother for passing the little jar to me while I had stood silently, biting my lip, watching the group in the center of the village as they made their plans to go after Gid.

"You okay?"

My eyes shot to the crack between the flaps of the door. Lamech sat with his back to my tent, but I could see his head was turned so he could speak to me low over his shoulder.

"I..." What was the point in lying? He had obviously smelled the salve. "My legs hurt."

He turned and moved one of the flaps aside a little, and the shiny salve made it obvious where I had used the medicine.

His lips went tight. "Wait here," he said tersely.

Where did he think I was going to go?

Many of the other men were still moving about, setting up camp in the twilight. Lamech moved easily among them and looked very comfortable here in the wilderness.

I felt uncomfortable and out of place. Maybe Zeke had been right about me staying home.

It wasn't long before Lamech was back. He knelt on his bedroll and set down several rocks before securing the flaps of the tent back with the ties.

Taking one of my ankles, he pulled my leg out flat and placed a rock on top of it.

I flinched. "It's cold!"

And it was dripping water down my leg.

"It's from the stream. Hold still."

He placed a few more and did the same to the other leg, and then he looked up at me, probably regretting bringing me along. I couldn't read what was in his eyes. He rubbed the side of his mouth with his thumb.

"How long have they been hurting?"

I didn't want to tell him. Twisting my lips, I said, "Before we stopped in Orihah."

His brow rose as he realized I hadn't made it more than a few hours before my weakness had started to show. He was regretting his offer to watch out for me.

"You can do like this. If it feels good." He reached out and started to massage one of the smaller rocks across my shin.

I sucked in a breath, and the motion of the rock stopped.

"No, it's good," I said.

22

He hesitated, as if he were deciding whether or not I meant it, but after a moment, he started the massage with the cold rock again.

Motioning to the other leg, he said, "You do it."

I reached out. Putting my fingers on a rock, I began to move it over my leg like he showed me. I couldn't say it felt better yet, but perhaps his remedy would work and I would feel better by morning.

One of the rocks tumbled off my leg. I replaced it, but it fell off the other side. Lamech replaced it. But again, it rolled off, and I giggled as Lamech pick it up and tossed it out the door.

He might have been smiling, but he had his eyes on my legs, and suddenly I felt very self-conscious again.

"The rocks are getting warm," I said.

He nodded and began gathering them up. Soon he had taken them and gone again, and I wondered if any of it had really happened.

But I ran my hands over my cold shins. It had happened. He had seen my need and offered me a remedy, without any censure, without so much as a smirk.

I pulled the ties on one side of my door, but Lamech was back with more rocks.

"Do the same thing again," he said brusquely and loosed the other tie so the flap fell closed, leaving me alone in the tent.

I lined up the rocks on the ground and lay on my stomach, letting my shins rest over the rocks. It seemed easier than balancing them all. They stayed cool for quite a while, and soon I had fallen into a deep sleep.

"You should ask for help if you need it," Lamech said

the next morning when we were moving away from camp.

His voice was hard and annoyed.

"I didn't need help."

He scoffed.

"I had medicine."

He sighed, rubbed the back of his neck. Was he conceding?

"But thank you. For the rocks."

Looking away from me, he shrugged it off. Was he so annoyed he wouldn't even look at me?

"I think it helped," I mumbled, feeling like a nuisance.

"I'm going to go talk to Jashon," he said abruptly.

I bristled. "You don't need my permission."

His eyes narrowed.

"If you want to leave, just go."

Scowling, he said, "Go walk with your sister," and he jogged away.

He gave it like a command, but my legs were burning and my breaths were already short. I had never traveled much farther than into the market in Melek from my home in the village. It had not occurred to me that I would not be strong enough to make the journey to the Land of Nephi, but the pain and fatigue were quickly making it very clear.

I glared at Lamech's back. And then I glared at my sister. I couldn't catch up to either one of them, so I trudged along behind the others until I could barely see them and our scouts at the rear caught up to me.

"You okay?"

I glanced back and my face got hot.

When Darius and Mahonri were at my side, Dare asked me again.

"You okay, Sarai?"

I nodded.

They were both quiet for a moment.

"Why are you falling behind?" Mahonri asked.

Mahonri was a friend of my brothers. He lived in the nearby village of Antum, and I had seen him often in our village. He had a scar that cut across his cheekbone from one of the battles he had been in, and one of his hands didn't work right, though I had never heard exactly what was wrong with it. It was one of those things people never really talked about.

I didn't want to tell them I was in pain, that I was weak and unprepared to be on the journey. We were still close enough to home that Zeke might send me back.

"I'm not fast like the others." I gestured ahead to where everyone else was disappearing beyond a rise in the terrain.

They were quiet again.

"I'll get faster," I said.

"You'll have to." Mahonri could be brusque with people. He didn't have very much patience, but he had never been mean to me. Even now, his words were just a fact, and he didn't say them to hurt my feelings.

I looked ahead at the empty trail, glanced at Darius, and thought of the ease with which everyone else seemed to be traveling.

"I know," I sighed.

I *would* have to get stronger.

3

I wasn't really lost.

Just a little turned around. I knew the general area I was in—somewhere in the wilderness south of the Land of Manti. And I knew which direction I was headed—south.

No. North.

I threw another pebble into the Sidon River and sighed. I had been second guessing myself for three days. I was unable to move forward with my impulsive plan, and yet still unable to talk myself completely out of it and turn back.

My son was out here somewhere, and I had to find him and bring him home.

I sighed in frustration and drew back my wrist to throw another pebble into the water when I heard the sound of...laughter? A girl?

I had been alone so long that any sound was a surprise. I dropped the pebble and scurried into the trees, too scared to peer out at the river, but doing it anyway.

If anyone was around, they would surely stop here at the river for water, but the road passed by the river farther north. Who would come to the headwaters? I was three full days past Manti and two days past the last Nephite settlement.

But I had lost Ardon's trail, and I was a little lost myself.

As I watched, the laughing woman emerged from the trees on the opposite bank. She was beautiful with brown curly hair and was followed by a man in buckskin pants whose eyes crinkled when he smiled at her. The woman fairly danced to the river and filled both their water skins while the man leaned against a tree and watched her.

They were in love. I was observing one of the simplest acts of love, to bring water to another.

I debated with myself whether or not I should confront them, perhaps ask for directions, but they were gone before I made a decision. Disappointed, I nearly stepped from the trees to follow them when I noticed another couple had taken their place on the bank.

Not knowing what else to do, I went instantly still, pressed myself against the large mahogany tree, and peered around at them.

They were not in love with each other.

"He shouldn't have married a girl he couldn't take care of," said the man, "when he was unwilling to give up his consuming career to provide for her needs!"

"I wouldn't have let him!" exclaimed the woman.

"Then you are both fools," he accused. "He could be dead, or die before we reach him!" He made a sound of frustration and lowered his voice, but it was no less harsh. "And now there is a child!"

"I may be foolish, but I am not the only fool here." She gave him a hard look. "It's just as foolish to covet what your brother has."

They were facing each other on the bank, but the woman turned from him and clenched her fists in her dress. She had her back to him, but I could see her eyes were shut tight and she was indeed carrying the child he spoke of, her belly round with it.

The man was partially turned away. I couldn't get a clear view of his face, but he was undeniably masculine. Thick, muscled chest and arms. Scars visible even from where I was hiding. Angry expression. Chestnut-colored hair that fell loose to his shoulders.

Something about him was familiar to me, as if I had seen him before. But I couldn't have. I had never even left my village.

The woman took a deep breath. "I shouldn't have said that."

"How long have you known?" The man shifted his weight from one foot to the other, but his voice held no inflection.

She looked woefully back over her shoulder at him. "A long time. I think I knew it the night we rescued Isabel."

"Well." He cleared his throat, and he wouldn't look at her. "You are only half right. I love you both." He turned on his heel like a soldier, pausing to speak before he strode away. "I'll leave you in peace, but don't stay here long. Gid would have my head if I let anything happen to you and that child."

The woman stood still for a long time, and I remained still too, watching her and feeling guilty for doing it, but now was not the time to make myself known.

She was pretty, beautiful really, with wide-set eyes and charcoal-colored hair that had moved like liquid when she had whirled away from the man.

The man who loved her and clearly had no right to.

After a time, the woman turned toward the river and crossed her arms over her chest. I noticed the blade that was strapped to her upper arm. She glanced around, as if recognizing something, and then moved toward a large rock on the bank. Having had a child myself, I knew her feet must be aching, and I thought she might sit on the rock to rest them. But instead, she knelt next to it, placed a hand on the rock to keep her balance, and leaned forward to dip her other hand into the river. When she withdrew it, it was dripping with strings of algae.

She looked at the algae in her hand for a moment and then brought both hands to her face and began to cry quietly into them, restrained, as if even alone she could not let herself grieve fully.

My eyes dropped to the ground. I felt uneasy. I was intruding on something very private.

I made a move to step away, to leave and let the woman grieve in peace, but my dress brushed the bark of the tree, and the woman looked up at the scuffing sound it made.

I saw her tear-stained face for just a moment before I ducked back into the shadows of my hiding place behind the tree.

I didn't hear the sobs anymore, and when I ventured a look, she had gone.

As the day went on, more people came to the river for water, mostly men. They must have been traveling together and camping close by. I was very curious to know why they were there. I wasn't brave enough to approach them, but when night began to fall, I followed a tall man back to their camp.

I got close enough to watch them, to listen to them, but though they were pleasant and friendly with one another, I didn't know if they would be friendly to me.

There were about twenty people in the band of travelers, and I counted six women or girls. Two guards were employed at all times. Some of them were clearly Nephite.

Some, clearly Lamanite. Others, I couldn't tell for sure. This made it very difficult to decide whether or not I should approach them and ask for assistance, but heaven knew I needed it.

I watched them closely while the last of the light played off the trees, trying to determine what they were doing way out here so far from any settlement, and more importantly, which direction they were traveling.

I bit my lip as I watched the man from the river—not the man with the laughing girl, but the one with the girl who had been crying. He sat apart from the others with a dark-eyed younger man who was clearly Lamanite, though the twilight made it hard to determine much more than that—I couldn't make out either of their features. They talked quietly to each other, but each one periodically glanced up. Broad-shoulders, I nicknamed him, glanced toward the girl from the river. Dark-eyes aimed his glances at a brown-haired girl who was easily the youngest among them. She couldn't have been more than fourteen or fifteen.

When the girl from the river approached the men, Dark-eyes nodded to her, got up, and left. Broad-shoulders regarded her warily. But she sat by him and they bent their heads together to talk in relative privacy.

It was nearly dark, so I decided to return to my own little camp on the other side of the river. The travelers were clearly staying until morning, and I would have the night to decide what to do.

I lay awake for a long time that night, deep into the second watch. Alone in the woods, I thought of Ardon, my son, my boy, my baby, alone somewhere in the night.

I thought of that morning eight days ago when we had

been in the fields working together. We were laughing and the sun was bright, almost too bright. I had shaded my eyes with my hand, looked at the sky to judge the time, and then I had left him working alone in the field and gone home to fetch our midday meal.

If only I hadn't left him alone.

I sighed. If I hadn't left him alone, I would have been taken captive too.

I thought I heard a whisper in the night around me, and I became suddenly very alert. A shiver went through my chest as if eyes were watching me in the night.

Just the breeze in the trees. Only the whisper of God's breath, I told myself.

I determined to follow the group of people. Whichever way they traveled, they would lead me to somewhere, hopefully somewhere I could get my bearings and make the decision whether or not to carry on with what was turning out to be a foolhardy plan.

It was a reckless and hasty decision to follow Ardon into the wilderness, but to do nothing was unthinkable. I would be unable to live with myself. I would be unable to live at all, to take an unencumbered breath ever again, if I did not recover Ardon from the men who had taken him captive. I should have waited until the men of my clan came back from hunting, but I hadn't wanted the trail to go cold.

I said a prayer, entrusting my keeping to God and His angels until morning, and I made myself relax and go to sleep.

I awoke before dawn, readied myself quickly, rolling my bedroll and eating a cold meal, the last of the food I had brought with me, as I made my way toward the larger camp on the other side of the Sidon.

I hid a distance away where I could hear them. The band of travelers left their camp early. I waited a short time before I crept to the campsite, studied the ground and began to track them.

South, then.

I followed them southward for two days. They trekked overland and stayed off the main highway. The twigs and leaves showed their passage easily. I could tell they were trying to be careful, but the path of twenty men was hard to hide. They were all very good at hiding their tracks, and they were all doing it except for perhaps one of them. I might have thought one of them was leaving a deliberate trail if I hadn't suspected it was the inexperience of the youngest girl, the one Dark-eyes had continued to watch through the morning.

I stayed quite a distance behind, but I did see them from time to time, moving through the hills as we were, ahead of me. The group made excellent time. They were not traveling for leisure, and I appreciated that.

As the third morning wore on, I began to feel the odd sensation that someone was watching me, following me. It was no less than I deserved, following the others as I was, but it kept me on edge with the hairs on my neck prickling. The only question was whether some member of the group I followed had seen me and backtracked to see who I was, or whether my stalker was someone else entirely.

So it did not surprise me when I stopped to rest at midday, though I had no food left for a meal, and two men stepped from the trees and walked toward me. I experienced a moment of relief when I recognized the men were from the band I followed. One of the men was tall with brown wavy hair. The other was the man I had seen at the river. *Broad-*

shoulders. My eyes widened suddenly in recognition as it occurred to me why he looked so familiar.

He was the prisoner who had spoken so kindly to Ardon when his captors had marched him through our field.

"You!" I exclaimed before either one of the men could speak. "What are you doing here?"

He glanced at the other man in confusion.

"You're free," I said, rushing a little toward him, stopping short to clasp my hands together and beg of him. "Where is he? Where is my boy?"

To my dismay, he looked back at me blankly. He exchanged another look with the other man, who I finally glanced at as well, then he took a step toward me.

"I'm not sure I understand," he said gently, but his eyes said I was the one who did not understand.

"You're the prisoner," I said, now growing unsure of myself.

He had to be. I had seen him from the cover of the trees, but I was sure this man was him, the man who had been so kind to Ardon and taken the blow for speaking out to protect me.

One of the Lamanites had forced him to translate. "They want to know where your mother is, but do not tell him. Don't point. Don't even glance in her direction."

So Ardon had shaken his head and bravely said he did not know.

The Lamanite had said something, clearly something lewd. The man, *this* man, had replied tersely, and the Lamanite had elbowed him in the face and then tied Ardon to their parade of prisoners.

"Don't struggle," he had advised Ardon calmly after

33

shaking off the blow and wiping his bloody nose on the shoulder of his tunic. "It will not go well if you do. The less attention you draw to yourself, the more likely they are to leave your farm, your home, and your family alone."

I had been close enough to hear this. Why hadn't I run to my boy?

I must have paused for a moment to remember this because I turned my eyes back to the man before me. I quickly stepped up to him and touched his temple, cradled his cheek in my hand.

He had no bruise there.

I drew my hand away. "I'm sorry," I said and looked between them. "I...I thought you were someone else."

The other man broke into a grin. "And we thought you might be someone else." He easily placed a hand on my shoulder. "I am Kenai."

Broad-shoulders had been staring at me, probably coming to the conclusion that I was crazy, but jerked a little when his friend spoke and politely placed his heavy hand on my shoulder as well.

"I am Jashon."

"I am Salome," I told them both, though I was holding Jashon's gaze. He looked so much like that prisoner. It was unnerving.

"And who is this boy you seek?" asked Kenai.

"My son. Ardon."

"Has he run away then?"

I shook my head.

"Well he can't be far. He must be very young. We'll help you search for him."

"He is twelve, and he is not lost."

"But you can't be more than twenty!" Jashon burst out and then actually looked embarrassed, stepping back and rubbing a hand over his face.

I raised my chin a little. "I am old enough to have a twelve year old son."

Kenai adjusted the bow on his shoulder. "And where is your husband?"

I eyed them closely. I did not want to tell them I had no protection, no man to care what happened to me, but when they both stared levelly at me, Kenai with patience and Jashon with hard eyes, I knew there was really nothing for it.

"I have none. He is dead."

In a kind gesture, Kenai placed his hand on my shoulder again. "Be at peace. No harm will come to you by our hands."

I looked down, overcome with relief. He couldn't know how long I had worried his party would not be kind to me, though he was clearly aware that I was nervous about it at present.

Kenai moved and Jashon followed him to where I had laid my travel pack on the ground, and they both sat. Neither of them wore a travel pack, though I had seen that they both had them. I realized suddenly that they had been stalking me like prey for some time. When had they noticed my presence? When had they sensed I was trailing them?

When I hesitated to follow them, Kenai invited me to sit with them. I did but I kept my eyes averted, feeling awkward in my realization that they had been spying on me.

In a moment, a stick of dried meat appeared before me in a large hand. My eyes shot to Jashon, and he gestured for me to take it, bouncing it a little in his hand.

"Go on," he coaxed.

I had run perilously low on food, meat in particular because I did not know how to procure it in the wild. For two days I had been foraging what I could from the plants of the forest, and I wondered if they knew it.

"Thank you, Jashon," I said as I reached out for it. I took a bite and to my surprise it was not tough, but soft and very flavorful.

He tossed another piece to Kenai, who caught it easily, snatching it out of the air.

Once I had tasted the meat, I ate hungrily, and when I had finished it, Kenai passed me a corn cake and some goat cheese.

"Take it," he said when I again hesitated.

"How long have you been watching me?" I wanted to know.

"A while," Kenai admitted.

"I didn't feel your eyes until this morning."

"That's when we decided to confront you."

I nodded and ate the cheese. "This is very good," I said.

"My wife's sister makes it."

"You are lucky."

They both chuckled.

Kenai said, "I am lucky the other women of the village take pity on me."

I glanced up at him again in question.

"My wife..." he began, but when he could not seem to bring himself to say any more, Jashon finished for him.

"His young wife is a terrible cook."

This made me smile.

"And yours?" I asked Jashon. "Can your wife cook?"

His eyes dropped to the food in his hands. "I have no wife."

I looked down too, remembering suddenly that he was in love with another man's wife.

"Who is Gid?" I asked into the silence that had fallen.

Jashon looked up sharply, and I met his querying gaze.

"Gid is my brother." He paused, exchanged a look with Kenai. "What do you know of him?"

4

I nudged Isabel with my elbow. "It looks like your husband finally gave up hope on your cooking and found someone new."

She looked over at me and then followed the direction of my gaze to where her husband had appeared in the clearing.

Isabel got to her feet and hurried toward them, but she barely spared Kenai a sweet smile before placing her hand on the woman's shoulder.

"My wife, Isabel," Kenai said to the woman.

Eve and Melia ventured toward the newcomer, but I stayed where I was. I wanted to look at her freely.

This woman was older than me by at least ten years, maybe more. At first glance, she looked no older than Isabel, a few years older than me. But her figure was developed, the skin of her hands more weathered than Isabel's, and this woman had life experience behind her eyes.

After some of the initial introductions were done, Jashon nudged the woman to follow him to the center of our camp.

I gave her a little smile when she passed me. She smiled back and cast a nervous glance to Jashon as the men began to notice her.

Jashon found her a seat on log near the cook fire. The

men watched her with interest. Eliam and Jarom set down the arrows they were working on, and Muloki swept stone fragments off the thick, leather leg guard he used for cutting arrowheads. Soon, everyone was gathered around, sitting on their heels or taking a knee near the fire.

Jashon stepped forward. "This is Salome. She's from one of the southern tribes." He waited a moment while everyone murmured a greeting. "Her son is lost in the wilderness. She's been looking for him."

Salome had her hands clasped in her lap, and she blushed a little but shook her head firmly. "He's not lost. He was taken captive by a band of Lamanite warriors. I'm going after him."

She couldn't have known why, but this statement brought a sudden silence to the clearing rather than exclamations of outrage on the child's behalf.

Jashon folded his arms across his chest. "Tell them what you told me and Kenai."

She took a breath.

"Nearly a fortnight ago, it has been now, my son and I were working in our fields. He kept working while I went to our house to fetch the midday meal."

"So? Get on with it," grumbled Mahonri.

Salome turned and glared at him as she went right on with her story. She had a bit of feistiness in her that made me smile. I could never be like that. I was obedient and docile and well-behaved.

"I got the meal together, but when I tried to return to the field, I...I almost stepped out into the open when something, I don't know, something stopped me. I had a strange feeling. I can't describe it—foreboding, sickness, fear, I don't know—and so I stepped behind a tree and peered out at Ardon.

"He was working still, making the sheaves, and I almost stepped out again, and again something stayed my feet.

"That was when I caught movement from the corner of my eye. A convoy of men. They were not Nephite, or if they were, they were unlike any I had ever seen. These men wore only their breechcloths and had brown skin, though I thought it was to be expected since so much of their skin was exposed to the sun."

No one said anything, but looking around at the others I could see many of the men looked impatient, with their arms folded over their chests, their glances darting to Jashon.

"They marched through my field, with no regard for the plants they destroyed, directly to Ardon. Stupid child stood staring at them. He didn't run to me." She looked down for the first time. "And to my shame, I could not run to him."

Still, the men remained silent, but they could not sense, as I could, what this story might have to do with them.

When Salome didn't go on, I said, "Gid was with the convoy. He was a captive." Everyone looked to me when I spoke into the silence, and I was glad when their eyes went back to the woman for confirmation.

Keturah went to her knees in front of Salome. "Is it true? Did you see him? Did you see my Gideon?"

Salome met Keturah's gaze. "I saw a man who looked just like Jashon." Her eyes found Jashon as she said his name, timidly as if she were trying it out for the first time, experiencing the feel of it on her lips. "His hands were tied, not behind his back but loosely in the front." She held her wrists out to illustrate. "I remember thinking he was lucky."

"Gideon," Keturah whispered, but it was drown out by questions from the men.

"How do you know?"

"How could you see well enough from behind the tree?"

"What was he doing with them?"

"Was he traveling willingly?"

This last question garnered a lethal glare from Keturah. Clearly she thought Gid would never go willingly.

Salome was still looking at Jashon, beseeching him now with her expression to calm the men.

Jashon took a step forward and held up a hand. He was about to speak, but the men fell quiet, and he didn't have to. Then he met Salome's eyes again and gave her a small nod, inviting her to continue.

"One of the Lamanite men spoke to Ardon, but of course Ardon did not understand. Even as he spoke, the others brought your Gid forward. I didn't know why until he spoke to Ardon.

"He said, 'They want to know where your mother is.' He told Ardon not to point or indicate in any way, not to even look in my direction.

"Then he turned and said something I didn't understand to his captors, and one of them became angry and..." She hesitated, looked at Keturah and then back to Jashon as if he could give her strength to go on. She bit her lip and did. "He became angry and elbowed Gid in the face. His nose bled but he just wiped it on the sleeve of his tunic and told Ardon the men were going to take him with them and it would be better for all if he came willingly." Then she added bitterly, "Better for me, he meant. I've been following their tracks ever since, but I lost them at the Sidon. Their trail was obscured by the many tracks there."

Keturah took Salome's hand in both of hers and said, "Gideon will watch out for him. He will protect him if he can."

There was silence for a time while the men considered all she had told us.

"Well," said Kenai after a few moments had passed. "He has suffered no worse at the Lamanites' hands than I have at my wife's."

The tension broke and a chuckle rippled through the men. When they were courting, Kenai had once made himself so obnoxious as to provoke Isabel. Using a defensive move he had taught her himself, she had hit him in the face, and to the complete amusement of all the men, she had broken his nose.

Muloki took a step forward into the center of the group. He didn't have to say anything. His presence alone, his dark skin and his foreign clothing, was a reminder of the many things that might happen to Gid once he reached the Land of Nephi.

"There are men among my people who disagree with the treatment of Nephite prisoners. They don't like it, and they don't like being made to march on the Nephites against their will. But in time, Gid will make it into the hands of their rulers."

Melia spoke up. "His eventual fate will likely be sacrifice to the Lamanite gods, and his life in the meantime will not be pleasant."

"They will want him to be healthy enough for a sacrifice." Muloki grimaced. "So we do have some time."

But for now, we knew he was well enough. If we were on the same trail Salome had been tracking, we were going in the right direction. They had indeed taken him toward the land of Nephi, just as Muloki and the older men had said they would. They had not killed him and had in fact barely hurt him.

We traveled with more fervor that day, covered even more distance than planned, with the knowledge, the hope that we might find him. We were close, and now we knew it. We stopped for the evening meal but unanimously decided to push on until dusk. It was nearly time to stop for the night when Kenai strode up and walked beside me.

"Sarai, can Salome share your tent with you?"

"Of course," I said. "But hasn't she got one?"

"No."

"Okay. I've no complaint with that."

Kenai, though married to my older sister now, had always been like a brother to me. He had been Zeke's best friend growing up and though I thought they had grown apart after coming home from the war, they were as close as brothers again. I had never viewed Kenai in any other way. I would accept his protection, his advice, and his instruction in any situation.

"Thank you. And Lamech."

Lamech made a sound of question, but avoided Kenai's eyes.

"I've no idea what Salome thought she might accomplish alone in the wilderness. She knows neither how to hunt nor protect herself."

He left the sentence hanging with implication.

"I can't hunt either," I reminded him.

"I know. You should both be taught, and quickly."

Lamech continued to avoid Kenai's eyes, but after a weighted moment, he relented and looked into them.

"Fine," Lamech said simply after a moment, and Kenai

grinned as he left us to walk alone again.

"Kenai wants you to teach me," I said, realizing what their exchange had meant.

Lamech sent me a sour look.

"You don't have to act so put out about it," I said, turning away.

"I'm not acting."

"You're a jerk."

"Don't forget it."

"With your constant reminders? I'm not likely to."

Silence was his only response, but in the silence I thought of him bringing the cold stones to me. I thought of his arms and of his warm blanket wrapped around me. I thought of him prying Zeke's fingers from my wrist and entwining his own fingers with mine.

He was acting alright. I just didn't know what was an act and what was real.

When at last we stopped to camp, everyone was sweaty, dusty, and exhausted. The information Salome had given us had brought hope, but the excitement was wearing off. We had traveled a great distance, but Muloki said it was still a sennight until we would see the first Lamanite settlement, a place called Amulon.

Keturah made a noise that betrayed her frustration and crawled into her tent.

I was watching Keturah's friends, Lib and Ethanim, roll out their bedrolls at the door of her tent when Isabel approached me with Salome.

"Salome, this is my sister, Sarai. She will share her tent with you."

Salome was the same size as Izz but different, more

shapely than Izz. Her golden brown hair, damp now from a dip in the stream, was stick straight, and her face was very pretty, almost regal.

"Hello," I said lamely.

"I'm going back to Kenai," Izz said. "I will see you both in the morning."

I looked to Salome. "Hand me your sleeping mat. I'll unroll it next to mine."

She took off her travel pack and knelt. "I can do it," she said, her voice warm and tired. "Just show me where."

I pulled back the flap of my tent and gestured to the inside where my own bedroll was pushed to the side. She gave me a small smile and crawled inside the tent.

To give her a few moments of privacy, I stood and wandered over to Zeke and Eliza's tent. Eliza was already inside curled up on her bedroll, but Zeke sat on his heels at the door.

"Do I have a watch tonight?" I asked him. Keturah, Eliza, and Isabel had all been asked to take a watch. Even Eve and Melia had sat up with their husbands when they took their turn.

He shook his head. "Not until you can use a weapon."

Zeke had always been of the opinion that women had little need to know how to use weapons, even for hunting. But somehow, miraculously, Eliza had changed his opinion. I didn't know how to use any weapons, but only because I had never had the need. I could use a knife for cooking and other daily chores, but that was all.

"Kenai asked Lamech to teach me. Salome too."

"It will be to your benefit to have some skill with a weapon. Are there any you're particularly interested in?"

I frowned a little. "Not really."

"Not really, or no?"

"No."

"You'll have a better idea after Lamech lets you try some different things."

I nodded slowly, and when I didn't say any more, he regarded me more closely.

"Something wrong? It's not too late to go back if you're scared."

"No. It's just...do you really think I can learn to use a weapon?"

"Of course I do. You're smart and strong and capable."

This from the man who three months ago had thought women were made to feed the chickens.

"But I am just fifteen," I said, still unsure of myself.

"Ket was fifteen when she went to war. Jarom was twelve."

It was good not to hear pain in his voice when he spoke of Keturah. I wondered briefly how he felt about this expedition to save Keturah's husband, the man she had once chosen over him.

"They are both better than me."

The look he gave me was harder, sterner, but his words were gentle. "That is untrue."

I sighed and knelt next to him. "I had hoped I could be of use in feeding the men and seeing to their wash and their fires so they could concentrate on the important tasks. I did not anticipate having to use a weapon."

"I hope you never have need to." He regarded me for a long time, mulling something over. He waited so long to speak, I almost said goodnight and left. But finally he said, "You know I was an archer in Helaman's army."

I nodded. "Sure. Keturah said you were the best."

His brows went up. "She said that?"

"She brags about you all the time." I picked at a loose thread in the hem of my sarong. "Though not so much now that she is married to Gid."

He considered that for a moment, and I noticed he glanced toward her tent. "Well." He cleared his throat. "An archer has to have arrows to shoot. Otherwise, his bow does him no good. But, see, an archer can carry only a limited number of arrows in his quiver."

I kept picking at the thread, smoothing it down with my thumb.

"If there are two hundred men to shoot, how do you suppose I shoot them all if I can only carry twenty arrows?"

Just a few stitches would hold it in place.

"We had teams of men who saw to the care of the arrows and hauled them with us into battle."

I looked up, wondering what he meant to explain to me.

"Keturah once told me she didn't think hauling the arrows was a very important task. She thought it was too safe and required little skill."

"Does it require skill?" I asked, feeling like I was missing the point.

"Sarai, if one of the feathers on my arrow is misaligned, it will not fly straight. I will miss my target. I can do no good without the man who sees to my arrows. And so it is with you."

"What do you mean?"

"Don't think feeding the men and building their fires is unimportant."

I understood suddenly that he was trying to make me

feel useful and wanted. I could feel myself blushing with the pleasure of his compliment, even though he couldn't have truly meant it. I nodded. "Okay," I said softly, and then I got to my feet, surprised when my legs did not shake, and went to my tent.

Lamech's bedroll was spread out at the door of the tent, but he wasn't in it. I crawled over it and into the tent to lay down beside Salome.

"I'm tired," I said to her.

She laughed a little. "I am beyond tired."

"Kenai said you have been without food."

Her laugh faded, but she said, "I was."

"I'm sorry."

"I ran out two days ago. I've been foraging ever since, so I was not starving." She paused and added, "But it was not enough for all the walking I was doing."

"You don't know how to hunt game?"

"No. I've never had to. Though I'm thinking now I should have taken the opportunity somewhere along the way to learn."

"That's what Zeke says. My brother. He says I should let Lamech teach me. But, to be honest, weapons scare me."

"I am not afraid of weapons," Salome said, "but I have always been blessed to have someone who would supply me with meat. My father, then my husband, then my husband's cousins, the men of my clan."

"Clan?"

"All the people of my small village are members of my husband's family. Ardon was becoming a good hunter. He could snare fish, and he could thrash grain as well as a grown man."

48

"How old is he?" I was lying on my back staring at the dark, pointed top of the tent.

"Twelve."

"Chloe is twelve—my little sister. "How old were you when he was born?"

"I was sixteen."

Not much older than me.

"Keturah is right. Gid will take care of him."

"I hope so. Is he at all like Jashon?" Again, she said his name almost timidly.

"In many ways. I don't know Jashon as well as I know Gid. I've been staying with Keturah and Gid for almost a year."

"Why?"

"It's a long story."

"We have all night," she prodded, but yawned again.

"There was a boy at home I did not want to see."

"Ah."

We lay in silence for a moment.

"How did you know when you loved your husband?"

It took her a long time to reply, and I wondered if my question had been too impertinent.

"I barely knew him when we married. He was my father's choice, but I liked him well enough. I grew to love him over time. I respected how hard he worked for me and for Ardon. I respected his determination to fight for the Nephites' right to govern themselves, to be free from Lamanite rule. I know I loved him before he left for the war, in those few years we had together, but I don't think I realized it until after I found out he wasn't ever coming home."

She spoke slowly, really giving thought to her answer. She was so sincere, and I thought I wouldn't wait until she was gone from my life. I would love her right now.

She yawned. "You will know when you're in love, Sarai. Real love doesn't hit you like a bolt of lightning. Real love will grow like the tendrils of a vine around your heart, slowly and ever so much better if you nourish it." She rolled onto her side to face me and patted my hand. "Real love wouldn't have driven you from your home."

5

The moon was still high when I woke just before sunrise. I stretched and looked over at my young companion. She looked even younger in sleep, innocent and vulnerable, and I thought instantly of Ardon.

When Sarai woke a few moments later, I whisked the tears from my cheeks, but she saw them.

"Come on. You can walk into the woods with me," she invited as she stretched and leaned up on an elbow.

"Oh, that's not necessary. I'll be fine."

She smiled tiredly and rubbed the sleep from her eyes. "They won't let me go alone, and they grow more worried the closer we get to the Land of Nephi. Believe me, I would rather go with you than with Lamech."

"Perhaps your sister or one of the other girls," I suggested.

She shook her head. "They've all got husbands to walk with, and Keturah has Jashon."

"Jashon?"

"Sure. He's Gid's brother. He takes his responsibilities very seriously. If we don't get Gid back, I mean, if something happens to him, Jashon will probably marry her out of duty."

She was as sweetly naïve as she looked in sleep.

The morning was already warming up when we emerged from the tent. Others were stirring around as Sarai and I walked away from the camp to seek the cover of the trees. Lamech's bedroll was gone and so was Lamech.

"I'd like to wash up at the stream," I said when she turned back toward the camp. "Isabel says it is deep here."

She nodded. "Alright."

When I found the small river, I waded into it and began to wash off the dust of the trail, the sweat and the grime. I wished I could wash off the worry and sorrow and the heaviness in my heart. Many of the men from camp were there, so there was no privacy, but I managed to get clean enough to feel better.

Finished, I stood and waded from the river. As I stepped onto the bank, I passed Lamech and a tall man, young like Lamech, with square shoulders and dark hair that glinted blue in the sunlight. The two men were talking as they filled their water skins.

It was never polite to listen to other people's conversations, but men were coming and going, so it was clearly not intended to be a private conversation, and yet, what I heard did seem private.

"Let me help teach her," I heard the tall man offer.

"Not a chance," said Lamech coolly. "You *lost* your chance."

"What are you talking about?"

"You know exactly what I'm talking about."

I slipped quietly away into the cover of the trees. Of course I wanted to hear the rest, but I did not want to be seen gawking at the two young men.

"That's in the past. That's all over now."

"Why? Because her betrothal turned into a marriage? Tell that to Sarai."

"You don't know anything about it," the tall man said with mounting anger.

Lamech scoffed. "I know enough. I know you don't deserve her. You drove away from her own home."

"I did not drive her away," the boy growled back, clearly losing his patience. "She left because she wanted to."

"You're an idiot if you believe that."

"And you're an idiot if you believe she'd ever prefer you."

Lamech scowled, but I could see the insult hurt him. He attached his water skin onto his belt with a sharp, decisive pull on the ties.

"Listen, Darius. Leave her alone," he said. "You've hurt her enough."

The man's name was Darius. Was this the man Sarai had moved away from home to avoid? The conflict between the men wasn't funny, and Sarai's tender feelings were at stake, but I smiled to myself as Lamech stalked away and disappeared in the trees.

Wanting to get a read on Sarai's feelings, I chose a name at random from those I had heard around camp.

"What do you think of Mahonri?" I asked her when I was back in camp and we were eating the meal she had cooked.

"Mahonri? I don't know."

"You don't think he's handsome?"

I didn't know if he was or wasn't. I was sure I had not yet met him.

She glanced at a dark-haired man at the edge of camp. "Well, sure, I guess."

"You never thought of him as, you know, more than a friend?" I prodded.

She frowned, confused by my questions. "I barely know him. He's much older than me. I don't even think of him as a friend."

"And Darius?" I asked, lowering my voice. "What do you think of him?"

Her eyes fell to the ground and she shrugged sadly, looking so downcast my heart went out to her.

I touched her arm. "I might be able to help," I said.

Her cheeks had already turned rosy pink, but she shook her head. "He loves someone else. I could never be his first choice."

"Sarai, there is another young man who likes you very much, I think. Don't discount him."

"If you're talking about Lamech, you're wrong. He follows me because he promised my brother he would."

I laughed a little. "I think you greatly underestimate the power a woman can have over a man." Jashon approached us but didn't interrupt, so I added,

54

"She can influence him to follow the right path and persuade him to do good."

"Thank you, Salome. I will think on it." She offered a sweet little smile as she left me alone with Jashon, but I could see I had stumbled upon a tender subject and she was quite confused.

My eyes followed Sarai. She very much needed some guidance concerning the two boys.

Turning to Jashon, I said, "She is not much older than my son."

His eyes followed her for a moment too, and then he turned back to me. "I have a hard time believing you have a child so old," he admitted. "You don't look old enough."

I tilted my head and smiled. "I am probably older than you."

He actually laughed, the boyish upturn of his lips nearly turning my knees to liquid, something that had not happened to me in many years. It was unexpected, but welcome.

"I doubt that," he said. "These men all call me Zequinim."

Old man. I smiled at the nickname.

"You don't seem so old. My husband was twelve years older than me." I didn't know why I said that. Feeling the heat in my face, I changed the subject. "Were you in Helaman's army with these men?" I asked.

He regarded me for a moment, deciding whether to let the comment about my husband pass. After a moment, he gave his head a hard shake and said, "No. I was young enough that I had not made the oath my parents had, old enough that I was already gone fighting."

I knew that most of them were of a similar age and had been among the small army of men that were led to battle by Captain Helaman. We had heard of them in my village. But what was this oath he talked of?

Jashon glanced around and then tilted his head toward the woods, inviting me to follow him.

"I want to thank you for letting me join your traveling party," I told him when we were alone. "I acted rashly, leaving without my kinsmen."

He shrugged his big shoulders. "With Gid and Ardon together, there wasn't really another choice."

"Another man would have left me, forbad me to go to the Land of Nephi," I suggested. "He would have said it was too dangerous."

"It is."

"And so I appreciate your offer of protection and help."

He grunted. I had made him uncomfortable. And it was kind of sweet.

He cleared his throat. "When did your husband die?"

"Years ago. Where are we going?"

He glanced down at me. "I want to get the lay of the land from that rise there." He pointed to a tree-covered hill to our right. "We're doing a little scouting."

56

"Did you scout in the army?" I held the hem of my dress up a little as I stepped over a large rock.

"No."

"You're good at it. And good at spying, too." As he had apparently spied on me for several days without my knowledge.

His neck might have flushed a bit, but he only said, "Anyone can scout."

"I don't believe you."

He grunted again.

"Do you have much experience with women?" I asked, teasing him a little. It was obvious he didn't. He had yet to even be more than distantly polite. Though to be fair, it did seem that he was trying.

He stopped fully and turned to me. "What do you mean?"

I raised a brow. "Experience," I repeated. "With women."

I expected him to shrug again, maybe walk away, but he surprised me when he blew out a deep breath and said, "Only one. A very unavailable one."

My other brow rose. I certainly hadn't expected him to be so forthright about that. "Keturah?"

A quick grimace marred his features for a moment, but he put a hand to his chest and said, "Yes, though I fight it valiantly."

I couldn't help laughing at his self-deprecating sigh.

He shot me a shy kind of smile and turned to

continue up the hill. "I grew up with just my brothers and then went into the army. Not a lot of opportunity to go courting."

"You didn't seek out the company of women in any of the cities you were stationed at?"

"That wouldn't have been quite like courting. Just a distraction anyway."

"Truly? I thought soldiers liked...getting to know the local women."

"I belong to the church of God. The only business we have with unmarried women is courting them properly, and I wasn't at a point in my life when I was prepared to do so. I had little to offer but life in a tent traveling with the army."

"I've not heard of the church of God."

"But you have heard of Helaman's stripling army."

"Yes. Everyone has."

"And you did not know they were members of the church of God?"

"No, only that they fought when their parents wouldn't."

"Our parents lived in the Land of Nephi. Lamanite by birth, culture, religion, and heritage. A missionary came there and taught my people of the gospel of Christ. Ammon preached repentance and once our sins were cleansed by baptism, my people wanted to stay without sin."

"I see."

"All who were able and accountable made an oath

that they would sin no more. They buried their weapons of war and moved to the Land of Zarahemla for asylum."

"My people are of Mulek, born of Zedekiah, the king from the old lands. We came out from Zarahemla generations ago to keep our heritage pure, but I've not been there," I said. "What is it like?"

"It's large and overrun with people, but we don't live there. The Nephite government has given us the Land of Melek to live in."

We were nearing the top of the hill and Jashon put a hand out to stop me. "We need to approach the top with care." Our eyes met, and his reminded me of the greens and browns of the forest. "Now, just stay behind me, do what I do, and we'll see what is beyond this hill."

Jashon slid from tree to tree until we could see over the hill into a broad valley below. He crouched behind a small outcropping and beckoned me to follow. As he scanned the valley, he let out a low whistle.

"Look there," he said and pointed to the east.

I did, but all I saw was the blue sky and the deep greens of the thick vegetation that fell out before us, miles and miles of it. "What is it?" I asked.

"A campfire. See that thin wisp of smoke?"

"No."

I caught the corner of a smile.

"Well, it's there. We're in enemy territory now, so we can assume it's a Lamanite fire."

"But we are traveling with Lamanites." I said it almost as a question.

"No. They are all Nephite now."

"Just saying they're Nephite doesn't change their birth."

"Both my parents were born Lamanite," he reminded me. I was born to them in Shemlon. That's in the heart of the Land of Nephi—the heart of Lamanite territory."

He was born in Lamanite lands to two full Lamanite parents? I didn't understand. He was light-skinned and had chestnut colored hair, not much darker than mine.

"Are all the people we are traveling with of the same heritage?"

"Most. Muloki and Melia were raised in Lamanite holdings, but they didn't meet until they both came to Melek, both looking for different things."

"What did they seek at such a distance?"

"Melia was looking for her father. He had joined the church of God with the other converts of Ammon and traveled to Melek to avoid the religious persecution."

"I've heard of the people of Ammon. Ammonites. My husband spoke of them once." For some reason, I didn't want to keep bringing up Zedekiah, and I blushed a little when I mentioned him.

"Did you never leave your village?"

"My clan has several villages. But leave the clan? No, never."

"And you married within it?"

"Yes. Zed was my father's cousin's son."

I gasped when I realized what I had done. It was not respectful to speak the name of someone who had died, not when you were speaking directly about them, and especially not to an outsider.

We were still crouched low. Jashon had been scanning the valley and the surrounding hills, but his eyes shot to mine. He stretched out a hand as if he might touch mine. He hesitated for just a moment, but let himself continue. His fingertips were warm from the sun and moist with sweat.

"I'm glad you told me," was all he said, and he motioned for me to follow him as he slowly backed up.

"Why did you bring me with you?" I asked him when we were treading back down the hill. He put butterflies in my stomach with that smile of his, but I was too old not to be direct. There was no reason for me to be coquettish or shy, no matter what his smile did to me.

"I told you, there was really no other choice."

"I meant, why did you take me to the top of this hill?"

"Oh. I...uh...I thought we could talk."

Perhaps, like me, he was also too old not to be direct.

"Did you have something particular in mind?" I asked.

"Not really."

Not really. It hung in the silence between us as we stepped carefully down the hill.

Finally, not wanting to waste the time we had

61

alone, I said, "You told me about Melia, how she went to Melek to find her father. What did Muloki go there to find?"

"Keturah."

"But why? He's married to Melia."

Jashon's expression went blank. "I guess he didn't feel like waiting in line for Ket." After a moment, he cleared his throat. "Sorry. I didn't mean he doesn't love Melia."

I mulled that over as we came back into camp. Everyone was busy now, moving around, talking to one another, and curiously eyeing Jashon and me together.

Kenai spotted us and as he started toward us, he motioned for Zeke to follow him.

Jashon brushed my hand with his. I thought it was an accident.

"Salome."

I met the green of his eyes again and a curiosity there I liked.

"Thank you for the walk."

Something in his curious eyes, something in the way he had brushed my hand, perhaps to get my attention, gave me the impression that the walk to the top of the hill had not been for scouting the terrain, but for something else entirely.

But then I thought of Keturah. I thought of her at the river, squeezing her eyes shut.

I love you both.

I thought of her round belly and her missing

husband. I glanced at her, where she knelt near the cook fire, and even now all the men seemed to gravitate to her.

It is because she gives them food, I tried to tell myself. But she was so beautiful and fearless and generous of spirit, I didn't believe it.

"Is the way clear?" asked Kenai when he and Zeke drew up.

Jashon looked at me for a moment more and then turned his attention to the men.

"No. We need to travel west. There is a small war party to the east." He turned to speak to me. I felt the brush of his hand again, and this time, it felt intentional.

"Salome," he said, and I loved how he placed a heavy accent on the third syllable *may*. "Will you please go see to packing the camp?"

I thought the others had it pretty well handled. "Of course, but Jashon..." I glanced at the other men. "How do you know it is a war party?"

He looked me steadily in the eye. "I wish I didn't, but I just know."

6

The terrain began to change as the days wore on and we continued south. We had passed through thick wilderness that covered the north face of the mountains, but the south face was more rugged. Craggy and sheer drop-offs made our progress slow. The scouts spent hours finding ways around some of the steepest areas, and all the while, we were pushed to the west by the war party Jashon had seen.

"We should just confront them. We could win a fight. How many of them could there be?" one of the men said.

Jashon gave his head a shake. "We can't chance casualties. We need to save our men for Gid."

"We'll never get to Gid if they keep pushing us west."

"We'll end up in the sea before we hit any of the big cities."

Jashon smiled, but shook his head again. "We just need to move south faster." He turned to Jarom. "Is there any way we can get down this slope today?" He stepped closer to the edge of a deep crevice that spanned in both directions, giving it a dubious look.

"Not unless you can fly."

Jashon sighed and went to discuss it with Kenai, Zeke, and the handsome, darker-skinned Muloki. The gravel crunched beneath his feet as he walked. The sun was too bright, and the men had kicked up enough dust to make my head hurt.

I looked across the deep ravine. What Jashon had optimistically termed a slope was a sheer rock face. There was clearly no way around it. Ardon was on the other side of it. How had the Lamanites taken their prisoners down it? I shaded my eyes from the sun and studied the area. They had probably crossed farther to the east. Jashon hadn't said, but I figured we were more than a few miles off course.

"We'll just have to start down," Jashon called to the men. "And try to have everyone down by nightfall."

A few men grumbled, but only from fatigue. Everyone picked up their gear and prepared to move on when Jashon told them to.

Jashon was the only one who hesitated. As I pulled my wraparound on and situated it so it would not flap about as I climbed down the cliff, I noticed him watching me. All the other women, including Sarai, seemed to be paired up with a man to assist her. He was probably wondering just what to do with me. He scanned the available men, and after a moment, he walked back to me, his feet crunching the gravel between us again.

"Stay near Enos," he said.

I had heard the name around camp, but I didn't

know which man was Enos. It hardly mattered, but when Jashon approached one of the friendlier men, I was glad of it. I waited while Jashon spoke to him, and when Jashon gave him his assignment, his brows went up and he grinned.

Jashon's eyes narrowed with the strain of having to take us all down the cliff, but he quickly turned to help Keturah down to the edge and left Enos to come to me.

He put a quick hand on my shoulder. "You ready? I'm Enos."

"I don't need help," I said, feeling instantly ungrateful and foolish.

But Enos only shrugged and said "Then just follow me."

Saying I didn't need help proved to be not only pointless, but wrong. Even some of the men had to help each other over the rougher parts. The first section was steep but just loose gravel, and a sideways approach to it seemed to be all that was needed. I shook the small pebbles from my sandals and peered down the next section, where I could see the others were lowering themselves and each other over a drop, most going over on their bellies, some from a sitting position.

Enos sprang over it easily, if a bit ungracefully, and turned to coach me through it.

"You'll need to turn onto your stomach and come down backward," he said. "Find some handholds, there are a few, and set your feet into my hands."

I took a breath and did as he instructed, and I

understood why Jashon had paired me with someone strong and tall. There was no way I was getting through this alone. It would take all day, possibly into the evening, and I would have to trust someone I didn't know. But for some reason, I trusted Jashon—he inspired trust and loyalty—and so I put myself into the hands of the man he had chosen to help me.

Many of the obstacles had to be traversed one person at a time, so the going was slow. The men were quiet, watching how each obstacle was to be done, learning the ways to help their partner.

"Alright," Enos said. "Are you ready for this one?"

I gave him a small smile. There wasn't a choice, and we both knew it.

"I would fall down this cliff if it would save my son," I told him.

His smile was quick. "Hopefully you won't have to. Now, this time, you have to go over first."

Giving him a dubious look, I knelt near the edge.

"Sit, and hang your feet over the edge."

I had seen how the others had done it, practically walking straight off a large, flat-fronted boulder.

"Are you sure sliding down backward would not work just as well?" I asked, thinking I could do it the way I had done it before, the way I knew how.

Enos shook his head. "This is how they said to do it."

We were nearly the last ones down. The only people behind us were Keturah and Jashon and two men who were probably there to provide her additional help, though she never seemed to need it.

"Now, you have to slide off the edge. I'll hold you by the hands and lower you down."

I wiped my hands on my dress.

"Then, listen close. You'll have to find the foot holds yourself. And since you're not tall," he rubbed his thumb by the side of his nose and glanced over the edge, "you might have to fall a cubit or so before you can find them."

I swallowed. "Fall?"

He grimaced. "I will have to let go of your hands."

I let my eyes close, but I nodded. I would do it. I *would* fall down this cliff if I had to.

"They said the walls get narrow. Once your feet hit the walls, lean forward." He pointed to the blue sky in front of us. "There's a wall to lean against. Climb down the walls, and someone will be at the bottom to help you the rest of the way."

"What is the rest of the way like?"

"Don't ask. Remember what you have to do?"

I nodded. "Go over the edge. Stick to the walls like a lizard as I fall. Climb down them like a spider to an unknown, final terrifying step."

"You listen well. Here we go."

He waited for me to ease to the edge.

"Hands up," he said.

I put my hands over my head, and he grabbed my wrists from behind in a reassuringly vice-like grip. I

68

tossed a glance up over my shoulder, but it wasn't Enos's worried eyes I met. Jashon stood behind Enos, watching intently.

I took a breath and eased myself over the edge. My back scraped against the rock, but as Enos lowered me down, I could see the wall in front of me, the one I would have to lean against for balance.

"Okay," Enos called. "Can you feel the walls?"

"No!"

I felt panic welling in my throat because I knew he had lowered me down as far as he could reach.

But Jashon's voice came over the rock, calm and close as if he were lying next to Enos, farther down even.

"There are footholds on either side. Spread your feet a bit and you won't miss them."

"Okay." I was breathless, dangling there from Enos's hands, and my voice came out in a squeak.

"Salome."

Jashon's voice was warm.

"Take some breaths and tell us when you're in position."

I took three deep breaths and called, "R...ready."

As if I could ever be ready for such a thing.

"Let go of my wrists first," Enos called.

It was hard and went against every instinct I had, but I forced my fingers to relax. The moment I did, Enos dropped me.

I landed on two narrow ledges before I had time to be afraid. The free fall was only inches. I opened my eyes and looked around, trying to assess where I was. The rock in front of me came up to my chest, and I put my hands against it. Then I looked down and wished I hadn't.

"I'm good," I called up so they wouldn't worry.

"You're in the footholds?" Enos called.

"I'm starting to climb."

"Call up when you're clear."

Pressing my feet against the opposite faces of the walls in what was basically a hole Enos had dropped me into, and leaning forward onto the rock, I began to crawl farther down into the hole. Chancing a look over my shoulder, I could see the rock behind me, the edge I had eased myself over, cut back into the mountain, and it was clear if I had come over the rock on my belly as I had wanted to, I would have had nothing to lean against for balance. My heart filled with gratefulness, and my trust in these men increased.

I came to a point where the two walls angled farther in and the space got very narrow. A man called up from below me.

"Who's coming?"

I looked down, trying to see who was below me.

"Salome!"

"Alright, Salome. You're almost done. Are you ready for the final step?"

"More than ready."

"Okay, you'll have to slide down now. We'll catch you."

It was so steep now that it would be a freefall.

Whoever was down there had only called it sliding because the hole was so narrow I would be scraping against the walls. I thought of the trust I had felt just moments before, and I made myself do as he instructed. When my feet were through, I felt strong hands clasp around my ankles.

"Pull your arms in close to your body," he called up even as he began to lower me.

Remembering suddenly, I looked up and called, "Enos, I'm through!"

It was a moment before his echoing call came back. "Stand clear when you're down."

As I slid through the narrow space between the rocks, I felt several pairs of hands helping me—one even eased the hem of my skirts back into place. When I was completely down, sure-footed on the ground, I was looking up into Kenai's face.

It was just a moment before we heard the scuffing as Enos came down through the rocks, and Kenai pulled me out of the way just in time. Enos didn't need any help getting down.

Everyone else was starting to trail away, as the landing area was not large, and I thanked the men for their help and followed the others across the rocky terrain. It wasn't easy going. Many places required climbing down, but I didn't have to rely on Enos to help me as much even though he did offer his help frequently.

A clear stream flowed through the bottom of the ravine, and Jashon said it was a good place to camp.

"But there is a risk of flash flooding," Kenai said quietly when the others were busy with the fire and tents.

Jashon looked around at the thick green grass and shook his head. "We can't live in fear of what might happen. You know that. There are no signs of past flooding here."

Kenai sighed. "You're right."

"But send someone upstream to watch anyway."

Late that night, while Sarai slept softly, my heart was too heavy to sleep and I slipped from the tent we shared.

Only one man sat guard in camp, and I was glad to see it was Jashon. His eyes tracked immediately to me as I made movement in the stillness. His eyes were tight. The poor man was tired.

"I like that you sent a man upstream," I said quietly as I sat down near him.

He gave a stiff shrug. "Just a precaution. You're not afraid are you?"

I was, but not of flooding. I shook my head. "You're tired."

He grunted, but it didn't sound like a denial.

"Will someone spell you off?" I asked. "Take your place?"

He glanced at the moon and back into the dim coals. "Yeah. We all take a turn."

"I could take a turn," I offered.

A half smile touched his lips. "All the men take a turn."

"I can't sleep anyway," I persisted. "You could rest. If you want."

Despite himself, he let a yawn escape.

"I don't think so."

I sat up straighter. "Why not?"

"Can you use a sword? A bow and arrow?"

"I can scream the camp awake."

He let a surprised laugh escape, but it ended in a tired sigh.

"You don't trust me," I said.

He shook his head, frowning. "That's not it."

I licked my lips. "Then teach me to use a bow and arrow."

He took a deep breath through his nose and crossed his arms over his chest. "I could make arrangements for that," he said.

Arrangements?

"But that won't help you tonight," I pressed softly. "Just wake one of the other men."

The lines of his face softened. "It is my turn, Salome, and I will take it. Surely, you can understand it's a matter of honor with a man."

"A matter of pride, you mean."

He shifted and his fingers brushed mine. "It is mine to do," he said solemnly, and I gave up the argument.

I knew about stubborn men, and I was frankly surprised he hadn't already laughed himself off his seat at the suggestion of me standing watch while he slept, snug and warm in his bedroll.

The idea really was preposterous, and I couldn't help a small smile.

"You're good," I said. Just that, because it was true and the truth of it sat warm in my heart.

I felt his eyes on me as I stood and picked my way carefully back to Sarai's tent where Lamech lay on his back near the door. Even though his eyes were closed as I stepped past, I could tell by the scowl on his face, the hard lines and shadows created by the moonlight, that he was not sleeping.

"Think you could keep it down?" he said and rolled onto his side to face away as I knelt to crawl into the tent.

Jashon and I had not talked loud enough for the light breeze to so much as pick up our voices and carry them away. I laughed softly and murmured a goodnight.

That light breeze had blown a coolness into the air by the next morning. I was awakened by the sound of others talking outside my tent, and sleepily, I pulled my blanket to my chin and listened as I dozed.

"This one here," Keturah was saying. "The root is good to eat. Dig up as much as you can and pass it around equally."

"To everyone?" one of the men asked—Eliam maybe?

"It's heavy to pack, but it can be eaten raw."

"I know you've taught me which ones to eat before. I never remember."

Keturah laughed lightly, and I could hear her steps

through the grass as she moved on.

The sun was bright when I stepped from the tent. Squinting, I could see what we had not seen the night before, that we had set up camp in a very lush area with trees that bore fruit and underbrush that included leafy bushes and thick, knee-high grass.

"Come here," Jashon said when he noticed me alone, warming my hands at the fire.

I followed him away from the fire, away from the stream, and away from the camp. We walked along the craggy rocks we had descended the day before and stopped at a small mulberry tree that was tucked back in a deep, shady crevice.

"We need to pick some," he said stiffly. "Some for everyone."

Feeling relieved to be of some help to these people, and in a kind of payment for the safe travel and food they had offered so generously to me, I pulled up a corner of my skirts and began picking the berries with Jashon.

I dropped the berries into the drooping fabric of my skirt, and Jashon picked large handfuls, occasionally adding them to mine.

As I hadn't yet eaten anything in camp, I popped a few berries into my mouth, savoring the sweet and tart flavor, and noticed Jashon staring at me.

"Oh! Should I not have done that?" I said, swallowing down the berries. "Are we to give all we gather to the group?"

His eyes widened. "Of course not! I mean, of course you can eat from the land."

"Oh," I said again, lamely. "I think we have enough, unless you've got something larger to carry these in."

We both looked down at the berries in the folds of my skirt.

"Ah." He fished around in his satchel and came up with an empty linen sack, folded into a neat square.

"You had that the whole time?" I asked as he unfolded it.

He scratched the back of his head and then stood motionless and dumb for a moment. But then he jerked suddenly and opened the sack open so I could spill the berries from my skirt into the larger bag.

His hands brushed against mine, and I couldn't deny anymore what I had been feeling for days. Jashon felt awkward around women and it was very endearing to me. So very different from Zed, who could not understand why I did not immediately adore him.

Jashon wanted to talk to me easily, like Enos did, but he didn't know how to. Maybe I could do him a favor and flirt with him a little, because heaven knew he wasn't going to get any practice at it with his brother's wife.

7

Sarai

As we traveled, I kept picturing Salome's bolts of lightning. During the rainy season, I had seen much lightning, and the more I thought on it, the more I could see that my feelings for Darius had been like that. Bright. Jagged. Hot. Fizzled to darkness in an instant.

I got my food and sat down by Izz, inviting Salome to sit with us. I wondered if she would be more comfortable with Melia or maybe Keturah because they were older, closer to her own age, but Salome smiled and sat next to me.

For a while I ate in silence and thought of what Zeke had said about the man who carried his arrows. I wanted to help the men rescue Gideon because it was all I had to offer, not because I thought carrying their arrows was important.

"We'll pass Amulon first, in about a week," I heard Kenai say, and I focused in on what the men were planning.

"Have you been there?" asked Izz.

Kenai looked at his wife. "Once," he admitted. "Or twice. We'll start seeing more settlements after that, but we'll need to be careful to avoid going into them."

"I'll take Lamech into Amulon for information and supplies," said Muloki. "And Melia and Keturah. They won't look out of place. The city is pleasant, and the people are kind."

There was a chorus of disbelieving snorts.

"If we don't do anything unusual, we won't stick out," Muloki continued over the noise.

"Our clothes will," Keturah said.

"She's right," Melia agreed.

"I hadn't thought of that," said Muloki.

"When I went into Antiparah the women wore sleeveless tunics belted at the waist," Keturah informed us.

Everyone pondered this for a moment. Obviously none of the men had given the matter of clothing much consideration.

"I can modify your sarong," I said, "to look like that."

"Do you have needle and thread?" she asked in surprise.

"Of course. I carry my tools with me." I gave everyone a small smile.

"I can help," offered Melia. "Though I am not very good with a needle."

"Just tell me what it needs to look like."

Zeke asked, "What about the men? You and Lamech?"

Muloki slapped his leathern kilt. "This is fine." He looked to Lamech. "But we should lose the tunics. Now, so we don't look so pale."

"No problem," said Lamech, and both he and Muloki stripped their tunics off.

Melia took Muloki's tunic from him and folded it neatly. I watched as Lamech awkwardly wadded up his tunic to stow in his pack, and I wondered if he thought he was folding it.

"What about the rest of us?" asked Lib.

"There are caves," Kenai told him. "We'll find one, and the rest of us can wait there."

"And why go into the city at all? We could do without the supplies. We shouldn't risk it," said Eliam, a man I liked who possessed a pleasant disposition, a level head, and had once courted Isabel.

"I can find out if the war party passed through there. They will be as low on food as we are, and if they are headed south, they will stop for supplies in Amulon."

"And if they didn't stop?"

"We'll turn west and try the cities on the borders of Ishmael."

"This is impossible," Mahonri muttered under his breath. Everyone scowled at him, but he wasn't the only one who felt that way. The whole idea of locating where they had taken Gid, now that we were here in the Land of Nephi, was daunting. Half of us couldn't show our faces anywhere because our skin was too pale. Only a few of us knew the language. And other than a vague direction from Helaman and the information from Salome that Gid had been alive two weeks ago, we didn't know where or how he was. It was discouraging.

"You can leave."

Keturah was studying her fingers, but looked up when she spoke. She wasn't being harsh or judgmental. It was just an invitation.

"Nobody has to be here," she went on. "I appreciate your help, but I'll do it alone if I have to."

Mahonri cleared his throat and spoke again. "Look, I didn't mean it like that."

"Yes you did," someone called out, and there was a burst of nervous laughter from a few of the men.

"We don't even know what we're up against yet. It might be something as simple as a trade," added a stocky man from Keturah's unit they all called Reb.

"What do you mean, a trade?"

"We'll just trade Mahonri for Gid."

That eased the tension. Everyone laughed, even Mahonri.

"I'd do it, if it came to that," offered Lib stoically.

Ethanim rolled his eyes. "Get over her, man. She's married." His voice was wry. It was kind of a joke. Kind of not.

Lib caught Keturah's eye for a moment. "I know. But it's Gid. He's a husband, about to be a father, and I'm not. He's got a lot more to live for than I do."

Keturah leaned forward, shaking her head. "Lib, that's not true. Forget it. It's not an option."

"It *is* an option!" he insisted.

"No."

For some reason, when Jashon spoke, everyone always listened.

"Here's the plan. The women are going to modify two sarongs into tunics for Melia and Keturah. Sarai, can you make a leathern kilt for Lamech?"

I glanced at Lamech and nodded.

"Muloki, you've been teaching Lamech your language?"

They both nodded, but Lamech said, "I'm far from fluent."

"I'll do the talking when we purchase supplies," laughed Muloki.

"With our Nephite senines?" someone asked.

"Gold is gold. And it's not uncommon. The soldiers bring it back all the time."

Another chorus of snorts.

Jashon held up a hand. "Two more men to carry

supplies." He pointed to Jonas and Mahonri.

"Then Keturah doesn't need to go."

"Lib," Ethanim hissed under his breath. "Enough!"

Lib threw an icy glare at his friend, got up, and left the circle.

Melancholy fell over the group as we finished the simple meal. When I was done eating, I started rummaging in my satchel for the needle I kept pinned to a bit of leather.

"Sarai."

I looked up into Zeke's face.

He went to his haunches in front of me.

"Most of the men are going out to hunt."

I nodded. I knew we were getting low on food.

"Lamech is going to teach you to use some weapons while we're gone."

My eyes found Lamech. He wasn't looking at us, but seemed to be waiting. My fingers closed over my needle, but I said, "Alright. I will go with him if you think I should."

Zeke gave me a pleased nod and was soon disappearing through the trees with Jarom and the others.

"I'm not going to lie to you, Lamech," I said when we were alone in a small clearing. "I don't want to do this."

"Too bad. Nock your arrow."

Trying not to roll my eyes, I positioned the end of the arrow into the bowstring like Lamech had shown me. I felt awkward trying to hold everything together with my fingers and when I tried to lift the bow and take aim, my arms trembled. I tried to pull back the string, but it was so taut I could barely move it at all.

"Stop being a baby and pull the string back. Then I'll help you aim."

"I am pulling," I said through clenched teeth.

For a long moment I didn't hear anything but the birds in the trees above our heads.

"Truly?" he finally asked.

I lowered my arms and shook them out as I turned toward him. "Yes, truly," I said, my throat tightening with frustration. I felt my cheeks heat as I looked down at the arrow and fiddled with the fletching.

He took a step closer. Folding his arms, he looked toward the target he had set up for me. "Get into position again."

I sighed but did as he instructed. When he moved up behind me, I froze. I hadn't expected him to do that, but I should have. I could be so dumb sometimes.

He placed one strong hand above mine on the grip in front of us and the other over mine on the string. The string came back easily in my hand as Lamech pulled it with seemingly no effort. He smelled of sweat, but nice, and I couldn't put it from my mind that he wore no tunic to cover his chest at my back.

"Breathe, or you'll faint before you take your shot."

"Don't tell me when to breath," I said, annoyed and flustered.

He growled, and he was close enough that I felt the growl more than heard it. Lifting the bow a little toward the sky, he nudged my hand to the right. "Let go of the arrow."

I did, and it sailed straight into the target.

"Nice shot," said Jashon as he came through the trees behind us.

"Good job, Sarai," added Salome, who followed close on his heels.

Lamech took a quick step back, and when I looked to him, he was considering the arrow and nodding slowly. What a faker. Jashon and Salome had both seen him with his arms around me. The look Salome gave me, a cross between a girl's secret smile and a mother's concern, said as much.

"Lamech did it," I said. "I'll never get it."

Lamech as much as agreed with me when he didn't say anything, just stepped back and scrubbed a hand through his hair.

"Keep practicing," Jashon encouraged me, and then he turned to his brother. "You got this?"

Lamech nodded.

When Jashon left, Lamech lifted his bow from my grasp and began to show Salome where to place her hands and how to aim it. He showed her exactly how he had shown me, even placing his hands over hers, and all of a sudden, it didn't seem so special anymore.

I sat on a log near our satchels, Lamech's weapons, and the other supplies. The wind was rustling the leaves above us. I tilted my head back and watched them for a moment, then I closed my eyes and tried to forget about everything I was supposed to learn but couldn't.

"Sarai."

I opened my eyes to see Lamech standing with his hand outstretched.

"The arm guard," he said impatiently.

"Oh!" I slipped off the leather guard and handed it to him.

He returned to Salome and positioned the guard over her arm to prevent her skin from being hurt by the snap of the string.

Which she *could* pull back.

I sighed and put my head in my hands. Maybe I could get a rest while they worked.

"Where do you go when you do that?" Lamech sat beside me.

I lifted my head a little to look at him.

"You leave and don't respond when people talk to you."

I knew I did this sometimes, but I didn't realize Lamech had noticed.

"I don't know. Somewhere else, I guess. Somewhere better."

"That's why you always do it when you're with me."

I laughed a little and shook my head. "I told you, weapons frighten me. I'm not...it's not my...I'm not able to..."

He waited for me to finish, but there was really nothing left for me to say. I couldn't do it.

In one instant, he was watching me carefully. In the next, he held a knife in front of my nose.

I flinched.

"Take it," he said.

I looked from the knife to his face.

He took ahold of my right hand and placed it around the handle of the knife, squeezing it tight with both of his. "Just feel it," he said. "It's not going to hurt you."

I took a deep breath.

"Do you have a blade?" he asked.

"No. Why would I?" From the corner of my eye, I could see Salome aiming and shooting arrow after arrow.

"You don't even have a knife for cooking, cutting twine, general use?"

84

I shook my head.

"Then this is yours."

"Lamech, I can't take your knife," I protested.

A corner of his mouth turned up. "Funny, that's what your sister said. Only not in so many words."

"Get it through your head. I'm not Izz. I never will be. I'm not even like her."

"I know that," he said, his eyes widening.

"Excuse me if I don't like you calling me by her name."

"Oh. That," he said, remembering, and he dropped his hands from around mine. "That wasn't anything."

"Ha!" I set the knife in my lap. "That was you calling me by another girl's name."

"It wasn't like that. I'd just been thinking about her. I mean, about something she said...aw, nevermind, you wouldn't understand it."

"Why, because I'm not Izz?"

"Sarai," he ground out in exasperation.

Had I ever heard him say my name before?

"Congratulations. You remembered it."

"Grow up."

He ran a hand through black hair that fell loose around his shoulders. It was growing out again. When he was younger, he had worn it in two thick braids, but he had taken those out and cut it to his collar bone, which had transformed him from a kid with an attitude to a man with a brooding, intoxicatingly handsome stare. Which was one of the details I wished I didn't notice about him.

Salome was traipsing into the brush to retrieve the arrows she had shot, but I was sure she had heard every last word we had said.

Maybe she could help me make sense of it all later.

Lamech was detaching the knife's scabbard from his belt.

"You could put a strap through this and wear it around your neck," he said. "If you want."

I liked the idea of that and fingered the spot in the leather where I would place the cord.

"Here."

Lamech was holding another piece of leather in his hand. "I'll teach you the sling," he said.

I met his eyes.

"It's not as complicated as the bow," he said. "A bit harder to aim, though."

I reached out and fingered the leather strap. "Is it sewn here?"

He shifted. "It can be. A knot works fine."

Lamech demonstrated the slinging technique several times, fingering a stone into it, holding it in front of him, and then swinging it around over his head and letting go of one of the straps. He hit his mark each time.

"This will be a little long for you," he said when he handed it to me. "It's made to fit my arm length, so hold it up here."

"Why?" I asked, but I grasped it where he indicated.

"So you don't hit yourself in the face. I'll be back to get you later," he said and left us there to practice.

My skin stopped prickling when he left, and I looked to Salome. "You're a natural at that. You've never used a bow before?"

"Thank you, Sarai, and no, I have never used one. But I do find as I get older, my life experiences with some things help me to learn things I've never tried."

We fell into silence again, each concentrating on our own task. Salome shot arrows toward Lamech's target, hitting it occasionally, and I awkwardly tried to sling.

To my surprise, I started to get the hang of the slinging motion, and while none of my stones hit the target, many of them came close. I happened to glance behind me as I wiped my sweaty hands on my sarong. Lamech was leaning casually against a tree with his hands behind his back, but there was nothing casual in the way he observed. He watched our progress with an eagle's eye. I wondered how he had kept quiet about my terrible technique.

When he saw I had turned, he beckoned with a motion of his head. "It's time to move on."

I nodded, sent a glance to Salome, and tossed him his sling, which he reached up and caught with ease. When Salome and I had retrieved the arrows and returned the quiver and bow to Lamech, we walked back through the trees to find the others. The men had returned with enough meat for several meals, and most of them had their travel gear already strapped to their backs.

Every afternoon for a week, Lamech took Salome and me apart from the others and taught us where we should aim when we needed to hit an animal for food. He explained more about how to use weapons to protect ourselves, and he patiently showed us how to break free from a man's hold so we could run away from him should we ever need to.

The thought that we might ever need to know any of what he told us was frightening, let alone the thought that we might need it on this journey. Salome seemed to take it all in stride and she paid much heed to Lamech's instructions, but I felt awkward using all of the weapons and wished I could just gather kindling and prepare meals.

One afternoon, Salome was busy showing Keturah and the other girls a hairstyle she twisted up and secured with a slender stick, and she was not ready when Lamech said we should leave to work with the weapons. I suppressed a sigh and followed him.

"I think you feel most comfortable with the sling," he said as we entered a small clearing.

Lamech dropped the gear near a large boulder and turned to me with a question in his eyes.

I shrugged. "I guess." Figuring he wanted to work with that, I pulled my new sling from my satchel and then tugged the satchel over my head and dropped it near the boulder too.

He propped an arm against the boulder and leaned closer to me.

I tried to step away, but he had me kind of trapped. I held up the sling, and he glanced down at it.

"Don't you want to work with this?"

He shook his head slowly.

I frowned and realized how close he had me boxed in. "Then you want to show me another way to get away from you?"

A slow smile spread over his lips, but he gave that slow shake of his head again.

I swallowed. "Let me past."

"Am I making you nervous, Princess?"

"No."

It was a lie, and we both knew it.

I tried to step away again, but he shifted, subtly blocking my way. I wondered if this was meant to be a test of what I had learned so far, so I jabbed him in the ribs like he had shown Salome and me to do, and I darted away, smiling, pleased with myself.

But Lamech didn't praise me, and a dark look fell over the teasing that had been in his eyes. He stalked past me and started setting up a target at the far end of the clearing. Obviously I had failed whatever test he had meant to give.

I gathered small stones from the ground while he constructed a target from branches and some linen from the supplies. When he had it set and cleared out of the way, I began slinging.

From the corner of my eye, I saw him stretch against the boulder, placing his hands behind his head. His skin was browned like a mahogany bloom, and something about the rawhide tied around his biceps was really distracting.

"You should put your tunic on," I called over my shoulder, not daring to look at him outright.

"You heard Jashon. I need to make my skin brown."

His skin was brown enough.

"You're just trying to make me uncomfortable."

"Is it working?"

I took a deep breath. Of course it was working.

The leaves rustled behind me as Salome came through the trees.

"Your aim is getting better," she said to me, and I grinned because I knew she was right.

"You know what we do to boys who won't wear their tunic in my clan?" she said to Lamech as she passed me and walked toward him.

He shook his head.

When she reached him, Salome licked her hand and

slapped Lamech on the back. The sound of the slap was loud, and I could see there would be a welt.

"Salome!"

I ran toward them and gave her a dirty look. What a mean thing to do! But she just gave me a small smile, picked up the bow and arrows, and found a place across from the target to set her stance and start shooting.

"That's already red," I said indignantly as I softly ran my fingertips over the bright welt on Lamech's back.

"It's nothing," he said, but he rolled his shoulders as if he could shrug off the sting.

I knelt to pull a length of bandage from my satchel and wet it with water from my water skin. "This will take the sting out," I said as I rose and began dabbing the bandage against his hot skin.

"I don't need it."

"Yes you do. That was cruel of her, to hit you for no reason."

Lamech had been watching me over his shoulder, but I glanced up to see him giving Salome a puzzled look over my head.

"She was kidding. My brothers do it all the time. So do I, for that matter."

"Hit each other?" I removed the cloth and let his skin air dry while I rummaged in my satchel.

"Don't your brothers?"

I frowned. "Maybe." Had I ever seen them do that? Playfully punch or tackle? Isabel tripped people and thought it was hilarious.

"Jared and Daniel did it. That time before we left Orihah."

His words were soft, almost a murmur, and meant just for me. And he didn't try to hide the jealousy in them.

I glanced over my shoulder at Salome. "I don't understand it," I said. "I would never hurt someone just to be funny."

"I know."

My eyes shot to his again.

"Here. I've some healing salve left." I held up the little jar of medicine.

He shifted so I couldn't reach the welt on his back.

"It's fine now." He paused. "But thanks. Get your knife and we'll go over those moves again."

I set the little cloth to dry on the boulder and pulled Lamech's scabbard from where it hung under my tunic.

When we were ready to leave, Salome said she wanted to stay and keep working. Lamech didn't notice but she winked at me, and I knew she intended for me to have some time alone with him. It made me blush as we walked away from her, but Lamech didn't notice that either.

The meal was quick and soon it was time to leave again. I gazed south and wondered if we would ever find a settlement in this vast and endless forest.

I settled in near Izz and Kenai as, once again, we headed south.

Kenai looked around Izz. "Lamech says you've learned everything and you can stop the lessons now."

My eyes found Lamech ahead of us. Did he really want our time alone to be over?

"I very much doubt I've learned everything," I said, trying to smile.

He shrugged and grinned back.

8

Lamech and Sarai hadn't even disappeared through the trees before Jashon approached me from the other direction.

Shifting my weight, I adjusted the bow on my shoulder and then fingered a feather on one of the arrows in the quiver as he walked toward me.

"If you've time to come here and stare at me all evening, you've time to give me proper instruction. I'm not going to get it from your brother. He teaches pretty, young Sarai how to fight off men with her bare hands, and all I know how to do is stand still and shoot this bow."

A faint smile touched his lips. "You're hitting the target."

I shrugged.

A glint came into his eyes. "I saw what you did to Lamech. I almost fell over laughing."

I met his rare grin with one of my own. "They just needed a push."

He nodded slowly, as if he had not really considered they needed a push toward anything.

When the silence dragged on, I asked, "What are you doing here?"

His unreadable expression never wavered. "I don't know."

"You don't know, or you won't say?"

"I don't know."

"What are you supposed to be doing?"

He drew in a breath. "Watching out for Keturah."

I rolled my eyes. "Those other twenty men can't be trusted to protect her?"

"It's not just protection. It is my duty as Gid's brother to see that she has all that she needs, to take care of her, to be a comfort to her." He paused. "She seems strong, but she's worried. You can't imagine—"

I felt my eyes narrow. He was very wrong. I *could* imagine her worry. But I didn't need to imagine it.

"Oh," he said, ducking his head a little. "Sorry."

"Forgiven," I replied. The breeze blew through my hair as I walked toward him, and as I passed him, I brushed his hand with my fingers, an invitation to follow me, one I thought he would understand.

"My husband's kinsmen see to my needs and Ardon's. They provide us with meat and help us with our harvest. They are polite and good to me, all of them, but none is my particular comforter or friend."

"Maybe I am a better brother than they are."

I hoisted myself onto Lamech's boulder, shifting to get comfortable, and patted the space next to me. When he sat next to me, I leaned closer to him so our shoulders were touching.

"Maybe you are lying to yourself."

Jashon looked as if he feared I could see through him.

Maybe it wasn't such a good idea to sit this close.

"Come on," I said, sliding down from the rock and dusting my dress off. "Show me how to fight off a man with my bare hands."

His smile was back as he hopped down, but he said, "I hope you never have to."

He took his time explaining techniques I could use to break someone's hold on me, to get out of their grasp. He taught me where weaknesses could be exploited to my advantage and how to push the heel of my hand upward to break a man's nose.

"Never hurt someone unless you have to, unless it is down to your life or theirs. Try to inflict the least amount of damage that will still allow you to get away."

"How can I know what is the least?"

"It comes with practice." He glanced at the sun. "Here. One last thing for today."

I squared up to him and waited for his instruction.

"Take your belt off," he said.

Eyeing him curiously, I unknotted the belt at my waist and passed it into his waiting hand.

"If you can get this around a man's neck, and you pull it hard enough, he will pass out from lack of air. Once he is down, you'll have your chance to get away."

I watched as he demonstrated.

"It seems quite brutal," I said, feeling suddenly that I never should have come to the Land of Nephi. I should have run to my husband's brother and his cousins.

"It is kinder than death."

"What if I can't pull it tight enough, long enough for it to work?"

A look passed over his face, as if he had never had to consider he might not be strong enough to do something that had to be done. Then he bent and found a small stick on the ground. After tearing off the leaves, he twisted it up in the belt.

"Hold out your arm," he said.

He slid the loop of the belt over my forearm when I held it out and showed me how he could tighten the fabric by twisting the stick.

I winced when the belt got too tight, and Jashon immediately released the tension. "Sorry," he said as he lightly rubbed the red mark on my arm.

"You've taught me well," I said. "Maybe I'll wander away in the night and rescue Ardon on my own. Maybe I don't need your help anymore."

He leaned down close to my ear and said, "Maybe you are lying to yourself."

When the scouts came back with news of Amulon, I thought the men would discuss it among themselves, but they called everyone, even the women, to the cook fire to tell us what they had found.

Jonas, a man with brown hair, mild good looks, and beleaguered eyes did the talking for the men who stood behind him. "Amulon is a four hour walk from here. It is beyond that rise." He gestured to the southwest and most of us glanced that way.

"Is it in the mountains then?" someone asked.

Jonas gave a small shrug. "A mountain valley. We'll start to ascend as soon as we leave the camp."

"Are the rumored caves there in the surrounding hills?" Muloki asked.

"Yes," Jonas said. "It won't be difficult to hide all our men."

Keturah cleared her throat.

"Oh, give it a rest, Ket," Kenai said. "You know he means everyone."

"Well it wouldn't hurt him to say it once in a while."

Some of the men laughed.

"We'll march out after the midday meal," Jashon decided.

Muloki was as old as Jashon. He knew more about the area we were in and the people we were against, but Jashon was in charge. It was hard to explain, but the men accepted his command by tacit agreement and without question.

I thought it was because Gid was his brother. Rescuing him was his responsibility and his alone. Though of course, none of these men would let him do it alone. But I wondered, as I saw the strain constantly around his eyes, if he felt alone in it.

When it came time to pack up the camp, Sarai was immersed in sewing a leathern kilt for Lamech, one that was fashioned after the Lamanite style. I rolled her pallet for her and cleared the tent of her things. I passed the pallet out to Lamech who stood ready to drop the tent.

"What did you mean by that. With Sarai?" he asked under his breath as I helped him remove the few simple poles from the straps.

I leaned back on my heels, glanced at Sarai who was still intent on her sewing and paying us no mind, and turned back to Lamech. He wasn't looking at me, and I thought he might have a flush creeping up his neck. Was he still put out about the welt on his back?

"I guess I meant to draw out her true feeling," I said.

"It doesn't matter what she feels."

I put my hands on my hips. "Of course it does. At least you know now."

"Don't you see how that makes it worse?" He kept his

voice low, but I could tell he was quite upset.

"I'm afraid I don't."

He still wouldn't look at me, just kept his eyes on what he was doing as he rolled the tent and packed the other things tightly away for travel.

"She loves him." He didn't say who. "And I'm not good enough for her. She deserves better than both of us."

I wanted to put a hand on his arm, but I doubted he would receive it in the way it was intended. Instead, I said, "Lamech, the fact that you think you're not good enough for her, tells me you are."

He was finished with Sarai's things and dared to meet my eyes.

"She needs someone who knows her worth," I persisted softly. "She will need a man who never forgets it."

He pressed his lips tight together and looked at Sarai for a moment, then he gave a quick nod to say he understood and got to his feet.

9

Sarai

I scrubbed at my eyes. "I'm going to bed."

"We're not leaving early tomorrow," Jarom said.

I stared blankly at my brother, tried to shake the fog from my mind. I looked around. The sun hadn't even set yet. He thought I wanted extra sleep.

"The scouts are going ahead of us in the morning. They'll find Amulon in the hills and send a guide back."

"You're not scouting?"

He glanced at Eve and shook his head. "No."

I knew he had been a spy in the war. Kenai had trained him, and he was said to be the best. But Jarom's quick glance at his wife told me more than his words ever could. It was too dangerous for a man with a wife to go out ahead when there were others, ready and willing and capable, who did not have wives.

I nodded. "Probably wise. I'll see you in the morning then."

"But you haven't eaten any of your food," Eve protested.

"Didn't you like it?" asked Eliza. "I'm sorry. I thought I prepared it the way the men liked."

I gave Eliza a smile. "I didn't even try it. I'm sure it is delicious. Zeke is much smarter than Kenai."

Jarom snorted.

"What do you mean?" Eliza asked.

"Zeke would not have married a woman who could not cook," Jarom said, completing the joke.

But it was a poor joke, because it was at Isabel's expense. I knew how hard she worked to make Kenai's meals edible. She wanted so much to please him. I myself had helped her many times. And just because she did not seem to be improving much was no reason to make fun of her.

It was easy to make mistakes like that when I was tired, when I was feeling hurt and vulnerable.

I quickly took some bites of my food, remembering how weak I had become when I wasn't eating well and what a difference it had made to my strength when I simply ate the extra food Lamech brought me. I didn't want to become weak again, but I looked between my brothers. "You two can fight over the rest of this." I set the dish down and got up. I had fed my brothers enough to know their appetites were, in a word, hearty.

To my complete surprise, Darius got up when I did and followed me to my tent. It had been nearly a year since we had been friends in the village, since I had gone to Gid and Keturah's to get away from him. *Him and his secret girl*, I thought with a grimace, and in my mind I saw him look up from her, saw the look on his face when he noticed me watching through the trees, paralyzed with confusion and hot envy. Would the embarrassment never fade away?

The tips of my ears burned, and I tried to shield my memories from showing in my eyes.

He said, "Sarai," and all my unwanted, unreturned feelings for him came back so suddenly and completely it was as if I hadn't spent the past year trying to forget he existed.

"What do you want?" I asked.

His eyes widened and he angled closer to me. "I want you to forgive me," he said very directly. "For whatever it was I did."

Whatever it was?

He glanced at the others, every one of them pretending not to listen, and lowered his voice. "We can't keep going on like this."

"Like what?"

"Like you barely speaking to me, barely even looking at me." His voice was still low, and I could tell he was trying to keep it from becoming harsh. Did it bother him that much?

"I thought that's what you wanted."

His brows furrowed. He was so handsome. I wanted to reach out and touch him, to smooth the worried lines from his face.

"No," he said, utterly perplexed. "I never wanted that. I thought we were friends."

Friends. Friends did not make their friends want to die of humiliation.

I looked him steadily in the eye. I kept my voice low, for despite everything, I did not wish to humiliate him. But, *friends?*

"We're not."

I almost broke when I saw the crestfallen expression on his face.

"You have no idea the way everyone looks at me. They think I hurt you and made you go away."

The way everyone looked at him? Was that all he cared about?

"You did," I said.

"Izz," he said, exasperated.

No.

"I am not Isabel!" I screamed at him, my voice rising with each word. And without looking at anyone, I ducked into my tent, unable to keep from crying before I got inside.

But it didn't matter. Everyone could hear me even inside the tent. There was nowhere to go, nowhere but the scant privacy of this tent—that I now shared with Salome. But when darkness fell, it was not Salome who crawled into my tent and lay down beside me.

I was lying on my side with my back to him, but a quick glance over my shoulder was all I needed to confirm who it was.

"Hey," he said.

I sniffed and waited for him to say *I told you so.* I thought of his steely grip on my wrist. He had been so determined that I stay at home, so certain that I would be too much trouble to look after.

I had wanted to pull my own weight, had planned to. I had wanted to do the camp chores so the men could concentrate on getting Gid free. I hadn't planned to act like the spurned, jealous little girl I was. I had only wanted to help.

I felt his hand on my arm. "Come here."

Come where? We were right next to each other. But his voice was so gentle that I lifted my head to look at him. My face was wet and streaked with tears, and my hair lay in strings across my eyes.

He sat up and motioned me into his arms. "Come here," he said again.

When I sat up, he surprised me by lifting me up and setting me into his lap. Then he awkwardly selected small chunks of my hair and smoothed them from my face with his big hands.

Hands just like my father's.

I turned into Zeke's chest, smelled leather and the sandalwood soap Mother and I made for him, and cried all over again. His kindness was more than I could take.

Eventually, he eased onto his back again, but held me close against his chest, exhausted and pitiful.

"Salome is sleeping with Eliza tonight," was all he said before I fell asleep.

I didn't sleep the whole night, maybe not even half of it. I woke and was surprised to find Zeke awake, staring at the inside of the tent and absently stroking my hair. I was uncomfortable and beyond embarrassed. I tried to move away, but his arm tightened around me.

"Darius didn't mean to hurt you," he said into the darkness.

I swallowed. "I cannot bear his friendship."

Zeke was silent for a moment. "What if he offered you more than friendship, Sarai? What if he returned your feelings?"

"What do you mean?" I asked tentatively.

"You like him too much. He could never live up to the way you see him."

"Yes he could. He does every day." I fingered one of the ties at the neck of Zeke's tunic.

I felt him shake his head. "No. No one can live for very long on a pedestal."

"What does that mean, Zeke?" I wasn't trying to be difficult. I truly was trying to understand what he had camped out in my tent to explain to me.

"Do you remember when I loved Keturah?"

"Of course."

"I loved a Keturah I had made up in my mind. I gave her qualities I wanted her to have, and I disregarded the qualities she had that I disliked. I made her perfect for me in my mind. And now that I can see more clearly, I see that she is not what I thought. She could never be right for me, and I could never be right for her."

"Right?"

He hummed, thinking. I felt it rumble through his chest below my cheek, steadying and comforting.

"We always have our agency. I am sure Keturah and I would have been fine, even happy, if we had married as our families wished. But...there was someone better suited for each of us."

"I agree," I said.

"Someone we couldn't see until we let go of the idea that our marriage was meant to be."

I took a breath. "I understand what you're saying, I do. But I don't think I can be just friends with Darius."

"I didn't think I could return to being friends with Keturah."

"How did you do it?"

"Well, the truth was, we had never been more than friends, not really. I took too long to realize it, wasted a lot of my life wishing for something I didn't even want. I did not do it the right way."

"What is the right way?" I whispered.

"Prayer, patience. A new perspective." He hesitated. "Perhaps you could look at other worthy young men."

"But I don't want any other man!" I said in a rush,

103

before I could think it through carefully. Lamech was probably sitting outside my tent as usual.

"Don't you?" he asked, too knowingly.

I didn't think he could see me blush in the darkness, and for that I was grateful.

"Why don't you give him a chance?" Zeke suggested softly.

"Because he's just like Dare—he doesn't want a chance, not with me."

"You're wrong," he whispered. "Don't give him qualities he doesn't have. Don't overlook the ones he does. Look at him the way he is." When I didn't respond, he said, "Get some sleep, Sarai."

"What about you?"

"It won't be the first time I've gone without sleep over a woman."

I couldn't help the broad smile that overtook my lips when he called me a woman.

"Thanks," I whispered.

I could hear two men at the main fire, the guards, talking in low tones. The fire crackled and the wind blew through the leaves high above our heads.

I yawned. "Eliza made you be nice to me, didn't she?" I said sleepily.

Zeke chuckled. "No, though she has much more compassion than I do."

Lying there with my brother's arm around me, with tear stains on my face, I doubted it. "You didn't want me to come."

He sighed. "Sometimes, Sarai, I act too impulsively. I charge forward before thinking things through."

I did that too. "Decisiveness is a good quality, Zeke."

"It can be bad," he said softly.

"So can indecisiveness."

I thought of the time Keturah had been unable to decide between Zeke and Gid and of how much pain it had caused my family, especially my parents who had been unable to plan the wedding of their oldest son to the girl of their choice. I had been witness to their private disappointment. I thought of my feelings for Lamech. I was unable to make the decision to move forward with them, because I couldn't let go of the idea of Darius. I didn't need to move on to another boy, but I did need to move on.

When I woke, Zeke was gone, but Lamech slept outside my tent. I didn't leave it right away. I held the flap aside and watched him sleep. Of a lot of the warriors here, I'd have said they didn't look as fierce when they slept, but not of Lamech. His brows shadowed his eyes and even in sleep they looked dark and brooding. His face was not slack, and his lips were set in a frown. I let my eyes linger on his frown—longer than I should have, but Zeke had said I should start looking at things with a different perspective. I was heeding the counsel of my elder brother.

"You can stop staring at me," the lips said.

My first impulse was to drop the leather and let it fall back into place between us. But I didn't.

"Make me," I said.

His frown turned into a smile. "I can, you know," he threatened.

I wondered why he enjoyed bickering so much. Didn't he ever want meaningful conversations, anything that was more than superficial?

I glanced out to where Salome was already starting the

fire and working with Eve and Eliza, and I remembered the smile, conspiratorial, she'd given me on her way into camp last evening.

I looked back to Lamech who was regarding me now with open, always assessing eyes.

I made a decision then.

"It's just that you're so handsome," I told him. And then I let the flap fall between us.

It was a mistake.

Lamech didn't know what to make of what I had said, I could tell. But he treated me the same as before—moderately kind, formal, and with an irritated undertone.

But as the morning wore on and the scouts did not come back, everyone seemed to be getting irritable.

Zeke had given me a good length of buckskin to fashion a garment for Lamech to wear into the cities, a garment that would make him unrecognizable as a Nephite. Melia had brought Muloki's kilt once for me to inspect. It looked to be a simple garment, but was quite intricate in the way it was cut and stitched. It was well-made and I could see that it would be comfortable for the wearer.

I had the leather cut and had done the initial basting, but by the time the scouts strode back into camp, I was nearly finished with the thing. Jashon called the group together to hear their report, and I continued my work while the others talked at the fire.

Jonas said, "Amulon is a four hour walk from here. It is beyond that rise."

"Is it in the mountains then?" someone asked.

Jonas paused. "A mountain valley. We'll start to ascend as soon as we leave the camp."

"We'll march out after the midday meal," Jashon announced, and the men set about packing up the camp.

Bent over my work, I knew I could finish if I just took a few minutes more. When at last I sat up to stretch my back and look around, I saw that Lamech and Salome had dropped my tent.

"Thanks," I said as I got to my feet.

Salome smiled. "You were working. It's no trouble at all, and Lamech did most of the work anyway."

Lamech only glanced up from where he was rolling the tent tightly.

Salome knelt to pack her own gear, and I stood for a moment watching Lamech.

"I've finished your leathern kilt," I said.

He glanced up again to the leather I held in my hand.

"It's different because the size is not adjustable. I can see why the men adopted the Nephite garments when they came to Zarahemla."

Finished attaching my tent to his own pack, Lamech stood and held out his hand for the garment. He unfolded it and looked it over. I watched as he inspected the stitching that, while decorative, was quite masculine. At least, I would never use such a blocky, large stitch on my own clothing. I smiled when he seemed pleased with it.

"I do hope it fits you," I said, uncertain now that measuring against Zeke's buckskins had been sufficient. I should have just measured Lamech. "I used Zeke's clothing as a guide."

"It's fine. Thanks." He gestured to my belongings that he had pulled from the inside of the tent and set aside. "Can you finish up?"

I nodded, and he left. I watched him say a few words to Jashon and then go off alone into the trees.

I didn't see him again until the men had us stopped at a cave near Amulon.

After Salome took a deep breath and crawled into the cave, Jashon turned and offered me his hand to help me step up to the entrance.

"Jonas is right inside," he said.

I lifted my chin. "I'm not scared."

"Good," he said after a slight pause. "You will need courage, young Sarai, for everything that is yet to come." And he pushed me gently toward the cave.

The truth was that I did feel a tinge of fear creeping up my throat, but I thought of Lamech and of Salome and of the things Zeke had said to me. I thought of how Father had let me come because he knew I needed to grow up. I thought of Keturah and her sword, of her baby and her imprisoned husband. I thought of the way Jarom looked at me, the way Izz always said what she wanted, the hangdog look Darius got when I couldn't talk to him, and I was sick of being timid. Being timid had never gotten me anything of worth.

Inside the cave, Jonas led me to the back wall to sit next to Salome, who reached over and squeezed my hand. It wasn't long before everyone was settled inside and a makeshift torch had been lit and propped in the center of the cave.

My eyes circled the cavern, locating my brothers and their wives, Izz and Kenai, Dare, Lamech. Most of Gideon's friends had gone to their heels in the darker corners, but Gideon's brothers stood near the light and talked quietly to each other. Melia and Keturah had both lain down to rest. It was cool in the cave, but the floor was hard and dirty, and I couldn't see myself sleeping here, where my nerves were jangling with Darius and Lamech in such close proximity.

When Lamech finally sat down, I decided to be bold and went to sit next to him.

I licked my lips as I got out Melia's sarong and a needle. "Does your leathern kilt fit?"

I could see that he was wearing it, but I hoped it was not uncomfortable for him.

"Like you measured me twice."

I couldn't help a smile. I had measured him more than twice with my eyes.

"I'm good with guessing people's sizes."

"You do it a lot?"

I nodded.

"Did you know you hold your tongue between your lips when you stitch?"

I blushed but grinned down at the fabric. "I know. I can't help it. Believe me, I've tried to stop."

"If it works, I say don't change it."

The light flickered, and I sewed quickly to finish the final seam. Knotting the thread, I bit it off. As I smoothed the garment over my knees to see it completed, the torch guttered out and the whole cave plunged into darkness.

"How long do we have to stay in the cave?" I asked Lamech as I folded the tunic in the dark. I remembered how Lamech had not even been able to fold his tunic in the light of day. It made me feel fond toward him.

"Just until Muloki gets back and we decide where we need to go. We can't move on until we know, and we can't stand out in the open so close to the city."

I moved a little so I was closer to him. I felt him go still, but I stayed where I was.

"Dak speck nakal?" I asked him.

I could feel that he turned to me.

"What?"

"I asked if you had the Lamanite language down yet."

"No. But you apparently do."

"Muloki taught me when I was little."

"You are still little, Princess."

This time when he called me Princess, it did not sound insulting.

When the men came through the cave's entrance with another torch, Lamech slid away, and Salome, having lost her balance in the dark, yelped and fell on one of the men in the far corner.

Jashon was standing over them but he turned to retrieve the torch from Jonas and listen to his report.

Darius caught my eye. He was scowling.

Lamech followed my gaze and cleared his throat. "You two will be happy together."

My eyes snapped to Lamech's. "What do you mean?"

"I don't know what you're doing over here, but—"

"He doesn't even like me."

"But you like him. You're crazy with it, Princess."

I shook my head. "I'm not."

His voice turned cooler, but he wanted it to sound like he was just giving me advice. "Look, don't use me to try to get back at him."

"I'm not," was all I could say.

He just gave me a hard look. Then he got up and went to join his brother.

10

Keturah lay down on the dirty floor to rest. I stared at her for a moment before I slid along the floor toward her.

"Here," I offered. "Rest your head in my lap."

She was tired enough that she accepted without qualm. "Thank you, Salome," she said sleepily.

I watched as Jashon left his brother's side, discreetly giving Lamech and Sarai as much privacy as possible, and came toward us. I wondered if Sarai was a match he approved for his brother. It did seem as if he might have finally noticed his brother had an interest in the girl. I looked down at Keturah and smoothed her long slick hair from her face and neck, and I felt sorry for Jashon because he had been unable to pursue a match for himself.

I reached out and began to rub slow circles into Keturah's lower back, and she made soft sighing sounds.

"I remember the discomforts," I said softly to her. I looked up to meet Jashon's eye as he went to his heels at her feet. "You are brave to come so far in your condition." I said.

"Foolish," she mumbled into my lap.

I smiled, still watching Jashon as he opened his water skin and began to wash her feet with such tenderness that tears pricked at my eyes.

"No," I assured her. "You love Gid with all your heart. Like me, you had no choice but to come."

"Mmm," she said. I couldn't tell if she agreed with me or if having her back and feet attended to drew the hum from her lips in relief.

"Would you like a wrap for your shoulders?"

"No. I'm hot."

I kept rubbing her back and smoothing her hair from her moist brow. After a time, I felt that she had fallen into sleep. Jashon sat slowly back on his heels and held my gaze for a long time.

I felt a touch on my shoulder.

"Stretch your legs. She can rest her head on my lap for a while," Lib said softly.

The torch had burned low and the light was very dim. Most of the conversations had ceased, and it did seem strange to talk above a whisper in such soft light, and Jonas had not returned with the torches yet.

I looked around at the others.

Sarai and Lamech still sat together, and Sarai was bent toward the light, sewing. She was remaking a sarong into a sleeveless tunic. Sarai's stitches were quick and sure. She knew how to sew, was confident, and obviously skilled in it.

I stood and moved to the far side of the cave because I wanted to be near the torch. After a moment, Jashon joined me there in its flickering light.

The cave was sufficiently sized to hold all the people that sat quietly within its walls, but it was not large. At least that's what I told myself when Jashon stood next to me and it felt too close. I could feel the heat from his body. He smelled of earth and sweat and leather.

I tossed my hair over my shoulder, looked up at him and said quietly, "You're standing too close."

"No, I'm not."

"Yes, you are. I can practically feel your breath on my skin."

"Then take a step back."

I looked at the floor behind me. Several of the men sat there, already with their knees pulled up to their chests to make room for me.

"If I move back, I'll fall into Joshua's lap."

"You're welcome any time," Josh invited good-naturedly, and the men laughed.

Jashon glanced around me at the men.

"See?" he said, "Josh will catch you if you fall."

I almost wanted to do it—to let Josh trip me and to fall into his lap. I almost wanted to see the look on Jashon's face when I put my arms around Josh's neck and pretended to have hurt my ankle or my elbow.

I stared at Jashon, fighting desperately to keep the smile from my face. My kinsmen saw to my temporal needs, food and shelter, but they did not overly concern themselves with my happiness, mood, or enjoyment of life, and so it had been so very long since anyone besides Ardon had teased me.

I went still and numb when I thought of my son.

Jashon's smile was in his eyes, but he immediately noticed the change in my expression, and he searched my face for the reason. His smile faded before it reached his lips.

Of course he knew why I couldn't laugh.

He reached up to wipe a tear from my cheek in the same moment the torch guttered out.

We stood like that for long moments listening to the murmurs of the others and the slow, deep breaths of those who rested. Jashon's fingers moved on my cheek. He tilted my face up to his, and I could see his profile in the small light from the entrance, his shoulders blocking out much of what little light there was, his long hair falling forward as he bent toward me.

I felt his breath on my cheek and his lips brush over mine. His voice was the merest whisper against my ear.

"Now you can feel my breath on your skin."

There was a scuffing sound at the opening of the cave and bright light shone through as the men moved away the brush they had used to conceal the entrance.

Suddenly, my feet were kicked out from under me and I tumbled backward. But Jashon's steady hands caught me and lowered me gently into Josh's lap.

A moment later, Jonas came through the entrance with a new torch that sent light into our dark corner, and I looked up into Joshua's surprised smile.

Muloki reported that the market in Amulon would not take place for three days hence, and Jashon feared we were making our presence too obvious with our comings and goings from the cave.

I overheard him talking to Jonas. "Take some men and go search for a better cave. Bigger, farther from the path of the guards."

Jonas seemed to be the busiest of the scouts, in and out of camp at all hours, inviting men to go out with him, telling others to stay, and almost all the reports to Jashon came from him.

It did not take him long to find a cave he felt was safe for our extended stay near Amulon.

The new cave was much larger with a larger entrance that allowed in more light, but the features of the land and hills and rocks hid the entrance well.

For the past weeks traveling with these Ammonites, I had stayed busy. I had gotten to know these people, their generosity of spirit and their courage. I had learned to shoot a bow and how to defend myself. I had taken a watch in the dark of night, prepared meals, hauled water, found kindling—all manner of camp chores. When I was talking to the others or listening to them I didn't dwell so much on Ardon, though the constant worry for his safety sat heavy in my chest.

Waiting in the cave, with the absence of work to be done and movement, gave my mind time to wander and left my heart free to fear for my son. As my traveling companions sat together and talked quietly in the cave, careful to keep their voices low so they wouldn't echo, I leaned against the rough wall and closed my eyes.

Ardon was a good son. He was growing into a good man.

Zed's father and his brother, Jacob, had wanted to take Ardon away after Zed died.

"The boy needs to be trained in the ways of the chief," Anias said when he had seated himself at my hearth soon after the men returned with news of Zed's death.

My throat had tightened. As if it wasn't bad enough that Zed was gone. I tried to give my voice an air of authority.

"You may take him and teach him during the day, but he has no need to sleep away from his mother."

Jacob leaned back and crossed his ankles, ready to be insolent and argue it out, but Anias sat up straighter, seeming somehow unsure.

Could it be possible he wasn't sure of the right course for Ardon? I could manipulate even the slightest waver in his resolve. I took courage from the thought.

"He's but a boy. I will raise him to be fair and you will teach him to be courageous and decisive."

They glanced at each other.

"You could solve the problem by marrying again. You are mine. I will find someone suitable."

Someone suitable for Ardon, he meant. Someone suitable to raise the boy who was next in line to rule the clan.

And *you are mine?* It was intolerable!

I sat stone still, not daring to give away my feelings. None of Zed's kinsmen were suitable to me, and it was not likely Anias would approve of a man who wasn't his kin. He might if it were just for me, but not for his grandson. That was the way of it. Anias was the chief, Ardon's grandfather, and with Zed and my own father both dead, he was my protector. His word was law, and his decision would be carried out surely and swiftly.

You could solve the problem by marrying again. *You* could solve the problem.

You.

I studied the older man carefully. He was implying that I had some degree of control here. He wouldn't say it outright, not in front of Jacob, but I heard it, saw it in his eyes. If he had wanted me to marry one of his other sons, he would have told me so at the door and the people would already be gathering at the main fire.

Still, I had to tread carefully.

Give me the right words.

"You are wise to seek to resolve this."

That pleased Anias. So far so good.

I turned to Jacob. "And I know you have houses and

means to support many wives and children. You are successful and respected."

He nodded.

I tried not to frown at his self-important smirk.

"I thank you for giving Ardon of your time and imparting your knowledge to him. I will need provisions for Ardon and some small provisions for myself only. I have no need of legal arrangements." I glanced between them and tried to look very accepting. "I know your word is binding."

Jacob frowned, but Anias looked amenable.

"Perhaps it is too soon to take another husband," Anias said, clapping a hand on his knee as if it were settled.

I stayed silent.

He rose, and waited until Jacob had risen too.

"We make an oath unto you, Salome. You will have all the provisions you need. Ardon will live here with you, if you agree that he will be trained up in the ways of the clan."

"I would not have it any other way," I said, keeping my voice steady.

When they left, I went into the next room and just looked at my sleeping son. He was barely toddling about. How could they think to take him from me? To say nothing of my own feelings about it, Ardon would not understand why his mother was gone, why he was in an unfamiliar place with people he barely knew. And offering me a marriage that was nothing but a legal agreement so I could accompany my son to his new home? Not acceptable.

I would be alone here, lonely perhaps, but at least I would not be someone's unwanted second or third wife.

"Gid believes she can do anything, but I think even he would stop her now."

My ears perked when I heard the men in the cave talking about Keturah. I opened one eye to peer at her. She was sleeping.

"I think we can spare enough men to stay with her somewhere until the rescue is done." I thought that was Joshua.

"But it is my responsibility to rescue Gid."

That was definitely Jashon.

"Then let it be our responsibility to save Ket from herself." *Ethanim.*

"She won't like it." *Jarom maybe?*

"If we were still sixteen and under Helaman's command, I'd say make her finish what she started, but we're not. We're grown, and she is a woman with child, with Gid's child, not some scrappy girl pretending to be a dirty warrior." *The one they called Reb.*

"She was as good as you and you know it." *Lib.*

"Alright." *Jashon.* "I'll think on it."

I heard scuffles as the men dispersed to other parts of the cave, but Jashon and Lamech stayed near.

"You can't have her in your sights at all times," Lamech said, his voice much lower than the others had been.

"It's my responsibility."

I peeked up to see Lamech shaking his head. "Not any more than it is mine. And I have a clear conscience doing much less for her than you do."

Jashon sighed. "You could do it less grudgingly."

"I keep a proper distance, and you would do well to keep one also." He was silent for a long moment. "Don't kid yourself. Dead or alive, Gideon is the only one she will ever want."

Dead or alive.

If something happens to him, Jashon will probably marry her out of duty.

I rolled over and tried to fall back into sleep.

After two days of inactivity, Muloki took his wife and Keturah, Lamech, Mahonri, and Jonas into Amulon to attend the market for supplies and information. If they could at least find out the direction Ardon and Gid had been taken from here, it would be of great help to us.

Both Keturah and Lamech ducked out of the cave with Muloki, and I could see in Jashon's rigid shoulders he didn't want them to go. I could see in his eyes he wanted to go with them. But it wasn't possible. His presence in the Lamanite city would be both noted and suspect.

He paced around for a while, but eventually sat near me against the wall. His knees were up, his elbows on his knees, and his hands in his hair.

I scooted closer to him.

"You should try to rest," I said.

He snorted. "Not possible."

"You have to trust in their good sense, in Lamech's ability to keep her safe."

He was quiet a moment. "It's not about trust."

It was about caring too much for Keturah.

"You have to let her go."

"Stop telling me what I have to do!"

Several heads turned at his sharp tone, but he lowered his voice to a harsh whisper.

"Do you think I want this? Any of this? This horrible trip? Caring for my brother's wife? I do *not* want it, but it falls to me!"

He was looking down at his hands, acting as if he had already failed, but his jaw was set and his breaths deep and steady, and I knew that if rescuing his brother and my son was within his power, he would not fail.

My mind went back to Jacob on that day Anias had come to take Ardon away. He had stayed silent, but he had not agreed with his father. He wanted me to live in his household and to raise the little chief himself, to have power over us and dominion over my decisions. I thought he also wanted to wrest control from his father and rule the clan the way he wished, but the toddler in the next room had more right to rule than he did.

"Of course I don't think you want it," I said. "But it is those who do not want power to whom it should most rightly fall."

He leaned back, straightening his legs in front of him.

"I'm not jealous of Gid for what he has, only angry that he values it so little he can leave without a backward glance."

"I doubt he doesn't realize the charms of his wife."

Jashon winced.

But I laughed a little. "If he is anything like his brothers, he knows exactly what it is for which he fights."

He shook his head. "He wanted to be a soldier long before he met Keturah. He wanted to go with me to Teancum and the battles in the north, but I wouldn't let him. I told him he had to protect the farm."

"And did he?"

"Of course. Until the Ammonite militia formed. I guess he couldn't help himself any longer."

"So now he has turned the tables on you. It is your turn to protect the farm."

"The farm is one thing."

Keturah was another.

"You bear your burdens well, Jashon. Do not let fear crowd out your faith in your god."

He looked down at me and raised a brow.

"I may not share your religion, but I would be blind not to see the courage and fortitude your faith gives to you and your men." I reached out and smoothed my fingers over his. "Do not let it fall by the wayside because of one hard experience."

I wished I could see the green of his eyes as he studied my face. It was too dim in the cave, especially in our dark corner, but I had memorized the color and every fleck of brown and gold in them.

"The others—Lib, Joshua, Ethanim—they love her because of the way they know her from the war. They lived together, ate together, slept and fought beside each other. They all owe their lives to each other many times over. But I admit, I do not know her in that way."

I didn't know what to say. Tell him to leave his brother's wife on the farm and find his own life? He could never do it. The farm was his birthright, and he would have the larger portion someday. I just squeezed his fingers, hoping to give him some support, though I didn't feel I had much strength to offer. I was weary, and I was worried.

We sat a long time like that, hands connected, giving comfort, taking comfort. I was relieved when he seemed to relax, to rest, but when Muloki entered the cave, Jashon's sharp eyes shot to him instantly. In a second he was on his feet in front of Muloki.

"We found them."

11

With the first rays of light that filtered through the entrance of the cave came time for Muloki and the others to go into the Amulon market.

My heart pounded as I watched Lamech duck out of the cave with the others. Eventually, I drifted back to sleep, but woke to the sound of Muloki's excited voice.

"Here now. They're in the city now."

Was he talking about Gideon?

I rubbed my eyes and peered at the others through the flickering firelight.

Jashon did nothing more than close his eyes and let his chin drop to his chest. It looked like defeat, but it was relief. Maybe prayer.

Muloki's eyes glowed. "They're camped on the outskirts of the city."

The men were on their feet. Melia stepped through the door of the cave, followed by Keturah. Ket went to Jashon, and he pulled her into his chest with one strong arm. Then his other arm went around her, and he held her tight. The news was good, and the embrace did not seem unusual, but Lamech watched his brother and sister-in-law with a speculation in his assessing eyes that made me look at them again.

Jashon pulled away and looked into Keturah's face. "You saw him?"

She shook her head. "Jonas and Mahonri."

Jashon found Jonas in the dim cave. "Are you sure? It was him?"

"It was him."

Everyone was talking at once.

Jashon squeezed Keturah's arm but left her and went to the men. "And the boy?" he asked.

Mahonri nodded, but his eyes turned to Salome, who followed Jashon, her hand at her throat.

"He's there," Mahonri told her. "And he is well, under the circumstances." His words to her were kind, almost tender, and I smiled, knowing already that he was not as hard as he made people think he was.

"Are there soldiers in the city?" one of the men asked.

Muloki folded his arms over his chest. "It's one of their outer strongholds. The place is crawling with them." Most of the men sobered, but Muloki said, "We'll follow them out into the wilderness again. It will be easier to stage a rescue when our numbers are equal."

Zeke and Kenai edged forward.

"How far to the next settlement?" Zeke asked.

"Helam."

The men turned to look at Melia.

"I remember passing this way with my grandfather. It's a two day journey."

"Can a rescue be staged in that amount of time?"

"Not if we have to stay a day behind them to avoid detection. And we'll only run into more cities from there."

"Why do we have to avoid detection? We can fight."

I left the men to work out the details and began to pack up the camp.

Jashon sent men to spy on Gideon's captors, and when

they left the city, we put Amulon quickly behind us. The Lamanites traveled on the road now, south toward Helam, but we followed discreetly in the wilderness to the west.

The terrain remained the same, and I wondered how two different peoples who dwelt in the same fertile land could be so different. When I looked at the lush vegetation, the useful plants, the weather patterns, and the stars in the night sky, I saw the hand of God. Could a whole country of people be blind to these things?

"You're getting stronger," Lamech said when the sun was high.

We hadn't been traveling in silence, but he had not said anything like that before.

I blushed with pleasure, but said, "It is just a natural consequence of the hard travel."

"Which you have done without complaint."

I peered at him curiously. Was he angling toward something? Did he mean to ask me to do something I wouldn't like?

But he didn't say any more, and I didn't know what to make of his lovely compliment, what I was sure was a very high compliment from someone like him. He could have said I was pretty or even smart, and it would not have meant as much.

When evening fell, Kenai led us into a protected glen. The long canyon had high walls and a rocky cliff at the far end. The grasses were soft and green, and a narrow but deep river wound through it.

"There's no way out of this canyon," someone said. I didn't look up from the fire to see who. "If Lamanites come to the entrance, we'll be trapped."

"We've got enough spies out to give us proper

warning," Jashon said. He pointed to the tops of the cliffs. "And there is a way to escape, but we won't do it unless we have to."

"Where is it?"

"I didn't see a way."

"It's hidden, like the entrance to this canyon." I looked up to see Lamech. "But it's there."

"Could the women do it?"

"Why would you even ask that?" Keturah set another small log on the fire, irritation evident in her voice.

"Now simmer down," Jarom laughed. "You're in kind of a condition if you hadn't noticed."

She snorted. "I've kept up so far, haven't I?"

A lot of the men sent each other guilty glances or looked at the ground. All of them avoided her eyes.

"I have." She sat up straight. "I have," she said again.

When no one else would speak up, Lamech did it. "You're pushing yourself too hard. Losing the baby will not help. Gid would kill every one of us." Keturah made a note of protest, but Lamech talked over her. "He would not trade the baby's life for his own."

"You dishonor your husband to think otherwise," Jashon said quietly.

Keturah looked between Jashon and Lamech and from them to the other men in disbelief. Exasperated, she said, "I'm not going to lose the baby."

"You've been walking twenty miles a day for weeks," said Kenai.

"And you're not eating enough," Izz added.

Confused, defeated, too tired to protest further, Keturah said, "What would you have me do? We're already here." She looked around at the men again. "You've already talked about it, haven't you?'

Jashon cleared his throat. "I think it would best for you and Gid's child if you stayed here and rested while we continue on and complete the mission."

She shook her head, not in protest, but in disbelief. "It won't work. You'd have to leave too many men. It would put the mission in jeopardy. You need all the men for the rescue."

"If you'd just let me go—" Lib began but Jashon broke in calmly.

"If you want to go, then just go. You don't need my permission to kill yourself."

There was a low growl. I thought it was an animal until Ethanim turned on Lib, moving suddenly and pushing Lib in the chest. "I swear if I hear you say that one more time I'm going to punch you in the face!"

Lib pushed back and jumped to his feet. Ethanim jumped up too and swung his fist at his friend. It wasn't the best way to deal with differences, but I doubted anyone blamed him. I didn't like violence, but even I didn't blame Ethanim. I was about ready to take a swing at Lib myself. His wallowing over Keturah was almost whiny at times and had begun to get annoying.

Lib evaded Ethanim's fist and before either of them could get in another swing, men were holding both of them away from each other. The friends—I knew they were best friends—glared at each other as they struggled against the men that held them.

"Someone's got to drive some sense into you! You can't covet another man's wife! You're in serious danger of losing the Spirit!" Ethanim lowered the volume of his voice, but kept talking. "You know the commandments. Lib, you can't do this." He paused, stopped struggling, and then spoke very slowly, paying no attention to all the rapt faces staring at them. "She made her choice, and she belongs to Gid."

Lib wrestled free of the men who held him. He glowered at Ethanim and stormed off toward the dark edges of the canyon.

Keturah got awkwardly to her feet and went after him.

I heard Jashon speak because I was near him. "Dare," he said very quietly, and his whole command was in that one word.

Darius left the campfire and followed his sister, his back disappearing into the night, and that was the last time I saw Darius for a long time.

When plans were made and the men put out the fire, I got into my tent and waited for Salome to enter, but she lingered near the coals with some of the men, so I closed my eyes and listened to Lamech breathing outside my tent.

You are getting stronger. And you have done it without complaint.

I was still awake when Salome slipped into her bedroll. When she just lay quietly and sighed, I asked, "Is something the matter?"

"I thought you were asleep."

"I'm not."

"What are you thinking about?"

Was Lamech outside the tent? "I bet you can guess," I whispered.

"Did he do something that troubles you?"

"No." I hesitated. How could I say it? I knew the words would sound awkward and silly, but I reminded myself that being too timid to ask for help had never done me any good. "He thinks...he said I was using him to strike back at Dare."

She took a slow breath. "Are you?"

Salome was the only one here with an outside view of it. If she thought I had been using Lamech to be vindictive, perhaps I had been. "I didn't think I was, but now I wonder. I didn't mean to. It is so very hard to know your own heart, isn't it?"

"It is, Sarai."

I lowered my voice. "Zeke wants me to think about courting Lamech."

I could hear the smile in her voice when she said, "I have to admit, I've noticed an affection between the two of you, but might I suggest waiting for him to court you when the time is right?"

"He won't."

"Then why would you?"

I rolled up onto an elbow, turning to her in the darkness.

"Why would you want someone in your life who doesn't want you bad enough to do something about it? Love, Sarai, friendship and relationships all take two people to make them work. If he is not ready, no matter the reason, you will fail at it, and it will hurt. On the other hand, when you are both prepared and willing at the same time, it will be the easiest thing you ever did, building a relationship with him." She paused. "Don't you think he is smart and capable?"

"Of course I do." Capable of everything but folding a tunic neatly.

"Then trust him, Sarai."

"I will try."

"He is the kind of man who will want to be in charge of a courtship. The question is, are you the kind of woman who can let him."

The answer to that question sent a lot more questions adrift in my mind, and when we finally fell into silence, I searched my heart, and then I prayed that I would not make any more missteps. I wanted to be patient and concentrate on the task at hand. I wanted to bring Gideon home.

I overslept, something that was unusual for me, and when I emerged into the daylight, it seemed the whole camp was arguing near the center fire.

"The only direction he'd have gone is west," Muloki was telling the others. "There are no major cities to the east."

"Not even on the coast?" Ethanim asked.

Muloki shook his head emphatically. "Nowhere warriors would have taken a prisoner of Gid's rank."

"But does Lib know that?"

Muloki looked as if he felt guilty. "We talked about it several nights ago, he and I. I told him Gid was most likely headed west toward Mormon and Ishmael, toward the great temple of the sacrifice."

"Then that's where he's headed," Zeke said.

"He might only wish us to think that," Muloki replied.

Ethanim exploded. "Well, we've got to find him before he tries something ridiculous!"

"He's going to do what he's going to do," Jashon pointed out calmly, but his lips were tight and the worry lines around his eyes had deepened.

"That's why it's up to us to stop him!"

Joshua, one of the warriors from Orihah that I didn't know very well, approached Ethanim. "We will," he said, his voice level, guarded like Jashon's had been. "Come on, let's go cast about for his trail again."

"Wait." Jashon stopped them. "Don't obscure the tracks that are there."

The men stopped and waited for instructions from Jashon. But the answer was obvious. If Lib had gone to offer himself in exchange for Gideon, no matter what direction, he must be stopped. But Gideon was being taken south, and he must be rescued.

"We should split into two groups."

Jashon started to protest, but Sarai spoke over him, directing her words to Muloki. And the words were foreign.

Muloki listened to her, then shared a look with his wife.

Everyone else was gaping at Sarai.

Muloki translated. "Sarai says we should send a group after Lib and a group after Gid. She will go with a group and I will go with a group. That way, each group will have someone who speaks Lamanite."

Everyone started talking at once. Sarai listened to all the voices but when she spoke, she directed her answer to her eldest brother, Zeke. "Muloki taught me to speak Lamanite when he first came to the village. I took to it, and I liked it, and so Mother and Father helped too. I know enough to speak easily with Muloki and Melia."

Zeke glanced at them for confirmation. At their nods, he turned back to his little sister.

"I believe you, but I don't think splitting the group would be wise."

Opinions began to fly, but in the end Jashon raised his hand and all the men became silent and attentive. I doubted any of them would dispute what Jashon determined to do.

"Look into your hearts."

That was all he said before he turned away from the men and began packing his belongings onto his pack.

While the rest of the men similarly packed their gear, Jashon knelt where the cook fire had been, removed the rocks that surrounded it, covered the ashes with soil, and raked over the area with brush to make it appear as if it had not been disturbed. The rest of us knelt with him and listened as he offered a prayer.

I looked around and found Kenai. Walking to him, I asked, "Is your sister not staying here? I thought the men had determined she could not go on."

He looked at me grimly, his lips tight. "When we split, we won't have enough men in either party to leave anyone here with her."

"Oh." It was as I thought. "I guess Lib didn't think of that before he went off to save her husband."

Kenai surprised me with a small smile. "Guess not."

Frustrated that tracking Lib and rescuing him from himself might delay me from going forward to find Ardon, I said, "Why should we save a man who rushes so recklessly into folly?"

Kenai—tall, lanky, jocular Kenai—looked down at me with compassion in his eyes.

Would Christ not go back for one of his sheep?

I looked at him curiously. I wasn't sure if I had heard the words because I had definitely not seen his lips move, but I said tentatively, "I don't know your Christ."

He knows you.

Again, I stared curiously at the lips that had not moved and then into the kind eyes that had spoken so clearly to my heart.

"Go on and get your things. We're moving out," Kenai said out loud and the moment was broken.

I went to collect my pack and satchel. Jashon was dividing the men into two groups when I returned to the center of camp.

"Muloki, Melia, Ket, and Salome, you're with me. Also Jarom, Eve, Darius, Jonas, Ethanim and Reb. We'll track Lib."

They all moved toward him.

"Kenai will be moving east. Isabel, of course, Zeke and Eliza, Eliam,   Lamech, and Sarai—you'll all be traveling with him."

The remaining people moved toward Kenai.

"What about the others?" Kenai asked, referring to the remaining men around the fire and those who were currently out scouting the terrain or guarding the campsite.

"Everyone here is with me. Everyone else will join you by midmorning beyond that east rise."

I looked toward the rise over which the sun was appearing. Then I looked around the fire. Enos was not in camp. I caught Jashon's eye but his expression gave none of his feelings away.

I watched as the women hugged each other goodbye. Melia took some leavened bread from her satchel and pressed it into Sarai's hands, then kissed her quickly and moved away. The men stood stiffly by, clearly ready to move out without the fanfare, but endured hugs and goodbyes from their kinswomen. Keturah hugged Kenai tightly. Melia laid a hand on each of their shoulders. Isabel, Eliza, and Sarai all hugged Jarom, and Eliza even kissed his cheek. Eve giggled and boldly kissed Zeke's cheek, making everyone chuckle except for Jarom who scowled, and I wondered if perhaps there was a joke among them I was not aware of.

"Alright already," said Jashon. "Zeke offer a prayer."

Everyone immediately knelt in the dirt, and as Zeke offered the words up to their god, I thought about the faithfulness of these young people. I knew that some would think they were foolish and that their efforts were in vain. I knew my kinsmen would be among those who thought this. I might even have been among them two weeks ago, but I had felt of the spirit of which they spoke so freely, which they claimed led and directed them, and I could no longer view their faith as futile. I believed God listened to them and answered their prayers.

I wondered what I might have to do to get God to hear and answer my prayers.

Look around you. I already have.

The voice was so sudden, so soft, so close that the hairs on my neck rose. My eyes sprang open. The others still knelt with heads bowed, beseeching their god for help.

Had nobody heard the words that I had heard?

When the prayer was done, everyone rose to their feet, and Kenai's band of men left to the east.

"Come on," Jashon said, and he swept us all up in a glance. "Let's go track down that fool of a boy."

At his mention of tracking, I laid aside the strange voice I had heard, intending to examine its meaning later. "Jashon," I said. "I can track."

He stopped, turned, and gave me an inquisitive look.

But I was confident in this, and even more confident because I had seen that these men did not overlook the skills of their women. "Show me where the men lost his trail, and I will track it."

"If only Gideon were here," Keturah sighed. "He can track anything."

Muloki gestured for me to follow him, but spoke to Keturah. "Liam taught both his boys to track, Ket. I think we'll get by sufficiently."

In a moment, outside camp, Muloki pointed to a track in the soil—a fresh print of the outside of Lib's sandal. I ran a finger over it lightly, memorizing it. I measured it against my hand, then against my foot.

"Are all the prints like this? Just the outside?"

"Most of them."

"And how long did he leave them?"

"For about a mile."

"And what geographic features will we find a mile from here?"

Muloki glanced that way and shook his head. "They don't change, if that's what you mean. More of the same."

Jashon boldly brushed my hand with his, and more than one of his men noticed.

"Let's go see for ourselves."

13

Sarai

Kenai led us first east out of camp and then south down a rocky hillside into a small canyon that led toward the rising sun. I didn't know how he knew where to lead us, but his steps were sure and steady.

"Does he look that much like your Darius? You can't take your eyes off him."

I refused to let Lamech bait me into arguing with him. He would have to find a new way to keep a wall between us if he wanted one there.

"I was thinking that he is very sure of our direction."

Lamech didn't say anything for a moment, but he finally said, "He was a spy in the army."

"Oh, yes, I've heard that. But here? In the Land of Nephi?"

Another moment of silence. "Kenai has scouted terrain to reach to all the seas."

"Have you as well?" I asked.

"No. I've not been to the Land of Nephi."

We walked on in silence for a time. After a while, Eliza came to walk by me. Lamech stayed by my side, not even pretending to give us privacy to talk.

Eliza was Zeke's wife. I didn't know her very well yet, but I liked her. My whole family had worried so much about Zeke after Keturah decided to marry Gid. His sadness had been deep and scary. We had prayed for his recovery for years, my parents always treating the sadness like it was an illness, and finally God had heard our prayers and sent Eliza to my brother.

"You are keeping up really well," she said to me.

"I've never been on a long journey." I readjusted the straps of my travel pack. "But I am becoming accustomed to all the walking."

"Zeke says you speak Muloki's dialect of Lamanite."

"I do. Not so fluently as he does, but he taught me when I was young. When he first came to the village, he did not know our language, so Chloe and I used to quiz him on his words. Then he would quiz us on words in his language. Chloe lost interest over time, but I took to it. Within six moons, he and I could have a full conversation in either language."

"It may help us now."

"It may," I agreed. "It's funny, but when I was demanding to go with the rescue party, the thought did not even occur to me."

"No?"

"No. I just wanted to go—because Gid is my friend. He—" my voice broke, but I swallowed and finished talking. "He took me in at a very hard time in my life."

Lamech snorted.

"He was like a brother to me," I went on, ignoring Lamech, "and a friend, and he stayed up many nights talking to me when I know he would have rather been with Keturah."

"I don't know him well, just a little from when he was a guard on my uncle's estate. He was diligent about doing his work there, but I spoke with him sometimes. It sounds as if he is very nice."

"He is. Except for when he is with Keturah, he is

rather...uncomfortable with women. He was raised out on a farm with just his brothers for company, and he never had the opportunity to be around girls. That's what he told me, anyway."

I felt Lamech's presence next to me, felt his full attention in our conversation—he didn't try to hide it—but he didn't say anything.

"He always treated me well," Eliza said. Then she grinned and caught Lamech's eye. "And how do these boys treat their mother? Are they uncomfortable with her, too?"

I laughed a little. "Not at all. They treat her both like a queen and like she is one of the men. They adore her. They are always joking with her, but they are quick to offer her due respect at the appropriate times."

"But they never had much practice with other girls. That is understandable then. We girls are very difficult to get along with, aren't we, Lamech?" She must have felt his interest in our conversation too.

I was eager to hear Lamech's response though I knew it would be something rude. But he surprised me.

"I find it difficult to get along with girls I like."

"Is that why you don't get along with Keturah?" I asked.

He gave me an odd look. "No. I don't get along with Keturah because she threw over Zeke for Gid."

"But Gid is your brother," Eliza said.

"And Zeke is my captain."

"But he's not been your captain in over two years."

He looked at us both, but spoke gently to Eliza. "I don't mean to be rude, but you cannot understand what it is to have a captain."

I don't mean to be rude?

138

Eliza looked toward her husband, hiking along with Kenai, Izz, and Eliam. "No," she said slowly, "But I do know what it is to hold Zeke's heart and not want to hurt it. I can sympathize with Keturah in a way you cannot."

Lamech actually seemed to agree. I looked back and forth between them.

"If I would have said that, what Eliza said, you would have argued with me for a day and a half," I pointed out. And it was true. He would have, and had done more than once on this journey.

He gave me a long look and said, "I'm going to see if Kenai will let me scout ahead for a while."

He lengthened his stride and easily caught up to Kenai and the others.

Next to me, Eliza giggled.

"What is so funny?" I asked.

"He as much as said he likes you, and I can tell by the look on your face that you didn't understand what he was trying to say."

"What do you mean?" I turned my eyes toward Lamech. He hadn't said anything of the sort.

"He said he has a hard time getting along with girls he likes."

"Sure, but he didn't mean—"

She cut me off with another laugh. "And then he agreed he'd have argued with you for a day and a half about nothing."

Frustrated, I heaved a deep sigh. "Even if that were true, what am I supposed to do about it? Salome said it is not the time to court."

Eliza nodded. "Salome is right."

I sighed again. "And I agree," I confided. "But everyone has an opinion about Lamech and me, and everyone has differing advice. I'm beginning to think nobody knows what they are talking about."

"Well, every situation is different."

"I don't know what to do. I don't even know how to feel." I swallowed hard. "You know I've been trying to get over Dare, and Lamech thinks I am using him to make Dare jealous." I bit my lip. "So does Salome."

"Are you?"

"I don't know. That's why I'm glad we've separated and Darius is gone with Jashon."

"Jashon is intuitive." She winked at me.

"You think Jashon sent me with Lamech on purpose?"

She laughed. "I know he did. But I suppose the Spirit directed him for God's own purposes as well." When I sighed deliberately again, she placed an arm around me and said, "It will all turn out, Sarai. You must have patience."

"That's easy for you to say, Eliza."

"Do you think it was easy to love Zeke in the beginning? You know what he was like." She shook her head, her curls bouncing softly back into place. "No. He went to Uncle Helaman's so you wouldn't see. He can be the most stubborn man."

I laughed. "That's what Mother says." I looked at her, licked my lips. "Eliza?"

"Hmm?"

"Thank you. For telling Zeke what to say to me."

She took my hand, squeezed it tight, and tried to hide a smile.

Our spies met up with us by late morning. They were

supposed to report on the direction Gideon's captors were traveling, but they were running in fast and they came with an urgent warning.

I recognized Gideon's cousin, Enos, as he hurried toward Kenai and Zeke. Eliza and I exchanged a look and rushed to catch up so we could hear what was going on.

"A patrol of Lamanites ahead." Enos glanced at the women as he caught his breath. "They've already seen our company, and they've changed their course to confront."

"Coming out from where?" asked Zeke.

"There is a city called Laman beyond this peak," said Kenai, pointing to it. He didn't seem surprised that we'd meet a patrol here, but his voice was clipped when he called, "Sarai," and turned to find me among the men.

"Here," I said, hurrying forward.

He looked at me and took a deep breath. "I hope you're as good as Muloki says you are."

"Pray for me," I said.

Kenai glanced around at everyone. I knew it was an order to pray, but I doubted any of the men needed an order.

"Let's keep walking as if we were walking in to meet them," Kenai said. "Sarai, you walk with me. Everyone else, weapons at the ready, but not obviously. How many men in the patrol?"

"Ten," said Enos.

Kenai nodded. "We can fight if we have to. Sarai, Eliza, and Izz, if it comes to fighting, you get behind us as quickly as you can." He spoke almost casually, but I knew he meant every word and he expected his commands to be obeyed with exactness.

"Eliza can fight," said Zeke.

Kenai looked at his friend. He nodded once, but said, "Not unless it becomes necessary, Eliza. Got it?"

"Yes," she said, and we walked on until ten men came through the trees.

"Shalal!" I called merrily and ran forward to meet them.

One of the men at the head of the group held up a hand and they all halted behind him. I glanced at the others, keeping an almost silly smile on my face. I was so nervous but I hoped they would interpret it as my gladness to see them. Some of the other men wore only their breechcloths, some wore a longer loincloth made from animal skins. I had a moment's regret at giving Lamech such a hard time about going without his tunic in order to bronze his skin. The man who seemed to be the leader of the patrol wore a full leathern kilt like Muloki's and the sight of it, its familiarity, gave me a small measure of comfort, and I pretended I was talking to Muloki.

"I am so overjoyed to see men of the people," I said flawlessly in the language Muloki had taught to me, directing my words to the leader. "Of my own people."

The man scanned me curiously and let his eyes rest on my light brown hair, golden streaked now from the sun.

I blew a lock of it from my brow. "A defect of my birth," I said.

The man, who was older than Zeke and younger than my father, gave one thorough look at the group behind me. I glanced back to see Kenai standing shoulder to shoulder with Zeke and Lamech. The rest of the men circled Eliza and Izz, who peered around Kenai and gave me an encouraging, if worried smile.

"Where do you come from?" the man asked me.

I didn't know how to answer. Where was I born or where were we traveling from?

"These men are taking me home to Jerusalem," I said, the name of the city coming into my mind even as I said it. I moved closer to the man, keeping his eye contact. "I was abducted, taken captive by the Nephites. It is a rather long story, but my betrothed came for me and rescued those women along with me." I gestured to Eliza and Isabel. "These are their kinsmen, and in return, to keep their honor, they have offered safe travel to our destination, which we have accepted."

"Honor," the man snorted, crossing his arms over his bare chest.

Lamech eased up beside me, and a quick look told me he was glaring daggers at the band of men.

I cast a strained smile at the man who was now scrutinizing Lamech very closely. I could see his hand wanted to go to his sword, but he very obviously restrained himself, a clear token of trust.

"Lamech, what are you doing?" I demanded in our own language.

Lamech tore his gaze away from the band of Lamanite men, and when his eyes fell on me, they became very soft, like I had never seen them before. I felt myself blush when he stroked my hair down, leaving his hand at my neck, and said in clear and confident Lamanite, "I will deal with the men, my little princess." He turned back to the man. "You will forgive my betrothed. She is overcome with her happiness to be back in our homeland. She speaks out of turn."

The man grunted and looked warily between us, but a small smile twisted his lips. "My wife is much the same."

"Lamech," I began in our native tongue. "How are you—?"

"You can speak freely," Lamech interrupted smoothly. "The need to hide your identity no longer exists. We are among the people now."

His tone was gentle, almost as if he were consoling a child, which was more surprising to me than his miraculous ability to speak the Lamanite language. He put his arm around me and pulled me into his side as if to hug me, but he quickly whispered against my ear. "Do not speak Nephite to me—only to the others. And you must treat me as if we are to be married."

That meant I would have to show him adoration, and if I could not summon that, in the very least, I must show him esteem and respect. And I must not argue with him or do contrary to his wishes.

At least, I thought, not in front of these men.

Lamech went forward to clasp the leader's arm, but he hesitated for just a moment before extending his hand.

"I am of the Order of the Nehors. I hope I find myself among friends."

The man's brow went up, as did mine, and the men behind him murmured to one another. After he scrutinized Lamech, he held out his hand and Lamech gave him the same strange handshake I had seen him give to Muloki with a laugh the day we left the village.

"I am Lamech of Jerusalem. This impetuous girl is my betrothed, Sarai."

Impetuous. It was so far from an accurate description of me, it was almost laughable. My younger sister, Chloe, was impetuous. Izz, too, maybe, but not me. Lamech had called me impetuous, but he had said it with affection, and that made something warm start in my heart.

The man stared at Lamech for another long moment and then said, "I am Zaaron." He turned to the man next to him. After conferring, he turned back to Lamech, not giving another glance to the men who stood behind us—which was more than he gave to me.

This was very good. It would be a great dishonor to Lamech for any of the men to look at me now that they believed I was his betrothed. They all honored Lamech by averting their eyes from me during this initial meeting.

Zaaron didn't look at me because I belonged to Lamech. He didn't look at the rest of our band because they were Nephite dogs.

"Are you from the city Laman, then?" Lamech asked Zaaron.

"We are in the army there, but our service is done for the time. We are traveling home."

"Do the Nephites attack the border cities?" Lamech asked in genuine surprise.

"It is not unheard of."

"Jerusalem has never been attacked in my lifetime."

I thought this was a very unwise claim for Lamech to make. There was no way he could know that.

But Zaaron surprised me by laughing. He clapped a hand on Lamech's shoulder and said, "That is because you are very young."

The man next to him laughed also, an older man with missing teeth and a scar on his face. "But that is the time to acquire a pretty young wife!"

Several of the men laughed, but still none of them

looked at me. Lamech would let them know when it was acceptable to him for them to acknowledge me. But as I glanced up at them, I noticed one man, not much older than myself, Lamech's age maybe, openly staring at me. I quickly averted my eyes.

"You can travel with us as far as Ani-Anti. You can tell your friends to go home. Their duty is fulfilled. If they go now, they may go with our thanks."

I felt Lamech go still beside me. "They're not my friends," he bit out. Then he sighed, ran a hand through his hair. "But they have made an oath unto Sarai."

Zaaron's lip curled, but I could see he knew the men would not leave if they had vowed they would see me home. If he had made an oath, he would have seen it through also.

"What's going on?" Zeke asked, drawing up behind us.

Lamech turned to me expectantly.

I stared at him blankly for a moment before realizing what he wanted. "Zeke wants to know what is being said concerning them."

"Tell him these men of Laman wish them to return to their own lands."

I nodded and turned to relate the information, understanding why Lamech did not do it himself.

Zeke shook his head. "No."

"They might make you," I said.

"What's happening? What is Lamech telling them?"

"Lamech told them only the truth, that your people abducted me at the end of the wars, mistaking me for a Nephite because of my hair and light skin. He told them how he followed after me," I went on proudly, "and how he single-handedly freed me from the army's camp." I didn't know why I

146

was telling it this way, but I knew that I must not speak the truth, even in Nephite, and I willed them to understand. "And he told them of your oath to see me safely to my home in Jerusalem."

They all looked between me, Lamech, and Zaaron in confusion, but no one contradicted me.

"Our oath," Kenai said slowly. I could see he was trying to remember if we had talked about this in all our planning.

"Yes, because Lamech rescued your two women with me. I think these men respect your oath, but Lamech wishes to release you from it."

"We would not dishonor our women, our forbearers, our God, or ourselves. No." Zeke shook his head. "Tell Lamech we will not accept a release from our oath."

Kenai's voice was bold and clear when he added, "Tell him we will fulfill our oath to you."

I sighed deliberately and nodded, then turned to Lamech. But before I could speak, the young man at the rear of the Lamanite band scoffed aloud. Zaaron turned to look at him and groaned.

"Come forward, Tecumeni," he commanded.

When the boy came forward he scowled at Zeke and said, "Their oath is to their god. It means nothing." Then he looked directly at me, blatantly looked me up and down, and smiled before casting Lamech a wisely wary glance.

"Stand with the other women," Lamech commanded and staring intently at the young man, stepped in front of me.

I threw my eyes to the ground and moved to obey him.

"Stop!" said Zaaron. "Tecumeni will apologize."

"Uncle, I do not think they are what they say," Tecumeni protested. I could hear that his dialect was quite

147

different from the one we had been speaking, but I understood the meaning of each word very clearly.

Zaaron looked at us with almost embarrassment. "Nevertheless, we will extend them our trust. It is expected in the Order."

"But Uncle—"

"That is enough." Zaaron gave Tecumeni a stern look.

Tecumeni turned to Lamech and offered an apology that was somehow both grudging and smooth. "It is not you, Lamech of the Nehors of Jerusalem, that I do not trust. It is these Nephites. I fear they have lied to you."

Lamech gave Tecumeni another hard stare, and then he suddenly grinned. "That would be nothing I have not done to them."

Some of the men laughed, and, clearly pleased, Zaaron turned to Lamech. "We will escort your band as far as the village Ani-Anti. That is our home, and you may stay with us there to replenish your supplies and rest."

"My woman does not need rest," said Lamech. "She will travel until I tell her to stop."

I noted that Lamech still did not give his leave for any of the men to look at me in his presence. I didn't think the men overlooked it either.

"Sarai," he addressed me. "You may walk with the other women if you wish."

"Thank you, Lamech," I said and nodded to the other men, though they would not look at me to acknowledge it. I turned, and Zeke and Kenai stepped apart to allow me past them.

"Lamech says you may fulfill your oath," I told them.

"Good," they said in unison.

"Get ready to move out," Kenai called to his men.

"Wait."

I heard Lamech's heavy voice, and I was afraid I knew what he wanted. A custom my people still kept from the old ways, any man would want to solidify his claim to his betrothed in the presence of so many male strangers. My heart started to pound, and I almost laughed to realize it was pounding harder than when the band of Lamanite men had walked into view. I turned to face Lamech.

Playing his part very convincingly, he stepped forward, took my arm, and pulled me to him. He bent his head and placed a kiss on my lips.

I couldn't help but sway into him, and when he pulled away and looked into my eyes, I was still unsteady.

"We will be home soon, my princess," he said softly.

But he said it in Lamanite.

14

Salome

"We shouldn't have separated from the others," I overheard Keturah say to Jashon.

"You shouldn't second guess my decisions—especially not in front of my men." There was no heat in Jashon's reprimand. It seemed that none of these men expected Keturah to act appropriately and follow the social rules of politeness.

"The men would think something was wrong if I didn't question my captain."

"I don't believe that for one second."

I didn't either. Keturah was quick to do what any of the men asked of her—not that they really asked her to do much. She had a willing heart and was always eager to do her best and to make things easier on others.

"Believe what you will, but I still don't think it was necessary to separate. Lib is going to go straight to Ishmael and demand to see the king. We are going the wrong way."

"No, we aren't," I called out, my eyes trained on the evidence. At least, we weren't going the wrong way if we wanted to find Lib.

Muloki made it to my side first. "What is it?"

I pointed to a partial footprint embedded in a narrow patch of soil between two craggy areas. "Stop!" I said suddenly. "Don't mar anymore marks." I crouched down to see the track better. "But look around for more," I called to the men up ahead.

"It's all rock," Darius said dubiously.

"I found this one," I countered.

Everyone studied the ground around them, but Jashon joined Muloki and me. "If this is Lib's, he's headed west into the sinking sun."

"It's his," I said confidently. "See here at the heel? It's identical to his previous tracks. And I believe this one was not deliberate."

All the men looked at me.

"Because," I went on as I measured the track against both my hand and my foot to be sure. "We're so far away from where his trail left off. Those tracks were distinct and deliberately placed. This track is marred at the edges."

"Why did he want us to think he was going south?" Ethanim wondered aloud.

We all looked at each other. This track was directly west of the last one I had found and the one before that earlier in the morning.

"He'll turn north soon," said Melia quietly, and everyone turned to look at her. "Toward the Land of Nephi, the land of the very first inheritance."

"But why?" Ethanim was frustrated and clearly worried about his friend.

Melia exchanged a glance with her husband. "He just will," she said after a weighted pause, and folding her arms against a chill none of us could feel, she walked away without meeting anyone's eye.

The men shuffled their feet, shifted their weight, and

stared at the ground. Jashon rubbed a spot on his temple. Darius scratched his head. Ethanim fisted both hands in his hair and let out a yell of frustration. But when I caught the glimmer of tears in his eyes before he let his hands fall to his sides and stomped away from the group, I recognized it for what it was—pain and helplessness.

I knew the helpless feeling of watching a loved one walk away toward death or pain or imprisonment.

But Lib had done it knowing full well the outcome.

I started moving, catching Jashon's eye as I followed after Ethanim.

I was grateful to these men for their willingness to let me accompany them on their rescue mission, but since I had joined their group, I had started to care about each of them. It was impossible not to. I loved to watch the way they helped each other and cared for each other. It was not so obvious with the men as with the women, but they carried an esteem between them, a bond that none of them took lightly. They worked extremely well together, sometimes seeming almost as if they could read each other's minds.

The men of my clan were like this too, but there was something different about these men. I wondered if it had something to do with how often they prayed together, how they invited that spirit I had felt into their lives.

I had always prayed when something really bothered me, when I needed help, or when I was in trouble, but I wondered what difference I might notice if I prayed continually as these people did.

"Ethanim, wait!" I called after I had followed him across the top of the craggy hill we were on. I didn't know if he knew I was following him—probably—but he didn't let up.

"Go away," he called back over his shoulder.

I didn't. I hastened my pace instead.

When we had descended the hill and were out of sight of the others, he finally stopped, but he didn't turn around. I heard him sniff. He wiped his palms across his face.

I walked up slowly behind him. "It's okay to feel hurt," I said. "Our feelings are what make us know we are alive."

He cocked his head to the side, treating me to a portion of his profile. "That is what you followed me to say? Our feelings make us know we are alive?"

I giggled. "I guess so. Lib is your friend?"

"Lib is an idiot."

I touched his elbow, willing him to turn to face me, but he didn't. "What makes him an idiot?"

"Keturah. Every man who loves her is an idiot."

"I have noticed that quite of few of the men love her—"

He snorted. "Try all of them."

"All but you?"

He shrugged.

"You do not think she merits their loyalty?"

"Their loyalty, yes. Love?" He scoffed. "They are all fools."

I had seen that Keturah clearly valued her friendship with Lib, for she had a closer friendship with him than with any of the others, even Jashon.

"I think I see," I said.

Another scoff. "Oh yeah? Sure you do." His sarcasm fell flat.

He was jealous of Lib's friendship with Keturah, of his loyalty to her.

"You've been friends with Lib a long time," I said.

"Forever."

"He is your best friend, then?"

Ethanim cleared his throat. "He is closer than a brother to me."

"He was, you mean."

Finally he turned to look at me. His face was still wet and his eyes were bloodshot and slightly puffy.

"It was inevitable, you know," I said, "that you would fight over a girl."

He almost recoiled. "I don't want her!"

"And he can't have her, but that is not the point, is it?"

He shook his head. "No," he said quietly.

The point was that Lib valued Keturah, a woman he couldn't even have, over the friendship he had shared with Ethanim for their entire lives. It was probably not so clear in Ethanim's mind, but I saw it all very clearly because I was not close to the situation as he was.

I reached up and touched Ethanim's cheek, much like I had done so often with Ardon. I smiled at him. "He will be your friend again. You surely have enough faith in your god to deliver him from danger."

"Even if we find him before he turns himself over, it won't be the same."

"Perhaps no. But it would have changed anyway, so let him be noble in it."

He stared at me for a moment and then chuckled and spoke almost under his breath. "Noble."

"Yes," I laughed. "His gesture is a noble one. Almost as noble as it is foolish."

He laughed with me, nodded his head, and stared off to the north.

154

"We all have to grow up," I said. "He will learn from this, and it is not for you to stop him."

"Then why are we chasing him down?"

I grimaced. "It is not the life lessons we are trying to stop."

He swallowed hard.

"Come on," I said and offered him my hand. "Let's get back to the others. We're wasting valuable time. The sooner we find Lib, the sooner we can go after Ardon."

"Aw, Salome. I didn't even think... Lib's such an idiot."

"There's no need to apologize for him. Without you and your friends, I would still be wandering hungry in the woods of Manti," I said tightly.

He nodded. "Still," he said, and he stepped toward me and gave me an awkward hug with one arm. "Lay your fears aside. We will find him."

I wanted to respond, but I choked up, and in the end I just nodded and let him lead me back to the others.

Jashon was still studying the track when I approached it again. "How did you find this?" he asked me, almost bewildered.

I shrugged. "I have an eye for tracking is all."

Muloki adjusted the leather straps of his travel pack. They seemed to be rubbing awkwardly on his bare skin. "I'd say you do."

"So would I," Jashon muttered and looked up from the print. "Muloki," he said and ran a hand through his hair. "Tell us again how the Land of Nephi sits geographically."

"It is shaped as a dish and abuts the southern border of the Nephite lands. The two lands are separated by a strip of wilderness that extends from the east sea on one end to the west sea on the other." Muloki tried to motion with his hands in the air in front of him, but giving that up, he said, "Here, like this." He moved to a less rocky area, knelt, found a small stick, and drew a map into the dirt, orienting his drawing so the top of the map was north.

Jashon studied it as he drew a hand across his stubbled cheek. "And we are where?"

Muloki pointed to a spot near the middle. "As far as I can tell."

"And Kenai took the others in this direction." Jashon touched the map and moved his finger east.

Muloki grunted.

"Amulon is here?" Jashon indicated a point northeast of our current position.

Another grunt.

Jashon sighed deeply. "Alright. And Lib is on a trajectory that heads in this direction." He moved his finger west. He stopped it and changed direction, moving it due north. When he stopped again, he looked at Muloki.

"Ishmael."

"The capital city?"

"Yes."

I broke into their conversation. "He is going to the great Temple of the Sacrifice?"

They both looked at me.

"But they are not taking Gid and Ardon there," I said in confusion.

Muloki shook his head. "We don't think so. Not according to the scouts."

"And remember," Darius said, "Helaman said to go south."

156

"How does your Helaman know where they have taken my son? Why do you give so much credit to his words?"

Jashon stood. "Have the men eat and rest," he said to Muloki. Then he brushed my hand with his and said, "Follow me."

I followed him away from the others, walking slowly by his side through the forest. At last he found a fallen log and motioned for me to sit on it, which I did, and I turned to look up at him curiously.

"Helaman is more than a chief captain to us." He paused, rubbed his jaw. "You know the other men and I belong to the church of God."

"Yes."

"We believe that God speaks to man through chosen men, men who we call prophets."

"I did not know that."

"We believe Helaman is such a man."

"A prophet?"

"Yes. A man chosen by God to be his mouthpiece here on earth."

I bit my bottom lip. The idea was not so strange. "And you believe he spoke for God when he told you to travel south?"

"Yes."

"So you believe God wants you to find your brother?"

"Yes, of course."

"But why does he not set Gid free himself? Why did he allow Gid's capture in the first place? Why must you trouble yourselves, put yourselves in danger, to travel all this way to rescue him? It would be so easy for your all-powerful god to do so."

Jashon sat beside me, and I welcomed his nearness. He cleared his throat and then spoke softly. "You know of Captain Moroni."

"Of course. Everyone does."

"Years ago when I was fighting with Teancum, we got word of one of Moroni's great triumphs. See, he wanted to free the Nephite prisoners in the city of Gid. The Lamanites had taken not only men, but women and children. They held the city, and they would not let the people go. One night, Moroni was able to lower in weapons and supplies to the prisoners over the walls of the city."

He paused and to my surprise reached over and took my hand lightly in his. I responded by squeezing it more firmly, secretly pleased that he had foregone brushing my hand and held it instead.

"Why did Moroni not lower the ropes over for the people?" he asked quietly.

I shook my head.

"I pondered this question for many days. How easy it would have been for him to rescue the people. That was his aim. That was his goal and purpose. He had everything in place that night, and yet he left the people inside the walls."

"But he gave them weapons."

Jashon's burning gaze met mine. "And God has given us weapons that we might free our brother."

My chest suddenly felt tight and a lump formed in my throat. I knew what he said was true. I couldn't deny it, but I didn't even want to. I wanted very much for it to be true. I wanted very much for an all-powerful God to be aware of our situation and to care about Ardon's safety. I wanted very much for God to care about the ache and the guilt and the longing in my chest—to care about me.

"Not only did Moroni free the prisoners, he gained the city also. He had a greater purpose there that night."

He was saying that freeing Ardon and Gid was not the only reason he had embarked on this journey.

Jashon broke our eye contact and faced forward, giving me only his hard profile when he said, "Salome, who do I speak to about arranging for a marriage?"

"Who...?" The change in subject was so sudden, I didn't understand for a moment what he was asking. When I did understand, I had to bite off a grin.

"Yes, who might I speak to about marriage? Your father?"

I looked down at our clasped hands.

"My father-in-law," I said. "But he is unlikely to allow a marriage to Enos." I bit harder on my lip.

He turned his head to look at me. "No, Salome. I do not mean marriage to Enos." But he noticed the teasing glint in my eye that I couldn't hide. "Will your father-in-law allow your marriage to me?"

I twisted my lips in thought. "If you return Ardon to him, he will reward you."

His brows knit. "That's not what I mean."

"Good, because I would not agree to it."

He looked away again. "I see," he said. "You do not want to marry again?" He sounded so matter of fact, that I almost thought I had misjudged him. I almost thought I had not hurt his pride.

I squeezed his hand even tighter and covered it with my other one. "I would not mind a husband. But I would like there to be love between us."

"Salome."

I tilted my head and regarded him until he looked at me again. "Have you ever kissed a woman, Jashon?"

I did not think Jashon was given to blushing much. He might have then, but I was caught in his eyes and did not notice if he did.

"Kiss me," I said.

He didn't hesitate, but he didn't move quickly either. I let my eyes drop closed, and I waited for him. He breathed my name onto my lips before he touched them with his.

When I opened my eyes to look at him, his expression told me everything I wanted to know. I had hurt his pride. He had never kissed a woman. He did feel there could be love between us.

And he was right.

"Returning Ardon home safely will persuade my father-in-law. But you must persuade me."

He gave only a slight nod of understanding before he kissed me again.

"Muloki wants to get moving." A quick glance showed Darius standing in the trees behind us, turned away, trying to offer us privacy as he delivered his message. I understood why he would value and respect privacy. He had been caught in a similar situation, and it had caused all kinds of turmoil for him.

After he had accidentally called Sarai by her sister's name and she had screamed at him, I had noticed that many of those we traveled with were not as friendly with him. No one was unkind, but those close to Sarai had clearly taken sides. Interestingly enough, Isabel seemed to be on Darius's.

Darius waited for us and we made our way back toward the others together. No one said anything until Darius spoke.

"I am capable of seeing to my sister's needs in her husband's absence. You can feel free to pursue your...ahh...courtship."

"I will take that into consideration," Jashon said. "But still, I feel the responsibility heavily."

"Save Gid. That is your responsibility. And you also have a responsibility to yourself." Darius glanced at me. "To see to your own family's needs."

"I am a man without a family."

"Something you should be working on."

Jashon didn't say anything, but after a moment, when Darius had gone on ahead, he looked at me and grinned.

Muloki hailed us with a wave when we entered the small clearing filled with people, all of them ready to move out.

"I'll walk with Ket," Darius said quietly and then moved away to join his sister. We both watched him.

"He reminds me of Ardon," I said.

I kept my eyes trained on the ground for other signs that Lib had passed this way, but I saw nothing for a long time. I was thinking I should suggest we turn north when Jashon broke into my thoughts.

"I'm starting to think Lib didn't come this way."

I glanced up at him. "I was just thinking the same thing. I feel that we should turn north."

"And what makes you feel that way?"

"I don't know," I admitted. "It's just a feeling."

"When I feel like that, it's the holy spirit speaking to me."

I laughed a little. "But would your spirit speak to me?"

"Sure. He speaks to all men."

"Jashon!"

We both turned to see Reb running up to us from the east. He and Josh had been acting as scouts all afternoon. I looked beyond him but did not see Josh.

Not waiting for a reply, Reb delivered his message. "A band of men to the east. They've spotted us and turned to intercept us."

Jashon's brow rose, and he glanced at Muloki. "Are they Lamanite?"

Reb shrugged. "It's hard to say. Josh is circling and he'll trail them in."

Jashon nodded and pointed to Jarom and Darius, who both nodded and disappeared into the trees.

The rest of the men stopped looking for Lib's tracks and their hands moved to their weapons.

Jashon nudged me. "Walk with Keturah."

I obeyed his calm command quickly. Melia and Eve joined us and the men formed a kind of circle around us. Keturah handed me her bow.

"You'll have to draw from my quiver," she said. "So stay close."

Her own choice of weapon was her slingshot, which she slipped from her belt and fingered a stone into as we walked.

Some of the men had spears. They all had swords. Melia and Eve both held a knife.

We walked for a quarter of an hour before we saw the six men coming toward us. They moved quickly on a path clearly intended to meet with ours.

"Stand ready," Keturah breathed as we all came to a stop and regarded each other.

"That's not necessary," I said, and I raised my hand to

the newcomers, a search party if my guess was right. "Hello, Jacob," I called out.

His shock registered in his expression before he squared up to Jashon, who stood as the clear leader of our group.

"We've come in search of the woman," he said stiffly, indicating me with the sharp movement of a hand in my direction. "And the boy." His eyes were searching for Ardon. "We are prepared to fight."

I rushed forward, shouldering my way through Ethanim and Mathoni. I stepped between Jacob and Jashon. They both glanced at me but kept their eyes trained on each other.

I leaned toward Jashon and mumbled under my breath. "These are my kinsmen."

Lamech stayed with Zaaron and his men, traveling with them as they led us through the hills toward their village. He fit in well, and I often heard him laughing with the men. Zaaron sent out scouts at the front and the rear of our large party, and Kenai called ours in with a call our men used often, the shrill call of the margay.

The margay was a small wildcat that lived in our forests. It was beautiful and small with large eyes and spots like a leopard, but could be quite dangerous when threatened. My brothers and Keturah's brothers had been using this call for many years. I didn't know who had started using it first, but it was one of the many things our families had in common.

Eliza, Isabel, and I had fallen a distance behind the men by mid-afternoon. I knew that during the past weeks our men had been taking a slower pace to accommodate the women in our band—particularly Keturah—but I realized now just how much slower they had been traveling. Zaaron set a much more strenuous pace.

"Are you tiring?"

It took me a few moments to realize that the man who had drawn up near us was speaking to me. I turned to see the one Zaaron had called Tecumeni walking steadily just behind my left shoulder. He was moving silently, and I wondered how long he had been there without me sensing him.

"Oh!" I said, unable to hide my surprise. "No." I glanced at the other girls who were just as startled as I was. "Well, to admit to weakness, yes, a little. It's been a very long journey."

"Does your husband push you hard?"

Was he asking if Lamech hit me? I was frustrated that I understood Tecumeni's words but did not quite grasp his full meaning.

"He is not my husband," I said, sidestepping what I did not understand.

Tecumeni smiled. "Nor is he your betrothed."

I frowned. "Yes he is."

He gazed at me for a moment. "Okay," he said, but his skepticism was one thing I did understand. After a moment he said, "Introduce me to your friends."

I remembered how Lamech had denied friendship with these Nephites. But I had clearly been talking with Izz and Eliza all afternoon, and I had no way of knowing how much Tecumeni had seen—probably all of it—so I said, "This is Isabel." I nearly added, "my sister," but stopped myself in time by biting my lip. "And this is Eliza."

Surprising me, he raised a hand and nodded politely to them both. "Tell them hello," he said.

"You may tell them." I laughed nervously. "They can both understand a simple greeting."

He turned back to them. "Shalal, I am Tecumeni."

They both smiled at him and greeted him back in his own language. They glanced at each other and cast me identical knowing smiles. I couldn't help blushing.

"He's cute," said Isabel. "Too bad you're betrothed."

"Maybe he'll fight Lamech for you," Eliza said, smothering a giggle.

"Eliza! Izz! Don't even say such things."

I turned back to Tecumeni, embarrassed. He looked at me expectantly for a moment, and when I didn't offer any information, he asked, "What did they say?"

"They said it was nice to meet you." Then I bit my lip to keep from laughing at the absurd lie. When I looked away from Tecumeni, I caught Zeke's worried frown. Tecumeni caught it too.

"What's his problem?" Tecumeni asked offhandedly, not seeming particularly interested in what might be upsetting a Nephite.

"He is Zeke. Eliza's husband. I doubt he likes you flirting with his wife."

He chuckled. "Eliza is married?"

"So is Isabel. Kenai, the leader, is her husband." I pointed him out.

"The one with the scar at his throat?"

"You noticed that?"

He was silent for a moment until I chanced a look at him. "I notice everything," he said quietly, and I was caught for a moment in eyes that had turned serious. But then he grinned and said, "Like the fact that you are tiring. I'll go ask your husband to allow you to rest."

"He's not my husband," I said again lamely.

He laughed. "Don't worry. I'll tell him it's the Nephite women who tire."

I watched Tecumeni trot forward and speak to his uncle. Zaaron looked over his shoulder toward us, glanced up at the sky, and then nodded. He raised his arm in the air and men began to slow until all of them had stopped.

A few moments later when Isabel, Eliza, and I caught

up, Lamech was glaring at me with his hands on his hips.

Ignoring him, I left the women and walked over to Kenai. "It looks like we're stopping for a bit," I said to him.

He studied the terrain. "Do you know where they're leading us?"

"They're taking us to their village. It's near Jerusalem. I told them I was from there."

"Then the chances of breaking off from them are not good."

I chewed on my lip. "You could take the men—"

"Sarai."

Lamech was calling me, so I hurried to finish.

"You could take the men and continue to follow Gideon."

"Not an option," Zeke said as he drew up to us, and from the look in his eyes, I could tell there would be no discussing it.

"Sarai," Lamech called again impatiently. "Leave them to their meal."

Kenai turned to go to his wife. I turned to go to Lamech, but Zeke grabbed my wrist, much like he'd done the morning we left our village. "Sarai, what do you think you're doing?"

Lamech was there in an instant, pushing his body between us.

Zeke let go and backed away, remembering who was watching and that in this circumstance he could not act like my brother. "Sorry," he said, his hands out. "Sorry."

Lamech ushered me toward a copse of trees without turning his back to Zeke. I was aware that everyone in both bands was watching what happened. Lamech had done exactly the right thing. I glanced over to see Tecumeni watching very closely—noticing everything—with his arms folded, his eyes narrowed, and a sardonic smile playing over his lips.

"Sit," Lamech commanded me, sighing deeply and running a hand through his hair.

I did, still aware of so many eyes on us.

"Are you trying to dishonor me?" he asked, a little louder than necessary.

"That was Zeke," I protested.

Lamech glanced over his shoulder. "I was referring to your flirting with that boy."

I didn't have a protest to that. "Oh."

He sat down next to me and offered me some venison from his satchel.

"What did he say?" he asked quietly.

"Nothing. He was just...flirting, like you said."

"What do you know about flirting, Princess?"

I didn't like his tone. "Lots of boys flirt with me. At home they did and especially in Orihah."

"Just not the right one?" he asked snidely.

I knew he meant Darius. The question hurt me a lot more than I thought he had intended. Lamech never flirted with me either. I shut my eyes and turned away from him.

"This whole situation is a disaster," Lamech said after a moment.

I sighed and turned back to him. "Why? What did Zaaron say?" I lowered my voice. "He doesn't believe our story?"

"I don't know. He pretends to if he doesn't. I think he is suspending judgment."

"Tecumeni doesn't believe it." To Lamech's sharp

glance, I said, "But only because he, um, doesn't want to believe it."

Lamech stopped chewing his venison. "What, specifically, does he not wish to believe?"

"The betrothal."

He snorted.

"What? Is it so unbelievable that he might wish me unbetrothed to you?"

I felt his eyes looking me over. "No," he grudgingly admitted. "It's just, I'd love to see Darius's reaction."

"It would probably be similar to yours," I said smugly, keeping an eye on Zaaron's men—one in particular.

Lamech caught the direction of my gaze. He took my hand. "It's exhausting," he said.

"Speaking the language?"

"Worrying about you."

My eyes went to our hands. "Lamech," I began.

"It's just for show," he said. "You started this lie, now we have to finish it."

I didn't believe him. Not completely. Part of it was for show. Part of it was out of jealousy.

And jealousy was good.

"I wish I could walk with you," I said.

"You can. You can help pace us."

"Oh."

"You'll slow us down a lot, but we'll lose Eliza and Izz if we don't."

I took my hand back, reaching into my own satchel to make it look natural. But probably the scowl on my face gave away my feelings.

I handed Lamech a piece of the bread Melia had given

me, saying childishly, "And of course you wouldn't want to leave Izz behind," even though I tried to bite my tongue.

"You know, the reason I treat you like a little girl is because you act like one." Lamech leaned back against a tree, stretched his legs out in front of him, and crossed his ankles.

"You do it to keep me at a distance. And I'm not the only one who—"

"Who what?" he broke in, unable to resist an argument with me.

I caught my breath.

"Never mind. You should hold my hand again."

He reached out and pulled me up and off balance so I fell against his chest. Then he held me there. He put his lips into my hair and said, "Don't giggle at Tecumeni."

I nuzzled into his chest like I had seen Izz do with Kenai. "Why not?"

"Please tell me I don't have to explain all the reasons it's a bad idea."

"Well I don't want to offend him. Don't you think that's a bad idea?"

"The more you talk to him, the more chance there is to give yourself away, to make a mistake."

"You're talking to Zaaron."

"That's different. There's no way around it. And besides, we're both men."

I sighed. "What should I do when Tecumeni engages me in conversation?"

"Well, don't giggle for starters."

I smiled into his chest.

"You could argue with him. You're good at that."

"That's only for you."

"Tell him your betrothed will kill him."

I laughed and leaned up to look at him. "He's not afraid of you."

He grumbled. "I think you're right."

"And I think Zeke is upset with us."

"There's nothing we can do about that right now."

Zaaron and the old man with the scarred face were up and pacing. Kenai noticed them and stood, and soon everyone was preparing to move out.

"Come on." Lamech eased me away from him, got to his feet, and offered me his hand.

I wished it was as loving a gesture as he made it appear.

We traveled until late in the evening before Zaaron and his men stopped to make camp. The forest looked the same as it had for the past month, and I wondered that anyone could know where we were. Despite the constant fear they invoked in the pit of my stomach, I was grateful for our guides.

"Do you think these Lamanites were sent to us by God?" I asked Lamech as he walked me into the trees.

"You were in the Nephite lands too long if you are speaking of their God," he replied.

I sighed. Even alone we could not be real with each other. That was the problem with lying, especially with this lie. We had to keep it up all the time. Zaaron's men were surely watching us closely at all times. "It's just that Eliza and Isabel make it sound so real."

"Make what sound real? Their God?" Lamech asked and his voice seemed to hold little interest in the Nephite god.

"Yes. And all their beliefs."

"You worry me," he said. "There will be no more talk of

the Nephite god. Now, hurry. I'll be here when you are ready to go back to camp."

We ran into one of Zaaron's men on our way back through the falling darkness. Lamech greeted him by name.

"Shalal, Josiah."

"Shalal, Lamech. Zaaron sends a message."

"Speak it."

"Our men will take the sentinel duties tonight while your men rest."

Lamech waited a moment before responding. "They are not my men," he said tightly, "and I imagine they will run their guards as they have been doing. Nevertheless, it is a generous offer, and Sarai will deliver your message to them."

I watched the man walk away. "I don't like lying to them," I whispered.

Lamech cleared his throat. "Lying doesn't sit well with me, either."

"I wish we could tell them the truth. They seem nice."

Lamech shook his head. "I don't think it would be wise. Look at the way they treat the others."

I thought they were treating the others well. They had done nothing but ignore them.

"It is a stratagem only, Sarai. Sometimes necessary."

We paused to survey the camp as we approached it. Kenai and the rest of our group had set out their bedrolls on the north end. My tent, and one for Eliza and Isabel had been set up in the midst of them. The Lamanites had set their possessions on the south end. Most of them were sitting on their heels at a small fire, but I could see that their bedrolls were similar to ours, and for some reason, it surprised me that they had them.

Our elevation was high, and the air was cooling as the sun went down. I retrieved a blanket from my tent and followed Lamech to the Lamanite fire.

One of the men gestured vaguely to the north and laughed, "You prefer to sleep with the dogs?"

Lamech gazed at the tent for a moment. He didn't join in the man's laughter. "Despite being sons of a liar, they have been kind to Sarai because of their women." He paused and when he looked at me, his dark eyes were soft, and he didn't hesitate to reach out a hand to stroke down my hair again. He left his hand at my neck as he said, "I won't ask them to move the tent."

I realized then what kind of a predicament we were in. Zaaron and his men would expect us to be glad, or at least willing, to get away from the Nephites. But there was little chance that any of my kinsmen would let me sleep nestled among the Lamanites.

The old man came to us. I thought he might, I didn't know, *insist* we sleep on the south end of camp. I moved a little closer to Lamech. Yes, he annoyed me sometimes, but I trusted him to keep me safe. I trusted him absolutely.

The old man spoke in a lowered voice. "You are wise. It is best to keep the peace."

Lamech nodded, and turned to me. "Let's go inform the Nephites of the guard situation," he said.

He led me toward our men. "Tell Kenai the Lamanites will run the guard duty tonight," he told me.

I rolled my eyes and clutched my blanket to my chest as I approached Zeke, Kenai, and Enos. "Lamech and I are uncomfortable with this charade," I said as I pivoted around to make sure we would not be overheard by any of Zaaron's men.

"We were just discussing it," Zeke said. If anyone had a hard time letting a lie stand without correcting it, it was Zeke.

"It's my fault," I said morosely. "I've put you all in a bad position with my impetuous story."

Zeke reached out as if to put a comforting hand on my shoulder, something he did often, but pulled it back before touching me. "You did fine," he assured me. "We will make it work."

"Come on," Lamech said, casting a surreptitious glance back at Zaaron's men. "We can't linger."

Lamech shared a look with Kenai before we left.

"What did Kenai say?" I asked.

"He said we will talk later. We need to make plans."

I had expected to sit up at one of the fires like we always did, but Lamech led me away from both fires. He led me away from the tents and the bedrolls.

"Where are we going?" I asked him. "It's getting dark."

"Is it too much to ask you to just trust me?" he asked defensively.

I giggled. I couldn't help it. But I grasped Lamech's arm and said, "Don't be mad."

"I'm not mad."

"You sound mad."

"I'm not."

We came to the edge of a gully where we stopped, and beyond it in the distance we could see the last glimmer of light on the horizon. Lamech crossed his arms over his chest and looked out at the view.

"I was laughing because just now, when we were talking to the man with the scar on his face, I was thinking about how much I do trust you."

174

"His name is Anahah," he said absently. "You trust me?"
Did he sound unsure?

"I trust you absolutely," I said, I wasn't really thinking he would take the words seriously. He never seemed to take anything I said seriously. But I thought it went deep into his heart when I said, "I know you would die before you let any of these men hurt me," even though I said it a little offhandedly as I gazed at the horizon lit like an ember.

Something about his silence told me I was right. After a moment, he took the blanket from my arms, unfolded it and draped it around my shoulders. He stood behind me and held it in place there.

I pulled the blanket tighter around myself, wondering if this—being alone together at the edge of camp—was only for show. I knew he would say it was. That was the problem.

Saying anything was the problem. Words seemed to be our problem. It never mattered what either one of us said, it always ended in an argument.

"How are you doing with the Lamanite language?" I asked into the night.

"It astounds me," he said quietly. "It is beyond my abilities, but I find that though I understand the meanings of all the words, very distinctly, I don't always understand exactly what certain phrases mean."

"I have that problem, too," I admitted and hesitated. "It's like with us."

"What do you mean?"

I licked my lips. "I understand the things you say, Lamech, but I don't always understand your true meanings." I paused. "And I think it is the same for you."

He didn't deny it, and I felt him edge closer to my back.

After a moment, his hands moved from my shoulders and he slowly, carefully, wrapped me in his arms.

I wanted to lean back into him, but I didn't. I was afraid to move a muscle. I knew this was only partially real, if it was real at all. He would pull away again. He would say something sharp, frown at me sullenly, or stalk away without looking back. If only there was a way to talk without words, like Kenai did with his eyes. Maybe something like that would work for us.

The horizon was still glowing, but it would fade soon. Grasping for courage, I turned in his arms. I could only stare at his chest and feel my throat tighten. I would do it. I would say what I could not say with words. Feeling my lashes brush against my skin, I looked up into the face of this boy who had annoyed his way into my heart. He was frowning down at me, but his shadowed eyes were curious. My heart was beating too fast and my breaths were getting shallow. It had to be now. Letting my eyes fall to his lips, I lifted my chin, and I kissed him.

He had kissed me that afternoon, but it hadn't meant anything, not between us anyway. Not like this kiss.

Because this kiss meant everything.

It was everything I couldn't say to him and everything he couldn't say to me, and I loved it, but I knew that the moment the kiss ended, he would start denying the true meaning of what his lips were saying so much more eloquently than when they spoke. I must have dropped the blanket because my arms slid around him. I barely registered his bare chest, but I did feel his wildly beating heart.

I was doing that. I was making it beat like that! He was the one who could expertly wield weapons in defense of all he valued. He was the one whose muscles felt like stone under my hands. And he was the one who would fight to the death before letting harm come to me.

But I was the one with real power.

In the moment I realized this, I prayed *let me wield this power wisely.* And then I drew in a breath and backed away from him.

I glanced around his shoulder at Zeke, who stood in the firelight with his hands on his hips, squinting into the night at us. It was hard to read his expression with the firelight behind him, but I was pretty sure he was scowling.

"The Nephites are ready to kill you," I said.

Lamech took another moment to look tenderly down at me, a moment that I wished could last a lifetime, before he said, "It's because they all love you. And I can't blame them. Come on, I'll take you to your tent."

There was no doubt about his bravery, I thought as I glanced again at Zeke.

Lamech left me at the door of my tent before joining the other men in the shadows beyond the reaches of the firelight. Zeke gave me an assessing look before he followed them.

I was about to crawl inside my tent when I realized I didn't have my blanket. Turning, I walked back toward the gully to retrieve it, and even though no one was paying attention to me, I felt my face heat with embarrassment remembering why I had dropped it.

And then my face went scalding hot when I saw Tecumeni walking toward me with the blanket, neatly folded in his hand.

16

Jacob stared at me for a moment, and then he looked back to Jashon.

"What is the meaning of this? Jashon, why do you have my brother's wife, and where is my nephew?"

I turned to look at Jashon then too.

Everyone was completely silent. Jashon's kinsmen were curious, and mine were confused.

I didn't know how Jacob knew Jashon, but I wanted to tell him at least that Jashon had not abducted me. I couldn't do that. I knew Jacob, and I knew he would not like it if I spoke before he spoke to me, especially in front of all these men. His temper could be volatile. So I waited, and I edged a little closer to Jashon.

Jacob noticed my movement, and his eyes narrowed.

"A small Lamanite war party abducted Ardon from the fields. Salome tracked them into the wilderness but lost the trail. My men and I are tracking the same party. We found Salome in the wilderness." He hesitated and glanced at me. "Half-starved and lost."

Jacob's temper faded from his eyes. He would expect me to have gotten myself half-starved and lost. He would be pitying and condescending, but at least he wouldn't be angry.

"Did you not receive her message?" Jashon asked.

Jacob glowered at me. "A vague message from a child."

I grimaced. I had told his six year old daughter that I was leaving and the men would have to finish harvesting the field when they returned from their hunt, and I had only told her that much because she had been at the well when I had stopped to fill my water skin.

Jashon shifted his weight. "You tracked her?"

I took another long look at Jacob and his cousins—seven men altogether. Jacob was the oldest of Zed's brothers. They had two younger brothers, Neel and Hep, and four younger cousins, Zaph, Abel, Kimnor, and Jareth. Jacob, Zaph, and Abel were all married. I could either become a second wife to one of them, a third in Zaph's case, or marry one of the younger boys. This was the reason marrying again did not appeal to me.

The men were soaked with sweat and weary looking. They had likely run day and night to find Ardon and me—Ardon mostly. I felt guilty for not running straight to them. Despite my intentions to free Ardon quickly and return safely before the hunt was over, I should have told them.

Jacob gave a curt nod. "Her trail was easy to follow."

Jashon stared at Jacob for a moment. Then he shook his head. "That was ours. We left a deliberate trail for her—so she could follow us."

Jacob smiled as if he didn't believe that.

Jashon ignored the condescending in Jacob's smile. "Do you wish to join us in the search for Ardon?"

"Assist you? What is Ardon to you?"

"The Lamanite warriors also captured Gid."

Jacob's brows shot up. "Your brother?"

I could tell from his tone he knew exactly who Gid was, and he would easily discern what an unlikely and horrible situation it was. Jacob was rash sometimes, but he was intelligent and quick.

Jashon was so solemn when he nodded. How heavy this responsibility must feel to him. I lifted a hand to touch his, to offer him strength and solidarity, and to ask a question I could not voice. He looked down at me expectantly, but when I glanced pointedly toward my brother-in-law, he knew what I was asking.

"Jacob fought in Teancum's army. He is my brother in arms. Zaph too."

My gaze drifted away as I pieced together how the men knew each other. "And Hep," I said softly. My eyes found Jashon's again.

And Zedekiah.

But neither of us said it.

Darius, Jarom, and Josh appeared behind my kinsmen and came forward when Jashon gestured for them to do so. Ethanim and Mathoni came around from behind me, and Jashon began to make the introductions. I admired how he took command, how everyone obeyed him readily. I admired the respect he both earned and received.

"Salome."

"Oh!" I said, realizing they were looking at me. "Yes?"

Jashon spoke sternly. "You may go rest with the women. We will discuss our plans with Jacob and his men." Jashon never excluded the women from their planning councils. When he looked down and gave me a secret, tender smile, I realized that he knew Jacob as well as I did.

"My husband's brothers," I said in response to the questioning gazes of Keturah, Melia, and Eve when I joined them.

"Will they make you go home with them?" Eve asked in concern.

I smiled, but I couldn't keep the sadness from showing in it. "They won't go home without Ardon."

They cast glances at each other.

"That is the way it is in my clan. Ardon is very important to them because Jacob does not have any sons."

"So what?" said Keturah.

"Someday, Ardon will be the chief of our clan. That is, the chief ruler. He will have more responsibility than any child should have."

"But, he won't have to rule as a child, will he?" asked Melia.

I cast a glance toward the men. "Jacob cannot rule."

"But why not? His father is the chief, is he not?"

"Jacob is the eldest brother, but he cannot become chief because he does not have a son. That is our tradition. He cannot rule unless Ardon dies." I gestured toward my kinsmen. "And each of those men will give their lives before they let Ardon die."

"But he is young. He could still have a son," Eve pointed out. "If...if the worst happened."

I just shrugged. "The way it stands now, Ardon will rule when Jacob's father dies. They respect that. They honor it. I was lucky they did not take him from me when my husband died."

"But he's your son!" Keturah exclaimed, her hand going naturally to her round belly. "Of course you would raise him."

I gave her a wry smile. No, I had been lucky.

"What do you think they're saying?" Eve asked.

We all looked toward the men, and we didn't have to

wonder for long before Jarom came over and sat on his heels next to Eve. "Jacob's men will go after Ardon. They want to see with their own eyes that he is well, but they will wait for us before enacting a rescue."

Keturah took a breath to speak, but he held up his hand.

"If things go bad before we can catch up, they will rescue them both." He glanced toward the other men. "Their numbers are few, but Jashon seems to think them capable. They will leave a man at the caves north of Amulon. If Jacob is not there, we will follow him on. They know our signals."

"But—"

"They don't want to wait." Jarom took a small cloth sack from his satchel and handed it to Eve.

Before he stood to leave, I asked, "Will I have to go with them?"

"You don't want to?" He did not sound surprised.

My eyes involuntarily went to Jashon. I didn't even have to shake my head before he said, "I'll go see to it. Wait here, ladies." He grinned, kissed his wife on her lips with a loud smacking sound, and left.

The other women smiled at her, and Eve blushed. "Here, hold out your hands," she said. "The last of our pistakai nuts."

We shelled the nuts and ate in silence for a time until Eve said, "Melia, will you come with me to fill the water skins? It looks like the men are filling them over there. There must be a stream."

Grateful for their kindness, Keturah and I passed over our water skins and Melia and Eve took them and went in search of water.

I opened my mouth to speak, but Keturah spoke first. "You've got him confused."

I knew she loved her Gideon deeply, but I was not sure how she felt toward Jashon. She was aware of his feelings, though she never encouraged them and, in fact, her actions toward him sometimes bordered on ungrateful and rude.

"Why do you never thank him?" I asked, avoiding what she implied.

She paused with a broken shell in her hand, but then she tossed it away and said, "At first, when I thanked him, he perceived my gratitude as love." She put a nut into her mouth and chewed slowly. "It's easier this way. He understands."

"Does he?"

She could avoid hard topics as well as I could. She didn't answer my question. Instead, she asked, "Why have you not remarried one of your husband's kinsmen?"

I gave a soft, unladylike snort. "It would be like you agreeing to become Enos's second wife."

She made a face.

"Besides." I lowered my voice. "I didn't want any of my husband's kinsmen to raise Ardon. I do not agree with their views or many of their values. Especially not their parenting strategies. I wanted Ardon to grow up good and kind and fair."

"Are your kinsmen not kind?"

"In their way they are. Neel isn't so bad, but he's young." I brushed the broken shells from my hands.

"You gave up marriage so you could raise your son the way you wanted?"

"Believe me, it wasn't a sacrifice."

"I'm sorry," she said. "But did you not like being married?"

I shrugged.

She studied me until I became uncomfortable with her gaze. "You weren't married to the right man," she concluded.

I shrugged again. But I had noticed the women in this clan loved their men. I hadn't missed Eve's deep rosy blush when her husband had kissed her. Eve had not married the wrong man. None of the girls had, not even Keturah.

If anyone could stand the agony of having her husband captured, of not knowing of his well-being—it was Keturah.

But my eyes went to Eve and Melia. And I thought of Isabel, Eliza, and even young Sarai. They were all very strong. And it was not hard to see it was their faith in their god that made them that way. Any one of them might have stood as tall and brave as Keturah did.

I turned to her. "I saw you crying," I said. "At the river, when you were camped at the head of the Sidon. I saw you with Jashon."

She didn't say anything, and we both gazed at Jashon, where he talked with the men, catching up, sharing information, and finalizing their plans.

I cleared my throat to speak again, but she said, "I sprained my ankle on the march to Manti. With Helaman. It was pretty bad, and the men carried me the rest of the way." She laughed a little. "For three years, I worked so hard to become their equal in every way, and I couldn't even walk to our final battle."

She sounded so defeated.

"I'm sure they didn't mind."

A small corner of her mouth turned up, and she slowly shook her head. "No, they didn't. Corban told me they would have carried me to the moon in return for all I had done for them." She waved it off, not wishing it to appear as though she complemented herself or wished me to. "Gideon carried me to that spot on the river, set me on that rock to soak my ankle in the cool water of the Sidon. That day you saw me, I was remembering how long it had taken for the coldness of the water to numb my pain."

I hesitated because we didn't know each other well, but I reached out and placed my hand on hers. I knew she was thinking of her husband. I knew it was hard. I knew that, like me, she tried every moment of every day not to think of him and what might be happening to him.

"Sometimes, it takes God time to heal us," she said. "To show us the right path or work out our lives for the best."

"Or rescue us," I said quietly.

The leaves fluttered in the trees above us, all around us, and sunlight filtered through them to where we sat. Keturah smiled at me.

"Yes, it takes time for God to rescue us, because He must work through our hands and our wills."

I was beginning to see where these people got their strength. Whoever had taught them these things, whoever had taught them about this God, had given them much.

"Gideon carried me to that rock and he...he had seen how much it hurt me to face the raw facts—to have to choose between him and Zeke."

She was quiet for a time, rubbing a blade of grass between her fingers while my mind raced. I had not known she had faced such a decision. No one in camp had given away such information, but they were a clan, like mine, and there would have been no hiding it among them. They all must have known.

"Gideon yielded to Zeke that day. He took the choice away to spare me from having to make it."

In the first moment, I thought this had been selfless of Gideon. He had loved her. He had wanted to take her pain away. But in the next moment, I wondered if anyone had the right to do that for another person—to steal their opportunity to choose for themselves, to take away their agency.

I certainly hadn't liked it when my father had betrothed me to Zed without my consent—though I might have given it if he had only asked.

"How did you end up with Gideon then?" I asked her.

"Oh. My brother saw how unhappy I was, and he went in search of Gideon."

"That was kind of him."

She laughed a little. "Actually, I think he was tired of my moping around. I was not aware he had gone to Gideon or made arrangements with him."

"So he arranged your marriage without your knowledge?"

She frowned a little. "I never really looked at it that way. I always wanted to marry Gideon."

"Always? What about Zeke?"

"I was always expected to marry Zeke."

"You didn't like him?" I thought he was handsome and nice.

"No, it wasn't that. I loved him. I still love him. It was just a feeling I had."

I waited for her to clarify.

"I think I knew in the first moment I saw Gideon that he would be more to me than an acquaintance. I don't mean I fell in love with him then—that's impossible—only that something inside me changed when I saw him." She looked down into her lap. "Does that sound silly?"

"No, it doesn't."

"Do you think every girl feels that way the first time she sees the man who is to be her husband?"

"You mean like they were destined to be married?"

"No. Not exactly. There is always a choice."

"Even if it's not yours?"

She smiled wryly.

The men were getting to their feet and dispersing. Muloki scratched out the map he had drawn in the dirt, and Jashon and Jacob walked toward us. Both of them had their eyes trained on me. I got to my feet and waited for them to approach.

"Jarom said you do not wish to travel with your own kinsmen," Jacob said.

He sounded matter-of-fact, not accusing. I couldn't tell if he was angry or not. I wasn't sure how to phrase my response.

"I prefer to travel with the women," I said. "Even though it may delay finding Ardon."

"My priority is to the clan," he said. "It is my duty to find Ardon."

"I know."

"You should travel with the clan. How can we protect you if you do not place yourself under our care?"

I glanced at Jashon, who waited next to Jacob, feet shoulder-width apart, hands folded patiently in front of him. His face gave nothing away. Had the men decided I would have to leave Jashon's kin and travel with my own? Jacob might have insisted upon it. Jarom had told them what I wanted. Didn't Jashon care? Was he glad to hand me back over to Jacob? I hadn't thought I was much trouble to his men, but I was one more mouth to feed and one more person for him to worry over.

"Jashon is capable of protecting me," I said, a knot of guilt in my stomach.

Jacob turned to regard Jashon, but Jashon kept his eyes on me. Then Jacob turned back and gave a self-satisfied nod.

"And you wish Jashon to have charge of your care?"

My brows knit. Something was happening here, but I didn't quite understand what it was. I looked between them again, but there was really only one answer to give. "Yes."

Another nod. "Good. Then it is done. Jashon has agreed to let you stay with Ardon in the village."

Then I understood.

"Good-bye, sister." He stepped forward and laid his hand on my shoulder. Then he turned, raised an arm in the air, called to his men, and strode away to the south. His men fell in at his side, and I watched them walk away until they were out of sight. They really didn't want to wait.

Keturah held up her hands, and Jashon helped her to her feet. Looking curiously between us, she asked. "What just happened?"

Jashon looked at the ground, and his breaths were deep and slow.

He didn't answer her, so I cleared my throat, and said, "Jashon just arranged my second marriage."

17

"Lamech," I whispered into the darkness.

His reply came immediately.

"Sarai, what is it?"

I hadn't told him about Tecumeni, that he had seen us and heard everything Lamech and I had said at the edge of camp. I had lain awake half the night in worry, but it seemed silly now.

"Nothing," I whispered after a moment.

The flap of my tent moved and Lamech crawled inside. "What is it?" he asked again.

"I said nothing. I'm sorry. Go back to sleep."

"You've never called for me in the night before. Something is wrong, Sarai. Tell me what it is so I may help you." When I didn't reply, he said, "I *can* help you, you know."

"I know that!" I insisted. "It's just...I don't think you can help me with this. I only called to you because...because...you are the one who is here."

He was silent for a moment. "If it's about Darius, just say it quickly and I will give you my honest opinion."

"It's not!" I exclaimed and then lowered my voice back to a whisper. "It's not! You thought I called to you because I have a problem with Darius?"

"So it's not about Darius," he said evenly. "Tell me what has kept you up all night or I'm leaving."

"It's Tecumeni," I blurted. "He...it's the way he looks at me."

He sighed. "Sarai, men look at pretty women. Of course he is going to look at you. Just ignore him—unless you don't want to."

"Don't be stupid," I said. "Nevermind. I told you, go back to sleep."

"You know I wasn't sleeping."

I sighed heavily and rolled over, turning away from him. "I don't want to fight with you Lamech. I really, really don't."

I felt his hand on my shoulder, but I didn't turn to him. I was so tired of fighting with him about things that didn't matter.

"It's the middle of the night and we are fighting, *again*, over nothing," I said into my blanket. "Keeping me at a distance is one thing, and if that's the way you want it, then I accept it. But you hurt my feelings every time you talk to me."

"I'm sorry, Sarai. That's how it has to be."

He offered no reason? Why could he not be pleasant like Daniel and Jared back home? The silence stretched out between us.

"Why?" I asked in a small voice.

"Why? Why would I want to be your second—" He cut himself off, paused, took a breath. "Are you crying?"

"No."

"Why did you call me in here?"

Slowly, I rolled back and looked up at him through the dim light that filtered through the tent.

"You *are* crying," he said.

I set my jaw, wishing I could tell him that I had liked

190

when he kissed me, but we were camped with Lamanites—Lamanites!—and it seemed so unimportant.

He just looked down at me, waiting, I supposed, for me to finish telling him what had kept me awake.

"Tecumeni saw us tonight."

"That was the point."

I bit my lip and continued to stare up at him. He wanted me to think it was the only reason he had kissed me. He wanted me to snap at him so he could snap back. But I wouldn't. I did not like the feeling inside me when we fought.

Finally, he said, "That's part of our story. It is good for them to see us together." Then he added, "Especially Tecumeni."

"When you left me at my tent, I realized I had dropped my blanket. You know, when...when I was with you at the gully."

"When I kissed you," he said, remembering to keep his voice a low murmur.

I nodded, flustered to hear him say the words. I sort of thought I had kissed him. I bit my lip, thinking of it.

"So I went back for it," I told him. "And Tecumeni was standing there, in that spot. He gave me the blanket."

Lamech let out a breath. "What did he say to you?"

"He just said goodnight."

"Nothing else?"

"No. Nothing. But that is not what has kept me awake." The next part, I didn't know how to say. How could I describe the look in Tecumeni's eyes? How could I explain that the reason it worried me was the way it made me feel?

Because I liked it.

I liked the way it made me feel. I felt pretty when

Tecumeni smiled at me, when he turned to go, but couldn't quite drag his eyes from me. I felt so very feminine when his eyes appraised me and I could see his approval in them. And I felt desired when he glanced briefly toward camp, toward my tent where he assumed Lamech was waiting for me. I didn't feel useless and unskilled and unable to walk a path on my own.

Tecumeni had looked at the stars in the night sky, taking a moment to appreciate them, and I knew he was thinking I was as pretty as they were. It was there in his eyes when he stepped forward and held out the blanket. He didn't let it go when I reached for it. We had both held it between us, and I felt like I couldn't move because his eyes held me there. He was getting to me, and he knew it.

He had said, "Goodnight, Sarai," and I had swallowed, nodded, taken the blanket, and gone back to my tent. But when I was tucked in my bedroll, when I tried to close my eyes, I saw his eyes and his smile, and I wondered what would happen tomorrow.

It wasn't that I thought anything would happen with Tecumeni, that I wanted it to, or even that it was possible, because it wasn't. He seemed nice, for a Lamanite, and I reveled in the idea that he liked me and he was not afraid to show it.

There were many things I did not yet understand about myself and about men, but this I did understand. Lamech and Darius both liked me a lot, like Daniel and Jared did, but I was not the kind of girl either of them wanted.

Lamech denied his feelings for me. I didn't know or understand why. All I knew was I hated the way it made me feel when he deliberately pushed me away. What did he think would happen if we weren't fighting with each other?

And Darius had hidden our friendship from everyone. When Kenai had been courting Isabel, Darius had started talking to me at our family meals. We had become friends. We had. The trouble was, I had to keep convincing and re-convincing myself of that, but as it turned out, he was the one who needed convincing.

In the mornings, after I had done my early chores at the hut in the village, the ones Izz wouldn't do, I went into the woods. Sometimes I foraged for fruits or vegetables or roots for our meals. Sometimes I went to the stream to bathe. And sometimes I met Darius halfway to Melek and went to tend his flock of sheep with him.

I had come to realize since leaving the village that those long days in the fields, while I helped Darius mend fences or lead the sheep to greener pastures, even birth the lambs, all of that had meant much more to me than it had to him. I knew he liked having me for a friend, but he had never seen it as anything more, never seen a possibility of anything more, as I so stupidly, so naively had. Zeke was right. I liked Darius too much. I had thought him invincible, thought he could do no wrong.

And when he did, it really shook me up. I couldn't believe it at first. That morning I was so eager to see him. All the work, all the talk, all the attention was centered on Isabel and Kenai. And when the women of the village weren't talking about the wedding, they were talking about the beautiful girl Zeke had brought home with him from where he worked in Zarahemla. And I had just wanted to be with someone who would listen to me, who would *see* me.

But I had seen him and Izz. I had actually seen him try

to kiss her in the woods. She was about to be married to his brother, and he had tried to kiss her. I came around the bend in the path where we always met to go to the fields together. And there they were. They were embracing and Darius lowered his head to kiss her, but she gave him her cheek. He looked crestfallen, and when he couldn't catch her eye again, he looked away from her.

And that's when he had seen me—astonished, hurt, betrayed, devastated, all in the same instant. I turned and ran, large tears streaming uncontrollably from my eyes. Darius hadn't only betrayed me. To think that he could betray Izz and his own brother was completely unfathomable—he was honorable, he was perfect.

I didn't take the path. I turned and ran through the woods toward the river, to a place where water fell from a cliff into a meadow where I knew I could be alone. I had to think. I had to get there.

"Sarai!" He was actually coming after me. As if I wasn't embarrassed enough, did he want me to look him in the face while he told me he didn't want me? While he said he never had? How was it to be endured?

A quick glance back showed him tearing through the woods behind me. I knew he was faster and he would catch me in no time. But when I turned again, I saw Zeke. I would always be grateful to him for being there in that moment.

"Sarai!" He called to me cheerily and waved, but when he saw my face he dropped his hand and jogged to meet me.

"Don't let him follow me!" I begged. "Please, Zeke. Please." I looked into his eyes for a moment, willing him to do this one thing for me, and then I kept running.

Later, Zeke joined me at the falls without Darius.

But Darius had told him what happened, at least the part that didn't incriminate himself. I doubted Darius would tell my brother he had been kissing our betrothed sister. I didn't tell either.

After that morning, I had decided not to love him anymore. I would will myself not to love him. So, when Keturah had offered to let me come with her to the farm outside of Orihah, where I would never have to see him, I had gratefully accepted.

"Sarai." Lamech's voice gentled, and I refocused on our conversation. "Tell me what has kept you awake. If I can't help, I'll get Zeke. Or Isabel if you want."

"Isabel's the last person who could help me," I said before I could stop the words.

I cleared my throat, wishing I hadn't said that out loud. "What I mean is, Isabel wouldn't understand."

He's cute. Too bad you're betrothed. Maybe he'll fight Lamech for you.

"I feel very *pretty* when Tecumeni looks at me," I blurted.

Lamech was quiet while he mulled that over, but he wouldn't understand, and I couldn't say words that would make it clearer. I wanted to feel pretty when Lamech looked at me. I wanted Lamech to look at me like Tecumeni did. I wanted it to be real.

"I do not know what you mean for me to understand by that."

My lip was trembling. A lump formed in my throat. "You're going to succeed," I whispered. "You're going to push me away."

"To Tecumeni?" He almost laughed.

I rolled away from him. "Goodnight," I sighed.

He touched my shoulder, trying to roll me back. "Sarai, you're not seriously considering it, are you? Your family would never agree. You'd have to move to Ani-Anti." He thought it was funny.

"No!" I rolled onto my back in frustration. "He makes me feel pretty and *you don't.* Goodnight." I rolled away again and huffed.

"I think I understand," he said after a moment.

"You will never understand," I said, bitterness in my voice. "So save yourself the trouble of trying."

"Listen, Sarai. I didn't mean to hurt your feelings. You and me—together—it just wouldn't work. It's a bad idea."

His voice was resolute. He meant it.

"Why?" I challenged.

He made no attempt to provide an answer, just sat silently in the dim tent.

I turned to him and sat up. My long hair fell around my shoulders, and I swept it to one side. "You are afraid," I accused.

He scoffed.

"You are a fearless warrior in battle because you are afraid of me."

"Sarai, that doesn't make any sense."

"Look at me," I said. I waited until he reluctantly did it. His eyes were so shadowed that I couldn't even see a glint of light in them. But I knew he could see mine. I knew he could see the features of my face and the filtered moonlight on my hair. I let him look at me, and then I whispered, "I am beautiful."

He gave a slight shrug to one shoulder.

I determined not to let him make me angry. Not yet. "I am beautiful, and it terrifies you."

"Yeah, Sarai? Why would that terrify me?"

I didn't move, just said softly, "You're afraid you're like your real father—without control, without care, without reverence."

His stillness told me I was right.

"Sarai, it is you who does not understand."

"I don't believe you."

Suddenly, Lamech reached over and grabbed the back of my neck and pulled me to him. His hand was hard on my skin, and the kiss he gave me was nothing like the kiss he had given me earlier in the evening. It was urgent and hard and contrived. He kissed me so hard I tasted my own blood as my lip split against my teeth.

This wasn't building a wall. This wasn't pushing me away. This was a warning. It was his way of telling me to stay away from him, his way of telling me he wasn't good. This righteous boy wanted to show me he was as wicked as his Lamanite father.

But he wasn't.

I knew it. His restraint confirmed it. Other than the unpleasant kiss, the most he managed was a rather crude sneer when he abruptly ended the kiss and drew back to observe my reaction.

When I remained still, he turned to go.

"I don't believe you," I said again.

His eyes flashed. "Then why do you have your hand on your knife?" More than any other emotion, his voice held disappointment. He hesitated a mere instant and then ducked quickly out the door.

I didn't move except to touch my split lip with my fingers.

I finally understood what Delilah had said.

He is afraid to grasp what he wants, what he feels he does not deserve.

"Lamech!"

It was Kenai, and he was angry.

"What," he growled, "just *what* were you doing in that tent?"

Lamech did not reply. I could imagine the look on his face, knowing the mood he was in. I wanted to warn Kenai to be careful what he said. Lamech would not hurt me, not truly, but I wasn't sure that he wouldn't take out his frustration on Kenai, a man who could well defend himself. It might be just the fight Lamech was looking for.

I heard Lamech say something in Lamanite. I rolled my eyes and called out, "He says you are no brother of mine." Then I scrambled to get out of the tent.

Kenai looked me over thoroughly. "I am your brother in every way that counts. Tell him that." He jabbed a finger toward Lamech to accent his words.

"He says he is my brother in spirit," I said in Lamanite.

"He has no power over you here. Only I do." Lamech didn't take his eyes off Kenai.

"He says you don't have the right to protect me," I repeated.

"A fact he has taken clear advantage of this night," Kenai growled.

I couldn't believe we had to put on this charade even in the middle of the night. "Kenai, nothing has happened. Please go back to your camp."

"Sarai, every man in that camp," he gestured behind him, "will protect you with his life, even from your *betrothed*." He sneered the last word. "Shall I call them?"

"No, of course not."

"You're bleeding," he bit out as if I were too dumb to notice it for myself or to understand what he would think had happened inside the tent.

"I bit my lip," I lied.

He lowered his voice and put his hands on his hips in the familiar way he always did, and it was a small jolt of reality amid this farce. His voice was tinged with pity when he said, "You look like a frightened deer."

My eyes shot involuntarily to Lamech, and Kenai noted it with regret. My face heated.

"Don't lie for him," Kenai told me. His voice was gentle but firm now.

I saw men approaching from the Lamanite camp. This was a disaster, an utter disaster, and it was all my fault for creating this impossible story in the first place. Zaaron, Tecumeni, and two others had their swords drawn.

"Lamech," called Zaaron. "What is the trouble with this Nephite?"

Lamech kept his furious eyes on Kenai, but when he finally turned to Zaaron he said, "Kenai thinks to prevent me from entering the tent of my betrothed. He thinks to force his religion on me."

Zaaron laughed as he came closer. "Tell him she is not his concern."

"I did."

"So did I," I burst in. "He only fears for my safety. He has vowed to protect me to my home. He came when he heard me cry out. But he was mistaken. I am not hurt." I reddened when I realized they would all think I had invited Lamech into my tent.

Zaaron turned to one of the other men and laughed again. "I think we have interrupted a lovers' quarrel. Let's leave them to it." He turned to go and the others turned with him, all but Tecumeni, who was glaring daggers at Lamech. "My money is on the woman," Zaaron laughed to his men. Then he called back over his shoulder to Tecumeni, "Tell the Nephite he can go."

To my dismay, Tecumeni turned to Kenai and said in perfect, flawless, beautiful Nephite, "Your honor has been satisfied, but leave Lamech alone with his betrothed. They are legally bound, and your interference is not warranted and not welcomed."

If he was surprised that Tecumeni spoke and understood our language, Kenai hid it well.

But I recalled that Tecumeni had understood it in the very first moments of our meeting, when we had been speaking about the oath, the one I had made up. I should have realized it then. How grateful I was in that moment that we had all been keeping up the charade even in Nephite, and how sad I was that I had started the charade in the first place. I wished in my heart that I could take it back, but knew I couldn't. It was much too complicated now.

"Sarai?" Kenai was asking if I wanted him to call to the others.

I gave my head a slow shake. "Thank you, Kenai, but I am fine as always here with my betrothed."

Kenai looked into my eyes. *Your safety is our first priority. We can and will fight these men if necessary.*

I nodded that I understood.

He gave a long hard look to Lamech, and I was glad the message there was for Lamech and not me. Then Kenai left, and I watched him return to the Nephite fire that was now just glowing coals. Eliam was standing there, waiting for him, and they both sat and talked in low voices.

Lamech sighed in disgust, glared at me, and stomped off into the trees. At the last moment before he disappeared he sent a sharp command over his shoulder. "Sarai, get into your tent and stay there."

I stood awkwardly with Tecumeni. I looked at the door of the tent, but I didn't get inside it.

"I'll sit outside your tent until Lamech returns," Tecumeni offered.

I forced a smile. "That's not necessary. I'm not going back to sleep."

"Then come for a walk with me—to take your mind off...things."

I glanced at the night sky.

"The moon is bright enough. Come on," he coaxed.

Not only was the moon bright, it was nearly morning. I laughed a little. "You can't think that is a good idea."

He shrugged one shoulder. Though it was sheepish and sweet, it reminded me of the insulting way Lamech had shrugged not ten minutes before, trying to make me believe he did not think I was pretty. I snorted softly and glanced to where Lamech had disappeared. Tecumeni was surprised when I held my hand out to him, but he took it and led me away from the fires, away from my tent, and away from the safety Zeke and Kenai and the other men provided.

"Was Kenai right? Did Lamech hurt you?"

I touched my split lip with my tongue, tasted the blood there, felt the sting and said, "No."

We strolled along together past Tecumeni's kinsmen, where strangely, the sentries did little more than glance at us, ignoring us as we passed. It was like a dream, walking with this stranger, this enemy of my people, holding his hand of my own free will and enjoying it.

"There's no point in denying it. I can see as well as Kenai that he misused you."

"How?" I demanded.

He rubbed the back of his neck. "Your lips are swollen and rosy, and your hair is a mess."

"Oh." My free hand instantly went up to smooth my hair. It was not in the tidy knot I kept it in during the day, and I could only imagine how wild it must look.

"I am not your enemy, Sarai. I cannot change what is done, but I may be able to help you."

"What do you mean?"

"If you are Lamech's then you are Lamech's. But I do not believe you are."

"Why not?"

He squeezed my hand. "Or rather, I do not believe your heart is his."

"He is a very difficult man to love," I admitted.

"But he saved you."

"Mmmm."

"Perhaps you traded one prison for another."

I thought of Darius, how my feelings had been tangled up about him. I thought of Lamech, how they were in a tangle over him now. "Perhaps you are more correct than you know."

Tecumeni slowed and drew me to a stop. "I should

return you to your tent before Lamech cools off and returns."

"It might be a long time before that happens."

"I'm sorry he hurt you."

"He did not do anything to me I did not let him do."

"What are you saying? You allow him to be cruel to you?"

"He is to be my husband. I will always submit to his wishes for that reason alone, but also, he would never ask anything amiss of me." I looked away from him, and began to move back toward the camp. "And anyway, he is not cruel. He is the best man I know. It was all a misunderstanding."

He walked along beside me in silence until my tent was in sight. "I know that something is not right," he said slowly. "I do not know what it is. The pieces do not fit together."

I wanted to tell him the truth right then. In all my life, I had never dreamed there could be a Lamanite as nice as Tecumeni seemed to be. I wondered if Lamech thought all Lamanites were like his father, depraved and treacherous.

"I do not know what you are talking about," I said.

"You do," he insisted. "And I will hear it from you, but not this night I think."

I laughed a little. "You're a very strange boy," I said.

"A fine thing to tell your future husband."

My voice faltered with nervous laughter. "Now I really do not know what you are talking about."

He took the hand that he still held with his, the hand that felt so good in mine, and placed them both on his chest over his heart. "You will. In time, you will."

He lowered my hand, squeezed it one last time, and walked away from me, leaving me staring after him.

This whole thing was an absolute disaster.

The sun would be coming up soon. The third watch had passed, and the whole of the night was nearly gone.

No one was stirring yet. Only the sentries were awake. I decided to go into the woods myself and attempt to find water. My mouth was dry, and I wanted to splash my face, to wash the disastrous night off me.

I was thinking about forgiveness. I didn't blame Lamech for what he had done in my tent. I had prodded him into it. I had deliberately upset him, and I had suspected the wildness was in him.

But though he had been wild, he hadn't lost control. Not once, not for one moment.

He had been trying to show me why loving him was unwise, why it would be a mistake for me. He was doing only what he did every day—pushing me away. He had come to his breaking point and pushed me as hard as he could.

I could fall over backward or fight back.

But either response would take a great deal of forgiveness.

And not just on my part. I would be a little surprised if Zeke and Kenai and the others hadn't already half murdered Lamech. The ridiculous thought made me smile despite my melancholy, and when I smiled, my lip split again.

I found a clear pool at a natural spring and knelt beside

it. After I filled my water skin and drank deeply, I retrieved my little soap and a cloth from my satchel. I wet the cloth and put it to my lips, wincing at the sting, but the sting prompted me to bend over the pool and inspect my reflection in the soft light of the morning.

My lip was swollen, and I looked tired, so I splashed my face with water and followed that with a thorough wipe down of my body, uncovering body parts and re-covering them one at a time as necessary. It felt good and made me think of the stream at home behind our house. If I had been there instead, I could have packed up my soap in my satchel and gone home to ask my mother's advice.

I touched my lip gingerly and then pressed the cold, wet cloth to it again.

How could I forgive this? Well, that was not really the question. The question was *should* I forgive this?

I knew what the scriptures said, the prophets, the priests, my parents. The answer was yes, as many times as it took.

But my heart was already so broken and disappointed, and Lamech knew it.

So was it wise? I had a calm disposition, a desire to please others and see to their comfort and happiness. I liked to have peaceful surroundings. I always forgave. But I did realize that this trait made me seem, well, like a push-over, like I was weak. Some people went out of their way not to offend me because they didn't think I could handle it. And some people didn't care about offending me because they knew they would be immediately forgiven. Most of the time, I didn't really care either way.

But perhaps my desire for peace had given Lamech the

impression I did not care about him. And perhaps I would open myself to manipulation if I let this go, if I just forgave it and failed to take him to task over it, if I did not allow my brothers to avenge me.

Wasn't that what I had done with Darius?

I sighed. I had neither forgiven Dare, nor let my brothers avenge me. I hadn't dealt with my feelings, just ignored them. I never allowed myself to think of what happened, but somehow it was always in the back of my mind.

We can't go on like this. I thought we were friends.

"We're not." I whispered the lie aloud. It still felt bitter and wrong. He had been my friend, was still trying to be my friend, and I had let him down. It was I who had not acted the friend.

I should have given him the chance to explain. Five minutes. Just five small minutes for the boy I claimed to love. He had offered me the gift of his friendship, and I couldn't give him friendship in return because what I wanted was his love.

"Sarai."

I caught my breath and jumped, turning to see Zeke.

"You scared me!"

"You're like a skittish dear." I could tell by the tone of his voice that he already knew why. But he just went to his heels beside me and scooped up a handful of water. He drank it, drew his arm across his mouth, and then wiped his wet hand on his buckskin pants.

I busied myself returning my things to my satchel.

He held out a piece of venison which I took only because my stomach growled loudly. "Anything you want to tell me?" he said.

206

"No."

From the corner of my eye I saw him nod his head slowly.

After he thought for a few moments, he said, "Alright. We're leaving in a quarter of an hour. You should come get some food."

"Okay. I'll be there."

"Lamech has already packed your tent and bedroll." He studied me closely. I felt his assessing eyes roving over me. I knew what he saw. My split lip, tired dark circles under my eyes, an ashen face, slumped shoulders, and confusion in my expression. The same things I had just seen in the reflection of the small pool.

"Okay," I said again.

But I didn't go back to camp for the morning meal. I sat at the waterside, and I thought about forgiveness. I only looked up when I heard someone approach. I dragged my eyes from the water to see Zeke again, and Lamech was with him. Lamech's eyes widened and he looked suspiciously from me to Zeke and then looked at the ground between us. He had probably been under the impression that Zeke intended to draw swords and fight. He probably would have preferred it.

"Sit," Zeke said to him.

Lamech hesitated, clearly resented being told what to do, but finally went to his heels.

"Closer," Zeke instructed. "To Sarai."

Lamech did it.

Zeke stared at us both. I glanced at Lamech. Zeke crossed his arms.

"Just say it," Lamech said flatly.

Zeke unfolded his arms and went to his heels before

us. When he spoke, his voice was curiously calm and reassuring. "I believe your own conscience has said more than enough already." He paused. "Am I right?"

Lamech actually glanced at me. "Yes."

"I've known you a long time, Lamech. I remember the first day you were put under my command in Antiparah. Keturah actually came to me and asked me to be fair with you. She thought I would take out my anger at Gid on you."

"You never did," Lamech said.

Zeke shook his head. "And I remember when Keturah told me you had seen to most of my care while I was unconscious in Cumeni."

Lamech might have blushed.

"You cleaned my wounds. You gave me food and water when I could not do it myself. You and I, we've got history."

Lamech nodded.

"And so I know you would never deliberately harm my sister."

Lamech didn't say anything.

"Because I know you so well, I know you have your purposes. You have your fears and feelings of inadequacy, but you live by the Spirit."

Still, Lamech did not say anything.

Zeke cleared his throat. "I know what it is to try to develop a relationship under the prying eyes and well-meant expectations of one's family. I don't know what happened in that tent early this morning. I don't need to know. I don't want to know. It is between the two of you."

Both our gazes shot to Zeke. He smiled a little at us.

"Sarai has denied any wrongdoing. And unless she tells me differently, I will respect her wishes and your privacy." He paused again, letting that sink in. Then a small, reminiscent smile crossed his lips. "I spent an...*interesting* night in Eliza's tent once. But listen, the best thing you can do is be honest with each other—and yourselves. Truly honest."

I broke in. "I try to talk to him but he won't listen!"

Zeke gave Lamech a long, hard stare. "He will listen now. But ask yourself, Sarai, if you are truly listening to him in return."

I twisted my lips into a pout. "I'm listening," I muttered. "I just don't like what he's saying."

Zeke hid a smile, but then he cleared his throat, and for the first time, he looked uncomfortable. He lowered his voice. "Lamech, I offer this counsel as your captain, your brother, and your friend." He paused again and shifted uncomfortably, frowned deeply. "I know you have not taken Sarai's virtue—"

"I'm not a conscienceless brute!" Lamech burst in.

"You were trying to prove just the opposite!"

Zeke raised a hand. I didn't understand why he was smiling, though I did see why he tried to hide it. "I *know* you have not taken Sarai's virtue, but I can see you have taken her innocence. When a man takes a woman's innocence, he takes a certain responsibility upon himself."

He raised his brows in expectation, and Lamech looked at the ground.

"I'm going to go get my breakfast, but there is one last point on which I want to be very, very clear. Lamech, if the two of you should wish to make this betrothal real, you would be welcomed as a brother in our family. I already consider you my brother. Father and I have already spoken of a match between the two of you, and he and mother would be very pleased to have you for a son."

He got up to go.

I got up too. "Thank you, Zeke."

He turned back to me and leaned in to place a kiss on my forehead. "You will have no more interference from me unless you seek it."

I nodded and started to cry. His kindness was sweet after the night I had been through.

Zeke smiled sadly, but didn't attempt to stop or dry my tears. He walked away with strength and confidence and left me alone with Lamech.

I turned away so Lamech wouldn't see me crying. But when I bent to collect my satchel, Lamech snatched it up.

"I'll carry it."

My argument was on the tip of my tongue.

"Please, Sarai, just let me."

I straightened and let him have the satchel. When he stood, he placed a hand on my shoulder and turned me to him. I couldn't look into his face. He didn't ask me to, just brushed my tears away and let his thumb brush over the split in my lip. He applied a little more pressure and pulled it out a bit to inspect it. Reaching into his own satchel, he withdrew a small jar.

"Leah's," he said.

It was all he needed to say. Keturah's mother made healing salves that I would always trust.

I did meet his eye as he dabbed some onto my lip, and it was more intimate than anything he had done in the tent.

He didn't ask for forgiveness, though I could see he wanted to. I thought I felt one of the tendrils Salome had spoken of grasping hold of my heart, and I hoped he could see my forgiveness in my eyes.

"There," he said, his voice coming from deep within his chest. He searched my face carefully. "Don't cry." He was almost tender. He couldn't quite manage it, but even his attempt surprised me. I expected him to fight even harder now, to push me away even harder. I expected him to sneer at me or just ignore me altogether. But I guessed what Zeke had said was really getting to him, or the Spirit was, because he looked remorseful and sounded repentant when he said softly, "I have disgusted you."

I couldn't respond to that. I knew that he had wanted to disgust me, to reverse the feelings I had started to have for him and make me hate him. I didn't know what he would do if I told him it hadn't worked.

I managed to shrug one shoulder, but tears spilled from my eyes anew. "You win," I said. "You have proved your point. I'm sorry..." I swallowed hard, "I'm sorry I didn't listen to you before."

One side of his mouth turned up in a self-deprecating smile. "*You* are apologizing to *me*?"

"I prodded you. I tempted you."

He shook his head firmly. "A man is always responsible for his own actions—for his reactions. You don't *get* to apologize to me, Sarai."

I had begun to edge away toward camp but faced him and put a hand to my chest, saying earnestly, "But I *feel* sorry. I'm entitled to feel what I feel. Can't you even respect that?"

He took a step back. "Of course. Of course you may feel what you want. It's only that you have done nothing wrong. You couldn't wrong me, even if you tried."

I stared at him. Did he truly think that?

"Don't place me upon a pedestal, Lamech. Don't."

I didn't walk with the Lamanite men or with Lamech. I didn't want to slow the pace. I wanted to get this whole experience over with. For a while, I walked with Isabel and Eliza, but they clearly wanted to ask me questions. I thought maybe Zeke had told them not to because their obvious avoidance of the topics of last night and Lamech and their forced cheerfulness were unnatural for them. Izz, for one, never avoided a topic if there was something she wanted to know.

After enduring that for a while, I fell back and walked alone. I knew the guards somewhere behind me were watching for danger so I just plodded along behind the others. It was early afternoon when perhaps the most dangerous thing that could have approached me did.

"Hey."

"If it isn't my future husband," I said, smiling for the first time that day.

Tecumeni adjusted the bow on his shoulder as he laughed.

I glanced up ahead at Lamech.

"Are you and your betrothed still fighting?"

"It's his favorite pastime." That at least wasn't a lie.

Tecumeni frowned, considering Lamech's back for a moment. Lamech walked beside Enos, and they appeared to be having an earnest conversation. I could only guess what it was about. "He doesn't seem to fight with anyone else. Not even that ugly Nephite."

I frowned too. "I guess I'm just lucky." I snapped a bunch of leaves from a tree as we passed and began tearing them apart at the veins and letting the pieces flutter away behind me.

"How old are you?" he asked me suddenly.

"Fifteen."

"That's barely old enough to be betrothed."

I should have lied.

Where had that thought come from? I had never been tempted much to lie. It was true—what my mother said—that once you committed a small sin, you opened the gates for the adversary to tempt you to greater and greater sin.

I just shrugged. "How old are you?"

"Eighteen."

"Where did you learn to converse in Nephite?"

"Where did you?" he challenged.

"From Eliza and Isabel."

"How long were you captive? How long did it take Lamech to find you?"

He waited a moment, but not long enough for me to respond, only long enough for me to realize there was no good answer. Then he said, "Eliza and Isabel don't speak Lamanite," as if he were accusing me of something.

"I taught them a little."

"Yes," he laughed. "How to say hello."

I giggled. That truly was all they knew how to say.

"They both like your Lamech—though I can't see why. Even after last night."

I squinted up at him. The sun was behind him so I couldn't discern his expression. I raised a brow in question.

"Isabel defended him quite staunchly, in fact. Her husband, I'm sorry to inform you, is prepared to kill him on your behalf."

"He takes his oath very seriously," I said, unable to control a small smile. "But, how do you know this?"

He shrugged and tried to look nonchalant. "I hear things."

"Ha! You eavesdrop, you mean."

Voice lowered, he confided, "It is part of my job, Sarai. Why else do you think I have been trained in their language?"

I paled, actually felt the blood drain from my face, wondering what else he had heard.

He pretended not to notice my pallor, though he couldn't have missed it.

"Did you know he calls her Izzy when they are alone?"

I giggled again and swatted him with the remaining leaves I held. "He does not. Nobody has ever called her Izzy."

He feigned surprise. "But, how do you know this?"

"She told me," I snapped out.

His grin said he did not believe me.

Lamech had been right. The more I talked to Tecumeni, the more likely I was to make a mistake and say something I shouldn't.

All I had wanted to do was help Gid, and all I had done since embarking on this journey was...was...well, I had learned to use a bow, a sling, and my knife. I had sewn the tunics quickly and efficiently, and the way they draped over the shoulders had turned out quite pretty. And I was translating for the men who were leading us through this wild land directly to Jerusalem, one of the places Muloki thought they would take Gideon.

The only real mistakes I had made, other than the enormous lie I had concocted, were with Lamech and Darius. I should have left Lamech alone, and I should have forgiven Darius.

I sighed.

"Alright, I'll stop teasing you," Tecumeni said.

And I was making a mistake by letting Tecumeni befriend me. "It would probably be best if you did not tease me at all." I glanced again at Lamech. "Lamech is not very happy with me just now. He's not even speaking to me. You'll just anger him more. He is not used to other men looking at me."

"I'm not afraid of him." He said this in a casual way that made me think he truly was not afraid of Lamech's brooding dark eyes the way I was.

"I am, and I am the one who will have to bear his ill-temper." But not like I was leading him to believe.

"Sarai, are you saying what happened last night was because of me?" The teasing in his eyes disappeared.

"No. It wasn't about you," I said, maybe too quickly.

He grunted his reproach. "Well, he doesn't seem to be talking to anyone right now. He's just been glaring at everyone and walking away. Honestly, I don't know what you see in him."

Usually, Lamech behaved at least tolerably with everyone but me. "What do you mean he's not talking to anyone?"

He shrugged. "No one but that Nephite."

Talking to a Nephite? I caught Tecumeni's knowing gaze. What did Lamech think he was doing? He would ruin everything.

I tried not to sound panicked. "Well, talking to you is not going to help. Go." I waved him away. "Go on and guard the back trail or something."

He laughed and returned to wherever he had come from, probably going to spy on someone else.

That thought put a knot in my stomach, but I put a skip in my step and hurried to catch up with Lamech. Enos saw me and immediately angled away to give us privacy. He ducked his head, but not before he cast me a small, encouraging smile.

I didn't waste any breath.

"Tecumeni says you are not speaking to anyone."

"I don't understand you." His voice was pained, and he spoke in Nephite.

I switched to Nephite, too, but lowered my voice. "What do you mean?"

"I mean I don't understand you."

I took a breath and blew it out slowly. "I guess I meant, why are you alienating yourself from our escorts? We need them. We need to stay on friendly terms with these men."

"You think I don't know that?" he burst out. But he took a breath too and glanced around. He lowered his head closer to mine adding another level of privacy to our conversation. "The Spirit has withdrawn from me. I can't speak to Zaaron and his men, because I no longer understand the language."

19

I couldn't look at Jashon. Not yet. Maybe not ever again.

"What does she mean, Jashon? What just happened?" Keturah asked, to which he gave her a hard look and just shook his head.

Jashon touched my hand, but then seemed to think better of it and folded his arms. "Come on," he said. "Let's go talk."

"Talking is not going to make it okay," I said under my breath, but I followed him toward the stream.

When we got there, we stood for a long time without talking. I knew he didn't know how to start. I could see him thinking about what to say. If I hadn't been mad at him, I might have taken pity on him and spoken first. But I was mad. I was embarrassed. And I felt guilty.

He had volunteered to marry me so I wouldn't have to go with Jacob and my own kinsmen. Betrothed to Jashon, I would be of his kin, of his family, and all would be right in Jacob's mind. And oh, how he must relish the idea of finally seeing me shackled to someone, as he had tried to see done for so long!

A betrothal would also secure Jashon a place in my clan, and he had volunteered to live amongst them so I could stay with Ardon.

I couldn't thank him. I wanted to kill him. A lifetime was too much to offer a stranger.

"I'm getting the feeling you are not pleased with the arrangement between me and Jacob."

I sighed, relented. "It is not the arrangement. It is the fact that Jacob can make this arrangement for me." I pouted for a moment. "The fact that you, a stranger, can make this arrangement for me."

"It was his condition. I agreed."

"You didn't have to do that!" I burst out. I took a breath, trying to calm myself. "He—Jacob and his father—have been trying to marry me off again since Zed died."

"I knew him, you know," Jashon said gently. His kindness was so hard to accept.

"I figured you did," I admitted.

"He was a good warrior, an excellent warrior. I respected him."

"I imagine he was. Excellence was expected of him. He was obedient and well-liked. He led our men out to battle with much honor."

"I liked him."

"Most men did. Or else they were jealous of him."

"Did you like him?"

"Well enough."

Jashon put his hand on my upper arm. It was warm and steadying, and I felt its presence heavily. "After the kisses we shared today, I thought you could like me well enough, too."

I blushed just thinking about the kisses. "It is not that. It is more complicated than that."

"It is so complicated that I am not intelligent enough to understand?"

218

"No. Yes. I mean, of course you are smart enough to understand. It is only that I cannot even put into words why an arranged marriage of this sort angers me so."

He reached up and stroked my cheek with the back of his fingers. It was difficult to stay angry when he was being so kind. But his kindness was part of the problem.

"Then just look at me," he said. "Your eyes will tell me everything there is to tell."

I laughed, but there was despair in it when I let him see my eyes. "Did you not have something else in mind for yourself, for your life? Some other woman? I hate that you are giving up your life for me and for Ardon, a boy you have not even met."

Then Jashon laughed, and there was hope in his. "But I knew his father, and I know you. I like you both. Your son will be strong and stubborn with a quick wit, a handsome face, and a ready hand to help others."

I almost had to smile at that, the description was so accurate. "Qualities you would like in a son?"

"Yes."

"Ardon will be the chief ruler of my clan. He cannot leave. I cannot go to live with your family outside the clan. Jacob would take him and raise him, but...I don't want that."

"Jacob told me of those things."

"And yet you still agreed. No." I shook my head. "It is too much for you to give up—your home, your birthright, your own family." It was unheard of. It was just not done.

He was very quiet for a moment, and then he said, "Salome, look at me."

I hesitated, but I raised my lashes and looked up into his face again.

"I wish I could say I was giving it all up—all those things you said—for you. Jacob's offer was opportune for me, so I took it. You are looking at a man without a home." He spread his arms wide. "Do you think I can live on the barley farm with Gid and Keturah?" He scoffed and turned away, then shook his head. "They have a home there already, and I will never be able to stay there."

"Because you love her."

"Because I love him."

I studied his face, trying to determine what he meant.

"I want my brother to care for his own wife," he went on. "That is how we come to love one another, by caring for each other, by serving each other, by suffering and striving and living together. A man should do these things for his own wife. Gideon has left me to do many of these things as he has pursued his career in the army. He is missing out on the best part of his marriage, and his absence has invited unwanted feelings between Keturah and me. She feels them too. But she won't if I go away."

"Well this is just convenient for you in so many ways," I said bitterly before I could stop myself.

"It was more than convenience, Salome."

He tugged me toward him and kissed me as sweetly as he had before. When he was done, still looking down at me, his hand still caressing the back of my neck, I took a deep breath and let it out slowly.

"One incredible kiss is not going to make me okay with this," I said, a dreaminess in my voice I couldn't quite mask.

I expected the comment to upset him, but his lips turned up in a smile, sheepish and proud at the same time, that made me laugh.

"Incredible?" he asked softly.

"Yes," I said, exasperated. "But I mean it. I'm not okay with this."

He became more serious. "What will it take to make you okay with it? Because it is done, Salome—I won't go back on my word—and I don't want you to hate every day of the rest of your life."

"I don't know."

"We'll find out, I promise. I believe there is enough natural feeling between us that we will both be happy."

I didn't say any more about it, but I knew he was right. We would be happy. I only wished that he had courted me, and we had fallen in love first, and Jacob had not been involved. I only wished it had nothing to do with Ardon, for I suspected a part of me would always feel that Jashon had only accepted Jacob's condition to be gallant and out of the same duty that drove him through the Land of Nephi.

"Tell me about the oath your parents made," I said to change the subject, to give myself time to accept what had happened. "You said before—on the rise that morning—that you would."

He looked at me for a moment, deciding whether or not to let the subject of our betrothal drop. Then he gave a slight nod and said, "The people now known as the people of Ammon, once lived in and around Ishmael, here in the Land of Nephi. They were Lamanitish in every sense—birth, heritage, tradition, religion. Ammon converted the household of Lamoni, a tributary king in Ishmael."

"What is converted?" I interrupted.

"Lamoni listened to what Ammon taught about God, he came to believe it, accepted it, and began to live it. Lamoni was Keturah's uncle, her father's brother."

"Oh." To top it all off, Keturah was of royal birth. "But what of the oath?"

"Ammon taught that God did not allow men to kill each other. The people followed his words, and after they had repented of their many murders and killings, they vowed they would never kill again."

"What is repented?" I asked.

"To repent is to repair your wrongdoings and never do them again. You must recognize your sins, feel sorrow, admit fault, and ask for forgiveness."

"And all your people did this?"

"Yes, and to seal their commitment, they buried their weapons of war in the ground."

I pictured men digging a large hole and casting in their many weapons, women in the attitude of prayer, and children of all ages watching their parents do this.

But Jashon said, "My father's swords were turned into plowshares and have gone blunt many times over tilling deep into the earth of our farm. Their purpose has turned to good, but many of my people were killed for their beliefs and many suffered during the flight to safer lands."

"What would compel your people to do this? To give up their traditions at such great cost to themselves?"

"The Holy Ghost."

"And what is the Holy Ghost?"

"The Holy Ghost is that spirit we talked about before, that spirit which confirms to us when something is right or good."

I had never heard the spirit called that.

"Like during prayer?"

He smiled. "Yes, like during prayer. Have you felt such feelings?"

I had, many times since I had met him.

"You have," he said, and I could tell he was very pleased. "It's okay." He read the look on my face. "It means God is speaking to you."

"But I am not a member of the church of God."

"All men and women are God's children. He will speak to us all, and guide us if we will but listen."

I bit my lip, wondering if I was prepared for what God might say to me. "I think the others are ready to leave," I said.

Jashon sent a look over his shoulder. The others were ready to leave, but he reached out and brushed my hand with his. It made me smile. Getting bolder, he linked his fingers with mine and tugged me toward him. Smoothing my hair from my face, he kissed my forehead and whispered, "It will all be okay, Salome. I will make it so."

I believed him.

And I let him hold my hand as we walked back to the others.

I was accepting a sympathetic look from Keturah as I hefted my travel pack up. I felt its weight disappear and turned to see Jashon lifting the pack onto my back.

"Oh!" I said in surprise.

But Jashon merely flashed me a smile. Then he turned and lifted Keturah's pack for her.

I watched Jashon help Keturah with her gear. The men had been right—her energy was flagging. She was working too hard and likely draining strength from the child within her. I looked at her pretty features, gaunt just now in the afternoon heat. And I thought about what Jashon was trying to be for her—her companion, her friend, her protector, her strength. I thought of the strain it put on their own relationship, how close they had become despite both their efforts to avoid feelings developing between them.

I could be jealous. I could envy what they had together—which was my first inclination—or I could be of help to their situation.

I reached over and placed a hand on Jashon's arm. "The tent. I should be carrying it." They both looked at me. "Since we're sharing it now."

I knew Keturah had insisted upon carrying her own supplies. Something inside her could not stand to show weakness to these men. It was something in their shared past, in the experiences together that prevented her from accepting and acting her role as a woman—at least with these men. But she was currently performing her most important role as a woman which was bearing a child. She couldn't deny it. She couldn't deny her feminine nature, and the men didn't, though they did try to yield to her wishes when possible. And one of these wishes was to carry her own tent.

"Okay," was all she said, and Jashon took immediate advantage of the opportunity to get the heavy article off her pack.

"Thank you," he mouthed before we set off, and I felt not only gladness in helping him, joy in assisting Keturah, but what I suspected was Jashon's Holy Ghost because my chest felt warm like it did when the men prayed.

I decided to do what their Holy Ghost told me to do.

I walked with Keturah for the rest of the day and when we made camp for the night, I did what I could to ease her burdens. Things that Jashon normally did for he, I did instead.

When I crawled into the tent that night after sitting up to listen to the men confer, Keturah was already nestled in her bedroll. But she surprised me when she spoke without opening her eyes.

"You may not like him, but you will make him a lovely wife."

"I thought you were sleeping," I said as I nestled down into my bedroll. "I wish he hadn't sacrificed himself for me, but it would be impossible not to like him."

"I know." She yawned. "I find it difficult myself."

"I know." I drew my blanket up under my chin. "You must depend on me now. Let Jashon rescue your husband."

"After he rescues Lib."

"The man who would sacrifice himself for you," I mused.

"Foolish man," she muttered, but there was fondness in her voice.

The next day, I picked up Lib's trail again. I would have said it was impossible if I hadn't first heard someone breathe that we were being led by the hand of God. I thought about that and decided it was as easily true as not.

Jashon had sent scouts ahead, and finding the trail clear and easy to follow, Mathoni had run back to inform him. I had never seen Jashon deliberate when there was a command to give. He just gave it. He never let the men see him unsure, so I knew that he was about to do something he didn't want to do when he stared at his sandals for a time and then wandered off into the woods alone, presumably to pray about his choices.

"I want you to stay here with Ket, Melia, Muloki, and a few of the other men," he said to me when he returned.

"Whatever you feel is best," I said dutifully. "But why?"

His eyes were soft when he looked at me, but he squinted into the distance. "Lib's clear trail indicates he is being careless now. He thinks he has lost us. He can only be a half day ahead. We can overtake him if we run."

My eyes went to Keturah.

"If we wait any longer to overtake him, he'll make it into one of the cities. You've seen him. He'll be taken straight to the prison. And besides, it will only take a few men to subdue him."

I almost asked if he thought it would be necessary to subdue the man, but I could see in his eyes that he was joking.

Once Jashon had made his decision, it wasn't many more minutes before he took Ethanim, Joshua, and Darius and began to run to the north. Jarom, Reb, Mathoni, and Corban remained with us. Muloki led us to a shaded area protected from view on three sides and Reb produced a small ball from his satchel that the men began tossing and kicking around.

"What is that they're doing?" I asked Keturah.

"Have you never seen it done before?"

I shook my head, captivated by their skill..

Keturah moved into their circle and Corban tossed her the ball. She bounced it off first one elbow then the other. She hit it with her knee and caught it on the outside of her heal. Turning to smile at me, the tossed it up and caught it on the inside of her ankle. Then laughing, she lobbed it over to Reb who caught it easily and continued on with the game.

"It's a game we played a lot when we were young, during our time in Helaman's army. When we weren't working, we were playing."

"Will you teach me?" I asked. "What is the ball made

of? I think Ardon would like it."

She smiled. "We were all Ardon's age when we began playing. The ball is made of leather and filled with dried beans. I will show you how to make one. I've made plenty."

"Does Gideon play?"

"Sure. He's good at it, but he would rather spend his energy on weapons. I mean, on work instead of play."

"What will happen with Lib?" I asked.

"Jashon will find him. He thinks we headed south, so he's being careless with is tracks now."

I had seen his carelessness in his trail. "And when he finds him?"

"I'm not sure. But he will not let him try to trade himself for Gideon."

"Why does he think Gideon came this way?"

"The king lives in Ishmael. He supposes that they would bring a captain of Gideon's rank straight to the king."

"And why won't they?"

"I am not sure, but I know our scouts are following them to the southeast, and I know Helaman told us to go south. I trust Helaman with my life."

"And with Gideon's?"

And Ardon's?

"Of course. Gideon is one of his sons. He would never lead us astray. It would be impossible."

"But how can he know? Why would it be impossible?"

"Helaman is led by the spirit, and the spirit would never give him a wrong impression."

"I have felt this holy spirit," I confided.

She looked at me with bright eyes. Gone was the gaunt and tired look from them. "It is wonderful, is it not?"

I shifted a little on the rock I sat upon. "I must admit I have my concerns. Such as, if I feel this holy spirit, must I do the repenting and must I abide by the things it tells me?"

"Mmmm," she said. "That is a tough question. Melia?" She leaned back to get Melia's attention. "Will you come here?"

Melia joined us under the big shade tree and sat with her knees drawn up, her arms wrapped around them. She wore her pretty red sarong modified in a tunic style, and smoothed it as she sat.

"Salome has questions about conversion. I thought you might be able to answer them better than I can," Keturah told Melia.

"What do you wish to know?" Melia turned to ask me.

I shot Keturah a glance and she gave me an encouraging smile, but she didn't speak for me. So I said, "I fear that if I feel the holy spirit, I will have to do this repenting Jashon told me about."

"You don't have to do anything you don't want to. That is the beauty of Christ's plan. But you must realize that each choice you make comes with a consequence."

I frowned, thinking of all the choices that had been made for me by my father, my parents, my husband, my husband's kinsmen. I had suffered the consequences of those choices as well, though they weren't my own.

"What is Christ?" I asked.

"Christ is the Son of God. He will come into the world to redeem us from our sins."

The Son of God.

"Why do we need a redeemer? What is a sin?"

Both women smiled. "I think we'd better start at the

beginning," Keturah said. She called to the men.

"I took a long time to accept these teachings," Melia informed me. "So I understand your questions."

The men went to their heels near us, curious and still tossing the ball to each other.

"Let us see if we can explain what we believe before the others return." Keturah cocked an eyebrow at the men in a challenge.

Corban began, and I sat in rapt attention as they explained the gospel of Christ to me beginning with a man called Adam.

20

I looked at him in horror as it dawned on me what he was saying. They would expect him to talk to them. Panic rose in my chest. If the spirit of God had given him the Lamanite words, then the Spirit had taken them away.

"Just repent then." I said. "Fix it!"

The concern on his face was real.

"What if it's not that easy?"

"What if it is? Everyone's depending on you. Gid's depending on you."

He huffed. "Gid's probably got a plan of his own. He's not waiting on us."

"Then what are we doing here?" I looked around. "With them?"

He rolled his eyes.

"Lamech, what is it about me that puts you so on edge? What is it that frightens you so much? Is it something I can change?"

"You can't change who you are," he said quietly.

"Zeke said we should be honest with each other. And the truth is, Lamech, the reason I get testy with you is because you confuse me so much. You hold me close for a moment, and then you push me away."

"I know. I'm sorry. It is not your fault."

Had I heard him right?

"It is. I've acted like the child I am."

"And I have acted like the wicked man I am."

"A wicked man would never have had the gift of tongues in the first place," I insisted quietly. And then I realized why Lamech did not feel he was good enough for me. He didn't feel he was good enough for anyone. "Don't you know God loves you?"

His jaw tightened.

Immediately, I pulled him to the side of the trail so the others could pass us. Most of them tried to avoid staring, but I met many sets of eyes. I thought of what Zeke had said about trying to have a relationship with everyone looking on, everyone giving an opinion, everyone scrutinizing the things we did. I put them all out of my mind, and I took both of Lamech's hands in mine and squeezed them.

"Lamech, go into the woods. Reconcile yourself to God. You cannot be led by the Spirit until you are worthy of it once more."

He shook his head. "True repentance takes time and thought, prayer and action. I cannot just do it on command."

"You must! All it takes is sorrow for your sin. Are you sorry for what you did?"

"Do you even know what I did?"

I dropped my eyes when I said, "You kissed me and you cut my lip."

His laugh was a little ragged. "Don't you think it's strange, Sarai, that the Spirit would not withdraw from me when I participate in this massive lie we have staged, but it leaves when I kiss you?"

My eyes shot up to his. "But we are lying to preserve our safety! We are lying to save Keturah's family, and God has said that we may protect our families unto bloodshed."

He gave me a strange look.

"I know the teachings of the prophets." I folded my arms. "Other things too. I'm not as stupid as you think I am." I withdrew a few steps and turned to watch everyone else as they made their way ever farther south.

"I don't think you're stupid, Sarai." But the way he said it, halting and sheepish, made me think he hadn't exactly thought I was smart, either.

"You think a woman who is pretty cannot be smart."

"Have I ever said that?"

"It's okay," I said. "Everyone thinks that about me."

His voice gentled. "No they don't."

It wasn't a comfortable topic. "Well anyway," I said, not wanting to talk more about it, "we are lying for a good cause."

He smirked, but it turned into a small laugh. "I know it doesn't sit well with you. Your conscience eats at you." He was plaintive and quiet for a moment. "A kiss is meant to show love, Sarai. When I kissed you in the tent," he swallowed, "I used that kiss for a purpose it was not intended for."

"Why *did* you do it?" I asked him. I thought I had a pretty good idea. I touched my tongue to the cut on my lip.

Lamech noticed it because he was watching me closely.

His eyes shone with self-loathing, humiliation, and tears he did not allow to fall. "What I did is unforgiveable."

"No. It is not." I reached up behind his neck and pulled his head down next to mine. "It is not unforgiveable."

We stood like that, hearts in our throats, until Lamech asked, "Can *you* ever forgive me, Sarai?"

"I already have," I said. I felt so warm inside, and I wanted him to feel the same way. I wanted to share it with him, but I knew I couldn't. It was a feeling he would have to find for himself. I settled for twining my arms around him, like the tendrils of a vine, and I held him close to me in an embrace, so close, because he needed it.

He did not know that God loved him, but he would know that I did.

"Now go," I said. "You know what you have to do."

He back away awkwardly. "You need to catch up," he said and jerked his chin toward the disappearing band of men. "Your brother can protect you."

I found my kinsmen in the distance and smiled when I realized I *was* strong enough to catch up. "I will," I said. "Now go."

Lamech looked deeply into my eyes, his nostrils flaring as he took a ragged breath. Suddenly, he stepped forward, put a hand in my hair, and kissed my forehead. He pulled away and fingered the cut on my lip. "Someday, I will be worthy to kiss your lips," he whispered.

And then he went into the woods alone.

I didn't bother leaving the trail for the cover of the woods. I just dropped to my knees where I was and prayed for Lamech.

Lamech hadn't begged me for my forgiveness, but in the hours since he had treated me so roughly, he had shown that his heart was aching and broken, he had shown both remorse and sincerity. Having experienced a broken heart myself, I would never have wished one on Lamech, but this was a very good thing. God could bind up the broken-hearted, but He could not do much with the stiff-necked.

Not that Lamech was particularly stiff-necked. I had seen him kneel to pray. I had heard him pray, heard his fervent proclamations of courage and honor and faith. I knew he relied on the guidance of the Holy Ghost. I knew he followed the counsel of the prophets. I knew he heeded the commandments and upheld the Title of Liberty. I knew he believed in God.

So how did he not know God loved him?

"Sarai, are you okay?"

I looked up to see Tecumeni and the man Lamech had called Josiah coming toward me through the long grasses.

I got to my feet and tried to offer up a smile. "I fell behind."

Tecumeni looked around. Did his eyes linger on the place Lamech had disappeared in the trees? He turned and said something to Josiah so quickly that I didn't understand it.

"Josiah will help you catch up. I'm supposed to stay on the back trail."

I looked at Josiah's stern face. He was handsome, in a way, I supposed, but he put fear in my heart. His hair was shorn very short so that I could see his scalp. He wore no tunic and was greasy with the oils that deterred the biting bugs. But he was tall with square shoulders, dark, interesting eyes, and a nice smile I had actually seen a few times.

Josiah was already starting to walk away.

"Okay," I said to Tecumeni, and he waved me off but seemed to be distracted, his attention caught by something off the trail.

"Can you run?" Josiah asked when I caught up to him.

"Run?" Uh...if we go slow, I guess."

He looked me up and down and might have sighed.

"Come on then."

I followed him in the direction the others had gone. I

felt unease with him and wished Tecumeni had gone with me and left Josiah to cover the back trail. I wondered why he hadn't. But Josiah kept his distance and only spoke to me when necessary, and even though I had to stop for periods of rest to catch my breath, I was able to run beside the Lamanite warrior.

When we made camp that night, Lamech was not there. Nor was he there when we set off again in the morning. I traveled with Eliza and Isabel, but occasionally caught up to travel with Zaaron and his men to converse with them, hoping to keep communication open in Lamech's absence. I even ate my midday meal with them.

"How much longer until we reach Jerusalem?" I asked Zaaron as I bit into a piece of fruit he had given me. I had never seen or tasted one like it before, but it was fleshy and sweet and I savored it.

"If we set off early tomorrow morning, we will eat our midday meal in Ani-Anti. Jerusalem is a half-day's journey from there."

"On what day is the market in Jerusalem? May I buy this fruit there?"

Some of the men laughed.

I licked some juice from my hand. "I take it I may not buy this at the market?"

Zaaron gestured with the knife he had used to cut my fruit in two and pop out a large pit, indicating something over my shoulder. I looked and beheld a tree burgeoned with fruit like the one I had just eaten.

"Only a fool would buy them in the market when he can pick them anywhere for free."

I shrugged and willed my face not to turn pink.

"Do you expect Lamech to return soon?" Zaaron's question was posed casually, but I could sense his deep curiosity. Why would a young man like Lamech travel into the Nephite lands to rescue me and then leave me with two random bands of strangers without a word to either leader?

"I don't know," I said honestly.

"He's gone off to sulk," said Tecumeni.

"He's gone off to hunt," I countered. "He will be back when he is ready. Lamech always has his reasons."

Tecumeni rolled his eyes.

"Leaving me under your protection is a sign of his trust in you," I pointed out.

"Leaving you under our protection is his way of avoiding what is difficult. He is a coward. You should end your betrothal with him and marry me."

I knew his words were in jest, but they made me angry.

My voice was low and steady when I insisted, "Lamech is the bravest of men. And I could never marry a man who was such a poor judge of character."

"But you'll marry a man who misuses you."

I glared at him. "Why do you care?"

Zaaron and the other men were looking between us.

Tecumeni sat up a little straighter. "I should think it was obvious."

I stared at him, shook my head.

"You are a girl who needs protection, and your kinsman won't do it."

Had he said kinsman or kinsmen? Had he meant Lamech or the band of Nephites? What had he heard? What did he know?

"I do not need protection from Lamech."

Tecumeni scoffed. "He is the only man here you do need protection from. Even the Nephite dogs see it."

Finally, Zaaron cleared his throat.

"I'm sorry," I said quickly, glancing at Zaaron but addressing Tecumeni. "I provoked you. You are entitled to your opinion, but please, don't speak ill of my betrothed in my hearing. He is a man who walks alone much of the time. Having a wife will be an adjustment for him. His heart is pained and grief besets him, and there are many things about him which you do not understand." I turned my eyes to Zaaron. "He is harsh with me, but only because he has not yet learned to be gentle. Please. Suspend your judgment."

All of the men quietly finished their food and then found excuses to leave. Zaaron got up last, leaving only Tecumeni, and as he walked past me, he patted my shoulder.

"Maybe we could see each other sometimes after you get back to your home," Tecumeni said, choosing to abandon the subject and the anger from a moment ago. "I can go to Jerusalem any time."

"You could come to the wedding."

"I was thinking maybe sometime before that."

"No," I said. "No." I shook my head. "It would not be appropriate."

He gave me a long, hard stare. "When we get to my village," he said slowly, "you will meet my family." He watched me closely. "And my betrothed."

"Your...what?"

"Her name is Alena. She is Zaaron's daughter."

"And you are betrothed to her?"

Another long, hard stare. "As betrothed as you are to Lamech."

I held his gaze, but I swallowed hard. I did not know what to think about that declaration. I gathered my things and got up to go.

"Wait." Tecumeni got to his feet, went to the tree, and picked several of the fruits. He brought them to me and took the liberty of slipping them into my satchel for me.

"Thanks," I said. Feeling off balance, I went to find Izz and Eliza.

Ani-Anti appeared out of nowhere. One moment we were in the trees, and the next moment, we were walking into Ani-Anti. It looked eerily similar to my village back home, but in a way, that was comforting.

Zaaron turned around and walked back to me. "Your Nephite escorts can stay here at the edge of the village for the night. No harm will come to them, but they must leave in the morning. I will send a guide with them to the border."

I looked first to Isabel and then to Eliza. Then I shook my head. "They won't want it. They knew the risk when they started their journey. And they will want to take me clear into Jerusalem."

Zaaron grunted and nodded. "It is unwise for them to go into the city. I cannot protect them there. You may come with me now."

He turned to enter into the village, so I quickly said, "Just a moment. I would bid these people goodnight. Isabel and Eliza are my friends."

Zaaron eyed me for a moment. I couldn't tell what he was thinking. "Do it quickly."

I did. I turned and hugged Isabel fiercely. "I have to go with him," I whispered. "To his home I think. I'm to be a guest in his home, and you are to stay here overnight." I indicated

238

the place we stood at the edge of the village and turned to Eliza to embrace her as well.

Then I went to Kenai and reached up to put my hand on his shoulder in what would be seen as a formal farewell, but I spoke to both him and Zeke. "I'm to stay at Zaaron's home. I will come back in the morning and you may escort me the rest of the way into Jerusalem. Zaaron says it is not safe for you to go into the city. He can't protect you there."

There was misgiving in both of their expressions. They didn't want me to walk into that village alone. Kenai folded his arms. "I actually wish Lamech had returned."

Lamech would have been invited in with me.

Zeke only said, "Go with faith, Sarai. Be bold. The Lord can give you courage."

I nodded and turned to go.

Kenai spoke up again. "And Sarai, tell them we neither want nor need their protection."

"Then you are stupid," I said, but a grin stole over my face.

I was surprised when Tecumeni did not come to walk next to me as I entered the village with his kinsmen, but when I saw the girl who must have been Alena run out to meet him, I thought I understood why. I watched them closely as they embraced, as Tecumeni took a step back and asked her a question. I watched her bright eyes absorb every line of his face as she looked up at him and answered. She gestured back to a home behind her, which was a very large tent made from skins.

A home Isabel would be happy in, I thought to myself.

When Zaaron and I reached them, he embraced the girl as well. He picked her up and twirled her around once before setting her down, which set her into gales of giggles.

"Alena," Zaaron said. "Meet Sarai. She is our guest for the night."

Alena greeted me with a smile, but threw a curious look to her father and then to Tecumeni who was standing as far away from the rest of us as he could without appearing rude.

"A traveler," was all Zaaron told her. "Sarai, this is my daughter, Alena."

In no time, all the people from the village emerged from their homes to greet the returning warriors. I recognized Tecumeni's mother because she hurried toward him with outstretched arms, a trail of young children on her heels. The oldest girl, tall and pretty, gave me a friendly smile while her mother greeted Tecumeni. When it was her turn to greet him, Tecumeni gave her an awkward sideways hug. He said terse greetings to his brothers—fourteen and ten maybe—but lifted the youngest ones into his arms and ruffled their hair.

"My nephew takes good care of them," said Zaaron, noticing where my attention was centered.

I felt my face heat. "I have little trouble believing that. He has been good to me. But where is his father?"

"Dead in the war."

"Many of my people died in the war too."

I felt him looking at me. I had said the wrong thing again.

"My kinsmen," I corrected. "And where is your wife, Zaaron? I would like to meet her."

He looked around.

Alena giggled. "She has only gone to the cistern, Father."

When Zaaron's wife returned to the village with a large basket full of wet laundry, she set it down and hurried to her husband. She didn't show her exuberance as her daughter had with Tecumeni, but I could see that she felt it.

She clearly loved her husband—the savage, sword-wielding Lamanite warrior—as much as my mother loved my father.

Sansan inspected my light skin and hair, but she welcomed me with warm hospitality. After she gave me my midday meal with the others, I said I wanted to explore their village and they waved me away. I was curious about this foreign village, but more than that, I wanted to give them time alone. It had been so long, months Tecumeni had said, since they had seen each other, embraced each other, spoken to each other. I didn't want to interfere with their reunion.

I wandered around and then went to the edge of the village and waved to Eliza when I was able to catch her eye. I wanted them to know I was okay. I hoped it would ease their concerns.

When I got back to Zaaron's home, I saw Alena hanging the wet laundry on lines strung between trees behind the strange tent.

"Oh, you mustn't do that," she protested when I pulled a tunic from the basket and began to drape it over the line. "You are a guest."

"A guest who owes your father much."

Her lips twitched as if she might smile. "Well, don't let my parents see you."

Together we finished the chore quickly. As I hung the last item, she said, "Let's go see Tecumeni."

"But his family hasn't seen him in so long," I said.

She rolled her eyes. "*I* haven't seen him in so long."

I guessed that was true, so I didn't argue anymore, and I followed her down the main path of the village to the tent where Tecumeni's family lived. We found them finishing up their midday meal.

When Tecumeni heard Alena's greeting, he looked up and our eyes met, but his eyes quickly shifted to Alena's.

"Let's go swimming in the cistern," she said, bouncing over to him like a little hopping magpie.

He glanced at the sky, but before he could reply, Alena insisted, "There's plenty of time."

"Sarai has been traveling for a month. She is tired."

"And so a swim will feel nice. She can wash her hair."

"Alena."

"She said she wanted to go. She said she wanted you to take her."

21

Salome

When the men came back early that evening, Lib was with them.

My heart rejoiced at the sight of his golden hair catching the slanted rays of the evening sun as he walked amid the men. But I was angry at him too, for delaying us from pursuing Ardon. And I didn't understand why no one else was angry with him—with the possible exception of Ethanim who was still stomping around camp.

Keturah actually ran out to meet him, throwing her arms around his neck and hugging him tightly, a hug that was awkward because of her belly and his height, but not because of all that had happened. I watched her curiously. Did she not think she encouraged his feelings for her with her actions? Those feelings that had caused so much trouble and delay for us all.

But as I continued to watch through the evening, I noticed that for her at least, it had not gone beyond the hug. She did not touch him at any other time. She did not give him lingering, teasing glances. She managed to preserve her friendship with Lib by preserving the distance between them. This was how she was with Jashon, too. It was how she was with all the men, something she had probably learned while she had lived among them in the army.

It was how I handled Zed's kinsmen, too. I had always

taken care not to let them think I was open to marriage, but I stared glumly into the fire thinking that perhaps I had deprived Ardon of something he needed because of my aversion to being ruled by a man I didn't love.

I became aware of whispers in the night behind me, and as I strained to hear the words the men said, I realized they were not intended for my ears. When some of the men questioned the impulsiveness of his betrothal to me, Jashon told them about Jacob, but not the things I knew of him. He told them terrible things Jacob had said on the night of Zed's death. Things he had said while drunk about going home to his brother's widow. Tasteless things that Jashon spoke of with clear disgust, and the other men murmured their understanding.

"You look awful sad tonight."

I looked up. "Oh! Jarom, I didn't see you."

He dropped to his heels next to me and tossed another small branch onto the fire. Sparks shot up through the night, the breeze swirling them and setting them off in different directions. Did he want to know if I had overheard them? Did he feel sorry for me? Did he think I was unworthy of his friend? I didn't feel I owed him an explanation for my pensiveness, but I found myself giving one anyway.

"I'm feeling guilty." I looked up at him, at the light flickering on his face, then back into the fire. "I was thinking that now, since Jashon will be Ardon's father, he will be more inclined to save him."

Jarom actually laughed. "That doesn't make a difference. We will save him whether he is one of our sons or not."

I twisted my lips. "I know."

"Salome?"

I looked up again, straight into Lib's face. His eyes bore a pensiveness that matched my own.

"I would like to take you for a walk, if you will agree."

My brows lifted a little, and I looked again to Jarom. He gave me a nod. "See you in the morning, Salome."

I stood and followed Lib to the edge of camp. We walked slowly around the perimeter in the dim night to get a little privacy, always keeping the fire in sight.

"I want to apologize to you," Lib said. "I mean, I want to ask you to forgive me."

"Me? But what for?"

"I delayed your search for your son by my actions. I'm sorry."

I bit my lip and thought for a moment. "I accept your apology, and of course I forgive you. I don't understand, but perhaps it is not for me to understand."

"Thank you," he said after a moment of silence. Awkward silence. "Thank you," he said again more quietly.

"These men did not have to come after you, and I did not have to come with them. It was hardly your actions that caused the delay."

He laughed bitterly. "I am leaving in the morning. I just wanted to tell you of my regret before I left."

"You can't leave again! I'll tell the others. I'll tell Jashon of your plans!"

"I worked the plans out with Jashon. Darius is going with me to Zarahemla." He scoffed. "Guarding me there, is more like it."

"But...why?"

He was quiet for a moment, but I sensed he was trying

to figure out how to tell me something important. Finally, he said, "When a girl was assigned to our unit in Helaman's army, the others and I were upset, to put it mildly. I can't possibly explain the resentment and confusion we all felt. The thought of that skinny little girl fighting beside us in battle was almost more than we could bear. It was unthinkable. It was insulting."

"I thought you were all friends," I said. "I thought the men liked Keturah."

I could hear the smile in his voice when he said, "It took a while."

"What made you change your minds?"

"You've met her. You've eaten her corn cakes."

I smiled wryly.

"That was the first thing we liked about her. But before that, before she even joined us on the training field, our captain, Seth, came to Ethanim and me and assigned us this incredibly strange, incredibly impossible duty. He wanted us to stay with her every minute of every day. Guard her. Befriend her."

"And did you?"

"We obeyed our captain's command to the letter. Ethanim told her we requested the duty, but it wasn't true. I upbraided him for the lie, but he insisted she wouldn't let us do it if she knew the truth. I reluctantly agreed, because I felt she would have lost trust in her captain if she thought he didn't trust her."

"It sounds as if he didn't trust her."

"Oh, he did. It was the men he didn't trust. The blessing was ours—to earn by obedience—much more than it was hers. And well, anyway, she kind of grows on you."

"But now you're leaving."

"I've spent so long protecting her, watching out for her, serving her. When she went home from the battlefields, I thought it was over, but then she and Gid married, and Gid brought her back to Orihah. Ethanim and I fell into our old habits whenever Gid went to work in Zarahemla. He was gone from the farm for fortnights at a time." He paused. "I don't know how he could stand to leave her," he added quietly.

"It sounds like he is the only one who truly trusted her."

"I never thought of it like that." He ran a hand through his hair. "And well, anyway, I cannot stay here, so I am going to Zarahemla. I have a friend there who builds boats. Big ones. Huge sailing vessels. I want to help him. He asked me to assist him with the designs, but I turned him down because, well, you know."

"Sailing vessels? Truly? That sounds exciting!" I said. "I have never seen such a thing."

"Hagoth wants to build a ship that will hold many people within it so that he might colonize the lands to the north. He wants a fleet of ships for trade and the movement of supplies."

I could tell this was a subject that interested Lib, and I thought sadly about the things he had missed out on because of his obsession with protecting Keturah, perhaps the only woman in the Nephite lands who didn't need protection. I listened to him as he told me about this man Hagoth and all his plans until Jashon joined us.

He took my hand, but spoke to Lib. "Are you sure you won't continue with us on our journey?"

"No, and I'm sorry. But I feel it will be best to remove myself from this situation. I'm sorry I cannot assist you in freeing your brother."

Jashon just shook his head. "See to your own needs." He lowered his voice and put a hand on Lib's shoulder. "Your life is as important as Gid's. God loves you. He wants to see you progress and find happiness. Reconcile yourself to His plan for you. If you must go now, you must."

Lib nodded and offered his thanks to Jashon. Then he leaned around Jashon and spoke to me. "Again, I am sorry, Salome."

"And again, my forgiveness is freely given."

I didn't see Lib any more after that. In the morning he was gone, and Darius with him.

"They're not going to sail away on those boats are they?" I asked Jashon.

He shrugged. "I think Lib's main interest is in building them. Darius is only going to see him safely to his friend—"

"Hagoth," I interrupted.

"He's only going to see him to Hagoth—that's for my peace of mind and Ethanim's—and then he plans to visit a friend in Antionum."

"Who does he know in Antionum? Isn't that in the east?"

"A man from Helaman's army, Seth. I didn't know him."

"The captain?"

"Do *you* know him?" He was teasing me.

"Lib mentioned him," I laughed. "But I want you to tell me something."

"Okay. If I can."

"You can. What does it mean to reconcile yourself to God?"

He smiled. "To be reconciled with God is to accept and follow the righteous plan He has for your life."

"But did the men not just teach me of agency?"

"Of course you may always choose your own path. But you will find the most joy when you accept God's will. Your wills can actually become one."

"So you think marrying Zed was part of God's plan for me?" But before he could answer that, I quickly changed the subject. "Why did Darius go with Lib?"

We were on the trail south again. We were going back to Amulon, where we hoped to meet up with Jacob, Neel, and the others. Muloki led us on a more direct route, one he said was shorter since we no longer had to follow Lib's misleading tracks.

"He offered to go and Lib accepted."

"But..." But Gid had yet to be saved, and Darius had yet to reconcile with Sarai.

"There was a need. Darius saw to it. He does what has to be done."

"But he left other things undone," I countered.

He was quiet, and I thought he had no answer to that, but after a moment, he looked out into the horizon and asked, "What did you have to leave undone to come on this journey?"

"Well, the unharvested field of course, but Ardon is a child. Do you think I made the wrong decision?"

"Oh, there is no doubt you made the right one. But so it is with Darius. He set aside the unimportant, the things others could do, the things that would work themselves out, the things of his own desires to attend to the thing of the most immediate need." He paused again, though we were moving swiftly through the terrain. "I will never hold his kindness to Lib against him."

"You are a good brother."

He didn't say anything, and his guilt hung heavy in the air between us.

"It's not like you think it is—with Ket," he said.

"That is not what worries me," I replied. Truly, when I had opted not to harbor jealousy over Jashon's affection toward her, it had disappeared. I licked my lips. "About our marriage, I mean. I admire your devotion no matter what has been driving it."

He huffed. "And what does bother you then?"

"How guilty I feel."

"Why would you feel guilt?"

"I heard what you told Muloki and Jarom."

"Aw, Salome." He sighed. "I wish you hadn't overheard that."

"Because you don't want me to know why you really interceded with Jacob? Because you had to marry me to keep him from taking me with him and marrying me himself?" *If you could even call it a marriage*, I added silently to myself.

"No, Salome, so you wouldn't think what you're thinking now."

"You would keep it from me?"

He shook his head. "Because it's not true. Up until I ran into Jacob, my best chance at marrying you was rescuing Ardon and praying your father-in-law could be talked into giving you to me as a reward."

"Are you saying you want to marry me?"

"I asked you to before we ever ran into Jacob."

He had a point. A good one. "I guess I forgot that."

"Nice to know it meant so much to you."

I laughed a little. "Jacob makes me crazy."

"I guess you heard he wasn't my favorite person either.

250

I wouldn't let him near my sister, if I had one, and I won't let him near you."

"That sounds very noble," I said dryly.

Jashon glanced around, taking a quick mental inventory of all his men. It was a habit with him. He couldn't stop watching over these people. I looked around too. Keturah was with Melia, and Muloki talked with Ethanim behind them. Most of the other men were spread to the flanks watching the terrain for signs of enemies or settlements we should avoid. Jarom and Eve walked hand in hand a distance behind everyone else.

Jashon rubbed a hand over his jaw. "You've noticed, I'm sure, that Lamech is not my full brother."

"It occurred to me," I admitted.

He stared straight ahead. "When I was eleven—"

I quickly put my hand on his arm to stop him. "I believe one of the girls told me—when we were discussing the skill of tracking. And now, I believe I can put the pieces together. You don't have to revisit it."

"I revisit it daily," he said quietly. "My parents' ashen faces. My father's clenched jaw. My mother's tears. The destruction of our house. They took our food stores, even our clothes." He paused, cleared the emotion from his throat. "I have killed many men in defense of freedom since that day, but..." He trailed off and just shook his head.

But that was the one he could not forget.

I slid my hand down his arm to hold his hand. I wanted to slip my arm into his and put my head on his shoulder, but we were not out for a casual stroll. We were moving much too fast, nearly jogging through the hills.

"I told Gideon to stay at the farm, to help our parents.

The funny thing was Gideon was nine, and Mother had always wanted more children. She thought of it as a blessing, almost from the first, and Gideon and I took off to seek revenge on our brother's father." He scoffed self-derisively. "We had not yet mastered forgiveness. Not like you."

"Like me? What do you mean?"

"I have seen your tremendous capacity to forgive."

"It is..." I shrugged. "It is how I am. It is easy for me."

"Then you have a gift."

I acknowledged his comment with a smile. As a girl, I had been unable to understand why forgiveness was so difficult for others to offer. As I had grown, I had begun to suspect that I was the unusual one. I had forgiven my father, and every day with Zed had been an exercise in forgiveness.

"I think the more annoyed you are with someone, the easier it is for you to forgive them."

I laughed, wondering if it was indeed true.

"I was counting on that for myself."

He was teasing me, but I could sense his unease. He thought he had irreparably offended me by arranging our marriage.

"Jashon," I said. "Of course I am not angry with you. I shouldn't have allowed myself to become so upset. I acted ungrateful for your sacrifice, and I—"

His hearty and genuine laughter cut me off. "Marrying you will not be a sacrifice."

I waited while he finished laughing. "Nevertheless," I continued, "I am grateful for your intervention."

"Do you want to know a secret?" he asked. "Jacob always made me crazy too, but running into him yesterday was, well, it was just my lucky day."

There was one more thing I wanted to ask Jashon before I let the matter go.

"Jashon?"

"Hmm?"

"When you said the men in the army liked getting to know the local women, did you mean all the men?"

He wouldn't look at me, an action that spoke much louder than his soft reply. "Yes." He took a breath. "I thought you might ask that someday. I had already made up my mind to tell you the truth, but of course I hoped you would not ask."

"I think I knew it anyway."

"I knew Zed had a wife at home."

"You probably knew him better than I did."

"Longer maybe. He was the chief commander of his own men, and I mainly saw him at councils." His gaze trailed off into the distance, and I knew he was in his memories of a time he had not thought he would have to remember.

"What are you remembering?" I asked.

He shrugged, as if to shrug it off, but started talking as if he couldn't help himself. "One night, he'd been drinking. I had actually given him my ration of wine. He said his wife—you—wouldn't mind if he found another girl. And the way he said it, I could tell, he was sad about that."

I didn't have to wonder if what he said was true. I knew it was. The only time Zed ever drank to excess was when he was feeling really low.

Zed had chosen me out of all the girls in all the villages. He came to our home, handsome and important, and I had peeked around the door when he was talking to my father. In truth, I had been pleased and flattered by what I heard. But my father had agreed on the spot, without seeking my opinion, and by the time I was married to Zed, I resented both him and the marriage. I hadn't understood that my father could not have refused someone of Zed's status. I was young and stubborn, and I had pouted too long. I withheld my love from my husband, even though it had been right there in my hands to give.

"He missed you, and in his way—"

"Thanks." I put my hand on his arm to keep him from going on, from talking about things we should let die with Zedekiah. I smiled a little, the best I could do, and we hurried on toward the caves west of Amulon.

Neel was waiting there when we arrived late in the evening, dusty, tired, and thirsty.

But I knew that if the rest of us were tired, Keturah would be utterly exhausted. So why was she preparing an evening meal for all the men?

I went to where she knelt near the fire mixing the sticky dough for corn cakes. Pulling her hair back over her shoulders for her, I twisted it up and secured it with two thin sticks from my satchel.

"Feel cooler?" I asked.

She sighed.

"Get away from this hot fire. I will make the meal. Perhaps Jashon would take you up onto that outcropping to catch more of the breeze."

Jashon stood conversing with Muloki, and I caught his eye as I spoke. As I offered Keturah my hand to help her up, Jashon came immediately to us with a questioning quirk of his brow.

"Keturah needs the cool breeze from up there." I pointed. "Here, take my water."

254

Jashon glanced over his shoulder at the outcropping. He took the water skin I held out and then left with Keturah. I watched as he helped her up the rocky incline.

"How fast can you cook those?"

I turned to see Jarom going to his heels near the small fire.

"The fire has to be out before full dark," he added. "The scouts found travelers to the west. Too close for comfort."

It wasn't the first time we had run into travelers and avoided them, and I knew their safety precautions by then.

"I don't actually need the fire, just its heat. I only need some coals to keep the stone hot."

He nodded and started moving the coals with a stick. After a moment, he followed my gaze to see what I was staring at.

"She loves Gideon, right?" I asked and then bit my lip to stop any more foolish things from coming out.

"Completely," he said. "Turned me down for him, so she must have fallen hard."

I laughed and finally tore my eyes from the couple on the rocks. "Not you too!"

One side of his mouth turned up in a kind of sheepish smile, and he gave a half a shrug. "My affection for her was more a way to strike back at Zeke, but yeah, she turned me down flat." He smiled fully and deeply then. "Gave me a bloody nose, too."

I remembered how Eve had kissed Zeke on the cheek when we had divided company. And I remembered Jarom's scowl, which had been quite real amid so much teasing from the others.

"Was there..." I wasn't quite sure how to phrase my

question, especially since it wasn't any of my business, but decided to just ask. "Was there something between Zeke and Eve?"

"No." He didn't reply beyond that, just frowned, shifted his weight and stirred down the embers again, so I didn't press him further about it.

I flipped the first two corn cakes off the hot stone and passed them to him. "Enjoy," I said.

"I plan to." His smile was back, and I noticed that when he got up, he took the cakes to Eve and shared one with her.

I fed the rest of the men before the light from the fallen sun faded, and then I went to my bedroll. No fire. No tents.

We left early the next morning and all but ran southward in the path that Neel directed. We passed Mormon, reaching it much more quickly than we had the first time a few days ago, and by midday, we met Zaph at the head of a vast, treeless plain.

He signaled to us from a distance, and as we approached him, an idea occurred to me.

"Jashon, with the extra men of my family, we have enough, don't we, to leave some with Keturah? Just look at her."

His eyes were filled with worry when he turned them to her. "I don't think she would stay. But I will ask."

I shook my head. "Don't ask. You will have to issue a command."

22

In the morning when I woke, only one man was sitting in camp. Jashon had taken Gid's kinsmen and gone on without us, hoping to move faster without Keturah. I looked around for the other men that remained—Ethanim, Josh, Reb, Corban, Mathoni—but I didn't see any of them.

I lay very still and stared quietly at him. I didn't want him to know I was awake. I watched as he poked at the coals in the fire pit and scrubbed at his eyes. But it wasn't very long before Keturah said, "Morning, Mahonri."

I looked more closely at him. A thin scar cut across his cheekbone, but unlike some unsightly scarring I had seen on returning warriors, his scar made his already handsome face much more interesting. The last time I could remember seeing him was in the cave in Amulon.

"I thought you'd never wake up," he groaned. "I've been watching the back trail alone for four days."

Keturah sat up and wiped the sleepiness from her eyes. "Why didn't you wake me?" She was clearly used to taking a watch in the night.

Mahonri's eyes dropped pointedly to her mid-section.

"Lie back down," I advised her.

She waved me off and said, "You could have awaken Salome."

"I don't know Salome."

Keturah gave an annoyed little huff at his curt tone and rolled her eyes.

"I'm going to sleep now," Mahonri said. "Expect a knife at your throat if you wake me." And with that, he moved to the bedroll he had already spread a short distance away and fell promptly asleep.

"He's pleasant," I remarked.

"I don't know why he's like that," Keturah said quietly. "Underneath it he is actually a very nice person."

"Like Lamech?"

She had to think about that.

"Why don't you two get along?" I began to coax the hot coals Mahonri had been tending into a small flame. I didn't want it to get large because I didn't know where we were or who might be around us.

"I am willing to get along. I think...I guess he just prefers to be with other people."

"Does it bother you?"

"It did at first. Now I have come to expect it."

"Has he always been this way with you? Distant like he is?"

"Yes, from the first moment. His eyes slipped over me that morning as if I wasn't there, and he has never seen me since."

"He is the same way with Sarai," I said. "I worry for her. He will not be an easy man, and she is so..." I tried to think of the right word to describe her. Innocent? Malleable? Inexperienced?

"She wishes to please," Keturah filled in. "She cannot figure out what makes Lamech happy—because nothing does—and it confuses her. She doesn't know who she is if she is not serving and seeing to the comfort of others, but Lamech won't let anyone help him. He cannot be at ease in her company, because he is not at ease with himself."

She shifted uncomfortably and then lay down, brushing some leaves and twigs off of her bedroll as she eased herself down onto it.

When she started to breathe again, I asked, "Did you sleep at all last night?"

"Very soundly."

I cast a quick glance at her as I poured some water into a small dish to heat over the fire. She looked rested enough.

"Well, try to rest some more. No telling what the day might bring."

I poured a handful of dried beans into the water, a pinch of achiotl to flavor them, and then I broke a piece of dried venison into the bowl, reflecting back to when Eve had given me a large ration of the provisions Muloki had brought back from Amulon, insisting they were mine—I only needed to carry them myself. They had quickly depleted. We would have to make at least one more stop for supplies on the way north.

I glanced at Eve and Melia, who still slept near each other on the far side of the fire, and I felt bad I did not have any more food to prepare for them. I had to give what I had to Keturah. She had the most need of it.

"Were you scared?" Keturah asked after a long, quiet moment.

I knew what she was asking. "Yes, but quite unnecessarily. There is no need for you to fear it."

"That is what my mother says."

"She is right."

"Things often go wrong." She turned onto her back,

smoothed a hand over her rounded belly, and stared up into the leaves overhead.

"True enough, but there is no sense in worry."

"I wish Gideon was here. I wish the baby was here. I want this trial to be over." She turned her head and offered me a smile. "I never was very patient. Headstrong, that's what Micah always called it."

"Micah?"

"My oldest brother."

"Did I meet him?"

"No. He stayed to watch over Gideon's parents."

"Are they ailing?"

"Oh, no. Not that. They live in the borders of the land, far from the other towns and villages. They are frequently bothered by small bands of roaming Lamanites, but all it takes to discourage raids is someone who will shoot an arrow or two at their feet."

"Which Gideon's parents won't do?"

"No, they won't."

I brought her the bowl of food. She sat up, leaned back against a log, and accepted the bowl with a grateful smile.

"What are they like? Gideon's parents."

She took a bite and smirked. "Jashon's parents, you mean."

I looked down at my hands. "Jashon's parents, then. What are they like?"

"They're the best people in the world. I really admire the way they deal with hardship."

"Will it be a hardship if Jashon does not come home?"

She did take a moment to think, but I wasn't sure it was Jashon she was thinking about. She finally answered. "Liam and Naomi have four grown sons, and all four have chosen life in the army. They are reconciled, I think, to the idea of one of them not coming home."

I was trying to picture them in my mind. Liam would look like Jashon and Gideon, wouldn't he? I wondered which of his mother's features Lamech had. And there was a younger brother—Shad. Who did he look like?

My own mother had died of illness when I was young, and my father shortly after my marriage. It had been a long time since I had had any parents other than Zed's father.

"Are they excited for the baby?" I asked Keturah.

She nodded, a wistful expression on her face.

"Keep eating," I said.

"But you have had nothing," she said, though she did take another bite.

"I thought I would wait and see if the men brought in any game."

"Are we out of food?"

I thought of the limited supply in my satchel and thought probably everyone else was just as low. I had received the largest portion at Amulon, and I had very little left.

"No, but we should be careful with what we have left. I wonder where the other men are."

"One will be to the north, one south. And one will be on that rise right up there."

She pointed to a large hill a distance away.

"There?"

"Sure. You could see everything from up there." She took the knife from the sheath on her arm. The handle was beautiful jade but the blade was black as night and looked wickedly sharp. "Here. Watch."

She held the blade out until it caught the early light and flicked it in a series of quick movements. I watched her, but she nodded toward the hill, indicating I should look there instead.

In a moment, I saw the flashes of light in return.

"Nothing to report," she said and went back to her meal.

"Which one is up there?"

She shrugged. "Not Joshua." She gestured in the other direction. "Good morning," she called out to him. Then to me, she said, "It looks like you won't have to go hungry after all."

I turned and watched Josh come into camp carrying two dead rabbits by their ears and a cedar bark bag filled full. He handed me the bag without a word and went to his heels to skin the rabbits.

"It's rice," I said when I looked inside the bag.

He glanced up from his work. "We found a slow stream with lots of it last night, but we had to wait until this morning to thresh it." Before I could ask him how they had done it—usually it required a canoe of some kind—he looked back to the rabbits and said, "It was abundant on the banks."

"Who is on the hill?"

"Reb. Ethanim helped with the rice. He's scouting to the south now. He will signal when he sees Jashon. When the sun is up, Corban is going to scout north to find the quickest way out of this valley. Mathoni is circling the perimeter."

I glanced at the sleeping warrior on his bedroll.

"Mahonri is going to sleep until tomorrow." He chuckled. "I think he's been awake since the caves at Amulon. And I am going to make a real fire and cook up some rabbits for my girls."

262

Keturah gave him an affectionate smile. "How come you don't have a girl yet, Joshua?"

Color appeared on his cheekbones instantly.

"You do have a girl!" Keturah laughed.

"Nothing official yet," he said. He flashed us a grin but kept his hands busy preparing the meat.

I turned my attention to cooking the rice while Josh told Keturah of a girl at home named Desiree who made him laugh, who only did what he asked half the time, and who had never told him he was handsome—though he very clearly was, and somehow, this seemed to be the thing about her that impressed him the most.

"Is she pretty?" Keturah asked him.

"To me."

"I bet she's the prettiest girl in Orihah."

Josh gave his head a shake. "I cannot see why that should matter. She is beautiful where it counts."

"Well then, does she love you?"

"I cannot see why that should matter either," he teased.

In the middle of her laugh, Keturah sucked in a sharp breath. Josh glanced at me but otherwise pretended not to notice.

"Is it safe to have such a large fire?" I asked quickly.

"We haven't seen any sign that it is not," he replied. "For the time, as long as we burn the driest wood, the danger is small."

"It is hard to wait for the others to return," I said. "To not know what is happening."

Keturah let her breath out.

So did both Josh and I.

But Josh continued. "There should be three groups of

men—Jashon's, Kenai's, and Jacob's. Each group will have an assignment, an area they are to clear of guards or sentries or other impediments. By the time Gid and Ardon are free, they should be able to run freely back to us."

"They can coordinate all that?"

"They have all been trained extensively in just such a thing. If Gid is able, he will already have a plan of escape. He might be waiting until the time is right."

"But what can he do?" I asked.

"He can note which of the other prisoners might aid him, even if it did not lead to their own escape. Even some of the guards might find it distasteful to hold a Nephite prisoner of war who has done nothing wrong."

"And what will happen to him? No one ever says."

"The truth is, no one knows for sure. If his captors intended to kill him themselves, they would have killed him before he ever got to your farm."

"And what of Ardon? What will happen to him?"

"He will be rescued."

I smiled at his confidence, but said, "If he is not rescued, I mean."

Josh turned to Keturah. "She doesn't know her betrothed very well, does she?"

Keturah shook her head. Turning to me, she said, "Jashon would never come back here without your son. His son now." Turning back to Joshua, she said, "It is strange to think of Jashon as a father."

"The zequinim? He is everyone's father."

I knew what he meant. Everyone went to Jashon with their concerns, and Jashon made it his responsibility to see to the needs of everyone he considered to be under his care.

Keturah sucked in another breath.

It hadn't been long enough since the last time, so I didn't ignore it again. "You need to breathe through those," I reminded gently—but firmly.

She nodded and tried to.

When her breaths came more easily, I motioned for her to lie down. "It is too soon, and those pains are too close together."

But she shook her head. "If it is going to happen now, there is no stopping it. And besides, I need to go into the trees."

It surprised me how easily Keturah talked of this, going into the trees. It surprised me that a girl referred to so often as headstrong would agree to being accompanied—even to request it of her men. I couldn't even imagine what life had been like for her in the Nephite army. But as I had observed the way these people did things, I began to understand their observance of rules, even rules they had made for themselves. They were very strict to obey that which they thought was right. It kept the camp running smoothly, and I could see how their lives at home would be just as peaceful. They kept themselves free and unencumbered by following the commands of their leaders.

Josh got up and helped Keturah to her feet, and then I walked with her into the woods. When we came back, Eve and Melia were awake and talking quietly to Joshua. Melia was stirring the rice and Eve was mixing a small batch of the corn flour into dough.

"Lay down," I instructed Keturah, who had had two more pains while we walked into the forest to see to daily needs.

I couldn't deny that I was worried. According to Keturah, the baby still had two full fortnights before it was to be delivered. I could attend the birth, I was sure of that, but if the child had problems, I was not sure I could provide the proper care for it. I would do my best, though. She deserved it. And I would be the child's aunt, after all.

While Keturah lay on her side, I rubbed her back in slow rolling motions. She listened to the others talk, and every so often she would interject a comment, but her voice was tight and her breaths came quick.

By early afternoon, I was sure the child would be born within the day. Even the dogwood didn't seem like a good idea if this was a true labor.

"Just think," said Eve, "in no time, you will have Gid's son in your arms."

Keturah smiled at that—everyone knew she wanted a son—but everyone knew it would be safer for Gid's child if he stayed in the womb.

The day went slowly, and despite the eminent birth, peacefully. It was warm, but we were comfortable in the shade. Eve and Melia walked down to the stream to wash tunics. Mahonri slept while Keturah and I talked.

"We will be sisters," Keturah said almost absently while staring up at the fluffy white clouds. "I don't have any sisters. Well, except Melia."

"What do you mean?"

"My mother, a widow, married a man several years ago. Melia is his daughter. But she and I have never lived together and are much more like friends than sisters."

"Is there a difference?" I had never had sisters, either, or many friends.

She giggled. "I guess I wouldn't know."

"I wouldn't either, so I suppose we can make this—between us—whatever we want."

She smiled at me and I went back to sewing the small leather ball for Ardon with a needle Sarai had given me.

I thought about young Sarai and wondered where she was. I hoped she was safe. I hoped she was getting along with Lamech.

"I think something is happening," Keturah said after a time.

"Hmm?" I looked up and scanned the camp. Nothing had changed. Mahonri still lay sleeping, snoring lightly. The clouds still drifted lazily overhead.

"Can't you feel it? Here," she said, putting a hand to her chest. "Something is happening with Gideon. Today is the day they will rescue him."

She couldn't know that, but I didn't see any reason to dispel her optimism. "Have you always been in tune with him like that?" I asked, not knowing what else to say.

"Not with Gideon. It is the Holy Ghost that speaks to me, like we talked about."

I sat very still and concentrated, trying to feel this impression she claimed to feel.

"I don't," I said. "I don't feel it. When the men pray I have a warmness in my chest, but I don't feel that right now."

"It is a very good thing that you can recognize that feeling, but the Sprit can speak in different ways. It feels different depending on its current purpose."

I frowned, thinking about that. It was all very confusing. I thought I had understood the things Keturah and Melia and the men had taught me.

"What does it feel like right now?" When the question came out, it sounded as if I didn't believe her, and I wasn't sure if I did.

"It feels like a sense of foreboding."

"But I have had that since the moment Ardon walked away."

"It is heavier than that, sits more deeply in my heart, and it brings me comfort instead of worry."

"How can foreboding bring you comfort?" Now I really didn't believe her.

She frowned and whisked away some sweat from her brow. "Perhaps is it more like impending than foreboding. It is hard to explain a feeling. Can you explain how you feel about Jashon?"

I put the final stitches in the ball. "No."

"Sometimes, I don't think our language has the words to adequately describe the holy feelings. It takes practice to learn to discern the spirit."

"And I have not had it."

"Not yet." She smiled at me, confidence gleaming in her eyes. "But you will. Your heart is ready to receive it, Salome."

When Eve and Melia returned, they decided they would lay down for a rest. The day had been uneventful, but a welcome respite from the hard traveling we had done. The warm sun made me want to sleep too, but as I moved to my own bedroll, I caught a look that Keturah exchanged with Joshua. Her face was pale, her eyes were pleading, and her voice was thin.

"Josh?"

He was chopping logs with a grim face. What I thought

of as a peaceful respite had made him restless, but when he looked at her, his worry seemed to fade into resolve. "Salome, will you wake Mahonri, please?"

"Absolutely not."

He straightened and frowned.

"He said he'd put a knife to my throat if I woke him."

Josh laughed and got up to do it himself. "I am not afraid of Mahonri's knife."

Mahonri didn't pull the knife, but he was irritated at being woken up.

"I need you to assist me with a blessing," Josh said gravely.

Mahonri stilled, nodded, and rolled to his feet. His eyes went instantly to Keturah, and I could not, *could not*, believe the compassion I saw in them. I watched curiously as he went to Keturah and knelt near her.

"Hey," he said gently and smoothed her dark hair back from her face. He bent and placed a kiss at her hairline. "Worried?"

She nodded.

Of all the men, this was the one she chose to show her weakness to, this ornery man who didn't have a kind thing to say to anyone.

I sat on my bedroll and pulled my knees up, encircling them with my arms. I felt like I was intruding on something private, but I couldn't look away from what was happening. I felt that feeling of impending, the one that comforted, and I knew something very important was about to happen. Who were these people? How did they evoke these strange feelings inside me?

Josh knelt on the other side of Keturah and they both

set their hands on her head. And then Josh did nothing more than pray.

I had heard these people pray a hundred times by then. I had been struck in the heart, even down to my soul, by the intensity and warmness of their holy spirit. But no other prayer had been like this.

Joshua called down the very powers of heaven and told Keturah the child would not come until it was safe and the child was fully developed in every way, and commanded, actually commanded, her body to stop the birthing process. He told her she would feel comfort until her husband returned and gave many more instructions on the manner in which she should treat her husband when he returned, specifically that they were to pray together for direction. I realized that Josh did not seem to be talking to God in his prayer. He was talking to Keturah. This blessing, as Josh had called it, was almost like a prayer from God, to her, through him.

Was Josh like the prophets they spoke of? A mouthpiece for God here on earth?

When Josh had concluded and said amen, the men shifted, and they laid their hands over the child in her womb. She folded her hands peacefully there above it over her chest, though tears streamed down her face as Mahonri spoke words to her child, commanding him to remain comfortably within his mother's womb until he was grown large enough to survive. He blessed him with faithfulness, with intelligence, and with love for his fellow men.

And he called him by name.

Gabriel.

When the men were done, my throat was so thick with emotion I didn't know if it would ever ease.

270

I watched as Mahonri squeezed Keturah's hand and then went back to his bedroll, fell onto it, and began snoring again. I watched as Joshua took the knife from Keturah's arm and signaled the man on the hill. He waited for a signal in return before he slipped the knife back into its sheath and returned to stack the wood he had cut. He gave me a modest smile, but I only managed to swallow hard in return.

And then I lay down and thought about what had just happened.

23

I gaped at Alena. I had never heard anyone blatantly lie to get what they wanted. When I saw Tecumeni reconsider, I marveled that she knew him well enough to manipulate him this way. Instead of being jealous of his feeling toward me, she used it to her advantage.

Tecumeni introduced me to his mother, Charlot, and then asked her if she would mind if he left for the afternoon.

"Take Ava and Caleb with you," she said. "But I want the little ones to nap."

Caleb looked to be about Alena's age, which I thought was around thirteen or fourteen. But he was already tall and strong like his brother. He seemed steady and smart, and he had smiled at me when we had been introduced. Ava was near Isabel's age, maybe a little older, maybe even older than Tecumeni—I couldn't tell. She had very dark hair which she wore in intricate braids and knots. I liked both of them right away.

"How long have you been traveling with Tec?" Ava asked me.

Tecumeni walked ahead of us with Caleb, and Alena bounced along between them, giving almost her entire attention to Tecumeni.

As I watched her, I wondered if I had been that way with Darius, if he had seen me that way, if he had thought of me that way. I had certainly felt giddy like that when I was around him. I knew I was more demure than Alena—that was just my nature—but still I wondered.

"Was it a long time?" Ava asked again when I didn't respond.

"Oh. Sorry. No, it wasn't. Just a few days. From Laman."

She nodded. "That's where the army is camped."

"I heard that. But a lot of good an army at the border did me."

"What do you mean? The army protects us."

The Lamanite army was for protection? No. The Lamanite army came into my country to attack, to usurp power, and to kill and murder and maim because of the false traditions of their people, because they believed they had the right to rule over us.

Didn't they?

"A band of Nephites abducted me. Lamech tracked us and rescued me."

"Who is Lamech?"

"My betrothed." My blush came fast and hot, not because I was speaking of a fake relationship, but because Lamech was conspicuously absent when he should have been there.

Her face showed disappointment. "Oh. I thought you might consider Tec."

"But..." I looked at Tecumeni in confusion. "Tecumeni said he was already betrothed."

Ava followed my gaze. "To Alena?"

I nodded.

"Our parents have always harbored a kind of hope that they would marry. But, just look at them. Everyone can see they are not a good match—everyone except her. So far, Tecumeni only tolerates her. They still hope that when she grows up a bit, Tec will like her better."

"Why would he say it then?"

She giggled a little. "Perhaps to make you jealous."

"Me?"

"If I know my brother. And he is my twin—I think I know my own twin. Besides, I've already seen the way he looks at you."

"He has become my friend. He is very easy to like."

"I noticed." She cast a meaningful glance at Alena.

"Would she not accept Caleb instead?"

She motioned forward to them. "He does not even exist for her. Not like that."

"Maybe as she matures. Maybe as they both do."

"Maybe." But she sounded doubtful.

"Do you have a betrothed?" I asked her.

"No."

Her quick, emotionless reply confused me. All the girls I knew in Melek loved talking about which boys they favored. The light had left her eyes, so I didn't ask her more about it, just followed her to the deep pool they called the cistern.

I had never seen a cistern before, and when we arrived at it, I could see immediately that I would not like swimming in it. The only pool I had ever been in was the shallow pool at the base of the waterfall near Melek, where I could see and touch the bottom. This pool looked fathomless.

"Don't you use this for drinking?" I asked.

They all laughed.

"Of course not," Alena said. "That would be gross. We use the wells for drinking."

A stone ceiling nearly covered the cistern with a large pocket of air between the water and the top of what was essentially a cave.

I thought of hiding in the cave at Amulon, and I thought of Lamech and of moving closer to him in the dark.

What are you doing?

And I thought that perhaps I *had* used Lamech to strike back at Darius—just a little—to make him feel the jealousy that I felt.

"Come this way," Tecumeni said. "There is a way to get in down here."

"I don't want to get in the water," I said quietly to Tecumeni as we climbed down to the entrance. "I don't know how to swim."

"I'll help you." His offer was simple, friendly, and genuine. "It's not like swimming in the sea. The water is still."

Hearing a loud splash, I craned my head around the cliff to watch the ripples until Alena emerged from the water. Her smile was instant, and I watched her with interest.

"Is the water deep?" I asked when Tecumeni and I stood together at its edge.

"Yes."

I didn't move.

"I said I would help you."

"I know." I stared down into the water, and then I looked at Alena, Ava, and Caleb who were all playing in the water already—wet, cool, and uninhibited.

"You think Lamech would get mad? It's not like he's here to see."

I looked up at the censure in his tone. "No." I swallowed. "I am afraid of it—of the water."

He didn't reply for a moment, and when he did, he only held out his hand and said, "Trust me."

He was a Lamanite! Of course I could not trust him.

But he just looked into my eyes, and for some reason, all I could think about was the disappointment in Lamech's voice after he had kissed me in my tent. *Then why do you have your hand on your knife?*

But this wasn't Lamech.

"What do you know about me?" I asked, and I asked it in my native tongue, Nephite.

His gaze didn't waver, his expression didn't change, but I thought a small light lit in his eyes. His dark hair was cropped short, almost shaved at the sides—shorn, probably, when he had been in Laman with the army. He wore a string of beads around his neck, and his hand was still out between us.

He answered me in his own perfect Nephite. "I know your brother respects Lamech. I know Lamech seeks his own brother. I know Lamech did not go off to sulk, and I know your betrothal to him is not real."

He knew.

He knew everything. So why didn't panic hit me? Why didn't fear choke off my air?

I put my hand in his.

Because I trusted a Lamanite.

I had barely time to register his smile before he said, "Hold your breath," and jumped into the cistern, pulling me with him.

The sensation of complete immersion in the water was strange at first, but almost comforting, like being wrapped in a cool blanket. I was weightless for a moment until I felt a tug on my hand and Tecumeni pulled me with him back up to the surface. When I opened my eyes, Tecumeni was grinning at me. His wet hair was spiky, and water dripped from his eyebrows and pooled in droplets on his lashes. He reached a hand up to smooth some stray strands of hair from my face, though most of it was still secured in the knot at the nape of my neck.

"Are you okay?" he asked.

I slipped down into the water and sputtered.

"Kick your feet," he said.

I tried, but I kept sinking. I felt his arm slip firmly around my waist. Being so close to him was strange and forbidden and unfamiliar, but his strength and surety were a comfort to me, and when I had placed an arm half around him too, resting my hand on his shoulder, my fear vanished and I enjoyed the coolness of the water. Tecumeni towed me toward the others using his other arm. I felt his legs kicking beneath the water, too.

"Have you never been swimming before?" Alena laughed, as if the idea was preposterous.

I shook my head. "Near my home there is only the—" I pretended to cough then bit my lip. I had almost told her of the waterfall. Hadn't Tecumeni said something about the sea? Were we close to the south sea? I shook my head. "No."

Tecumeni pulled me a little closer to him.

Alena and Caleb dove and swam together, but Ava glided to the bank and came back with a strange, sticky looking substance in a slender hand she held above the water. She slid around behind me, and after she had deftly untied the cord that bound my hair, she began working the substance into it.

I didn't think it wise to ask what it was. Any true

Lamanite girl from Jerusalem would have known already, and her ministration felt so soothing, I just closed my eyes and let her do it.

When I no longer felt her hands in my hair, I opened my eyes to look around at her, but Tecumeni was watching me so closely—almost affectionately—that I couldn't look away from him.

"Hold your breath again," he said suddenly, and he grabbed me close to him and plunged us both down into the water. When we came up again, he turned me in his arms and inspected my hair. "I think it's all out," he declared.

"That was very sweet of your sister," I told him.

"That is her way."

I craned my head around to see her—it was almost as if Tecumeni was deliberately keeping her from my sight. But after a moment, he loosened his hold and let me turn. Ava was on the narrow bank. I could not see Caleb at all, but Alena was halfway up the cliff, crouching to keep us in view.

"Come on, Tecumeni. Let her finish her bath alone," Alena called. She didn't seem jealous like I expected her to be, just possessive, like she knew he was hers and I was not of consequence.

He lifted his hand from the water and waved her off. "I'll wait for her. She doesn't know her way back."

That seemed to satisfy her well enough, and she left.

Ava sent us a sly smile and left too.

It was suddenly quiet in the cistern.

The light from the opening played on the water, but we slowly drifted out of it. Tecumeni seemed content to tow me around the edges of the cistern. After a while, I could help propel myself through the water, but I kept a hand on his shoulder to keep from sinking. The only sound was the water dripping and splashing as we moved through it and its soft echo off the walls.

In a dim corner, Tecumeni leaned back in the water. "Here," he said. "Lay across my chest. We'll float."

I looked at his lazy smile, at the veiled look in his eyes, and knew I could not lay across his chest.

"No." I held onto a jagged piece of the stone wall and edged away from him, feeling the buoyancy of the water.

"It's okay. No one is here. Ava will keep everyone away."

"Why would she do that?"

"I asked her to."

"Oh."

He reached out and tugged me toward him. "Come here," he coaxed.

"No, Tecumeni."

I felt wet and small, but unafraid.

Tecumeni studied me, and I sensed his disbelief, his confusion.

I tried to explain. "It would not be appropriate."

He moved up in the water so he was facing me again. "Sarai," he said gently, meaning to entice me. "I know you do not belong to Lamech."

"I do not belong to you either."

The quiet in the cistern was calming, even as our conversation alarmed me. I had trusted Tecumeni. I still trusted him with my safety, but he knew nothing of the gospel of Christ or of my values and rules. And for the first time, floating there in the beautiful, peaceful, dim cistern with a very handsome—a dangerously handsome—boy, I wanted to keep the rules. I wanted to hold fast to my values because they were right and good and for my protection, not because my parents said I must or because I felt I would disappoint them if I disobeyed.

Still, I was in the water, and I could not get to the bank alone.

"What do you know about me?" I asked him again, breaking the silence. My native Nephite rolled off my tongue and sounded strange here in this foreign land.

"I told you," he replied, switching between the languages as easily as I did.

"You told me what you know of Lamech."

A smile curved his lips.

"You can cook and sew and walk twenty miles a day."

I shrugged. "Anyone might know that."

"You know things about people that others do not take the time to notice."

He raised a brow, watching for my reaction, but I only waited for him to continue.

"That rawhide is not a necklace." He swam closer. "You wear a knife around your neck."

My hand went to it under the water. "It is Lamech's."

He nodded as if he had suspected it and noted that I still wore it, even in the water. "You do not like the feel of a lie on your lips, and your smile is so pretty it makes me ache inside." He paused. "Especially when you smile at me."

I blushed deeply and quickly, but then the absurdity of his statement hit me, and I burst into giggles. He couldn't be serious. He was teasing me. But he kept a straight face, and it made me wonder.

"You're a liar!" I accused with more laughter.

He waited for my laughter to die out as he towed me toward the light that still filtered in through the entrance. When we got to the bank, he clutched me at my waist with both hands and lifted me out of the water to sit on the edge of it.

He looked up at me and said, "I'm not the liar, Sarai."

My smile quickly disappeared. I looked solemnly down at him, this friend I had betrayed before I even met him. "I'm sorry," was all I could say. I couldn't explain.

He put his hands on either side of me and lifted himself out of the water, held himself there before me, studying my lips as if he might kiss them. Then he lowered himself back into the water without touching me.

He swam back into the pool and stopped in the middle. Turning his head to the side, he instructed, "Wait for me at the top of the cliff." And then he kept his back turned to preserve my modesty as I got out of the water and stood in my wet, dripping sarong. I watched him for a moment, treading water with his back to me, and then I picked up my satchel and climbed the cliff.

Maybe he did know of my values.

I had time to wring out my tunic and stand in the warm breeze long enough to half dry before Tecumeni appeared.

"I'll set up your tent so you have a private place to rest before the evening meal. It will be a long affair, as Sansan will want to feed her guest well."

"Okay."

I thought we were nearly back to the village when Tecumeni said, "Sarai, wait."

I turned to look at him. He was stopped near the large trunk of a pinyon. He was breaking open the cones, prying them open with his knife.

"What are you doing?" I asked as I watched his hands closely.

"You have to stop asking questions like that."

I sighed. "I am not much of a liar."

"That's an understatement."

"Does anyone else know?"

"How would they?"

"You didn't tell anyone?"

"No."

"Thank you."

He had a handful of seeds and passed them to me. "It doesn't mean I won't. Put these in your satchel."

I did and then waited for him to break more of the brittle cones with his fingers. He tossed away the bits of cone and placed the nuts in my open hands.

"Are you ready to tell me what you and your people are really doing here? What is so important that you've traveled a month into your enemy's lands to accomplish?"

"What will they do to me if you tell?"

He didn't look at me, just kept breaking the cones open. "I don't know."

"Well, you won't like the feel of a lie on your lips either. I understand that you must do what you must do. You will feel better if you are honest."

He looked sharply at me. "Don't you understand? It's not about honesty. It is about duty. My commanders did not teach me the enemy's language so I could keep the information I find to myself."

"But you are not with the army now," I said feebly.

He just gave me a hard look and rolled his eyes.

I had to laugh. "You look just like Ava when you do that." But the weight of what he was saying, his dilemma, his inner struggle, did not escape me. "She said you are twins."

That seemed to amuse him.

"Aren't you?" I asked.

"Usually she tells people she is my older sister." It wasn't funny, but the way Tec said it made me laugh.

"And is she?"

"Only by moments." He passed me another handful of nuts.

When I had plenty of the strange nuts in my satchel, enough that their weight was noticeable, Tecumeni brushed his hands off and asked, "Do you trust me, Sarai?"

"Unwisely, I do."

He gave a slight nod, a slight smile. "I know what will feel better on your lips than a lie," he said, and then he bent down and kissed me. He was very gentle, his lips were soft and expressive, and it was a very sweet kiss. But that was all.

He straightened and peered down at me. "That's not how you kissed Lamech."

"I know Lamech a lot better."

He quirked a brow. "Do you?"

"Not really," I admitted on a grin.

"That was a little like kissing my sister," he said with disappointment tingeing his voice. He rubbed a hand across his jaw.

"Do you kiss your sister a lot?"

He laughed.

"I have a sister too. She's a lot more fun than me." I frowned and added, "You would probably like her. All the boys do. Chloe is a lot like Alena."

He shook his head firmly. "Not interested."

I hid a smile. "Tecumeni, why did you tell me you were betrothed?"

He shrugged uncomfortably. Glancing then toward the village, he abruptly changed the subject. "Listen," he said. "When we get back to the village, I won't see you alone any more. This is it. Goodbye, I mean."

"Then I must thank you," I said.

He shook his head again. "No, don't. Don't thank me." He gave me a pained look. "Just...Sarai, just trust me. That is how you can thank me, if you feel you must."

"I do." My brows knit. "I told you I do."

He gave me a long look. "Okay."

We started again toward the village. "I hope you will be very happy with Alena," I said, and he laughed.

"How could anyone be more fun than you?" he teased.

The evening meal was a long affair as Tecumeni had warned, but it passed in a blur and before I knew it, I was lying in my tent alone. I wished for Lamech. I wished for my brothers. Even Darius would have been a comfort. I was lonely, but I knew I didn't have to feel alone. I prayed in my heart, and I felt better.

Deep in the second watch, I heard movement outside my tent. When I dared to push a corner of the flap aside, I saw Tecumeni and Caleb were lying on their bedrolls staring up at the stars. They talked quietly to each other for a time—I thought Tecumeni was telling his brother about his time in the Lamanite army—and I felt just as if my own brothers were sleeping outside my tent. I thought of how he had offered to sleep outside my tent that first night in Lamech's absence. He knew it would be a comfort to me. Of all the men in the Land of Nephi, God had sent me Tecumeni. A tear slipped from the corner of my eye, and I finally fell asleep.

In the morning, I found a stream by myself. I knelt and drank deeply from it and then filled my water skin. I studied my reflection in the small trickle of water. Same large eyes as Mother, same pale skin as Cana, same honey brown hair as Chloe, except mine never escaped its knots as Chloe's did. There wasn't a drop of Father in me, nor of my brothers, nor of Isabel. It was too bad Izz was not the one here in the Lamanite village of Ani-Anti. With her long black hair and exotic dark eyes, she would have fit in perfectly.

The shrill call of the margay cut through the trees. I looked up quickly, searched the forest around me. Nothing. The forest was still.

But in a moment, the village came alive.

24

Salome

"Wake up."

Mahonri's voice was quiet, but not gentle.

I opened one eye and peeked at him.

"Maybe you'd like to find my knife at your throat," I mumbled.

"Do you want to go get your son or not?"

I opened the other eye.

"I'm leaving now. You can come if you're ready in three minutes."

I sat up and glanced around and then up at the sun. Everyone in camp was resting and the sun was in the western half of the sky.

"What do you mean?"

"I can't sit here doing nothing any longer. I'm going where the fighting is. You coming?"

I couldn't sit here doing nothing any longer, either.

Swiftly, I got my things together while Mahonri waited impatiently at the edge of camp.

"I wish it was me."

I kept packing but turned my head at Keturah's soft words.

"I guess I've had my adventures," she said with a tired smile.

I pulled my wrap-around over my shoulder and

checked to be sure the knot was tight before I knelt beside her. "You've many more adventures to come."

She smiled wanly. "He won't wait. Go quickly."

I nodded, got to my feet, and trotted after Mahonri as he disappeared into the trees.

I glanced behind us. No one else was coming. I wanted to ask him a million questions, but just said, "Why are we leaving?"

He was moving quickly. "I don't know about you, but I'm a pretty incompetent midwife."

"I don't doubt that, but why are you bringing me?" He could have slipped away without me, would definitely have preferred it, and we both knew it.

He looked over to catch my eye. It was brief, but it was deliberate. "My mother raised me by herself."

That was all he said about it, but it was all that was needed.

He looked me over pretty thoroughly. It might have seemed rude, but he said, "Can you run?"

"Not as far as you, but yes. Let's get moving."

He might have smiled as I started into a jog.

With just the two of us, we were able to move quickly. He did spend some time waiting for me to catch my breath, but we got into a rhythm and made good time.

"Do you know where we're going?" I asked when the sun began to fall behind the hills.

"Not really."

"You inspire confidence."

He reached out for my elbow and pulled me to a stop.

"Breathe," he said through what was either a pant or another half smile.

I put my hands on my hips and bent a bit at the waist to ease my back, and I concentrated on taking in controlled, deep breaths of air.

He pulled something from his satchel and when he caught the last rays of the sun with it and signaled to the south, I could see it was a piece of dark obsidian. He waited a moment, scanning the horizon, and then signaled again.

"There," he said after a moment. He pointed to the southeast, but when I looked there, I didn't see anything but the pink sky of twilight.

Mahonri signaled once again, and this time I did see a flash in the distance.

It wasn't ladylike, but I spit on the ground between us and wiped my mouth on my sleeve. "What does that mean?"

"Remember where you saw it?"

I nodded.

"We're headed that direction. Can you navigate by the stars?"

Several bright stars were already starting to appear.

"Not well."

"We'll have to slow down, but we can be to that spot by dawn." He pointed to where I had seen the flash of light.

"Dawn?"

"You slept half the day."

I shrugged and got my water skin out.

"Not too much," he said. "You'll get a cramp."

I spit again. "I think I know how to drink water," I said as I tipped it back.

He almost smiled again.

I swallowed. "How do you know that was our men signaling back?"

"We have a kind of password, a series of flashes. Whoever that was gave the correct signal."

"Oh." That was rather simple.

"Come on," he said. "We've got a battle to get to."

I tied my water skin to my belt again and followed him. "Do you think there will be fighting?"

Mahonri shrugged. "We might be able to free them without fighting. But when one gets the chance to fight, he fights."

"You would kill another just to see your own kinsman safe?"

"Gid's no kin of mine."

"That's beside the point."

He actually laughed, and the smile seemed so natural, I wondered why he didn't smile more.

"I don't love killing, Salome. Every good man loathes it."

"You think you're a good man?"

"Of course."

"You seem like you might not care about being good," I said.

"It's not so hard to make right choices."

"It's so easy even you can do it?"

He laughed again.

"Do you think this is the right choice, to try to make it in time for the rescue?" I thought of what Keturah had said, had felt. Maybe it had already happened.

"I do," he said confidently.

"And to bring me?"

"I wouldn't have awaken you if I didn't think it was right."

It was full dusk by then and Mahonri was guiding me confidently through the dark. He was a stranger, and I trusted him completely.

"Do you think it's the right choice for us to be alone in the dark?" I teased.

"I have no designs on your virtue," he said. "Do you have designs on mine?"

"No." My smile turned into a laugh I couldn't hold back. Was this even the same man who had threatened my death if I woke him up?

"Then we're good."

By dawn, we were atop a grassy knoll and Mahonri used the first rays of the sun to signal ahead.

I waited with baited breath for a return signal.

"What did they say?" I asked when I saw it. There were many flashes, and I wondered if it was a more complex language than just a system of symbols.

"They're stopped. They're making a plan."

He signaled again, and when the return flashes came, he said, "If everything falls into place, it will happen tomorrow night."

What would happen? What were they planning?

"We have to sleep now. Can I trust you to keep your hands to yourself?"

A smile formed on my lips. He was delightful when he wasn't brooding. I clenched my fist and punched him in the shoulder. "No."

The travel was hard, unlike any of the traveling we had done so far in the larger group. Just the two of us moved much more quickly through the wilderness, and I had to wonder how much faster Mahonri would have been moving if he had been alone. He didn't bother looking for places it would be easier to take the women through. He didn't bother going large distances out of his way to avoid obstacles. He just led me over, under, or through them, assisting me when necessary but allowing me little rest. Knowing that some kind of rescue was to take place, I wouldn't have taken rest periods even if Mahonri had insisted on it.

"Maybe we should have left sooner," I said. My feet slipped in the loose soil as we ran down a hill. Mahonri made it look easy. Even all but falling down the hill, he looked graceful. My legs were tired and exhaustion and dehydration were beginning to set in, but I would not quit.

He was quiet for a moment. "Maybe, but even I have to sleep."

Periodically, he exchanged signals with whoever was ahead of us, flashing his obsidian and watching the distance for a response, which he always received.

"Are we getting closer to them?" I asked. I rested one knee on a boulder as I rationed out a little water from my water skin.

"We are. They've stopped outside a city."

"Is that where they've taken Ardon and Gid?"

He swiped a forearm across his brow, then put his hands on his hips and bent slightly to breathe deep. When he stood again, he shrugged.

"We're only a few hours out. You should be able to rest before they stage the rescue."

"Will I be able to help?"

Reaching out, he felt my water skin. "I don't know. It depends on what they have planned," he said as he passed me his own water skin. "Drink," he said when I hesitated.

"I don't want to be in the way." The water in his water skin was warm, but it was plentiful, sweet, and most importantly, wet. I passed the water back. "Do you think Jashon will be mad? That you brought me?"

He took his time taking a draw of the water and tying the skin to his belt. Looking toward the sky, stretching his back and neck, he said, "No. Not mad. And I don't answer to him anyway. I'm here for Ket."

I watched him from the corner of my eye as we set off straight up a hill. "Are you one of her many admirers then?"

"Not in the way you think."

"What do you mean?"

"Do you know who she is?"

Who she is?

"Gid's wife?"

"Her parentage, I mean."

"I...I guess I don't."

"Your son is to be the next ruler of your people. Keturah's eldest brother was to be the next ruler of ours. He was to be our king."

"Oh," I said dumbly. No wonder they all revered her. No wonder they respected her as if she were a princess.

"We no longer have kings," Mahonri went on. "But the people know who she is. For generations, my family has been guarding hers."

"Oh," I said again.

"I guess it's in the blood. I had to stay with her."

"So why did you take me and leave?"

"Because I had to leave."

I would have laughed, but his face had gone dark. He wasn't joking.

292

"I think her brother is in danger."

"Kenai?"

He grunted.

We were coming around the bend of a hill and a city came into view.

"Look! There!" I pointed to a sprawling settlement in the distance. Manmade buildings towered over fields and homes that sat in a large valley, and walls surrounded it all. Beyond it, farther to the south, I thought I saw the glimmering of water. "Is that the sea?"

Mahonri pulled up and we both looked on for a moment. "I think it is. Come on. No time to waste."

As we drew close to the city, he withdrew his obsidian one more time and shined it with the soft cloth he kept it wrapped in. "We have to be more careful about signaling now," he said as he made a final signal.

A quick flash came back.

"We meet north of the city," he interpreted for me.

After that, Mahonri changed. He stopped talking so much, retreated into his thoughts. He was concentrating, preparing himself mentally. I looked at him closely. He wasn't sad, just focused. Perhaps this was how he distracted himself from the terrible work a soldier was expected to do.

He pushed onward until we were approaching a very large city from the north. We had passed other smaller settlements, always giving them a wide berth, but nothing compared to this city, and when I saw the size of it, it made complete sense that the Lamanites would have brought their prisoners here.

When we were drawing close, Mahonri called out to his friends using the call of an ocelot or a wildcat, a call I had heard Jashon's men make from time to time. It was meant to be a communication. Sure enough, a call came back, and it was close. We were nearly upon them.

Mahonri gave me a half smile and led me toward the sound.

The northern outskirts of the city were thickly wooded, but it wasn't long before we saw two men coming toward us through the trees. Relieved to recognize them both, I smiled at Jonas and Eliam.

"We didn't know you were coming," Eliam said to Mahonri.

"I didn't know either," Mahonri said.

All three were silent for a moment. Then Jonas said, "Gid is being held inside a prison near the center of the city. Our plan involves getting men inside the prison. They will go in as prisoners."

"He says he'll volunteer," Eliam added.

Mahonri let out a breath. "I feared something like that would happen. Felt it."

"What do you mean?" I turned to Jonas. "Who will volunteer to be taken prisoner?"

"Kenai," Jonas said quietly.

"Is Gid here then? In the city?" Mahonri glanced at me. "And the boy?"

A brief grin crossed Eliam's lips, but then it was gone. "They are."

I closed my eyes to keep back sudden tears. Now was not the time, but exhaustion had set in, and the tears pricked at the corners of my eyes anyway.

Jonas and Eliam kindly overlooked it and turned to lead us toward the others who had set up a camp in the trees.

While they talked, I couldn't keep my eyes from searching ahead for a glimpse of Jashon.

"Kenai's men met up with a group of Lamanite soldiers headed home from the city Laman. Sarai convinced them she was Lamanite and they formed a tenuous partnership. Kenai and his men are camped outside their village, a morning's walk from Jerusalem."

"That's the city we saw from the peak? Jerusalem?"

Jonas nodded.

"One of the Lamanites has been..." Jonas trailed off for a moment, scrubbed at the back of his neck. "He's been helping. Giving us information."

Mahonri snorted in disbelief. "Why would he?"

The two men glanced at each other.

"An interest in Sarai, we think," Eliam admitted.

"What?" *Sarai?* "He hasn't hurt her, has he?"

"No! Nothing like that," Eliam said quickly.

"This...spy, I guess he is...he has connections. He found Gid and the boy and offered up a plan for getting them free."

"A plan that will put our men in the prison?" Mahonri scoffed. "And why do we trust a weasel who would turn on his own people?"

"He is curious." Jonas paused. "About the holy spirit."

I thought Mahonri might scoff again, but he didn't.

Jonas took a breath. "Anyway, we're waiting for nightfall. Almost everyone is here."

Everyone. That meant Jashon and Enos. It meant Ethanim, Kenai and Zeke. Muloki and Jarom. It meant Isabel and Eliza must be here, along with Lamech and sweet, young Sarai. But when we approached the circumspect group hidden in the trees, I didn't see either Lamech or Sarai.

For a moment I didn't see Jashon either, but when my eyes found him, I didn't look farther. He didn't look up from his conversation with Zeke right away, but when others greeted Mahonri, he shifted his eyes to us.

Should I smile? Should I wave?

I ended up turning to Mahonri.

"Thank you for bringing me here."

I had spent two days with him and hadn't noticed the color of his eyes. They were a brown that reminded me of fall leaves. When he held my gaze, I thought of bringing in the harvest, the crunch of the fallen leaves, sitting near our fire with a blanket around my shoulders and seeing Ardon's face in the firelight.

"I hope your boy is okay."

I gave him a smile and turned as Jashon approached us. I would have to accept whatever he said. If he said I couldn't be a part of this, I would have to find a way to be okay with it. But I wasn't above begging.

Before Jashon said anything, he turned me by the shoulders and led me away from the others, men who didn't look surprised to see either Mahonri or me.

I hadn't realized I was so worried about Jashon's reaction to me being there until he pulled me into his chest and my worry eased. His hand was in my hair and his cheek was against the top of my head when he said, "You're a sight for sore eyes."

"Is he here? Have you seen him?"

I hoped it did not offend Jashon that I asked after my son instead after his travels or well-being, but I found I could not help it.

He pulled away and found the worry in my eyes and

296

maybe the relief when he answered my question instead of asking after Keturah.

"We've had eyes on him since Amulon." When I frowned, he said, "These men, Salome, and my men have run over these hills with messages and directions."

"Mahonri showed me how you could find each other over distances, with the flashing obsidian."

"And did you talk Mahonri into bringing you?"

Would he be upset if I had? But what could he really expect? He was the one who had rescued me after the first time I had set off on my own.

"He offered. I accepted. He is a good guide."

Jashon was quiet a moment, and from the way he searched through the small crowd of men, I wondered if he was perhaps upset with Mahonri.

"Is that anger in your eyes?" I asked.

His smile was quick and warm as he shook his head. "No, Salome."

But the look was still in his eyes.

"She was well when we left," I offered so he did not have to ask after Keturah.

"My brother's wife?"

Of course. Who did he think I meant? Who put the strain around his eyes and the tightness in his jaw?

"The men, Joshua and Mahonri. They said a prayer over her and the child." How to describe it? It was like nothing I had ever known. "Mahonri commanded the child to stay unborn. The holy spirit was there."

A brow went up. "Then it's as it should be. We might have thought of that before."

"Your preoccupation has not been small," I said.

A full grin spread over his face and he took my hand. "You're generous."

There was a commotion among the men, a small shifting of attention, a low murmuring.

Someone else had just arrived in camp. One of Jashon's spies, no doubt, but when two men came closer, I was relieved to see that one was Lamech. A younger man flanked him, and it was he who caused the reaction in the men. Lamech found his brother easily and led the other man toward us.

The man was young, maybe eighteen, nineteen at most. He seemed like a boy to me. His head was shorn and his chest was bare. He looked very much like the Lamanites I had seen that day in my field, but I knew that to hide among the people in this land, the men had gone to some length to wear the right clothing and look the part. Sarai had spent hours fashioning clothing for this purpose, and even Lamech was wearing something similar to the young man.

Jashon stepped away and addressed the newcomer.

"You are Tecumeni," he said, clearly having been informed the boy would be arriving.

"I am."

"Tec, this is my eldest brother, Jashon," Lamech said.

The two eyed each other a moment. Tecumeni's lips twisted wryly into a smirk.

"Is it done, then? What Lamech said?" Jashon asked.

"It is."

"So you've done it? You've put her in prison?" The other men stepped aside as Zeke, wild-eyed, pushed his way through the crowd that had gathered.

Tecumeni said nothing as he gave Zeke a slow, assessing look.

"Sarai's elder brothers," Lamech informed him quietly as Jarom stepped up beside Zeke.

Jarom's eyes weren't as bright with anger, but they definitely held worry.

Tecumeni turned to Lamech. "These are to be your brothers?"

Lamech didn't exactly blush, but his shoulders stiffened and he swallowed hard.

Tecumeni offered an arm clasp to Zeke. "We meet again."

Jarom frowned as his brother reluctantly took the arm. Zeke didn't release it when he should have, and upon looking more closely, I could see he gripped Tecumeni's arm very tightly in his big hand.

But Tecumeni took a step closer and dipped his head to allow for a bit of privacy when he spoke. "I have set the plan in motion. She will be as safe as I can make her."

"In the prison?" Zeke asked.

Tecumeni cocked his head. "Didn't Lamech explain?" He glanced to where Lamech had stepped aside to confer with his brother.

Zeke all but growled. "He did."

Seeing the arm clasp and that Tecumeni had been accepted into camp, many of the men wandered back to what they had been doing. Knowing the plan would soon go into action seemed to be all they needed. Jashon turned to talk to Lamech and Muloki. I recognized most of the men from the past weeks, though I didn't know many of the names of the men who had split from us and gone with Kenai. Isabel and Eliza must have been resting in the single tent that was set up a short distance away.

Zeke finally eased his grip.

"She will be locked in a cell by herself, away from the other prisoners. We can't get anyone else into that cell, the one with the window. It has to be a woman."

"She's just a girl!"

Tecumeni went on as if Jarom hadn't spoken. "She will have the weapons and the food."

"Does she know what to do with them?" asked Zeke.

Tecumeni snorted. "Well, surely she can figure it out."

"She's just a girl!" Jarom insisted again.

Tecumeni looked between them. "A smart and capable one. Trusting. Loving. A girl who will do anything to save her friend."

"What do you mean by *loving*?" Zeke's voice was low and threatening.

Reacting to their hostility, Tecumeni glared at the brothers.

Trying to appear as though I was not eavesdropping on this conversation about Sarai, I made another scan of the camp. Most of the men had returned to making ready their weapons. I caught a glimpse of Jacob and my kinsmen on the outer fringes. They kept to themselves, but they were ready to help save Gid and willing to accept help for the sake of Ardon. Everyone was here and ready to rescue their kinsmen, to fight if necessary.

"She is a girl who has not known enough love," Tecumeni said.

Both of her brothers scoffed.

"And I suppose you think you can offer it to her?" Jarom said.

"Of course not. Her heart is with the Nephite dog." A

surreptitious glance caught Tecumeni indicating Lamech with a nod of his head.

"Tecumeni," Lamech called over. "Explain again how it will go to Jashon."

Tecumeni said a cool "Excuse me," before turning to consult with Lamech, Jashon, Muloki and Kenai.

That night, when things were quiet, I said to Jashon, "Do you think that young Lamanite's plan will work?"

Jashon let his head fall to the side so he was looking into my face. "I do."

"You don't think it is a trap?"

"It crossed my mind."

"You can't have missed that no one here trusts him. Why are you going along with it?"

"My brother vouches for the Lamanite."

It was a simple statement, it might even be that simple in his mind, but come tomorrow, it may have complicated outcomes.

"Besides, it is a good plan. It will work."

Confidence showed in his eyes, reassuring me, but then something else came into them. Regret. Tenderness.

"I wish I had met you in a time and place I could have courted you the way you deserve."

I gave a little shrug. There was no point in wishing for what could not be, and he was the one who deserved a traditional courting. He was getting a very poor deal in me, a jaded wife with a half-grown son who was not of his own blood.

He rolled onto his side and reached over to touch my cheek. Despite the many listening ears, he was bold and said, "Do you think you could ever love me?"

Was I imagining the stillness, the collectively held breath? I hadn't realized the men were interested in what happened between Jashon and me, but I should have. I was a girl they found in the wilderness, and he had agreed to marry me so I could continue to travel with his men instead of my own kinsmen, who were going to the same place! Of course they wondered why he had done this.

And I wondered why he thought he was so unlovable.

I leaned forward to close the inches that separated us and kissed his lips. The kiss was chaste, but it seemed loud in the silence. He was as conscious as I was that my bedroll lay in the midst of twenty warriors for my protection. But what none of them knew was that the kind of protection I needed was exactly the kind his kiss provided me.

"How could I not love a man who exemplifies his Christ so well that he has made a life of doing for others what they cannot do for themselves?"

He swallowed, and his eyes followed me as I eased back to my own blankets.

The morning broke uneventfully, but the men were quiet, reverent even, because they knew there would be fighting in Tecumeni's village. Men would be taken prisoner. Sarai would be taken prisoner.

It was barely mid-morning when Zeke and the others trailed in.

"They're wounded!" I said.

Many of them were wounded, but on closer inspection, most of the wounds were quite superficial.

I helped where I could, and as I moved among the men, I was sad to see that Enos, Mahonri, and Kenai were not among them. I offered Isabel a smile and then pulled her into a hug. I knew how she must be feeling.

"Is Kenai in the prison then?" I asked her.

She nodded. I had been among these women for a fortnight, and it did not surprise me to see the strength and determination in her eyes.

By late afternoon, Eliam and Jonas trotted into camp. Quickly searching the faces, they found Jashon and went to report to him.

"It all seems to be going as planned. Kenai and the others are within the prison walls, and Tecumeni has Sarai settled in a locked cell away from the men."

"I wish it was me in the prison instead of Sarai," I said to Isabel.

"So do I."

Her long black hair, normally tied back in a knot, was loose around her face, and I wondered if she had not yet had the time to do it up and out of the way.

"Jashon says that come the night we will be running from the city. Let me put your hair up."

She smiled gratefully and turned her back to me so I could secure her hair at her nape. But we had hours yet to wait, so I took the time to make it pretty.

When I was done, Isabel put a hand up to feel the knots and twists.

"It's a shame you didn't have daughters," she said.

"You do beautiful work," Eliza said, admiring the pretty hairstyle.

"Just keeping my hands busy," I said, and I found another stick to secure my own hair up off my neck. It was not as intricate as Isabel's, but it would keep me cool.

"Are you very nervous?" Eliza asked, but she didn't wait

for an answer. "I don't blame you, but have faith, and soon it will all be done."

"I have learned much from your people of faith and patience, but perhaps we could have a prayer together?"

The other women looked at each other and knelt up onto their knees. I let Eliza say the words for me, but when I said, "Amen," I meant it wholeheartedly.

At last, the sun began to dip into the western sky. We rested and ate well, and when the last rays of light were hitting the tops of the trees, Jashon said it was time to go.

25

I grabbed my things up and ran toward the Nephite camp at the outer edge of the village. I stood where I thought it had been. I tried to catch my breath, but my fear made it impossible. I turned around and around looking for signs that this was the place my kinsmen had slept the night.

"Sarai."

I turned with tears in my eyes to find Tecumeni and another man. Tecumeni's face was stricken and gray, and his bare chest was covered with blood.

I ran to him. "You're hurt!" I exclaimed as I rummaged in my satchel for the last of my bandages. I began to wipe the blood away, but Tecumeni gripped my wrist to stop me. His grip was tight and unyielding, and I couldn't help but think of Zeke's hand gripping me in the same way all those weeks ago. Zeke had grabbed me out of concern.

My hand stilled. I dared to look up at him, and he just shook his head.

"Bind her, and let's get moving," the other man growled impatiently.

But I barely noticed his impatience. "What has happened?" I whispered. I looked back at Tecumeni's bloody chest. "What has happened?" I choked out again.

Tecumeni threw a look back over his shoulder. "Go. Tend to Sansan," he insisted. "I can see to the infiltrator."

The other man hesitated, but only to sneer at me. Then he turned and ran back into the village.

Tecumeni might have sighed. He spoke to me in Nephite. "I'm sorry—I have to bind you." He held a long rawhide thong in his hand. "Turn," he commanded louder in Lamanite.

I just stared at him in disbelief until he grabbed my wrists and tied them together in front of me. "Nevermind. In front will work just as well." The remainder of the binding cord was so long it dragged on the ground.

"Tec—"

"Do you trust me?" he whispered.

I swallowed. Nodded.

He gripped my wrist again and dragged me forward into the village. Fear consumed me. My feet wouldn't cooperate.

"Where are you taking me?" I asked.

"To the prison at Jerusalem." He picked up the end of the cord and tugged like I was a little slave girl. I stumbled forward. "It takes half a day, but it's a pretty walk."

A pretty walk? I almost laughed at the absurdity of it.

"Where are my kinsmen?"

He cast me a sidelong glance. Passing across the main path of the village was not the place to discuss it. Tecumeni kept quiet while his people stared at me, yelled obscenities at me. Some of the women came forward and spit on me or on the ground at my feet. My eyes widened and my stomach dropped when several boys came into view at the edge of the village. Caleb was among them, and they were lined up with stones to throw at me.

I heard myself whimper, but I could not stop it.

As we approached, Tecumeni calmly raised a hand, but the words he spoke to them were so fast and sharp I couldn't understand them. The boys stood their ground angrily, but let us pass. I kept waiting to feel a stone on the back of my head.

"What did you say to them?" I asked shakily.

"I told them to drop their stones. I told them that Zaaron and I brought you to the village, and they would have to stone us first."

I gasped. "Would you have let them stone you?"

He scoffed. "Before I let them stone you."

"Tecumeni." I began to sob in earnest. "Is Zaaron alive?"

"I don't know. He was, but...I don't know yet." He cleared his throat. "We approached your kinsmen early this morning, before first light. Zaaron wanted to apprehend them and get an early start for the prison in Jerusalem."

"But they fought," I stated dully.

"They fought," he agreed quietly. "They have a mission to fulfill. I did tell my kinsmen that. I told them everything. Zaaron and Anahah could not understand. They could not see past the deception."

Maybe it was because I was not a native speaker of his language, maybe it was the way he absently rubbed his hand over his chest or the way he wouldn't look at me, but I had the feeling he was not being truthful.

"But I was the one who deceived them!" I said. "It was my lie! I deserve to be locked in the prison for what I did."

"Your Lamech is quite practiced in the art of deceit."

I shook my head. "No. He did it to help me. And the Spirit assisted him—he doesn't speak your language at all—so it couldn't have been wrong."

Tecumeni let my statement ring through the forest around us. I had no idea what he was thinking. Of course lying was wrong, but I wondered about Tecumeni's opinion of lying, his perspective, what he had been taught to believe. He valued duty over honesty, I did know that, and Alena hadn't given lying a second thought.

Finally, Tecumeni asked, "What is the spirit you speak of with such confidence?"

Could I explain it to him?

"Do you believe in God?"

"God?"

I bit my lip. "The Great Spirit, then?"

He surprised me when he said, "Yes. I believe in a great spirit."

"This is God," I told him. "The Holy Spirit is a feeling God sends to us to tell us when something is right or good. To warn us of danger. To comfort us when we are sad or afraid. To lead us in the right direction."

The forest was eerily silent. I longed to hear another call of the margay. I had always disliked its high-pitched scream, but just now, it would have been a comfort to know if my kinsmen had gotten to safety.

"Is this the feeling I have when I am near you?"

Tecumeni's question took me completely off guard. It embarrassed me until I thought to ask, "Do you only feel it around me?"

"No. I also have this feeling around your Nephite brothers." He glanced at me, and added reluctantly, "When I spy on them."

"Yes, that is the Spirit," I told him softly.

"And I suppose this is something only a Nephite can

possess?" he asked bitterly.

"No!" I said. "No! We are all are invited to come unto Christ, to reconcile ourselves to God through Him."

"Who is Christ?" The curiosity in his voice shocked me. He really wanted to know how he could hold on to what he had felt, how he could feel it again. He hungered for it.

And how could I keep it from him, this knowledge I was so lucky to have, even on a journey like this, as he dragged me away to prison? Perhaps one could not properly court on a journey like this, but one could certainly share the gospel.

And so I did. I began at Adam and I told Tecumeni all the doctrines I had read in the scriptures, all the gospel I had learned from the priests and from my parents. I told him of the conversion of the people of Ammon, of their oath never to fight against God or man. He stopped me there.

"But your kinsmen are among the people of Ammon, and yet they fight." A storminess passed through his eyes, but it was a confusion I could dispel.

"The young generation, those of my generation, did not make this oath. Instead, the boys made an oath to protect those who could not protect themselves, even unto death. My kinsmen are not afraid of death, because they know they will be with God forever."

"How can they know this? How can you?"

"Faith, Tecumeni. Faith in God and in that Holy Spirit who bears witness that He is."

Tecumeni drew up to a stop, stared at me for a moment and then motioned over his shoulder with his chin. I looked and beheld the city Jerusalem beyond him. "And you will need to have faith in me now, Sarai."

"You can't just let me go?" I glanced back in the

direction of the village. All the people had already seen him haul me away. Couldn't that be good enough?

"No," he said quietly. "I am honor-bound to bring you to the prison. The others will be waiting there with any of your kinsmen they were able to apprehend."

I sighed and nodded sadly.

"Besides, you will be safer within the prison walls than you would be in the forest by yourself."

"But...won't I be...sacrificed...or something?"

He laughed. When he tried to stop, he couldn't. But at last he said, "Not until the full moon," and then he laughed again. I started to wonder if I had placed my trust in the wrong man until he nudged me in the ribs and said, "That was a joke."

"Obviously a funny one," I said, but I didn't get it.

He sighed heavily, sobering quickly. "Come on. Let's get this over with." He started to walk away.

My feet wouldn't move again. "Tec...Tecumeni," I called out. When he turned and regarded me, all I could make myself say was a feeble, "I'm frightened."

He moved back to me and put a hand to my cheek.

"Will you..." I swallowed hard past the lump in my throat. I cast a glance toward the city in which lay a prison I would have to walk into. "Will you hold me for a moment?"

He had the foresight to pull me into the cover of the trees, but didn't waste any more time pulling me against him. I lifted my bound wrists and he ducked under them so my arms were around his neck. When I was safe in this Lamanite's arms with his hands splayed over my back, I began to cry.

"I could cut the binding," he said after a few moments, "but I would just have to tie it again before we reach the prison."

"It doesn't matter," I cried into his shoulder.

He held me close to him for a long time. "Whisper a prayer to your God," he suggested.

I nodded, but all I could breathe out was, "God, make me brave."

When I had cried all I could, I felt better. I felt the warmth of the Spirit, and I lifted my face to Tecumeni's worried frown.

"There is not another way," he said. He awkwardly but gently rubbed his thumbs under my eyes until all the tears were wiped away.

"I understand," I said, though I didn't. "Take me there now." What choice did I have if he was set on taking me there?

"Okay," he agreed, but the only movement he made was to lean down and kiss me.

This kiss was different. It was more than sweet and friendly and awkward, as the last one had been. There was so much more meaning in this one, more meaning than I understood. It was not inappropriate—I would have kissed him that way in front of my father—but it was confusing. He was trying to comfort me, maybe trying to give me something else to think about, but I thought it brought him a measure of comfort as well. He didn't like what he had to do.

"Take me there now, Tecumeni, before I lose my resolve." I lifted my wrists so he could duck under them again.

Trepidation filling my chest, I walked to the city in silence. As Tecumeni led me down off the hill, our path met up with a larger road. The gates were thick and wooden. The guards there looked me over when we passed though and questioned Tecumeni, but not extensively. People in the city glanced at us, but nobody seemed to care overmuch about

Tecumeni's stoic face or my tied hands. Tecumeni did not lead me down any of the many side streets I could see, just straight into the heart of the city.

"This city is huge." I couldn't help the observation. "Bigger than my home by many times."

"And where is your true home, Sarai."

I had told Zaaron I was from this city. "Not here."

"We've not traveled halfway into it."

Then Jerusalem was even bigger than it appeared.

I didn't know how to feel when I saw Kenai, Enos, and Mahonri bound and waiting at the thick wooden gates of the prison yard. I was comforted, knowing I was not alone here, but scared for what might happen to them.

And I had absolutely no idea how we would get out of here.

All three of them looked relieved to see me, but when Kenai moved to come to me, a guard pushed him back against the wall.

"Where are my kinsmen?" Tecumeni asked as the two guards eyed me with identical looks that made my skin crawl.

"They've gone off to celebrate their capture," said one.

"While my uncle dies?"

The guard shrugged, but the question made him turn to Tecumeni and give him his full attention.

"I am Tecumeni of Ani-Anti, kinsman to Zaaron. We are of the Order." The man's eyes widened and he glanced at the other guard who stood up straighter. "These men can go in the work details until the courts are done with them. After that, I don't care what fate befalls them. The girl is mine." He let his gaze skim over me. "I will take my vengeance from her."

The guard laughed a little. "Tecumeni, the courts are a

year behind! You will be waiting for *vengeance* a long time!"

Tecumeni stared the man down. When the man's posture weakened, Tecumeni said, "Put her in a cell inside. I expect her protected from the swine for guards you have here. She is mine. Do you understand?"

The man nodded.

"The men can go in the yard with the other criminals."

As I watched the silent guard lead Kenai, Enos, and Mahonri away, I wondered who on earth Zaaron was that these men gave Tecumeni, his young nephew, so much respect. Wasn't he just a man from a tiny village? I remembered when he had insisted that Tecumeni trust Lamech because he was of some kind of Order. I remembered how he had cut the fruit for me and popped the large pit out with his knife, and how I had foolishly revealed that I had never seen such a fruit before. And I remembered wondering aloud if God had sent us these Lamanites.

As the other guard took hold of the binding at my wrists, I caught Kenai's gaze.

We will come for you. Be prepared.

I had always loved that Kenai could communicate this way. Some said he spoke with his eyes. Some said he could read your mind and place thoughts in it. But I knew his amazing communication was nothing less than the Spirit speaking heart to heart.

When I felt his words, I knew Kenai's capture was part of a plan, but when as I sat alone in a tiny stone cell, I wondered what I could do to prepare for it.

I looked around. The guard hadn't taken anything of mine, only led me away from Tecumeni and the others and locked me here. He hadn't spoken to me, touched me, or really even looked at me after Tecumeni had claimed me as his own. I shuddered at what Tecumeni had implied he wanted with me, at what he had made those men believe.

But I remembered him turning his back so I could get out of the cistern. *Wait for me at the top of the cliff.* And I remembered when Mother told me people's actions meant much more than their words. *Ye shall know them by their fruits, Sarai.*

I still had my knife hanging around my neck, hidden under my tunic, and Tecumeni knew it. I still had my satchel and inside it the healing balm for my lip, a little venison, five of the large, fleshy fruits, and handfuls of the nuts from the pinyon cones. I even had my full water skin.

I turned my back to the door and eased my knife out. Carefully, I cut the rawhide cords that bound my hands. Finding the nuts in the bottom of my satchel, I slipped some of them into my mouth and felt my chin wobble as I tried not to cry when they hit my empty stomach. *Oh, Tecumeni,* I thought.

I noticed a small window above me, really just a shabby hole in the wall. When I stood on my toes, I was able to see out into the yard where the men were kept. I knew Kenai had been captured on purpose. I knew Enos and Mahonri were with him in this prison for a reason. My imprisonment here was a complication they would have to work out, but I had no doubt they would.

This was all part of a plan, but I didn't know what the plan was for until I saw Kenai through the window, embracing Gid in the shade of the far wall. My eyes were not deceived! It was Gideon!

I wanted to fall to my knees and weep in relief, but instead I sounded the margay's call.

I was not sure if I did it right because I had never done it before. The sound felt strange in my throat. Though I watched carefully, the men made no move to indicate they heard it, but something in their postures told me they did. I waited and after a long time of casually searching, Kenai finally met my eyes through the window. He gave me a quick reassuring grin, and then he turned away.

I turned away too, and suddenly, I knew why I was there.

I pulled my knife from its scabbard and made a slit in my sarong, feeling a moment's pause because of the work I had done to modify it into a more Lamanitish tunic for myself. With a sigh and a few good pulls, I ripped the bottom portion of it off. I had never shown so much of my legs—even alone in the cell I was embarrassed by it—but I needed the fabric. I reached into my satchel and found my needle pinned to its bit of leather. I pulled a long fiber from the torn fabric to use for thread, and I set to work.

I got halfway done before I looked around the floor. There it was. The rawhide—so much of it that Tecumeni could tow me like a slave girl through the village. I smiled to myself and said a quick prayer of thanks.

When Kenai eventually approached my window, I had the slingshots ready and a small cloth bundle filled with the nuts. I had the fruits halved with the stone pits left in their centers. Gideon looked gaunt. It was clear he had not been eating as well as the rest of us had..

Kenai was leaning on the wall to the side of the window so I couldn't see him, but I could imagine his sharp eyes roving over the yard, assessing the guards as he talked to me.

"Gid says the best time to escape is between the second and third watches."

"Tonight?"

"If everything is in place. Gid already has a plan, and the men on the outside are making preparations."

"Okay."

He didn't respond, and I thought he might have left, might have had to leave so his actions didn't look suspicious to the guards.

"Kenai?"

"Yeah, Sarai?"

"Don't forget me."

I heard his chuckle. "That would be impossible. Thanks for the clever weapons."

"Will they help?" I asked uncertainly. They were sewn out of cloth after all, not like the leather one Lamech had shown me how to make.

"Yes," came the firm, appreciative answer. "Get some rest."

"Okay."

I sat down and ate what I had left. Then I lay back and tried to rest like Kenai had suggested. I knew it would be a long night if everything went according to plan.

You would go without knowing the plan?

I smiled at the question Lamech had intended to be derisive. God had revealed my part of the plan to me when it was time and not before.

26

It took over an hour to walk to the city in the dark. We stopped in view of the lights that burned at the north gate. It shouldn't have, but it surprised me how silently twenty men could move through the night.

One of the men gave an owl's call, and two men materialized out of the darkness. Lamech and Tecumeni were welcomed with silence. Eliza and Izz fell out to the side with Muloki as if it had all been orchestrated, and Jashon leaned down to speak quietly into my ear.

"Do you want to wait here with the other women?"

I had left my village alone to track Ardon, had suffered fatigue and hunger and fear to rescue him. I had all but fallen down cliffs and had agreed to marry a perfect stranger. I had run for two days with Mahonri so I could see my son safe. Waiting outside the gates would be safer, but all I said was, "No."

Jashon seemed to understand. He slipped an arm around my waist, and we stood together, watching the lights, and waited for the time to be right.

We had followed the Lamanite abductors for many miles, all the time preparing and watching. This was our best chance to save Jashon's brother and the boy who would be a king, a chief and leader of his people, and, feeling the strength of the men who surrounded me, I was glad we had waited.

I couldn't tell in the dark, but when the first group of men set silently out toward the lights at the gate, I realized they had formed themselves into groups according to their assigned tasks.

Zeke and his men would secure the gate, ensuring it would be open to us on our way both into and out of the city.

Many minutes passed, maybe close to an hour, before we saw a quick series of flickers in the lights and heard the distant call of the ocelot cat. It was time to go.

"Stay close to me," Jashon whispered as we set out into the darkness, as if I wouldn't have anyway.

Jacob and his men fell in silently behind us. Though different from the Ammonites in dress, custom, and religion, in this, this love and duty to their kin, they were the same.

If I understood it all right, Tecumeni and Lamech would take care of the guards at the doors, and we would clear the guards in the prison itself. The way would be clear for Jacob's men to enter the prison yard and find Ardon, preferably without awakening the other prisoners.

There had been some discussion about letting other prisoners out as well, but as we could not judge upon their guilt or innocence, they would have to stay. A mass exodus would certainly be noticeable.

As for Ardon, I knew him to be guiltless, and while I felt for the other prisoners who were perhaps there under similar circumstances, I had no qualms about taking Ardon from these walls.

When we got to the city gates, they stood ajar. Jarom eased them open just wide enough to slip through. No guards were present to stop us, so the men eased the gate open even more so we could hurry through.

Then Tecumeni led us through the shadows a long way down the main road, turning neither right nor left. Finally, he stopped us and told us to wait around the corner of a large building.

"A quarter of an hour," he said. "That's all we'll need to get her out."

Sarai.

Just as Tecumeni and Lamech were about to slip around the corner out of sight, Jarom's hand shot out to grab Lamech's arm. A look, perhaps words I couldn't hear, passed between them, and then Lamech was gone, running after the Lamanite boy who was about to betray his people for Sarai.

When we heard the signal to move in, the men moved on silent feet toward the prison. No guards stood without the doors, and when Jarom tried the heavy door, he found it unlocked. It swung easily and as he eased it open, flickering light fell out onto the ground.

I followed Jashon, with Jacob directly behind me. The atrium we entered was eerily silent and empty. When we turned down a wide corridor, I saw why and wrinkled my nose at the smell of blood. Four guards lay dead around an open doorway. I glanced in as I crept past, and the dim moonlight from a small window showed it to be an empty cell.

"Cover the light," someone said, and a cloak went around the torch on the wall.

A warm hand squeezed my arm. I turned to see Jacob ease past me. He didn't meet my eyes, but if I wasn't mistaken, his touch was meant to reassure me.

Jacob, Neel, Zaph, all of them moved quickly beyond me until no one was left but me and Jashon, who now held the cloak around the torch.

"I can take care of the torch," I said. "You didn't come all this way to stand here doing nothing for your brother." I pushed him away and grasped the edges of the cloak. "Go on."

He hesitated for a moment. I realized this was a sacrifice he had agreed to make when he had agreed to let me come to the prison, but it was too much and unnecessary.

After an indecisive moment, he relinquished his hold on the cloak.

"We'll need the light when we come back through, but keep it dimmed."

I nodded and edged him farther down the hall toward the door that Tecumeni had said would lead to the main part of the prison, the yard where the men were kept during the sweltering days.

I certainly knew how to dim a torch, and standing on my toes holding a dark cloak around it was not the way.

But no sooner had I dropped the covering than two guards came from a side corridor. Their slow steps indicated they had no knowledge of what had happened here, and indeed their eyes widened when they took in the bodies of the other guards, the sticky blood that covered the floor, and me standing in the full light, reaching for the torch.

One of them said something to me, perhaps asking what had happened or why I was there or who I was, but when I couldn't answer, their eyes shot to the open cell door and confusion turned to anger. They thought I was Sarai.

As they rushed forward to put hands on me, I grabbed the torch and plunged it into the bucket of water that sat below it, sending the corridor into darkness. I dashed for the door at the end of the corridor and wrestled it open. All but tripping into the courtyard, I managed to pull the heavy door closed behind me. I dove to the side and made three quick, desperate cries as close to the little ocelot cries as I could make and then went as still as possible and tried to control my breathing.

When the guards didn't come out immediately, I imagined them tripping over the bodies of their comrades, and then I imagined they were probably finding a fresh torch to light.

If they came out here with a torch, they would see me immediately. They might see the other men moving about the yard, dispatching guards and breaking through locked cell doors in search of Gid and Ardon. Despite the four dead sentries inside, I knew the plan had been to spare lives if possible. When the guards came out here, they would alert the others, and there would be much more fighting than Jashon intended. My eyes were trying to adjust, but I couldn't find a place to hide in the dark. I tried to think quickly.

It went against every instinct I had, but I made my feet move back toward the door. I slipped my belt from around my waist and wondered futilely if I would be strong enough. The guards had to be stopped, and I had to stop them. I only hoped that when the door opened, it would be just the two of them again and not a full unit of trained fighters.

It wasn't long before the door did open and light spilled out as a torch preceded them. Just two of them. They didn't see me, and it occurred to me that I could slip back into the prison behind them without their notice. But I thought of Jashon out there in the yard, searching for Ardon, and I knew I would do what must be done.

Gripping my belt between my hands, I leapt at the man who was not holding the light. I clung like a burr to his back and pulled my belt tight around his neck. He made a noise that alerted his partner, but I pulled the stick from my hair and twisted it into the belt to wrench it tighter around the guard's neck.

He stumbled backward and fell to his knees, but he was still struggling. I twisted the stick again and prayed he would pass out.

The other guard had his sword out with the tip toward me, but he still held the torch. He eased toward me and said something I did not understand.

"Stay back!" I commanded him, but of course he did not understand me either.

We faced each other for long, charged moments until the guard I held slumped to the earth. Instantly, while his eyes were still on the fallen man, I let go of the stick and belt, scrambled up, and snatched the torch from the surprised guard's hand, twirling toward him and preparing to fight. He lunged at me, but I swung the fire toward him, and he jumped back.

"I don't want to, but I'll do it," I said to him, trying to keep my voice calm and low. "All I want is my son."

He lifted his sword as if he would advance on me, and I jabbed at him again with the fire. Surely one swipe of his sword would cut the torch in half, but the fire was still a threat.

The man on the ground was starting to rouse. He moaned and tried to make it up to his elbows. Curses! I hadn't been able to hold the belt tight enough or long enough.

But suddenly, the man was down again and Jashon was flying toward us with his own sword raised. The fight was short-lived as the guard had barely turned from me when Jashon got a hit to his dominant arm. To his credit, he didn't drop his sword. He squared his stance and raised his sword again to fight while his free hand rose to cover the wound. But Jashon used the man's weakness to his advantage and soon had the sword flipped away.

Spitting curses, the man fell to his knees for mercy, and Jashon let him have it with a quick blow to his head that knocked him out but did not kill him.

He looked at me, breaths coming fast, and said, "Time to go."

"But...Ardon..."

"Not yet, but they will be right behind us."

I looked over my shoulder into the dark yard where I could see dark shadows moving carefully about.

I looked back to Jashon, trusted the surety in his eyes, and I followed him back through the door into the prison.

He took the torch from me and set it in the sconce on the wall.

"I can dim it," I said as he stepped over a body toward the atrium.

"There's no one to see it now."

So that was where his confidence came from. There was no one to stop them from finding Ardon and Gid.

"Alright," I said and followed him past the grisly scene.

I quickly explained what had happened, how the guards had walked in on me, how I had bolted out the door, how I had half choked the first guard and held off the second. "But, the first guard was coming to. Did you knock him out again?"

"No. It was one of the men with a sling. You were pretty lit up there. The moment the light came through the door, our eyes were fixed on it."

"You saw what happened?"

He paused just inside the door that led to the street.

"You are a warrior any boy would be proud to have as a mother, and a women any man would be proud to have as a wife."

I barely had time to love the look in his eyes before he opened the door, peered out, searched the street, and left the prison, pulling me behind by the hand.

Staying in the shadows near the side of the road, he led me back toward the city gates. I hated to leave without Ardon, but the firm grasp of Jashon's hand gave me strength, and I knew he would not lead me away unless he was sure that Ardon would follow.

In this situation, I had to accept that I alone could not save my son. I had to accept that he was the Lord's son first, and he had prepared men to save him and equipped them with the skill and experience to do so. He had sent them to me in the wilderness.

I held on tight to the hand of my betrothed husband, and determined to be grateful and not disappointed. I would see my boy again when the time was right.

The city gates were just as we had left them, but Zeke was standing in the shadows to the side. It startled me when he spoke to us.

"Where is Sarai?"

"She should have passed already," Jashon said. "Didn't you see her?"

Zeke stepped forward. "No, but we've had a bit of a problem keeping the guards quiet." He gestured over his shoulder.

"She was gone from the prison cell when we went into

the prison," I said, hoping to offer some news that would ease his worry for his sister.

Zeke gave a nod, but paced and ran a hand through his hair.

"It looked as though Lamech had some trouble with his guards. They had to kill four. And Salome had some trouble as well."

Zeke blew out a breath. "It seems nothing has gone easily tonight." He paused. "Almost as if they were expecting us."

"No!" I blurted out. "The guards who came upon me were completely surprised. I could see it on their faces."

"Maybe they were just surprised to see four dead men on the floor," Jashon said.

I smiled at his sarcasm. It wasn't like him.

"Get going," Zeke said. "We'll follow when we've seen everyone safely out."

It wasn't long before we were in the forest again. We walked in silence. My heart was beating wildly and I felt the warmth in my face at the thought of Ardon being free to return home with me. Would I see him before the night was over?

Nothing seems to be going easily tonight.

I remembered Zeke's words, and I tried not to get my hopes up. As long as he was free, tomorrow would be soon enough to see my boy.

"I'll leave you with Muloki," Jashon said. "But I feel I should go back."

"Is something wrong?" Did he know something he was not telling me?

"No. Just a feeling. I just want to see it done." He

paused. "We might not meet up again before morning."

I had been feeling that possibility, too. "Alright."

"If Muloki says it's time to leave, go with him and know I will see your son safely to you."

Jashon only talked to Muloki for a few moments before he disappeared again into the darkness. I glanced at the moon. It was still several hours until the sun would rise.

27

Sarai

It was dark when I awoke to a scraping noise outside my cell. I heard muffled voices, but I couldn't make out what they said.

There was little light coming through the small window. I craned to see the position of the moon. I had slept the entire afternoon, evening, and half of the night. I had not taken time to make any preparations!

But even as I berated myself, I realized that the best way I could have spent my time was sleeping. There would be a long night ahead, and there was no telling what would fill it.

The voices were closer and I strained to hear them.

"Samuel said the wait for justice would be a year, and I have already grown impatient. I believe I will take my vengeance out of her now."

Tecumeni. And I thought my lies had been ugly. But I shut my eyes and said a quick prayer of gratitude that that sweet boy even knew how to sound crass.

The men were laughing. Tecumeni's words were slurred, almost as if he were inebriated.

"I've brought a friend," he laughed. "Double the vengeance."

I sat up. Who had he brought with him? Not Zaaron. The man who had been with him when he had found me and bound my wrists? His brother—the one who had been standing at the edge of the village ready to stone me? The idea did not bring me comfort.

There was a moment of silence, then a small scuffle, a muted thud, and then the sound of the bar being moved from my door. I shielded my eyes from the light of the torch as Tecumeni held it in the doorway. But it wasn't Tecumeni that stepped into the tiny room and looked eagerly around.

"Lamech!"

I was up and in his arms in an instant. When he held me against his chest, so firmly against his heart, I knew that whatever else the night brought, it could not hurt me. He would not allow it to. I held him so tight, and I felt every emotion he had in the tightness of his hold on me. It was powerful, but brief.

His words were curt. "Get your things. We have to move."

I quickly grabbed for my satchel where it lay on the floor, felt for my knife, assuring myself it was around my neck, and followed him out the door.

"Avert your eyes to the left wall and keep them there until we are outside of the prison," Lamech instructed. He took my hand and ran toward the entrance of the building.

I kept my eyes averted, but I couldn't escape the smell of blood, lots of it, as we ran past the dead guards.

When we were outside the heavy door, Tecumeni closed it as quietly as possible, extinguishing all the light that had been inside, and we were in utter darkness. Lamech pulled me back against the wall, probably where the guard had pushed Kenai earlier that day. We waited. I wasn't sure what we were waiting for until I heard it. The owl. It was another one of my brothers' signals, one they used when the margay was compromised, and I wondered if perhaps the margay was not normally heard in this city.

"Muloki has cleared the outer entrances and the road to the gates of the city," Lamech said. "Let's go. Sarai, you just need to run. Just run into the darkness where I lead you, and go as fast as you can."

"Okay. Tecumeni?"

"I'm here. Do as your betrothed says, Sarai."

I did. I held onto Lamech with all the strength and courage I had, and I did not let go. I couldn't have because he was holding me just as tightly. I worried about Kenai and Gid and the others. I wasn't sure if Ardon was with them. I wondered how they were escaping, if they were, and where they were at. But Lamech had said only to run, and I trusted him.

Tecumeni ran behind us. I could hear his footfalls as he ran, could hear his breath when, after our long sprint, it began to come in soft gulps like mine and Lamech's.

When we neared the gates of the city, we hid in the shadow of the walls and Tecumeni sent up the call of the owl. I would not have believed it wasn't a true owl except that I stood right next to him. When we heard the return call, I felt Lamech tug my hand again.

"Can you run farther, Princess?"

My breaths were still coming heavily. "As far as I have to."

He hesitated. They both did.

"I'm okay," I insisted in a harsh whisper.

They didn't waste any more time deliberating. By tacit agreement, they both took off running again, and we all ran straight through the wide open city gates. I didn't think about how the gates came to be open or where the guards were. I wanted to look for Jashon or his men, but I could see nothing in the darkness, and soon we were in the hills. We didn't stop until we were deep in the cover and relative safety of the trees.

I bent, with my hands on my knees, to catch my breath. When I could speak, I asked, "Are we waiting for the others?"

"Kind of," Lamech said.

"What does that mean?"

"We're waiting for the signal that they are out of the city, but we will travel separately to Amulon. It will be harder to track us."

"Are you taking us clear to the border?" I asked, turning to Tecumeni.

He didn't answer for a moment, and then he only said, "Yes."

"Here's a log you can sit on," Lamech offered, exchanging a look with Tecumeni over my head. "It shouldn't take the others long, though." His voice turned apologetic. "It won't be a long rest."

The clouds moved then, letting a little more of the moon shine through. I sat on the log trying to smooth my tunic down past my knees. Lamech leaned against a tree with his arms folded and one ankle crossed over the other. Tecumeni stood guard with his back to us. Nobody said anything.

Long minutes passed before we heard the margay.

I looked to Lamech. "What does that mean?"

"Shh." He didn't say it harshly, and he and Tecumeni were so still and silent that I stayed quiet, too.

Over the next moments, we heard the margay again and the owl three times. The final call of the owl was very close, and Tecumeni slipped into the trees toward it.

Still, Lamech did not move or make a sound, but when Tecumeni came back into view, Lamech let loose with the shrill call of the margay.

He came to me and held out his hand. "I hope you've caught your breath."

I understood that we would be running. "But Gid, is he out? And the others?"

"Yes."

The beautiful word hung in the night air.

Lamech tugged on my hand. But I glanced between him and Tecumeni. "Should we not thank God?"

Tecumeni hesitated, but Lamech met my eyes and dropped to his knees.

I followed him, feeling the dirt, the bark, the rocks, and the grasses cut into my bare knees and shins. Tecumeni even came to us and went to one knee as Lamech uttered a hasty but sincere prayer of thanks.

His prayer was as brief as his embrace had been in my prison cell, but it was just as powerful. I felt the spirit of God flood the forest around us, and I knew that no man who wasn't reconciled with God could evoke it so strongly in a few uttered words. I looked up at Lamech's outline in the darkness next to me.

"Can you run?" Lamech asked as we followed Tecumeni into the wilderness once more.

"I'm not a weakling, and I can see in the dark as well as you." I was frightened and uncertain of what we were running from, and though I didn't mean it to, it sounded testy. I thought Lamech would sulk and run behind me, but he ran at my side, adjusting his pace to mine, and when I began to tire or slow, he kept the pace and encouraged me along.

We ran for a long time through the darkness. I expected to fatigue quickly because of my long journey, but the daily exertion had built my muscles and my endurance, and I was able to run swiftly away from the dangers behind me.

Tecumeni drew up several times and each time, Lamech passed me his water skin to drink from before I could reach for my own. The moon was nearly setting in the sky, but sunrise was more than an hour away. Tecumeni drew up a final time and Lamech offered me his water again, but I shook my head and refused it. He had given up enough of his for me. Instead, I drew my own water skin from my belt. I took a long drink, and seeing that he had replaced his without drinking, I offered him mine.

He had not taken these opportunities to drink for himself, but he accepted my water skin and drank, squeezing my hand when he passed it back.

I looked at him again, studying him more closely in the increasing light. What was different?

"You can stop staring at me."

I was almost sure he was joking with me. I shook my head. "It's not that." Not just staring I meant, not just a casual look at someone I hadn't seen in a while. I was looking for something that was not there.

"Then what is it?"

"It's just..." *It's just that you're so handsome.* Our eyes met but I dropped mine quickly. "It's just that you look different."

He scrubbed a hand over his jaw. "Did I forget to shave?"

I thought he intended me to laugh, but it sounded so strange coming from him, I couldn't—couldn't even pretend to. I studied my feet. "It's the scowl. It's missing."

"He still looks ugly to me," Tecumeni said, and that did make me laugh.

"As ugly as you," I shot back.

Tecumeni grinned. "Let's find a place to camp."

"You two are rather friendly," Lamech said when camp was set up and Tecumeni had gone to check our back trail.

"He has befriended me."

"I noticed."

"He is promised to someone," I said. "And their betrothal is more real than ours."

"Then why was he kissing you?"

I gasped. "You saw that?"

"Couldn't take my eyes from it."

I didn't know what to make of that. But I didn't belong to Lamech, and I didn't owe him an explanation. I found myself making one anyway.

"That was only out of kindness. I asked him to..." I licked my lips. How embarrassing it was to say it out loud. "I asked him to hold me, just for a moment, before he took me to the prison. For comfort. I was scared, Lamech. He proved my friend, and he did me a kindness." That didn't seem like a good enough explanation. How could I make him understand? "It was a kiss of apology—for having to imprison me. I didn't think I would ever see him again, not like that. It was a kiss of goodbye." I took a breath.

Lamech waited until what I had said sank deeply into my own heart.

"Are you saying," he asked slowly, "that two friends

might share a kiss that means something besides love between them?"

He didn't needed to ask. I knew who he was talking about and was embarrassed to realize he knew the whole story. Perhaps Darius hadn't been as silent about it as I thought.

"Don't get me wrong, though. I still think he's about the dumbest man alive."

I sat up straight. "And why is that?"

Our bedrolls were side by side, separated by a narrow strip of wild grass. We were sitting next to each other, facing north, with all that had happened in Jerusalem behind us now.

Lamech looked at me, and I was right—the scowl was gone. "You offered Darius your love, and he didn't take it. He had one chance, and he wasted it." He paused. "When he would have offered his apologies, you wouldn't let him mend his mistake. I mean, you ran away so he couldn't. You wouldn't even give him the opportunity. And when you sent me into the woods alone to mend my mistake, I thought that maybe, since you hadn't let Darius make things right, maybe deep down you didn't *want* them to be made right."

He dipped his head and raised a brow as if asking me if I could deny it.

I had never seen him make such an expression before. I had never seen much beyond the scowl or a mask of indifference. I didn't know how to reply.

He moved close and dipped his head next to mine. "I'm not going to waste my chance, Princess." He kissed my cheek—a breath more than a kiss—and he lay down on his bedroll, turned over, and pretended to fall asleep.

When afternoon came, I woke. Tecumeni slept near us.

I looked over at Lamech, where he lay with his back still to me. "Lamech, you've got a cut on your back," I exclaimed softly. A gash was more like it.

"I noticed," he mumbled.

I slid closer to him and when I inspected the deep wound, it looked as if he had narrowly avoided being stabbed to the heart through his back. A smaller cut near his ear had caked blood around it but was shallow. "Oh, Lamech," I breathed. "What happened?"

He hesitated a moment. "Some Lamanites," he finally said, "are difficult to sneak up on."

My eyes went to the Lamanite sleeping on the ground. Did he mean Tecumeni?

I wondered what had happened between them and when. I knew that Tecumeni did not think much of Lamech. He did not like how Lamech treated me and hated him for being a Nephite and a liar. Lamech did not tolerate weakness in other men and had no love for Lamanites.

They hated each other. Didn't they?

I was naïve in some ways, but I knew that my presence, my very existence, made their ill feeling toward each other worse.

So how had they made their peace? How had it come to be that they combined their strengths to save me?

Lamech sat up slowly and ran a hand through his hair. It was clean and thick. I wondered if he had been to the cistern too. Alone, he could have easily overtaken our larger band of travelers and beaten us to Ani-Anti. Had he been at the cistern when I was? Just how long had he been following me?

And how much had he seen?

I reached for his satchel. "Do you have a bandage?"

"Yeah," he said. He didn't make a move to find it for me, just let me rummage through his belongings until I found the stiff white cloth.

I moistened the bandage, brushed Lamech's hair back, and wiped the dried blood from his ear and neck. He didn't protest, only tilted his head so I could better see the wound. When that was done, I shifted so I could clean the wound on his back. Fingering lightly around the edges, I could see the wound was deeper on one side and as long as my palm. The bleeding had mostly clotted and stopped, but it still seeped fresh blood in places.

"Lie on your side so I can pour water over it."

He made no comment and did as I asked, though I thought I detected a stiffness in his movements. He would never say, but it was hurting him a great deal. When he had eased onto his side, with his head propped on his hand, I began to clean the wound.

I gave him the bad news. "It needs to be closed with stiches."

"Do it."

I retrieved my needle and looked at Lamech, who waited patiently for my needle to pierce his skin. "May I have some strands of your hair?" I asked him. "That's what Leah would use."

"Yes."

"I'd use my own, but my hair is tied back in a knot."

"I said yes, Sarai."

He didn't move to pull them for me, so after I knelt there for a moment staring at his hair, I put my fingers into it. Isolating several strands, I pulled them out, then I smoothed his hair back down, sliding my fingers through it to sooth the place where I had pulled the hair. It was only a small pain, but the stitches would help heel up the larger wound, and both the pain and the stitches were essential if he wanted the wound to heal properly.

When everything was ready and it was time to put the sharp end of the needle into his wound, I stilled with my hand hovering over it.

"There is no other person—"

"I know. I know it has to be me."

He turned his head toward me a little. "No, Sarai, I meant I would rather have you do it than any other person. I know your stitches will be quick and sure." When I hesitated a moment longer, he said, "I watched you walk into that prison, Princess. You can do this."

"I don't want to hurt you."

"It already hurts. And besides, it won't hurt more than what I did to you."

"Don't beat yourself up over that."

"Just sew the wound closed."

I bit my lip, making my own wound sting, and I sewed Lamech's wound closed.

"I don't have any more bandages," I said when I was finished.

The stitching pulled but held when Lamech sat up. "It's best to leave wounds like this uncovered."

"Oh." I didn't know if that was true, but I figured he would know better than I would. He had probably seen thousands of wounds like this—perhaps even had some himself. "Should I put Leah's salve on?"

"Yes. That would be perfect."

Sifting through the items in Lamech's satchel again, I

found the little jar of medicine and smoothed some of the opaque cream over both of Lamech's wounds and dabbed a little onto my own.

"When Tec wakes, we'll—"

"Tec?" I interrupted. "I can see I am not the only one he has befriended." But that was obvious in the simple fact that the two men were traveling together. At first, I had thought they tolerated each other only for my benefit, but I was starting to sense now that it was more than that.

Lamech glanced at the sleeping Lamanite and only offered a shrug. "When he wakes, we will have to leave."

"Shouldn't we wake him now?"

"No. He has had too many sleepless nights."

Lamech did not have tolerance for weakness in other men, and he never showed compassion—though I knew he possessed both. I looked between the two of them, wondering just what had happened between them.

"Do you have any food?" I asked.

"No, but Tec does."

I wrinkled my nose. "I'm not going to steal his food." But I looked at his satchel on the ground next to him. I knew he wouldn't mind. He would be offended if I didn't help myself to his food. He wouldn't want me to be hungry. Hadn't he proved that in the hours before he'd taken me to the prison, generously giving me the nuts and the fruits, knowing I would need them? "What would I do? Just rummage around in his satchel?"

Lamech shook his head and laughed. I was humoring him, which was...different. He stood. "I'll go get something. Sit tight."

Sit tight?

"Alright," I said, frowning after him.

I'll go get something. I guessed Lamech was used to eating from the forest. But I wasn't helpless.

I looked around me. Tecumeni had found us a secluded place to camp, protected on all sides by thick trees or stone. The path that Lamech took out of the little clearing was invisible, and I knew I wouldn't be able to follow him.

I easily found some chay leaves—they were everywhere—and I almost laughed when I found the tops of the wild sweet potato.

It didn't take long for Lamech to return with a rabbit. I knew he could track and kill anything in this forest, but a rabbit was perfect for the three of us.

He smiled when he saw what I was preparing. I had seen him smile more in this one morning than I had in all the time I had known him. I liked it, but it was unsettling.

I set some food aside for Tecumeni and when I had satisfied myself that he would be well-fed before we continued our journey, I took out my needle and pulled a thread from my quickly fraying tunic and began to put a hem in it.

I felt Lamech's eyes on me, but I ignored them. I let him watch me for a while, bent over my work, before I glanced up.

"What are you doing?" he asked as if he'd just been waiting to be acknowledged.

He could clearly see that I was hemming my clothing. It was almost as if he didn't know what to say when he wasn't saying something mean.

I have a difficult time talking to girls I like.

His words came back to me, and the idea of it was endearing, but I tried not to make too much of it. This was Lamech after all, and his scathing tone would return.

"I'm wondering how to reach the back of my tunic."

"Why don't you change into another?"

"I haven't got another. My pack is back in Ani-Anti."

He gave me a strange look and pointed to my pack resting next to Tecumeni's. "Didn't you notice you were sleeping on your own bedroll?"

It was no wonder he didn't think I was very smart. "I was so tired..." I started to say.

But he just chuckled and waved it off. "Tec had your tent down and your pack readied the moment you left for the stream yesterday morning. I carried it to Jerusalem. I put your bedroll and tent on my pack and Tecumeni carried the rest when we escaped the prison."

"But Lamech! You carried the extra weight of my things even with that large wound?" And I knew he had gone as slow as he dared for me besides.

"I am at least one hundred times stronger than you, Princess."

I burst into laughter. He was teasing me, and even coming from Lamech—especially coming from Lamech—it was funny.

My laughter woke Tecumni. He opened his eyes, but when he saw us, laughing together, he closed them again and pretended to remain asleep.

Lamech tried to hide his smile, but he was pleased to have made me laugh.

I went to my pack and retrieved another sarong. "I'll go change over there," I told Lamech.

"I like the short one," Tecumeni said. When I glanced at him his eyes were still closed.

"Never thought I would agree with a Lamanite," said

Lamech, his voice light, but he gave Tecumeni the first fierce look I had seen on his face since the night he had kissed me in my tent.

I looked between them. They were handsome, young, strong, capable, and natural enemies.

"That is why I have to change it," I told them and turned and went alone into the trees.

28

Muloki, Eliza, and Isabel plied me for information, and I told them all I knew—about the gates, the dead guards, my altercation in the prison yard.

"Are you hurt?" Eliza asked.

"Not at all," I realized.

Suddenly, from out of the night, we heard a call.

"They're out," Muloki said. But before we could utter relief, he said, "Come on. We have to make tracks. I don't know how long before they will send men after us."

"After us? Do you think they will?" Isabel asked him.

"With four dead guards? Almost certainly."

"Are all the men out?"

"That call of the margay was to be the sign that it was completed successfully."

"Where is Sarai?"

"Probably not far from here. She's with Lamech and Tecumeni. She's safe."

I didn't think he could be sure of that, but he spoke confidently in his heavy accent.

When dawn arrived, we rested, but Muloki kept us moving north, doing what he could to minimize signs that we had passed—walking on stone when we could or through streams and small rivers. We moved with a sense of urgency.

Finally, Isabel asked the question I had been dying to

ask. "Shouldn't we stop and wait for the others?"

Muloki drew a battered forearm across his brow. "It's because we haven't seen anyone that makes me think we have to hurry."

Did he think something had happened? Or was he just taking precaution?

"I'd be killed three times by three distraught and angry husbands if I stopped and let danger find you."

"But what about our husbands? Where are they? Are they safe?" Isabel persisted.

Muloki was silent a moment. "Izz, you knew the risks when you came."

That subdued any lighthearted hope he had tried to give us, but in my heart, I thanked him for his honesty, even if it was not straightforward.

By the second evening, we had returned to Keturah and the others.

She noticed immediately that Gideon was not with us. "Is it done, then?" she asked Muloki as she hugged him and then moved on to Isabel, Eliza, and even me.

"We stayed back on the night of the rescue, were the first to leave. We haven't heard from anyone yet."

Keturah bit her lip.

The men had gathered around her, and Muloki told them all he knew of Tecumeni and his plan and all Jashon and I had told them of the prison in Jerusalem.

It wasn't until the next day that I felt another presence in the woods. *It could as easily be our men as the enemy. It could as easily be Ardon and Jashon as anyone else.* I wasn't even sure what I felt. I just felt...something.

"I think we'd better head back." Keturah was looking

into every dense patch of vegetation and frowning. A sheen of sweat covered her brow.

"Are the pains returning?" If they were, I would need to get her back to her bedroll.

"No. Nothing like that. It's just that something doesn't feel right."

I took a good look at her. "Yes, I think you are carrying the baby lower."

She gave a small laugh. "I meant in the forest. We need to get back to the men."

"I feel it, too."

We moved quickly through the forest, but Keturah kept the pace from becoming frantic. When we were back in camp, she signaled the man on the hill.

"He hasn't seen anything," she said, but the worry was still in her eyes.

Ethanim and Muloki hadn't returned from patrolling our perimeter, but Joshua sent Corban and Mathoni to scout for danger and he stayed with us himself.

"It doesn't seem fair that you should have to protect all six of us on your own," I said.

Joshua had seen to the care of all his weapons, helped haul water and prepared food for travel, walked Keturah into the woods several times, and he was now reclined against a log looking very little like a vigilant guard.

"Just because you cannot see the others does not mean they are not protecting you," he said.

"They are trained to do this," Keturah added. "They are trained to find trails left by others, to stalk, to hunt, to defend and protect. And that is why the unease I feel grows. They are not noticing the danger I feel."

I looked around the clearing. The breeze rustled the leaves in the trees and the clouds floated overhead, but nothing else moved. Keturah hadn't had any pains since the men had said the prayer over her. Everyone else was bored and restless and ready to leave at a moment's notice.

"I want to go up on the hill," I said, gazing in that direction. I bent down to retrieve Keturah's bow and quiver of arrows. "How long will it take me to get there?"

Joshua didn't move, but he became instantly aware. I thought he might tell me I couldn't go, but he didn't. "About twenty minutes. Walk directly southeast. Can you do that?"

"I think I can manage."

"Sound the margay before you get to the top. Otherwise you might find an arrow in your gut."

I was pretty sure I would get a warning shot first—maybe just an arrow in my foot or a tree next to my head.

"The call that sounds like an ocelot?"

"Same sound. Can you do it?"

"I'd do better with the owl."

"In the day?"

I just smiled as I took some of the rabbit Eve and Melia had cooked, and I walked out of camp. I was getting anxious to see Ardon. What if something had happened to him? What if Jashon was not able to bring him back? It was not doing my nerves any good to stare at the same things and think the same thoughts. I was restless and I had to move.

When I had hiked to the top of the hill, I got it. I could see why the men had someone stationed up here at all times. I could see everything in every direction.

I made a pretty good owl call, and I heard a low chuckle.

"Margay in the daytime, honey."

"Don't call me honey. Where are you?"

Reb appeared. "You're just in time." He tilted his head, inviting me to follow him. He led me through a thicket of brush and over a small brook, and from where he had made his small camp, I could see our larger camp down below and the terrain all around us.

"Look there," he said, and pointed to the southwest.

"That's them," I breathed. I handed him the food I had brought. "Why are they coming from that direction? How long have they been in sight?"

"About ten minutes."

I tried to count the people, but their distance from us and their movement through the vegetation made it difficult. "Are Gideon and Ardon with them?"

"Can't tell."

"So helpful," I said, but the hope in my heart was beginning to push away the worry and exhaustion I had felt for the past month.

We watched for another few moments in silence. "I'm glad I ran into you and your friends." Of course I knew Jacob would have found Ardon. But when I returned home, I would return with not only Ardon, but with my knowledge of the gospel of Jesus Christ, the influence of the Holy Ghost, and Jashon, a man who I thought could actually love me and see me for the person I was.

"When will they get here?" I asked Reb.

"By the time you get back to camp."

"Have they seen us? Do they know where the camp is? Will they recognize it?"

"Even if they didn't, I have signaled them already, and

Corban is leading them in."

Reb was small of stature and the top of his dark head only came up to my chin, but when I left the little camp in which he had been alone for so many days—save the occasional relief guards Joshua sent to allow him to sleep—I cast a look back at him and saw the soul of the spiritual giant that his short, stocky body disguised.

My heart was light and hopeful as I hurried back through the forest toward the larger camp until I heard movement from within a thicket of berry bushes. I stopped immediately and listened closely to discern the origin of the sound and the nature of its maker. My heart began to beat wildly when I heard the sound again. As quietly as I could, I ducked behind a nearby tree. The trees were slimmer here than in the lands near Zarahemla, and despite their pretty white bark, they provided less cover. I stood very still so my movement would not give away my position.

When I dared to peer around the tree, I saw it was only a deer. I almost walked on, but I turned back, drew the bow off my shoulder, positioned an arrow, and shot the deer. Then I hurried back to camp.

Reb had been right. Corban was just leading the men in through a small break in the trees.

My heart clutched inside me, and my breath caught as my eyes searched for Ardon.

He wasn't there.

The next man I searched for was Jashon. I vaguely noted Keturah running into the arms of a man next to him, but once my eyes met Jashon's, they held.

I hoped he didn't see contempt and accusation in my eyes, but I knew he saw confusion. He cast a quick glance at

Keturah and the man in her arms, a man who could only have been his brother, and then he came immediately to me. He took both of my hands in his and he didn't waste words.

"He is safe. He is with Jacob."

"Oh." It was all I could say. That and, "I killed a deer."

A broad grin spread over his face, and he did nothing but smile into my eyes until I smiled too.

"Come here and meet Gid."

Gideon was still kissing his wife when we approached them. All the other men were trying to avert their attention. I too wanted to step away and give them their privacy, but Jashon cleared his throat and waited for Gideon to give his wife one last soft kiss, look into her eyes, and then turn to us.

He didn't wait for an introduction. "Is this her?"

"Gideon! Be polite!" Keturah laughed through her tears.

"This is Salome." Jashon turned to me. "Salome, my brother Gid."

Gideon placed his hand on my shoulder and smiled. He did not smile as broadly as his brother, and his eyes bore a weariness that made me fear for Ardon. But he was pleasant enough, felt well enough to tease, had clear love for his wife, and he carried with him the spirit I had felt around all the other men. I liked him.

"We finally meet," I said.

In the moment our eyes met and held, I could see he remembered the first time they had met, that instant in the wheat field before he had told Ardon not to indicate where I was hiding—that instant I had looked out from the shade of a tree and silently begged him to take care of my son.

"Your son talks about you non-stop."

"I doubt that," I said, smiling, knowing it was not true

and loving the idea of it anyway. "Is he okay? Was he harmed?"

"He is fine. I kept him with me."

I didn't want to ask if the guards had tried to take him away or how Gideon had managed to keep my son safe. I only wanted to picture my son under the watch of this strong, brave warrior.

Gideon still had one arm around Keturah, but he tucked the thumb of his other hand into the belt at his waist. "And I hear he is to be my nephew."

Jashon was glaring at his brother. Was he still thinking I wanted out of the betrothal?

"He is," I said firmly. "And if you don't get Keturah off her feet, I am to have a nephew as well."

His eyes widened slightly as he turned to his wife, who just shrugged it off. "Mahonri gave me a blessing," she told him. "I had pains, but they have subsided."

"Come on then, let's go sit," Gideon coaxed and began to pull her toward the cook fire, which reminded me about the deer.

I brushed Jashon's hand, or I intended to, but he reached out and clasped my hand with his. "Will you help me bring the deer in?" I asked him. "I couldn't carry it."

I led Jashon up onto the hill and directly to the deer I had left there. He went to his heels and briefly touched its head. Then he fingered the arrow, wrapped his hand around it, and gave it a sudden, hard jerk.

"Beautiful shot," he said as he handed me the arrow.

Then almost gently, he picked up the deer and slung it across his shoulders. He stood and motioned me to precede him out of the thicket.

But when I did, he reached out a hand to my shoulder, stopping me. "Salome."

"Yes?"

His dark eyes filled with intensity. "Thanks."

I glanced at the deer's satiny ears. "We are low on food, and I thought you would all be hungry when you arrived. The deer was in my path and—"

He chuckled. "No, I meant...for everything."

I shrugged. "We'll just call it even," I said, thinking of all he had done to get Ardon out of that prison.

"No, Salome." He gave his head a small shake. "It is not a trade."

I bit my lip and searched his eyes for a long moment. I knew what he was saying. He didn't want me to feel that I owed him anything, specifically not a lifetime of matrimony. I didn't. And I didn't want him to feel that the only reason I married him was because of what he had done for Ardon.

"A partnership, then," I said, and I went up on my toes to kiss him so he would not have to bend with the weight of the deer on his shoulders.

But even with the extra weight, he met me halfway.

"I don't ever want you to think this, between us, is about Ardon," he said against my lips.

"I don't want you to think it either," I said and could not resist the urge to kiss him again. "It's like Keturah said." I instantly felt foolish for mentioning her in that moment, but I quickly went on. "I think I knew in the first moment I saw you that we would be more than acquaintances. A part of me did."

"Keturah said that?"

I stepped back. "About Gideon."

A teasing grin spread over his face. "The first time you

saw me, you thought I was Gid."

I tried to hide a smile as I remembered rushing to him and cradling his face in my hand.

"You know, his wife is the only one who still calls him Gideon."

"His wife and his sister," I corrected.

He grinned again—genuine, true, full-blown happiness—as we started again for camp.

"I think he will like having a sister," Jashon laughed.

"And Lamech? Will he like it?"

Jashon thought for a moment. "He will benefit from it."

I thought of the things Lamech had taught me—about weapons and hunting, about my careless behavior toward Enos—and I wondered if he would be the one who benefitted from our new relationship.

"When will we see Ardon?" I asked after a time.

"Tomorrow afternoon when we get to the caves outside Amulon. He's only about a mile to the east."

"A mile too far away," I said wistfully. "Did you get the chance to meet him?"

He was quiet again for a moment, and I wondered what he was thinking about. He adjusted the deer on his shoulders before he said, "I spent a long time talking to him. He reminds me so much of Gid when he was young—he even looks like him—when he was just my little brother, before we ever tracked that band of Lamanites, before we ever went to war." I looked up at him, studied his regret-filled expression. "Well," he added, shrugging his memories away. "I hope this experience hasn't changed him."

"So do I." I thought of Ardon's face and his hair, the color of budding mahogany blooms. I thought of the way he held his shoulders and the way he walked. I thought of his ever-ready smile and his easy acceptance of the role he must take as a leader. "He doesn't look like Gid," I told Jashon. "He looks like you."

He looked at his sandals. "Salome," he said. "Would you like having more children?"

"Of course," I replied. "Though none of them could rule."

He laughed. "We will leave that to Ardon."

"I had put it out of my mind, but I like children." Then a thought occurred to me. "Do you like children, Jashon?"

I thought he might have shrugged under the deer. "I've never been around them much."

"Well, there will be Gideon's child soon, and Ardon. You will get some experience."

"I'm going to leave the raising of Gid's child to Gid."

He didn't say any more, but I knew what he was thinking. He couldn't spend time with Keturah and her child.

"Well, perhaps for a while." His hands were both holding onto the legs of the animal, so I slipped my fingers into the belt at his waist—just so we would have a connection, so he would not feel he was alone in this. "But don't shun your family because the feelings are difficult to deal with. I intend for them to share in our happy times. We should share in theirs." When he didn't respond, I changed the subject. "Raising Ardon will be much easier now. His grandfather will respect your opinion much more than mine—even if they are the same."

Jashon grimaced. "I wish it wasn't like that. But I know for many men, it is. Your father-in-law is not unusual in his beliefs."

"No," I agreed. "You and your kinsmen are the unusual ones."

We were preparing the deer for cooking when I noticed a flash of light on the hill. I couldn't interpret the signals, so I nudged Keturah and pointed in the direction of the hill. "Keturah, what does that signal mean?"

She instantly dropped what she was doing. I stared at the deer flesh in the dirt at our feet, but she was moving into the open to get a better view of the flash.

"An attack!" Her voice was toned low, but it had the effect of a scream.

All the men's heads snapped up to read the signal.

"A possible attack," she went on, still watching the signal. "Hostile Lamanites. Weapons bared."

"Signal him back, Ket. Tell him to get down here." Gideon sounded surprisingly calm, but when Keturah had sent the signal with her black obsidian blade, Gideon said, "And get out of the middle of the clearing."

She came back to me. Eve and Melia joined us and Keturah urged us behind the trees at the side of the camp. "They're coming in from the south," she said softly. "Load the bow."

"Who do I shoot?" *And when, and how could I?*

"You'll know your target when you see him."

I shuddered at the coldness of the comment.

The men had their weapons at the ready. Some of them took off through the trees to the east and the west.

"They're going to try to surround the enemy," Keturah narrated for the rest of us. "They have about the same number of men as we have, and they are coming in quickly on a direct path."

"You could tell all that from the signal?"

"Yes."

Jashon, Muloki, Jarom, and Gideon stood in front of us, and the others flanked us. We waited long, tense moments to see what would happen. I hoped the men who had snuck into the trees could subdue an attack before it ever reached us.

"Do you think it is the guards from the prison?"

"No. Not professional soldiers anyway. More likely a family group."

"I have got to learn to read those signals," I said.

"Me too," said Melia.

"What is the point in having a lookout if he can't tell us what he sees?" Keturah's eyes were on the clearing and she spoke distractedly. I would rather have had her attention on the clearing, so I stopped making off-handed remarks and just waited.

And I did not have to wait long.

I heard the soft whir of an arrow, and one of our men went down.

29

Sarai

Lamech and Tecumeni were ready to leave when I came back to the camp.

"I thought we would wait for the cover of night," I said, but I let Lamech help me into my travel pack.

"No. We have to keep moving. The others will worry if we do not make it to the caves by the designated time."

"The others, are they okay?"

"The only thing I know is they are out of the city." He saw the disappointment on my face. "But yes, they are probably okay."

I had never heard Lamech say anything to placate or reassure—it was not really his way.

"Jashon had to leave Keturah with the men of her unit. He feared the baby was coming too early and hoped that with rest, she could prolong its time in the womb." He spoke of the baby neutrally, as if it were not a child that shared his blood. I wondered if he would be so indifferent when he held the baby, his little nephew, in his arms.

"Who got Gideon out of the prison?" I asked.

"Gid got Gid out of the prison. I told you he wasn't waiting on us."

"But who made the way clear? Who opened the city gates?"

"Jashon and his men went into the prison. Salome's

kinsmen showed up too. I think they followed her. Our men cleared the city streets, and Tec's men cleared the gate."

Tec's men. I looked around at Tecumeni, who just gave me half a smile and a small shrug.

I nodded. There were a lot more details I wanted, but I stayed quiet and tried to keep up as we moved swiftly through the terrain.

Tecumeni and Lamech took turns checking ahead and behind me as I traveled. I knew the care they were taking was not only for me, but I felt guilt for the extra work they were doing. I wasn't even carrying the full weight of my own pack, as Tecumeni carried my tent and Lamech my bedroll.

Tecumeni knew the area well and easily led us through it until darkness fell.

We had a small fire to cook some fish Tecumeni caught, but when he said he thought someone was on our back trail, we put it out and sat up talking in low tones.

"If there is someone trailing us," Tecumeni said into the darkness, "he is very good at it. He is hiding his tracks well. It's more of a feeling I have than anything I have seen or heard."

"I've felt it too," Lamech said. "But I can't find the proof."

I wished they hadn't told me of the mysterious traveler behind us. I appreciated their honesty, but I couldn't sleep for thinking of it. Lamech must have sensed my fear because I felt him pull the leather tie from my hair and stroke it back behind me. The sensation was calming. I thought I should probably protest, but I couldn't. Instead, I closed my eyes and fell asleep.

The next morning, I made corn cakes from the remaining corn flour Lamech had in his pack.

"It's a good thing we will pass through Amulon again. We need food," he said.

"I've never eaten these before," said Tecumeni as he reached for another one. I swatted his hand away from the cooking stone, but he didn't let that deter him.

I caught Lamech's eye for a moment. I knew he was watching Tecumeni tease me—and more importantly, me teasing Tecumeni back—but he didn't make any comment about it. Instead, he offered to fill my water skin. I gave it to him, and he strode out of camp.

As I cleaned up the morning meal and put out the fire, I watched Tecumeni take down my tent and secure it to his pack. I wondered why he was doing this for us—taking us to the border. Perhaps he merely wanted to assure himself and the Order that we were gone. Perhaps he cared about my safety. But he had been the one to place me in the prison. Why did he help rescue me from it, and why did he care so much about my safety? Because it certainly wasn't Lamech's safety he was concerned about.

I knew he felt affection for me. I felt it for him too. He was as easy to love as Lamech was difficult. He was open, friendly, and thoughtful. He was perceptive, and he acted with honor and integrity.

There was the possibility that he was leading us into a trap, but I thought of all that had happened since we had met him, and I knew it would have to be one elaborate trap.

I almost asked him why he was helping us, but he spoke first. "If we make good time, we will be to the gates of Amulon by the time the sun reaches there." He pointed to a spot in the sky just past the midpoint.

We were moving at least twice as fast as we had

coming south, and I knew if the men were pushing me that fast, it was because the danger was great.

"But Amulon is not really a place we can rest."

He grinned. "I can. And your Lamanite is pretty good. It gets better as you use it." We had been speaking in Nephite so Lamech could understand, but he switched to Lamanite. "Your husband's, on the other hand, has gotten much, much worse."

I had tried to explain to Tecumeni why Lamech could no longer speak his language, but I laughed and addressed his other point.

"You know Lamech is not my husband."

"But you wish him to be."

I stared at Tecumeni for a long time. I didn't know why he had kissed me that first time nor what I had done so wrong that made him dislike it. I didn't want to hurt him, but I had lied so much to him, and been so sick over it, that I knew I could only give him the truth now.

"Tecumeni, yes. That is where my heart lies. I don't know why."

He considered me, as if assuring himself that I indeed meant what I said, and I wondered if perhaps I was not using the language correctly. "He's lucky," he said earnestly.

It was hard for me to just accept a compliment like that, but it would be impolite to refute it, to deny it, especially when I knew he truly meant it.

So I just replied with a simple, "Thank you."

We heard the margay just seconds before Lamech walked into camp.

I had determined that I would leave Lamech be. Even though he was acting different, and I could see that his heart was lighter, I hadn't come on this journey to form a relationship, and neither had he. So when he came into camp, I kept my eyes on my work as if I didn't notice him.

"Tec!"

A woman?

I looked over my shoulder to see Lamech escorting a defiant looking girl into camp.

"Ava!" Tecumeni's voice cut through the little clearing. Was it surprise or reprimand in his voice?

Ava's darted around, and she threw her chin in the air. "I tracked you. Tec, what's going on? Why are you here? What are you doing with *her*?"

Her impatient voice was only accentuated when Lamech said wryly, "Tec, your girl is...nice."

Ava turned and stared at Lamech. Then she turned to me and demanded, "What did he say?"

"He thinks you are promised to Tecumeni."

Her lip curling, she looked at her brother. Tecumeni and I both laughed, and when I glanced his way, Lamech was looking at Ava and smiling too. I didn't like the way he was looking at her.

Lamech may look at whoever he wants, I reminded myself.

"Tell him I'm not."

"Don't bother, Sarai. She's going home right now."

"No I'm not. Not until you tell me what you're doing."

"Ava."

She looked around at us. "I'm coming with you."

"No you're not," her brother said.

She folded her arms, hitched a hip, and glowered.

"Would you like something to eat?" I asked her.

She didn't respond, but I could tell she was hungry.

I retrieved the last two corn cakes and passed them to Tecumeni. I did not think she would take them from me in the mood she was in. She obviously knew who I really was. "She will be more agreeable after she eats."

When Tecumeni had pulled her a short distance away, he gave her the corn cakes. She turned her back to me so I wouldn't see her eating them.

"His sister?" Lamech asked.

"Yes. They are twins."

He rubbed his arm. "She's not very nice."

"She was excellent to me before she found out I was a Nephite, a liar, and a traitor—before we killed her uncle. The two of them are close."

"Zaaron didn't die," Lamech said absently as his eyes assessed her, everything about her, while she argued with her brother.

They weren't so far away that we couldn't hear the argument.

"Why did you follow me? Mother needs you, Ava. She'll be worried sick that you haven't come home."

"She will be worried over you, too!"

"No." Tecumeni shook his head. "She knows I am about the Order's business."

My worried eyes shot to Lamech, but he just shook his head slightly, indicating he did not understand what they said, so I told him. He shook his head again, this time to indicate I should not make anything of the comment.

So I didn't. I stayed silent and listened to Tecumeni try to send his sister home. I was saddened that Lamech had not regained enough of the Spirit to understand the foreign language again, but I smiled when I thought that perhaps he did not understand because he no longer needed to.

Finally, Tecumeni strapped his pack onto his back and then came to me and lifted mine up, holding it for me to put on while he spoke to Ava. "I'm not coming back. Stop following me."

All four of us stood in silence, the impact of what Tecumeni said falling heavy around us, until the sudden call of the margay preceded the sounds of people coming through the brush. In a moment, Kenai, Isabel and Eliam walked into the clearing. The three of them looked at the four of us. Isabel grinned when she saw me. Eliam moved toward Lamech, and Kenai stood where he was and raised a brow.

"Morning all," he said.

I rushed to Isabel and we embraced the best we could with the large packs on. "I'm so glad you are safe," I told her.

"Me? You are the one who walked into the prison at Jerusalem of your own free will! I will never forgive you the worry it caused me."

"Did you have so little faith in the men to get me out?"

"Yes!"

"More Nephites! Tec, what is happening?"

We all turned at the anger in Ava's voice. Confusion warred with suspicion in her expression. He was her twin, and they were similar in height. She was not a short woman, but she looked almost like a child as confusion won out.

"Ava." He sighed in resignation and glanced at the sky to determine the position of the sun. "Walk with me. I can see you will not turn around until I explain."

He exchanged a brief conversation with Lamech and then escorted his sister out of camp ahead of us. I didn't waste time, just followed after them, leaving a distance to give them privacy to talk. We would travel as the crow flew, avoiding the many Lamanite cities we had passed on the way south, and be to Amulon by the midday meal if we hurried. I didn't know if dealing with Ava would delay us, but I did not want to be the cause of any delay.

After a while, I turned a little and asked Kenai, "Where are the others? Are they close by?"

"Zeke, Eliza, and Enos are the closest. They are east of us, traveling north. They will turn toward Amulon in another hour or two. The rest of the men are traveling in pairs, surrounding us on all sides."

"Why did you and Izz come to us? Lamech said we were less likely to be tracked if we stayed in small groupings."

"Izz wanted to see with her own eyes that you were safe."

"Why would Izz care?"

I knew it was a ridiculous question.

Kenai knew it too, and it seemed to confuse him. "You are her sister. She loves you." He paused and touched me at the elbow, waited until I looked at him. "Weren't you worried for her?"

The truth was I had given very little thought to anyone besides myself and my own concerns.

I glowered at Isabel over my shoulder. She was talking animatedly to Lamech, and as I watched, she playfully hit his still bare chest and laughed at something he said.

"Her easy friendship with him," Kenai said in a tone he had lowered considerably. "That is all it is, you know. She is friendly. It cannot be changed, nor would I wish it to be. Otherwise, she would never have befriended me. You know she keeps her true feelings inside, close to her heart."

I did know that.

I usually masked my bitterness toward her. I praised her to others and complimented her as often as I could. I patiently showed her how to perform domestic tasks—many of them more than once—and I tried never to criticize her efforts, remark on her inattention, or make her feel inadequate. I thought doing this would make the feelings I had go away, but nothing had worked. It wasn't as simple as that.

I looked away from her and Lamech, and glanced guiltily at Kenai.

I had hidden it for so long, but now I had shown my anger to Kenai, the one man I could not give an explanation to.

I knew it was jealousy. At least, I knew it now. I had always known in my heart that Dare had expected to marry Isabel. Likely, he had been expecting it for his entire life. Whether he had wanted it or not was beside the point, and I didn't really want to know if he had. The point was, when Isabel got married, I thought that he could love me. I had wished so hard for it, I had almost convinced myself the lie could be true. But inside, deep down inside, even a girl of fifteen can tell when love is not real.

"I worried that she would be sick over you going into the prison. She worries so much about you," I said, hoping to change the subject.

Kenai's laugh surprised me. "I'm not as bad off as I was in the days when you ran away from my brother."

I winced. That stung my pride, but I deserved it. When Kenai had first come home from the wars, he had been in a very volatile emotional state, but I knew as well as everyone else did that he had healed and was nearly his same old self.

I wondered if I had healed as much as he had, because run away from his younger brother was exactly what I had done.

"And I'm not as bad off as I was then, either."

He observed the direction my gaze kept taking. "Are you sure?"

I didn't answer. I didn't know. I was no longer sick over Dare, but I didn't like that Lamech could talk so easily with Isabel.

I have a difficult time talking to girls I like.

I took a deep breath and offered Kenai a small but genuine smile.

Ava was still with us when we found the caves at Amulon. When we met up there and started to fix a meal, she stayed silent, but Tecumeni offered to go into the city and obtain the supplies we needed.

"I've got to find someone to take Ava home anyway," he said, casting a strange glare at his sister. It was almost apologetic.

The men agreed, gave him what antums they had, and Tecumeni took his sister and headed toward the east gates of Amulon.

In another half an hour, Zeke and Eliza showed up, preceded of course by the margay's call, and the other men began coming into camp one or two at a time during the hours that followed. When several hours had passed, I was more than a little worried that Tecumeni would not come back with supplies, or that he would bring the Lamanite guard if he came at all.

We had not gone into a cave, but Kenai had found a large one with an opening that was easily obscured and we sat near the entrance waiting on Tecumeni, Jashon, and most of Jashon's band.

"Walk with me."

I looked up when I heard Lamech's voice.

That was all he said, and it was all that was needed. I went with him into the woods, but when our distance from camp increased and he did not suggest we return, I became nervous.

"Do you think Tecumeni will lead the guard out to us?"

He shook his head and gave me a look of disbelief. "Sarai, do you have any idea what that boy gave up for you?" I hoped I imagined the note of contempt in his voice, and I knew if it was there, it was for me and not the Lamanite who had been so instrumental in saving me and the others. When I didn't respond, he explained. "Tec betrayed his family, his heritage, and the Order of the Nehors. If he is caught, they will execute him, and not quickly or mercifully." He paused for a moment to let that sink in, but he needn't have. I was already starting to understand what Tecumeni had done. "He can't go home," Lamech added quietly.

"I didn't know," I said. "Because no one thinks I am smart enough to understand."

But if I had been smart, I would have understood the implications of Tecumeni's actions without Lamech having to explain them to me.

"That is untrue and you know it," Lamech said, and the tone of his voice made it sound more like a compliment than a reprimand.

I tried to change the subject. "Well then, do you really think it is safe for us to be out this far? Away from the others?"

"You don't trust me?"

"With my life," I said without hesitation. *But not with my heart*, I added silently. "I shouldn't have questioned it."

His lips twisted into a smile he couldn't hide. "If the patrol stops us, I'm sure you can come up with a believable story."

"Lamech," I protested, smiling a little myself. "That was the biggest lie of my life, and I hated every minute of it. I should have let the men deal with it."

Lamech stopped walking and reached for my shoulder to stop me, too.

"Sarai, the men did deal with it. Kenai commanded you to converse in Lamanite with the enemy, and you followed the command exactly. You did it with grace and intelligence, and most importantly, with the Spirit."

"Oh." Beyond that one word, I was speechless at his beautiful compliment. I knew I blushed deeply, and I looked down at my feet, which I couldn't help but notice were covered in dust from days of traveling.

"You reflect the spirit of God like a calm pool reflects the sunlight. That is why the boys in Orihah flirt with you. Your beauty and your sweetness are irresistible, and the Spirit you carry with you puts you beyond their reach." I could hear the smile in his voice. "Enticing and unattainable, that's what men see when they look at you, Princess. That is why Tecumeni could not resist saving you, why he cannot stay away from you even now. That is why I cannot stay away from you." He reached over and tilted my chin up until I met his dark, dark eyes. "That is why I love you."

He was so confident. So steady and strong, so sinfully handsome, and so sure of himself. His gaze didn't waver, his voice didn't falter, and his lips didn't hesitate to kiss mine.

I was so confused. I couldn't think it through. Hadn't I just decided Lamech was not ready to court me?

Or was it only I who was not ready?

I tried to tell myself we had never even had a coherent conversation, but it wasn't true. During the past weeks of travel, we'd had many conversations. During his visits home to the barley farm—which Naomi had noted with a small smile were longer and more frequent than they had been before—we had had conversations. Yes, lots of boys had flirted with me, but the only one I had thought I loved, the only one that had mattered, had rejected me. And even though the harshness of Dare's rejection was mostly imagined—he had, after all, left Isabel standing on the path and run after me to explain, to make things right between us, to preserve my good opinion of him—I still kept expecting Lamech to reject me in the same way.

No matter what he did or said, I expected him to reject me, and the truth, the real truth, was that I pushed him away harder than he had ever pushed me. And then I wondered why everything with him was so difficult.

He was the only one who could hurt me more than Darius had, and something in the warmness of his slow lips told me he knew it.

I didn't push him away then, standing there together in the wilds of the Lamanite lands—the lands of our fathers. I let him kiss me because I didn't know how to stop it, but I didn't let him kiss me a second time when, after regarding me with hooded eyes for a moment, he tried to.

"I...I don't think I'm ready for this," I told him. Then I added more firmly, "I'm not. I'm...Lamech, I'm not prepared."

He ever so gently set me away from him. I hadn't even

noticed his hands were at my waist, but I did notice when he did not remove them.

"Then prepare yourself. I will give you the full year—we both need it—but you've got only a month until we reach Melek."

I knew what he was saying. When we got back to the village, Lamech planned to make official arrangements with my father for a betrothal. But did he know what he was really saying?

"Are you...Lamech, are you certain?"

The look he gave me made me feel so young, so inexperienced, so unprepared, and so very pretty.

"I am at least one hundred times more certain than you, my little Princess."

30

Salome

I thought he was dead because he didn't cry out. I couldn't see which man had been hit by the arrow, had fallen to the earth, but in a moment Ethanim crawled into the trees.

It was a warning shot of sorts, a sick greeting. Shooting as they had from the trees, they could have killed him if they had wanted to. It made me ill, but the men seemed to expect it and even understand it.

Keturah instantly bent and began tending to the wound in his arm.

"A little to the left and they'd have hit you in the heart. Bandages girls?"

We all searched our satchels and came up with enough bandages to staunch the flow of blood.

But first, Keturah had to remove the arrow. She grasped it, but Ethanim stopped her with a hand on her arm. Her hands stilled as their eyes met, and he yanked the arrow out himself.

I winced and looked back to the clearing. The enemy had not yet shown themselves, but even as I watched, they materialized through the trees.

Bows ready, our men waited. They held their ground and waited.

I saw our other men moving into position behind the enemy. We had managed to surround them.

And then I heard a sound from behind me.

I flinched as a man—a Lamanite—ran toward us through the trees. He drew his bow from his shoulder and loaded an arrow into it on the run. I made a futile effort to draw up my bow, but he was moving too fast and barreled right past us, knocking Muloki off balance before he set his feet firmly on the ground between the two bands of men.

And he aimed his arrow at the leader of the other band.

Nobody moved.

The lone Lamanite said something to the enemy.

"He told them to go home," Melia interpreted softly to us, and I heard Muloki interpret for the men.

The leader appeared confused, but it was clear he recognized the man—he was not much older than a boy—who stood between us. Then his confusion turned to anger.

"What are you doing here? Protecting Nephites?" Melia whispered as the man spoke.

"These are not the men who killed Zaaron."

The leader of the Lamanite band glanced around at the Nephites surrounding him and his men. "A Nephite is a Nephite. You betray the Order to protect them."

"These men are under the protection of the Order. They are under the protection of Zaaron."

"Zaaron is dead."

"And you would dishonor him?" the boy shouted, but then he lowered his voice. "You have a habit of dishonoring the wishes of the dead, Josiah." There was absolute silence while the two men stared at each other. The enemy's leader, Josiah, pulled back harder on the bowstring he held. The boy spoke again. "Honor his wish. Go home."

There was quiet again while the man considered, but they both continued to hold their arrows trained on each other.

One of the other men spoke, and Melia continued to translate.

"He is no longer our brother, Josiah. You don't need to listen to him. Kill him! Avenge Zaaron's death!"

Still, the boy stood his ground and stared down Josiah.

There was another shout, but it came from outside the camp. And it was a woman.

"Stop it, you big babies!" Melia almost laughed as she repeated it to us. "Zaaron was not dead when I left the village. There is no need to avenge him."

Josiah, everyone actually, looked at her as she strode into camp from the west, apparently without fear. The men's eyes turned, but their weapons stayed raised.

"Put your weapons down. Tec is working under Zaaron's orders."

Tec?

I stood on my toes to see over Jashon's shoulder. I felt his controlled breaths and, though he did not take his eyes off the confrontation in front of him, I knew he sensed me there.

I caught a glimpse of the man who stood between us and this hostile group of Lamanites with his weapon drawn. Shaved head, bare chest and back, it *was* Tecumeni, the Lamanite who had helped us plan the rescue.

"Is this true?"

Tec raised his chin slightly. Other than that, he didn't move. "Yes. It's true."

"These are not the men you're looking for. Those men have already passed into Nephite lands. We tracked them. Tec is to spy among these." The girl gestured to us.

Couldn't she hear Muloki interpreting her words?

Finally, Josiah lowered his weapon a notch. "Is this true?" he asked Tec again.

"Yes, what Ava says is true."

Ava stepped to Josiah and put her hand on the bow until he released the tension on the string and let her push the weapon down. He held his shoulders back and regarded her silently.

"I need you to take Ava home," Tec said to Josiah. He cast a glance over his shoulder at us. "She is interfering with what I must do."

Ava whirled to face him, losing her composure for the first time. "No! I can help! And I'm not going with *him*."

Josiah laughed. "She got herself here. She can find her way home. Come on." He motioned to his men, didn't even glance at us, and turned and left the little clearing.

Tec and Ava stared at each other, and then they turned to us.

Despite the fact that all the men had their bows trained on him, the boy said calmly in perfect Nephite, "We meet again. This is my sister Ava."

None of the men moved. They had all heard him tell Josiah he was a spy.

Tecumeni actually rolled his eyes. "Lamech and Kenai are waiting at the caves near Amulon."

Jashon's posture relaxed and his head moved slightly as he glanced at his men.

"Kenai said to give you the call of the margay, but you'll have to forgive my negligence in my haste to get here."

Jashon lowered his bow, and the others followed his

lead. "Glad you made it out," he said.

Jarom stepped forward. "Where is Sarai?"

Tecumeni smiled. "I helped Lamech get his betrothed out of the prison. They are waiting at the caves already."

Betrothed? I met Eve's wide eyes.

"You also helped her get *into* the prison," Jarom said under his breath.

Tecumeni shrugged. "Part of the plan."

Jashon studied Tecumeni. "Whose side are you on?"

Tecumeni put his hands on his hips and took a moment to look at the men around him. "I am on Sarai's side," he said simply.

"Sarai!" Ava exclaimed, and she rushed forward to her brother, standing toe to toe with him. Melia's translation of her words did not contain the same vehemence as Ava's delivery. "I knew it!" Ava exclaimed. "I knew this was about her!"

"Be quiet," Tecumeni told her. "Do you want to show these men more of your bad manners?"

She glared at him.

"You interrupted my conversation with Josiah," he said.

"I saved your life!" She gestured to us. "And theirs."

"I had it under control."

When Muloki translated that statement, Jashon laughed. He sent two of the men to tail the Lamanites. "Make sure they leave." Then he turned to Tecumeni. "The women are cooking venison for the evening meal. You and your sister are welcome here. Are you returning to Jerusalem?"

The boy shook his head. "No." Then he hesitated, bounced his bow in his hand a little. It was the first time he had looked even slightly unsure of himself. "I can't go home. I am going north to the land of Zarahemla."

"Is your sister going with you?"

Tecumeni glanced at her. She didn't understand what the men were saying. "Unfortunately, I think she is."

Jashon nodded. "Alright. Melia?"

Melia was already by Muloki's side, and she turned to Jashon.

"Take care of Ava."

She smiled and stepped toward the girl, talking to her in even tones. I didn't know what Melia said, but the more she spoke, the more Ava's guard seemed to go down.

I looked down at Keturah and Ethanim, still on the ground behind us. She had his arm bandaged.

"I need to clean it better, but this will do for now."

"Is it very painful?" I asked him, struck by his stoic bearing of his wound.

"It throbs," he replied, then relented. "It feels like fire."

He could have been killed right in front of me. I choked back a small sob. "Our feelings are what make us know we are alive," I whispered past the lump in my throat.

He grinned, but when he saw my face, he got hastily to his feet. "Oh, hey," he said. "None of that. It doesn't hurt very much at all."

"Oh, Ethanim," I said in a way I could not control, a way that made him pull me to him with his good arm and hold me awkwardly for a moment.

"All he did was take an arrow in the arm," Reb said.

I laughed and stepped away from him.

31

Sarai

One hundred times more sure than me?

"How?"

What had happened to Lamech? How could he possibly be so sure he wanted to marry me? I was less sure than ever. I was less sure about this than I had ever been about anything.

Lamech looked at me for a moment, frowning. That was a Lamech I was familiar with. He stepped back from me and ran a hand through his long, loose hair. "Sit down." Days ago, the command would have irritated me, but his voice had no force behind it. It was almost like an invitation. It sounded, and felt, more like the way he had talked to Eliza that day he had told her he didn't mean to be rude.

I sat on a stone near us and waited for him to speak.

He paced back and forth with his arms folded, and I wondered if I could make it easier somehow for him to say whatever he had to say.

"Wouldn't you like to sit, too?" I asked.

He stopped pacing and sat.

I knew if we ever did get married, like he was talking about, I must learn to communicate with him. Lamech was a man that both my father and I liked, and it would be worth putting in the effort to do this. I wanted very much to make the right decision, but I knew I was not ready to make it.

Deciding to be honest with him, I said, "I don't understand how you can be sure of this, how you can even think it possible that we wed. I am more uncertain than I have ever been."

"Because of Darius?" he asked tonelessly, staring at his laced fingers.

"No."

"Because of Tecumeni?"

"No. Because of you." And before he could ask me what that was supposed to mean, as I just knew he would, I said, "When I go to sleep at night, you are the one I think about. When I wake, you are the one I look for. But when I'm sad, you are the one who makes me so, and when I cry, you are the one who draws my tears. How can I reconcile these things?"

The words, so personal, so achingly honest, embarrassed me, but I spoke earnestly because when we got back to my father, Lamech would ask to marry me. Father would say yes. Zeke had already assured us both of that. And at the moment, I couldn't agree to the betrothal.

He didn't attempt to answer. He probably couldn't. What he did say, in the warm voice I had so seldom heard, changed everything.

"Sarai."

It was only the one word.

My name.

When he called me by my name—like that—I changed. And I knew.

But it was only the introduction to what he intended to say. "How old were you the first time I came to your village?"

The first time he had been to my village was for his

brother's betrothal ceremony to Keturah. In my mind, I could still see him walking between Gid and Jashon. I could still feel the power of our eyes meeting. Still feel my own curiosity, my own terror at the sudden, intense feelings. And yes, I could still feel the basket full of fruit lighten as I lost my grip on the handle, the fruit all tumbling out onto the ground, rolling away. And I would never, ever forget Lamech's hand brushing mine as he helped me return the fruit to the basket or the deep frown on his face as he walked away.

"Thirteen, I think."

"I was seventeen. And in your tent, when you said I was terrified, you were right. When I first saw you, I was terrified. I was a warrior—I wasn't planning on falling in love with a child. Izz told me I would have to hurry if I sought a betrothal with you, and the fact that she noticed what I thought I was hiding so well really alarmed me.

"Izz told you that?"

"It's what most of our conversations are about."

He paused, letting me think on that information.

"Why did it scare you?" I dared to ask.

"So many reasons." Hesitantly he took my hand and began to stroke it with his thumb. "You were so young. I mean, I was too. But you, you were really young—and innocent and pure and trusting."

"You couldn't have known that in one look." I smiled. Surely he was not being serious.

"I did." I watched the brooding look come back into his eyes as he remembered. "It was only a feeling that I wanted to know who you were, but it was more than I was ready for."

I shifted uncomfortably. He was talking about things he couldn't possibly know.

"In that moment, the moment our eyes met, you felt it too—don't say you didn't."

He stopped stroking my hand and squeezed it tight. He leaned forward slightly, expecting me to respond.

"I did." I licked my lips and admitted, "I knew that you were brave and kind and filled with the spirit of God."

"How did you know those things?"

"I don't know."

"I didn't know either. I didn't know it was the Holy Ghost."

"The Holy Ghost? Telling you we were...what? Meant to be together?"

He shook his head, almost sadly. "Only that you were pure and innocent. I had just come from the war, and I was anything but. I felt like...like I couldn't wash it off me, like I would never be clean."

I searched his face for a moment.

"I became friends of a sort with Isabel because she was safe. I didn't feel those weighty things when I looked at her, and that made it easier to talk to her...than to you. But, she noticed. I don't know what she saw when I was near you or how she saw it. Anyone could see that every boy in the village would soon be coming to your father. Isabel said as much and encouraged me to be the first."

"Then why did you never speak to Father?"

The look on Lamech's face said it all. "I did."

I was more confused than ever. If Father would agree, like Zeke had said, would we not be betrothed already? And if Father had said no then, why had he changed his mind now?

I thought we should probably start back to camp, so I stood. Lamech stood too, but he did not let go of my hand,

and he did not start walking even when I did. He pulled me to a stop.

"I spoke to my father, and he took me to speak to Hemni."

I looked down and waited. It had to be true, but why had no one told me?

"I explained my feelings to both of them. They both recognized immediately the influence of the Holy Ghost. I tried to explain the promptings, but it was difficult because they had not prompted me to any action. It was a feeling only. Well, you know."

I did know.

"Hemni said you were too young, and he asked me to wait for the right time. He said that if the Spirit testified this to me, then it would testify again when we were both ready."

When you are both prepared and willing at the same time, it will be the easiest thing you ever did, building a relationship with him.

Up until a few moments ago, when Lamech had said my name, I wouldn't have believed I was ready. I wouldn't have believed anything he was saying. And I definitely wouldn't have believed he was ready.

But he *had* said my name. And I *had* felt what he was speaking of. And I *did* believe every word he spoke.

"Why did you insist it could not work between us?" I asked, challenging him.

"That's where it gets complicated." His dark eyes glistened with emotion, with self-deprecating humor.

I couldn't stop a small smile of my own. Yes, that was where it got complicated.

"I don't want to live in another man's shadow." A flush

crept up his neck. "First with Darius, more recently with Tecumeni, I thought your heart was engaged elsewhere."

"And what convinces you that it is not?"

"I'm not convinced." He looked down at me with an expression in his eyes that told me so much about what he felt. "You can spend the rest of your life convincing me," he said, and he pinched me in the side.

I squealed, and I let myself be happy.

He caught me as I tried to wriggle away. "I love you," he said.

"I don't blame you."

"And don't you have a reply?"

I shrugged and tried to catch my breath. "I might. You can spend the next month convincing me."

He stepped back and stood with his hands on his hips staring at me for a moment, a little incredulous, a little admiring. Not brooding at all. "Come on," he said finally, motioning with his head. "Let's get back."

As we walked back to the cave together, I wanted to say I loved him too, but I didn't say it.

I wanted to be sure.

I wanted to be sure this new Lamech would last.

Was that so wrong?

I had misinterpreted every single thing Darius had said and done. I had seen only what I wished to see. Like Zeke had said of Keturah, I had made up a false Darius and fallen in love with him. The real Darius had only been my friend, but his friendship was a blessing I had completely overlooked in my longing for his love.

I wasn't much older than I had been then. I definitely wasn't more experienced with men.

Yes, I just wanted to be sure.

I chewed on my lip. "Is it...I mean, do you...when you went away to repent..." I was saying it all wrong. "When you went away to pray, did you get the answer you sought?"

He huffed. "Immediately. I had barely even made it to my knees."

I had known he must have, but hearing him say it was such a relief.

"And then Tecumeni showed up."

Tecumeni! Who had been distracted by something in the woods and sent me away with Josiah.

"What happened?" I had to know.

Lamech ran a large hand through his hair and glanced at me, offering me a wry smile. "He spoke to me in his flawless Nephite, and he demanded to know who we were."

"And you told him."

"I considered not telling him, but I told him everything—about my brother, about you and how Muloki taught you his language, about the betrothal being part of a story—and he's so enamored with you, he bit on his fingernail and came up with the plan to get Gid and Ardon out of the prison."

"By putting me in it," I said, a touch of accusation creeping into my voice as I remembered the big guards at the door.

"Do you think he liked doing that?" Lamech's voice was sharp.

"No," I said quietly. "I don't think he liked it. But he is a very good liar."

"Much better than you."

"Lamech?" I asked. This was another thing I didn't want

to know, but had to. "Lamech, did Tecumeni give you the cut on your back?" I looked up at him. "Did you two fight?"

"He would be hurt that you even thought it."

"Oh."

"The guard at the prison. Tecumeni's name and his words got the door open, but we had to do the rest." He paused. "It did not go according to plan. We had hoped to have no casualties."

"You were hurt rescuing me."

He didn't reply, and the statement hung between us until we entered the camp near the large cave. Eliza and Isabel cast knowing smiles at each other, and to my surprise, so did Enos and Zeke and a few of the other men. Had they been talking about us?

Tecumeni returned with the provisions like he had said he would, but then he informed me, "I'm taking Ava home. I'll catch up with you."

I just nodded. It was a lot of traveling, but I knew if anyone could do it, it was Tecumeni. These lands were his home. That thought made me sad for him since he planned to leave them forever, along with his family, his birthright, everything.

He was giving up so much. He had done it for me, and I had nothing to offer in return.

That night when Lamech lay down outside my tent, I left the flap open so we could talk. "Does Tecumeni know that you seek a betrothal, a real one, with me?"

Lamech was lying on his back with his hands behind his head, looking up at the stars. "He knows."

"He's giving up too much for me."

"That is his decision. And it is already made, so don't

worry about what you cannot change."

"Are you so ungrateful for what he did for us that you can be so insensitive to his feelings?"

"No, but I hope you are."

"Lamech!" I hit him in the chest like I had seen Isabel do.

He caught my hand in his and held it there over his heart. "I'm not ungrateful, but I am not going to give you up now to some reckless kid, Sarai."

Our tone was light, both of us relieved to have our mission completed and on our way home, but we both realized Tecumeni's feelings would have to be dealt with.

"I'm going to introduce him to Chloe."

Lamech snorted.

"He will take one look at her and that will be that. You know how pretty she is, how it affects boys."

He shrugged a shoulder, but it meant he did.

We had to wait until late the following afternoon before Jashon arrived with his men. Tecumeni and Ava were with them, and no more was said about either of them going home. They were both welcomed in our band, but it seemed that most of the men trusted them warily. Ava stayed close to Melia, who interpreted everything for her.

I hoped that someday she could forgive me. Not just for my lie, but for all it had caused—Tecumeni leaving home, leaving his mother to raise all his young brothers and sisters alone, her own uncertain future, and possibly Zaaron's death.

Almost as if they had been watching for Jashon, another band of men walked into camp shortly after Jashon arrived, and Ardon was with them.

He went into his mother's arms not as a child would,

running and with tears, expecting to be comforted, but almost as a brother would, as if he meant to comfort and assure her. He behaved like an adult, clasping arms with Jashon and then with Gid.

Jashon introduced Ardon to everyone as the other band of men, apparently Salome's kinsmen, watched patiently from a distance.

"My brother, Lamech," Jashon said when he came to us.

Ardon's eyes lit. "Another uncle?"

When Lamech and I glanced at each other, Jashon clarified. "I am to wed Salome."

Lamech clasped arms with Ardon and actually smiled at him.

We finally began the long journey home the next morning before the sun rose over the hills to the east. In a fortnight, we made it to Judea, where we stopped to rest and acquire provisions for the rest of the journey. It turned out to be a place of separation as well.

Several of the men wanted to make a stop in Manti to see old friends, and Enos and Lamech planned to accompany Jashon to Salome's village for their betrothal.

Gid would join them later. He stayed with Keturah and their baby in Judea.

Gabriel was born into the world during the night before we left. When we went to Eve's childhood home to say goodbye, Keturah was sleeping, but Eve's mother, Ophelia, brought the baby out to us in the courtyard.

"Here," she said as she passed the little bundle to me. He was warm and sleepy.

The women all took a turn holding him until finally Salome passed him to Jashon.

"Gabriel," Salome whispered as she stroked his tiny head with the tip of a finger while he lay in Jashon's strong arm. "Baby Gabriel." She seemed enthralled by just his name.

When Jashon had held him, he passed him to Zeke. I watched Zeke closely. We all did, and I remembered again what he had said about developing a relationship under so many eyes. Gabriel was Keturah's child, her firstborn, but he wasn't Zeke's. He regarded the child with a serious expression for a while, and after Zeke had passed him to Jarom, he put an arm around Eliza, kissed her at the temple, and they walked out of the yard together to wait elsewhere.

Jarom, Muloki, and several of the other men all took a turn holding the baby. Kenai was especially eager, and I couldn't look away, though I felt I should, when he cried over the little thing, the baby who looked so tiny in his arms. Like Jashon and Lamech, he was the child's uncle, and I guessed it hit him hard.

Lamech was the last to hold Gabriel. Many of the others had gone to put their gear on in preparation to leave, but I went to stand by Lamech.

"I think he already loves you," I said.

Lamech cleared his throat, but he didn't say anything.

Finally, we left for the last leg of our journey. In the hills beyond Judea, we said goodbye to Salome, Jashon, Enos and Lamech.

Salome was smiling but sad when she bid me goodbye. "I am so glad to have met you, Sarai." Then she bent toward me. "Send word and we will come for your betrothal."

I glanced at Lamech. Salome laughed and hugged me.

Jashon put a hand on my shoulder and looked deeply into my eyes. When he found what he was looking for in them, he said, "See you soon, Sarai."

Lamech kissed me in front of all the others, much the way he had in front of Zaaron's men. It was brief, but it made me blush. I blushed even more when he whispered "Don't giggle at Tecumeni" into my ear. He observed the blush for a moment, a very small upturn to his lips, and he said, "I will see you in Melek in a week." Then he turned and left, following Ardon and his kinsmen into the hills.

He stood tall as he walked. He was strong and sinewy and his steps were sure. I didn't think there was a terrain that would slow him down. My eyes followed him as he walked out of sight. He didn't look back, but there was something powerful in the way he kept his eyes trained forward.

"Don't worry," Tecumeni said as he came up beside me. "I've seen you kiss him before."

And he has seen me kiss you. I bit my lip, trying to think of something to say. Something I could say if Lamech were standing next to me.

But Tecumeni was kind and he said, "I have followed my heart, Sarai, but you must follow your own."

32

We didn't stay long there after the men from Tecumeni's village left, just long enough to smoke the venison for travel. Tec and his sister showed us a quicker way to Amulon, where the entire rescue party planned to meet and then travel together through the wilderness back to our own lands.

I still had not seen Ardon. I believed Jashon when he said I would in Amulon, but I was unsure whether or not Jacob would bother stopping there.

"I fear Jacob will take Ardon directly back home," I said to Jashon while we waited near the caves with his kinsmen as more men trickled in one or two or three at a time.

"He said he would stop. Besides, he needs supplies as much as we do."

My fears were eased because I knew Ardon was out of the Lamanites' hands, but I would not rest easy until he was safe at home with me and things were the way they had been before.

But of course, things would never be as they had been before.

Jashon had done so much for me and Ardon already. He had saved me from starvation in the wilderness and offered his protection and escort to the Land of Nephi. He had committed to live in my village as my husband so I could stay with my son. He had brought me the knowledge of a savior, and he said he could love me—not for who my son was, but for who I was.

When Ardon came through the trees next to Neel, healthy and smiling, my world came right. He was young, but nearly as tall as Neel and so confident in who he was. He looked to be the leader of his men already, which was as it should be.

He found me immediately.

"Mother," he said as I embraced him, and he laughed when I wouldn't let him go, but I finally set him away from me so I could look at him.

He didn't look as gaunt as Gideon had, and I wondered if the lion's share of the food between them hadn't ended up in Ardon's belly. His tall stature was straight and strong, if a bit fatigued like the rest of us. His big feet were dusty like mine and his face and neck and arms were burned by the sun.

I felt Jashon's presence behind my shoulder and saw Ardon turn his eyes to him.

"Jacob told me of your plans," he said, smoothing over what might have been an awkward meeting.

Jacob and my kinsmen stayed back, kept to themselves at the edge of the gathering. I wanted to thank Jacob for telling Ardon what might have been hard for me to say. I only hoped he told it right. All that was left to me was the introduction.

"Ardon, this is Jashon." I turned to Jashon and took in the odd expression on his face. Nervous? Humble? I said, "My son, Ardon."

Jashon stepped around me and held out his hand to clasp arms with Ardon.

"You look like Gid," Ardon said as he took it.

"Much to his dismay, I am sure."

Gideon laughed as he came up beside his brother.

Ardon's eyes were steady. "I will gladly welcome any brother of Gid into my family."

Later, after Ardon had been introduced to some of the men and I was resting under a tree alone with Jashon, I said, "I was worried about what you and Ardon would think of each other."

"He's a good kid," Jashon said. "I already admire him."

"And he admires you," I said.

He shook his head. "He admires Gid."

"Well," I said, reaching for his hand. "It won't take him long to see what I do."

When Amulon was behind us, and the men from Tecumeni's village were well and gone, spirits rose and we made our way through the dense wilderness once more.

We stopped in one of the mountain cities in the southern borders where Eve's family lived and Keturah and Gideon became parents to their son, who they called Gabriel.

Eve's mother brought Gabriel out to be viewed while his mother slept. Keturah could not travel for two moons, but the rest of us planned to move on shortly.

"Are you sure you don't want to stay just a bit longer?" I asked Jashon as we left the city through the big wooden gates.

He nodded to several of the guards. "Why would I?"

Because it's Keturah's child.

"It's been such a long journey."

"My whole life has been a journey. Another few days won't hurt me. Do *you* want to stay longer?"

"Of course not. Ardon is leaving with Jacob."

"I could request for him to stay with you."

The rub of it was that Jacob would honor the request if it came from Jashon.

I shook my head. "There is no reason for Ardon to stay."

After we left the city, we climbed a rather steep ascent to the east. A road twisted up through the summits, but we did not stay on it.

Jashon pointed into a valley below us. "Manti," he said.

The city was barely visible for the distance and the twilight fast falling, but it was a welcome sight.

"And that is the Sidon!" I said, looking at the slim line of gray that wound its way down the valley.

"We're near the headwaters."

The land was very quiet and still. The light was soft. The breeze was cool and gentle. We stood together on a bluff while the other men made a simple camp for the night. Since the Sidon River was a mile or two out of our way, we didn't stop at it to drink from its waters or reminisce, but we camped at a lovely small mountain lake. There would be no tents, no lovely corn cakes made by their women's hands.

"Thank you for finding me," I said.

"I've been looking for you for many years."

"I wish you had looked a little harder."

He turned away from the valley to search my face. "Did you feel alone?" he asked and his hand came up to touch my cheek.

"I thought what I had was enough. My life. My son. It was a great victory for me to keep him to raise in my own home."

He tilted his head back toward camp. "That boy is courageous. He is a natural born leader. I saw him fight in the prison."

I winced.

"He is very much like his mother. You have raised him well."

It was a compliment he meant truly, and I warmed at his sincerity.

"And he is as suspicious of me as he should be."

"Oh!" I said. "He has not said anything amiss, has he?"

Jashon chuckled. "No. He is proper and confident and a little curious is all."

"I explained the necessity for us to wed," I said.

"He understands it perfectly, and yet feels some amount of guilt, I think."

"There is no cause for guilt." But even as I said it, I felt guilty myself. If I had just agreed to travel with Jacob, to sleep in the camp of my kinsmen, we all could have avoided this betrothal and the feelings of suspicion that accompanied it.

But I did not regret it.

"Let him feel the guilt," Jashon said, taking my hand in his. "It is his recognition of what you have done for him, and it will grow into gratitude."

I rose with the sun the next morning, resigned to another day of travel. I knew I was not the first one awake, but when Jashon and Ardon came up together from the lake with a string of trout each, I was surprised at the early hour of their rising.

I thought briefly of Zedekiah as I watched his son come toward me with the man who would be a father to him.

I am sorry he could not be a man of the clan, I thought,

but I have found the right father for your son, Zed. I have waited for the time to be right.

Ardon was done with the things of children and he needed to learn how to be a man, a fair and just leader—things I could not model for him. I thought of how decisive Jashon was, how he commanded respect among his men and gained their obedience through love, never asking them to do things he would not do himself.

Ardon had never clung much to my skirts, but as he grew, I felt him draw even further from me. In my heart, he could always be my baby, but I did not fool myself that his trip to the lake with Jashon had been anything but an interrogation into Jashon's character, even if he did not know it himself.

"Mother," he said as he held up the string of fish for my inspection. "They are cleaned already."

I smiled. "But you haven't any spears with which to fish," I said as I took them from him, my mind already running through the ways I could prepare them.

"Jashon showed me a way to catch them without."

"Really?" I looked to Jashon for an explanation, but his face flushed as if he were embarrassed.

"It is accomplished with much patience and quick reflexes," Ardon informed me with a sidelong glance at Jashon, and I wondered what on earth they had talked about while they caught the fish.

The others left the three of us alone while we cooked the fish together. Lamech stalked out of camp with Neel and Zaph, and Enos lay back onto his bedroll. He must have been the sentinel through the night. How good it was to have a family to count on.

392

Enos watched Jashon with Ardon, the ease with which they conversed, both of them comfortable but feeling their way, too. He smiled at me, gave me a playful wink, and then rolled onto his side away from us to let us begin to form our new family.

When the fish were ready, Jacob and the rest of the men were there ready to eat before I even said, "Fish is on." Perhaps I was not the only one for whom this journey had been arduous.

While the others ate, I approached Jacob, and for once, I didn't wait for him to acknowledge me before I spoke.

"I owe you an apology," I said.

His assessing eyes shifted from his food to me expectantly.

"For leaving the village without you. I had my reasons, though I know they will seem trivial to you in the face of Ardon's safety."

Always a man of few words, he looked past me to Ardon and Jashon.

"It has all come out well enough," he said, generously diverting my apology. He returned to his food.

"I think it has," I said slowly.

"A piece of luck running into Jashon," he said, and he seemed to be feeling his way, too.

I sighed and sat beside him, even though he had not invited me to. "I am resigned to the consequences of my actions."

He actually stopped eating. "Sister, you would be resigned to marry me, but the lightning in your eyes when you look at him..." He gestured to Jashon. "It does not convince me of your resignation."

He smiled slyly when I flushed.

"I know my duty, Salome, when it is time for duty, but do you think I know nothing of love?"

I thought of Haret, his wife, and wondered if I had ever seen love between them. Had I ever looked for it?

My thoughts must have shown on my face.

"Love is a private matter. I keep mine private."

"That is your right," I said with a smile I couldn't help. "But I think I shall shout mine from the mountain tops."

He finished his food and started to pick at his teeth. "You should shout it to him. He asked me if there was a way for you to get out of the betrothal. He thinks you don't want it." He deliberately avoided looking at me.

Was Jashon still thinking I wanted out? Or was it he who wanted out?

"When?" I asked. Recently or early on?

Jacob shrugged infuriatingly and threw his fish bones into the fire.

"Maybe I'll just shout at him now," I said, annoyed, and I got to my feet intending to shout across the camp. I would shout the camp awake.

But I felt a hand on my wrist. Jacob held me tight but tugged me gently back toward him.

"It is private," he said. "Just let him see the lightning in your eyes. You've been hiding it too long."

I could hardly credit his words. They were so unbelievable, I laughed and sat back down beside him.

"What will your father say? How will it be done?"

Jacob stretched out his legs and folded his arms. "He will be pleased. He has worried about you these many years."

"He has worried about the heir to his chiefdom," I said,

unable to hide the cynicism in my words.

Jacob looked surprised. "You have seen the chief only, and not the father. Perhaps you should spend more time with your father-in-law. You bring him sadness when you stay away."

Not wishing to be married off, I had avoided Anias whenever I could.

"Perhaps," I conceded. "Perhaps it is time for many things to change."

I loved returning to the village with Ardon.

Someone had finished harvesting our wheat and it was already starting to come in again, but we didn't stop at home before traveling straight to Anias's in the middle of the village.

The boys and girls ran the streets announcing our homecoming, and by the time we had reached Anias's home, he was standing in the courtyard, looking much older than I remembered him looking.

Anias came toward us, stumbling forward in his relief that Ardon was with us, but when he was near, I saw that his hands were not outstretched to Ardon, but to me.

"Daughter," he said. "You are home."

I tried to make sense of his words of welcome. I thought myself to be unimportant to him—just the mother of his grandson. But had he thought—he must have thought—that I had been stolen from our fields?

While the others looked on or greeted their own families, Anias took my face in his old hands, tears spilling from his eyes, so like Zed's.

"You are mine," he said. "You are mine."

Jacob had been right. Anias was pleased with Jashon, pleased that I had at last agreed to a husband. He welcomed

Jashon, Lamech, and Enos into his home and village with gratitude and hospitality.

But when he took us together to the fire with a blanket he brought from his home, I protested.

"Jashon doesn't really want... I mean, he was just..." I bit my lip and looked around at the crowd that had gathered without my notice. "Surely his family will want to see him married. He is the firstborn. They have their own customs and rites."

Jashon took the blanket from Anias and wrapped it around both of our shoulders as someone had obviously shown him how to do.

"I have brought my kinsmen to witness." He gestured to Lamech and Enos with his chin. "And now, I will be yours, and you will be mine. I will keep you warm with the fire of my heart, and you will let me."

The crowd sent up a joyous cheer, and it was done. I was a wife again.

"I know there are laws for marriage in your city, in your church," I said later when he walked me to our home with its perennial wheat fields.

"And there are legal bindings here, sanctioned and sealed by your chief."

"But I fear you will not feel married."

"We can do a ceremony at my home if it will make you feel better, but Salome..." He stopped and turned me toward him. "Salome, I have felt married since you touched my face and found no scar there."

He brushed my hand with his. I took it in mine and let him lead me home.

396

Sarai

As we came into Melek, Eliza suggested we stop at the falls to wash the hard travel off in the pool there. Everyone eagerly agreed.

Tecumeni and I shared a look. I knew we were both thinking of the cistern in Ani-Anti. Despite my feelings for Lamech, it was a special memory for me. In that clear water, Tecumeni had accepted my beliefs. He had both liked and respected me despite my terrible lie. He had made me feel beautiful, and he had given me the chance to stand up for what I believed. In Melek, everyone believed as I did. I had never had to depend on my own testimony. He couldn't know he had shown me those things or that it meant so much to me.

I couldn't help but go to him. It saddened me when Ava scowled at me and moved away to Melia's side, immediately making some comment about me. From her tone, I knew it wasn't nice. Tecumeni frowned at her, but I didn't want her to ruin my lovely memory, so I turned away.

"I will never forget that day in the cistern," I told him. It was the day I had hung clothing to dry at Zaaron's home with the girl who wanted to marry Tecumeni, the day he had given me the fruit with the large pits Kenai and Gideon had used as weapons in the prison. And it was the day he had told Zaaron and Anahah that I was a Nephite.

He was quiet for a long time, but just before we walked along the ridge that overlooked the falls from above he said, "Nor will I, Sarai. I will not forget what you taught me there."

Had I taught him something too? I didn't know what else could be said, so I stayed quiet as we looked down on the falls and the river.

We saw the figure of a girl standing straight and alone on a log that stretched across the river at the edge of the waterfall. Chloe, my younger sister, held her arms outstretched, her eyes lifted to the sky.

In the next instant, her arms came together, she bent her knees, and she dove head first into the pool below.

Tecumeni and I stopped in our tracks, and the others milled up behind us.

"Was that Chloe?" Zeke pushed past everyone to get a better view of the pool, and then he started running down the slope, sliding down it, actually, on his feet. Kenai was right behind him, but the rest of us hurried down the trail.

Tecumeni didn't follow until I tugged on his arm. His eyes were still fixed on the place Chloe had disappeared, but when I nudged him, they shot to mine.

My brows knit at his expression, but I said, "I don't think the pool is deep enough for a dive like that."

When he realized why everyone was concerned, why everyone else was hurrying down the path, he started running too. Making my way behind him, I thought a simple introduction to Chloe would be an understatement now.

Zeke was knee deep in the water and helping Chloe step out to Kenai, who offered a steady arm from where he stood on the bank.

"What did you think you were doing?" Zeke demanded.

His voice was pitched high with worry, and I knew she had scared him as badly as she had scared me.

Chloe looked around at everyone. She put her hands on her hips, which were clearly evident, wrapped in her soaking wet sarong. I had been gone a year, and she was no longer a little girl.

Zeke was angry, but Eliza laid a hand on his arm. He took a breath and glanced around. "I will see you at home," he said grudgingly. Giving Eliza an apologetic look, he added, mostly to her, "I will bathe in the stream in the village."

"I'll come with you," Eliza said and hurried after him, giving us all a disparaging smile.

Chloe looked around at everyone again. "I'm fine," she insisted.

Nodding, agreeing somewhat, at least for the time being, everyone else waded into the pool, which I could see now was much deeper than I remembered.

"Chloe," I said, when I noticed her and Tecumeni eyeing each other. "This is Tecumeni." I didn't add that he had saved me, saved everyone actually. I didn't add that he was a Lamanite—that much was clear anyway.

"You can call me Tec."

Chloe brazenly looked Tecumeni over, managing to do it in a dismissing glance. "If I call you anything," she said.

I stared at her. Who was this strange girl? Chloe was headstrong, wild, and adventurous, but she was not rude.

"This is Chloe, my sister," I said to Tecumeni. I shot her a look, telling her to behave, as I waded into the deep pool myself, leaving them alone.

In the village, everyone was happy to hear that Gid had been rescued, that he was well, and that he was a new father.

Leah wanted to go to Judea right away, but Muloki talked her out of it, insisting that Keturah and Gid were fine and would meet her at their home near Orihah in a fortnight.

It was arranged for Ava and Tecumeni to stay with Keturah's mother and step-father, who no longer had any children at home. None, at least, until Darius walked into the village a week later, dusty from travel and as handsome as ever.

"I want to talk to you," I told him at dinner that night.

He gave me a hard look, one that said he'd rather do anything else in the world than talk to me. "Okay," he said coolly.

It was beyond my comprehension at the time that he was cool to me because I had hurt him. How could I have hurt him? Izz was the one he loved, the one who had disappointed him, the one who had married someone else.

"At the pasture?" It was the one place I had shared with him, the place our friendship had really begun.

"We were friends, weren't we?" I asked him when we were there, sitting on a stone outcropping that overlooked many fields.

"Yes, we were." He folded his arms.

"I'm sorry I ruined it."

"You ran away when I needed you most."

I winced. "I was hurt, and I was too immature to handle it. I didn't know how to deal with that kind of disappointment."

He considered that for a long moment, staring out over the fields. "I was disappointed too, and not just about Isabel."

"I should have let you explain after...after..." I looked down at my hands in my lap.

"After you thought you saw me kissing your sister." His

words were flat and accusing.

"Yes, after that. I should have listened to you. If I could go back, I would change it all."

"You thought I would kiss my brother's wife! That is what you think of me?"

I looked up at the hurt in his voice.

He took a deep breath and turned to offer me a wry smile, almost embarrassed. "We are taught to avoid the appearance of evil. All that happened, it was my fault."

I couldn't believe it. It was my fault—all the hard, difficult, jealous feelings were my fault. Running away, not dealing with the situation, and not allowing Darius to, either— that was all my doing.

"I have felt so responsible, so guilty for making you leave your home and your family."

I felt sick at the thought, that he had felt guilt. Why had it never occurred to me before? I sighed. It *had* occurred to me. It was the whole reason I had run away.

I had wanted him to hurt as wretchedly as I had hurt.

If I had truly loved him, I wouldn't have wanted him to hurt. I would have done anything to keep him from hurting.

"If you couldn't bear to look at me, I should have been the one to leave. I'm older, there are places I could have gone—"

"No!" I finally blurted out. "I was wrong. I was the one who let myself stay hurt for so long."

He just shook his head. "I almost came to get you, to bring you home so many times, but the others told me to leave you be."

I shut my eyes.

"You can't even bear to look at me now," he said softly,

self-loathing thick in his voice.

I opened my eyes immediately. "It's not that," I said. "It's just...just that I wish you would shut up." A slow smile spread across my face. I couldn't stop it. "Let us agree to forgive each other. Please? Let us learn from our own mistakes and move on. I do love you Dare, and I want you to be happy. And I forgive you. And I'm sorry."

He looked down into his lap. "I love you too, Sarai. But..." he hesitated, and I knew what he would say. "But it is how I love your sisters."

He caught my sharp look.

"Even Isabel." He heaved a deep sigh. "There was a time, before Isabel and Kenai, when I thought something might, you know, develop between us." He was fidgeting, folding and unfolding his arms, wiggling his foot. "But when I saw what was happening with Kenai, that was it for me. I immediately cut off the idea of it, just erased it from my mind. It took longer to erase the feelings."

"But you did?"

"Yes, Sarai, I did. And then you happened."

I almost giggled, the term was so funny. "What do you mean 'happened'?"

He ran a hand over his hair and gave a defeated shrug. "I was starting to think something could develop between us."

"And then I left."

The horrible truth of it floated between us, but after a moment, it kind of floated away. It wasn't horrible. It was only a missed opportunity. God had provided me with a new opportunity, a better one, one that would benefit me and help me develop and grow into the woman God wanted me to be, and He had set it into motion long before I ever fell for

Darius—on the day Lamech had first come to the village.

When our eyes met—don't tell me you didn't feel it.

"I'm sorry I hurt you," I said.

"I'm sorry too."

I couldn't hide the regret in my voice. "I wish we didn't have to learn these things on our friends."

There was that word again. Friends.

He suddenly hugged me to him, held me awkwardly pulled in to his side. "That's what a friend is for," he said roughly. I heard his voice catch, and it set tears pricking at my eyes. I let them come, and I let them soak into his tunic. "That's what we are all doing here, just learning." He pulled back a little and I looked up into his face. "So we should go easy on each other, yes?"

I nodded, and I was really relieved.

"We're only stronger for the things we have learned."

I nodded again.

"When I see you with Lamech," he went on, clearing his throat, "it gets to me. You know? But I can see...while we traveled, you...when you're with Lamech..."

"There's something about him," I finished for him.

He relaxed his arms, but I stayed where I was, leaned against him in the circle of his friendship.

"There is something about the two of you together. Everyone can see it. I want that for myself." He squinted into the distance, but I didn't think he was looking at anything.

When we returned to the village, he walked me all the way to the gate of my courtyard.

"Friends again?" he asked.

"Friends always," I replied. "The strongest." And I turned and went toward my home alone.

My heart was heavy but it lit when I heard Lamech talking to my father on the side of the house. He must have just arrived from Jashon's. He certainly hadn't wasted any time.

It was wrong, but I went to the corner of the house on the pretense of taking off my satchel and laying it down there with several others. But when I heard them talking about Chloe, I was confused.

"When I talked to Zeke, he was quite upset about her antics," I heard Lamech say.

My father sighed. I could picture him putting his hands on his hips as Zeke often did. "She is obedient to the commandments, but she is high-strung and does as she pleases once her work is done. Nothing Dinah nor I do seems to sink in. She is being reckless and destructive to herself. We cannot figure out why. We do not know what would help her."

"I think she would benefit from the betrothal," Lamech said. "Though she is young. I think the steadying influence and the impending responsibilities might help settle her down."

The betrothal? Was Lamech speaking of himself? He was certainly stricter than my father, but it didn't make sense.

I felt a slow burning ache in my heart when I considered what I thought I was hearing.

But I took a breath. I only thought I was hearing it. I was eavesdropping. I only had half the story. I knew Lamech loved me, and even if he didn't, I had his word that he would speak to Father about me, not Chloe.

I determined to wait until I had all the information before I got upset. And to that end, I walked boldly past the corner of the house directly toward my father and Lamech.

Lamech's warm smile reassured me instantly. When I drew near, he put his arm lightly around my waist.

"Hemni says yes," he said. "And we will plan a long betrothal so you can have the time you need to feel prepared."

I smiled and looked to my father. He was pleased.

"Hemni, may I take Sarai for a walk?" Lamech asked.

With Father's consent, we walked out of the village.

"Is my father planning a betrothal for Chloe?" I asked.

"I suggested Tecumeni," he said.

"But why?" And why would my father take such a suggestion? From Lamech?

"Isn't that what you had planned?" He almost had a glint in his eye.

"Well, yes, but that was just a convenient way to divert Tecumeni's feelings from me."

He smiled, amused. "You are the worst liar. You put some thought into it."

"I barely know Tecumeni. You don't know him either, and Father knows nothing about him."

"We all three know the important things about him."

That he had given up everything for what he thought was right. There was only one kind of man who did that. Muloki. Kalem. My father. Zeke and Jarom and every one of my kinsmen who had gone to war, who had been willing to give their very lives for what they thought was right.

Tecumeni was in very good company.

Lamech led me down a path that was overgrown, narrow, and not very easy to follow.

Lamech had told me once that a path might not always be clear in the lands we were headed to. He couldn't have known how right he was. On our journey to Jerusalem, the path had not always been clear, but when I trusted in the people I knew I could trust, I learned that I had skills of my own that were valuable. I had helped the others return as much as they had helped me.

Months ago, I had told him I was capable of walking a path on my own, but as we walked the narrow path, I was happy knowing I would not ever have to. Lamech would walk it with me.

I was not surprised when Lamech and I ended up at the old training ground, and I smiled to myself because Lamech *would* feel most comfortable on a battlefield.

"I love it here," he said as we walked down the rows of plants that were now heavy with the fall harvest.

"I know. I followed you here once."

That slow smile took his lips. "You did, did you?"

I nodded, but turned to scan the place. "I didn't understand what you were doing here. All alone."

"You will never understand me. Save yourself the trouble of trying," he teased gently.

But I couldn't laugh. "Until I saw you fall to your knees." I looked back at him over my shoulder. "Then I understood."

The breeze rustled the leaves all around us, gently bending the plants. It seemed to surround us and bend us closer together, too. Lamech's hands came up to my face. His fingers slowly brushed against my chin, my cheeks, around my ears, behind my neck to the nape of it like the slow-growing tendrils of a vine. The kiss that followed was like water. The beating of his heart was the rich earth, and the love in his eyes when he looked at me was my air.

"A kiss is meant to show love," I whispered, repeating his own beautiful words.

I felt his lips, so close to mine, curve up in a smile. "Yes," he whispered, and he showed me again.

ABOUT THE AUTHOR

Misty Moncur wanted to be Indiana Jones when she grew up. Instead, she became an author and has her adventures at home. In her jammies. With her imagination. And pens that she keeps running dry.

Misty is the author of *Daughter of Helaman*, *Fight For You*, *In All Places*, and other novels in The Stripling Warrior series. Her stories are filled with tenderness and humor, and her characters are real, endearing, and memorable. Her LDS fiction titles will inspire you.

Misty loves to read anything with a romance in it, edit, type, stare out the window, and hang with her family. She lives in the wild west where she has yet to see a stagecoach or a gunfight, and is, frankly, rather disappointed about it.

www.ingramcontent.com/pod-product-compliance
Lightning Source LLC
Chambersburg PA
CBHW051312250626
47155CB00007B/2296